D1429191

30131 05761609 3

THE HAND
OF THE
SUN KING

THE HAND OF THE SUN KING

J.T. GREATHOUSE

First published in Great Britain in 2021 by Gollancz
an imprint of The Orion Publishing Group Ltd
Carmelite House, 50 Victoria Embankment
London EC4Y 0DZ

An Hachette UK Company

1 3 5 7 9 10 8 6 4 2

A CIP catalogue record for this book
is available from the British Library.

ISBN (Hardback) 978 1 473 23287 7
ISBN (Trade Paperback) 978 1 473 23288 4
ISBN (eBook) 978 1 473 23290 7

Typeset by Deltatype Ltd, Birkenhead, Merseyside

Printed in Great Britain by Clays Ltd, Elcograf S.p.A.

MIX
Paper from
responsible sources
FSC
www.fsc.org
FSC® C104740

www.orionbooks.co.uk

For Hannah.
I told you I wanted to be a writer.
You married me anyway.
I can't think of any greater gesture of affection.

I

Student

I

Naming

Grandmother woke me in the dead of night and told me to keep silent. She led me through the forest by half-forgotten paths. Paths the Sienese soldiers would not know. Sticks snapped beneath my sandalled feet and the wet roughness of the undergrowth brushed my calves. The cries of owls and foxes wafted through the cool, dark air. The stark light of the moon and stars cut through a cloudless sky and made the night feel all the colder. Sleepy confusion gave way to fear.

Did my mother know that Grandmother had taken me? And where? I wanted to ask these things, yet I dared not. An air of mystery clung to my grandmother, this old woman who lived beneath our roof yet felt like a creature out of shadowed myth.

Several nights earlier I had lain awake, swaddled in silk and cotton, listening to my grandmother argue with my mother on the other side of an oiled paper wall. My father had left on business that morning, and my grandmother's presence grew to fill the space he had vacated. She spoke more openly against the Sienese, and in turn my mother, married to a Sienese man, argued against her generalisations and blanket hatred.

It did not occur to me then to wonder why my grandmother chose to live with us, beneath a Sienese roof, with a daughter she despised and a son-in-law she hated. But I was only a small boy. I knew little of Sien and nothing of my grandmother's people, nor their gods, and never imagined that I would become a weapon in the long and bitter war between them.

'You and your brother were named at six years old, yet your son is eight and nameless,' my grandmother said, her voice muted by the paper wall.

'It was not a crime when we were named,' my mother said. 'There was no danger to it then.'

Their conversation made little sense to me. I had a name, Wen Alder, given to me by my father in accordance with the naming traditions of his clan and a proper continuity from his own name, Wen Rosewood. Why did I need another?

'If not now, then never,' my grandmother snapped. 'And then the only path left to him will be service to the conquerors. Would you rather he become some imperial bureaucrat, his mind turned to calculating the interest owed by starving villagers on taxes they will never be able to pay? That is the path your husband has set him on.'

There was a sob in my mother's voice. 'You will not have my son for your war.'

'Is it better to make him an enemy of the gods? An enemy of his own family?'

Crickets filled the silence between them. I was fully awake now, excited by whispered talk of gods and war. The only god I knew was the Sienese emperor, whose rituals I had begun to study with my tutor the previous year. I had seen demonstrations of his power at the New Year festivals, when Sienese sorcerers – Hands of the emperor – hurled spheres of iridescent flame to dance among the stars. I worshipped the emperor and venerated the sages alongside my father, as he had done with his father, and so on unto the origin of our clan in the misty depths of history. Of what gods did my grandmother speak?

'I will not make him fight,' my grandmother said. 'But would you deny your son half of his heritage?'

I did not hear my mother's answer, but as I followed my grandmother into the forest, stumbling half-awake along an overgrown path, I realised what it must have been.

The interlocking brackets of a roof and ceiling appeared through the thicket before us. The path led to a wicker gate – frayed and brittle after years of neglect – which was guarded by three stone wolves. One stood in the centre of the path. The others sat on their haunches on either side of the gate.

'The Temple of the Flame,' my grandmother said, then gestured to the twin seated wolves. 'Okara and his sister, Tollu. Their mother, Ateri the She-Wolf, the mate of fire. Learn their names, boy.'

I had always been *boy* to her. Never did she call me by my Sienese name.

She led me past the wolves. I flinched away from them, even as I committed them to memory as she had instructed. Ateri stood with her head lowered to lunge. Tollu was calm-faced and proud, with piercing eyes over a shortened snout. Okara was the most frightening of the three. A distinctive pattern of scars had been etched across his face, marring his right eye, and his teeth were bared in a vicious snarl. Later my grandmother would tell me the tales of these strange gods – of Ateri's wisdom, Tollu's nobility, and Okara's guile and ferocity. That night she led me firmly but gently by the arm past the wolf gods, through the gate, and to the temple.

Moonlight dimmed the red and yellow paint of the Temple of the Flame. Paper screens had been nailed over the windows long ago. Most were riddled with holes and one had been torn away by a falling stalk of bamboo. A colony of foxbats clung to the brackets of the ceiling and watched us with bright, glinting eyes. The stink of their guano filled the place.

Grandmother led me up the steps to the altar at the temple's heart. She unbound her hair and let its thick reddish-brown curls, tinted grey at the temples, flow freely over her shoulders. Like all Sienese children, the sides of my head were shaved. With a frown, she untied my topknot. My hair – so much like hers, though combed straight at my father's insistence – fell to either side and tickled the tops of my ears.

She wiped decades of dust from the altar with a swipe of her hand but did nothing else to clean the temple. This stood in stark contrast to the ritual cleanliness of the Sienese, which I had observed at my father's side. Our worship had revolved around incense sticks, finely carved and painted idols, and temples kept fastidiously swept, polished, and painted by obsequious monks. Worship could not commence, in the Sienese mind, unless the sages had been properly honoured and welcomed into the sacred space.

My grandmother's religion centred not around the rite and ritual I knew but around fire and blood. She bade me sit upon the stone surface of the altar, then produced a knife of black glass from her satchel. Sensing my fear of it, she drew her mouth into a line and set the knife beside me on the altar.

The illicitness of our actions, the stillness and silence of the night, and the strangeness of the other artefacts she removed from her satchel – a clay bowl, a writing brush, a sheet of rice paper, a stoppered gourd, and a scroll of wooden slats tied with leather cord – unsettled me. Again, I wondered why she had brought me here, and I yearned for my blankets, for this strange outing to have been only a dream.

She walked to the back of the altar and opened a small brass door. It was the only metal I had seen in the temple. She stared into the darkness beyond that door, her eyes distant, the crows' feet at their corners growing tight as her gaze narrowed on some distant memory.

'Once,' she said softly, 'a witch would tend this hearth day and night. Once, the First Flame still burned here, a kindling from the same fire that set man apart from beasts. Now, there is only old coal and ash.'

She stacked wood within the hearth, then reached into the darkness. I leaned over the edge of the altar, trying to watch her hand as it disappeared within.

She snapped her fingers, and whatever path my life might have followed before that moment, it changed. For the first time, I felt the intoxicating thrill of magic. It seized my chest with a feverish heat, raced up my ribs, over my shoulders, and down the length of my spine. The grain of wood and stone leapt out to me like the writing of an ancient god.

That heady sensation made me recall one of my first lessons with my tutor, Koro Ha, the previous year. We had been studying my pedigree, the list of my father's ancestors dating back to the beginning of our family. One of many texts I would memorise for the imperial examinations.

Though my father was a merchant of middling station, our family tree had at its root men of influence and power. Greatest among them was Wen Broad-Oak, who had been Hand of the emperor, a sorcerer and general who had helped to conquer the horse lords of the Girzan steppe. It seemed impossible that I, a merchant's son, could trace my line from such dizzying heights of power.

'Could I be Hand of the emperor?' I had asked Koro Ha.

'Perhaps, if you work hard,' he had answered, bemused by my childish ambition. 'It's an uncertain path from here to there.'

'Could you have been?'

That made him laugh. 'No, I don't think so. And I would not have wanted that honour, were it offered.'

I found that confusing. Always my father spoke of our ancestors as exemplars to which we should aspire. His mission

7

in life was to restore our family to the heights from which we had fallen, a task that required wealth – which he spent his days pursuing – and prestige – which I would earn through education and imperial service.

'Why wouldn't you want to be Hand of the emperor?' I asked Koro Ha. 'What honour could be greater?'

'Power always comes at a price,' Koro Ha said. 'I have heard – though I do not know it for true – that in exchange for the gift of sorcery, the emperor sees through the eyes of his Hands. Some even say that he hears the echoes of their every thought. In any case, I prefer to choose my own path through the world. Power is a burden I do not wish to carry.'

'That's just an excuse,' I said. 'If you could have had it, you wouldn't have let power slip through your hands. You failed, so you pretend you didn't want it in the first place. I'm not going to fail. I'll restore the Wen family and become the greatest sorcerer the empire has ever known.'

'Oh?' Koro Ha said, amused by the accusations of his seven-year-old student. 'Even greater than the emperor himself?'

That gave me pause.

'The second-greatest sorcerer,' I said.

Koro Ha chuckled and said, 'Well then, we'd best return our attention to your studies.'

The crackle of fire catching in dry wood rose from the hearth and the stone altar beneath me began to warm, drawing me back to the present moment. My pedigree had focused only on my father's line, but now I saw that there was power in my mother's as well. My grandmother was not Hand of the emperor, but she had wielded magic. A good Sienese child would have fled from such heresy and betrayed her to his father.

Ambition had already taken root in me, seeded by my father, but his desire to restore our family had never struck me to the heart. His plans for me were a burden I had laboured under since I grew old enough to feel the pressure of his expectations. I did my best to carry them, but only to do my duty as his son.

But at the snap of my grandmother's fingers, something gripped at the core of me and stoked my heart to fire. I wanted such power as surely as I wanted my next breath. When she conjured that tongue of flame, I felt for an instant a pattern uniting and constraining all things and her spell rippling through it like freedom itself. Nothing I had yet encountered in my young life – and nothing I would encounter, even reading the most profound volumes of the Sienese canon – held such a weight of truth and power. What could be worth pursuing, if not this?

Grandmother unstopped the gourd and poured clear, heady-smelling alcohol into the bowl, then unrolled the scroll of wooden slats, her mouth forming unfamiliar syllables as she studied it. Its slats were carved with strange symbols, smaller and less intricate than the Sienese logograms I had studied with Koro Ha. The last three slats were unmarked.

'Give me your hand,' Grandmother said. 'The one you write with.'

A pattern of scars that traced the seams of her right palm shone faintly, like the glimmer of moonlight on placid water. I had never noticed them before. Without thinking, I clasped my hands together in my lap.

'Calm, boy,' she said. 'I'll do nothing to you that wasn't done to me in my day, and your mother in hers.'

Fear of the knife made me reluctant, but she was offering a peek behind the veil of mystery she had worn all my life. More, she had given me a taste of magic, and in doing so had kindled a thirst for more – a thirst that would carry me, in time, to the heights of prestige and the depths of ruin.

I offered my right hand. She slashed me once. I yelped, but she held my wrist firm. Blood dripped from my palm into the

9

bowl of alcohol. At last she released me and I pulled away and studied the wound. It was shallow and followed the central crease of my palm. The scar would not be noticeable unless one knew to look for it.

'Look here, boy,' Grandmother said. 'I know it hurts, but you must watch. Your mother won't teach you. Someday you'll have children of your own. I can't make you name them properly, and I'll likely be dead by then, but let Okara eat my liver if I don't do everything I can to keep our ways alive. Now watch. And remember.'

I peeled my eyes away from my wound. She nodded solemnly and waited for me to return the nod before continuing. She cut her thumb with the tip of the knife, then stirred our blood and the alcohol together with the writing brush. When it was fully mixed, she painted a single stroke on one of the unmarked slats. Blood and alcohol seeped into the grain of the wood. She pressed the rice paper to the slat, then peeled it away and flattened it on the altar. I leaned in close, trying to understand what she was looking for.

'There.' She jabbed her finger at one angular smear, then another. 'Your name.'

With the bloody tip of the knife, she carved two symbols into the slat. They resembled the stains on the paper, but only abstractly. She said something in a flat, toneless language, then told me to repeat it. Though I did not understand the sounds I made, they resonated with me, like the power I had felt when she conjured flame.

'That's your true name, boy. Foolish Cur. The gods have a sense of humour, I suppose.' She pointed to the other slats. 'Here is my name, Broken Limb. A prophecy, I think. And your mother's, though she lost the right to it when she married that man.' The symbols on that slat had been scratched away. 'And your uncle, Harrow Fox.'

My gaze lingered on that third name, which evoked a hazy memory of my early childhood. Once, when my father had been away on business, a strange, dishevelled man had arrived at our home. Often my mother would send such beggars away with a kind word, a few coins, and a cup of rice, but at the sight of this man standing in the gateway of our estate she had been gripped by an anger that rooted her to the ground.

'You dare come to my home?' she had demanded, while I watched from the doorway of the reception hall. 'What, have you tired of sleeping in caves and bushes, hunted like the fox you are?'

The man smiled, showing a broken tooth. 'I thought filial piety was the highest Sienese value. You've no love for your brother?'

'There is nothing for you here,' my mother said. 'Go, before I send a runner to the garrison.'

He put up his hands, then retrieved a slip of paper from his sleeve. 'Give this to Mother for me.'

'I do no favours for you,' my mother said, with her lips thinned to a terse line.

'At least tell her to lie low,' he said, 'and that we're regrouping in the North, at Greyfrost, should she wish to join us.'

'I'll do no such thing.'

'Then you only put yourself in danger,' he snapped, anger flaring. His gaze moved past her to fall on me. 'Yourself and your son. They will come looking for me, and though you may wish to forget that I am your brother, the Sienese never will.'

The man had left then and Mother had gathered me into her arms and whispered reassurances, though she was the one afraid, not I.

Three days later, a Sienese patrol came to our estate and searched it. My mother's fingernails dug into my shoulders while the soldiers threw open chests and scattered her belongings throughout her apartments.

'Have you had any contact with the rebel Harrow Fox?' their captain demanded. No, my mother answered. Did she know the whereabouts of the fugitive witch Broken Limb? No, she answered again – truthfully, for the day the dishevelled man had visited our home, my grandmother had vanished, not to reappear until a week later, long after the soldiers had left my mother with stern instructions to inform them if she learned anything of her family's movements.

Young as I was, I did not understand why my uncle and grandmother were hunted, nor why my mother allowed my grandmother to live with us and yet refused to help her brother. All I knew was that, when my father returned and heard from his steward of all that had happened in his absence, his threats to throw my grandmother out of the house echoed through the estate.

'She is growing old,' my mother pleaded while I hid in the corner, fighting tears, knowing they would only stoke my father's anger. 'It is my duty to care for her. She's no threat to anyone. They hunt her for crimes committed long ago!'

Father had relented, with a promise that if soldiers ever searched his house again, my grandmother would find the well of his mercy dry. In the four years since they never had, and in fact it seemed at times that Father had forgotten that a fugitive lived beneath his roof – or, at least, pretended to have forgotten.

Grandmother was quiet for a moment, studying the names of her son and daughter, before she rolled up the scroll of wooden slats and said, 'There is one more thing to be done.'

She floated the bloodstained rice paper on the surface of the alcohol, then lit it with a taper from the flames in the altar and waited for the ashes to settle in the bottom of the bowl. Then she drank deeply of the mixture of blood, ash, and spirit before offering it to me. After I drank, she led me in the prayer chant of naming. The words were meaningless to me, spoken in her language, which I had not yet begun to learn.

It did not occur to me that our feeble names, carved in wood and sealed in blood, would one day ring out in the vast, columned halls of the empire.

2

An Education

Over the next four years, my grandmother taught me the culture of her people – our people now, for I had been fire-named. She taught me Nayeni, the language native to our country, and bade me always speak it when we were alone. Under cover of darkness we practised the Iron Dance, wielding dowels in place of swords. She taught me how to name the stars and how to read a trickle of water through the forest after rain. By night I revelled in her secret teachings.

In contrast, my ongoing Sienese education was a laborious slog. Koro Ha, my tutor, hailed from Toa Alon, a distant and destitute province of the empire's southern edge. My father, impressed by his high ranking and letters of recommendation, had brought him to our estate to prepare me for the imperial examinations, which would be held in Nayen for the first time in my seventeenth year. It was a task he had taken to with relish and efficiency. After two years of his instruction, I could read the 10,000 Sienese logograms and write half of them from memory. After three, I could recite the aphorisms of the sage Traveller-on-the-Narrow-Way when prompted only by page and line. After four, I had written commentaries on the classics of poetry – and then rewritten them dozens of times until they met Koro Ha's strict standard.

'He is a studious child,' Koro Ha told my father on one occasion when I was twelve years old, 'though often sleepy.' We had gathered in a pavilion overlooking the modest gardens of our estate. Father was home for a brief stay between mercantile adventures and had taken the opportunity to check on my progress. He and Koro Ha sat at a low table while I knelt nearby. My knees hurt, but I could not complain in front of Father. I craved his approval, for if I did well in his eyes he would be kind to me and have fewer harsh words for my mother during his brief stay.

Father stroked the wispy braids of his beard and studied me. I resisted the urge to glance at Koro Ha for reassurance. The smell of tobacco from Father's pipe mingled with the delicate scent of chrysanthemum tea. Koro Ha filled first my father's cup and then his own from the earthenware teapot, then set the pot aside for a servant to refill with steaming water. A third cup rested empty on the tray.

'What are the three pillars of society?' Father asked.

'The relations of father to son, husband to wife, and elder brother to younger brother,' I recited. It was a foundational aphorism, the beginning of any examination.

'What is the emperor to his people?'

'The emperor is father to all.'

'If the people starve, what is the emperor's duty?'

'To feed them.'

'If the emperor is threatened, what is the duty of the people?'

'To defend him.'

'If the people are endangered, what is the duty of the emperor?'

'To protect them.'

'If the people endanger themselves, what is the duty of the emperor?'

'To show them the right path.'

My father nodded, then filled my teacup. I sipped and met his approving gaze.

'He knows the principles well,' Father said.

'If I may, Master Wen,' said Koro Ha, bowing slightly. He turned to me and adopted the aloof attitude of a Sienese tutor towards his student, a reflection of the foundational elder brother to younger brother relationship. 'Continuing from your father's query, let me pose a dilemma,' he said. 'What is the relationship of the emperor to his ministers?'

'The emperor must command his ministers as a husband, and his ministers must advise the emperor as wives,' I answered.

'When a minister is concerned with the emperor's conduct, what is his duty?'

'As a wife may gently reproach her husband and propose a new course, in this way a minister may advise the emperor.'

'What if the emperor rejects that advice?'

'A minister must submit to the will of the emperor.'

'But what if the emperor is wrong?'

I nearly choked on my tea. I stared at Koro Ha, forgetting for a moment the rules of propriety. We had skirted around such questions in our lessons. He had presented me with thought experiments wherein I assumed the role of a wife married to a drunken fool, or a younger brother bound in loyalty to a tyrannical elder sibling, or a minister given some odious task by the emperor. These thought experiments were the most fascinating of Koro Ha's lessons, but I did not think my father would approve of them.

'Wen Alder?' Koro Ha prompted. 'If you require a concrete example, let us say that the emperor has levied too harsh a tax against one of his provinces. What if he has failed in his duty as father to his people in that province and they starve because of it? What if, when informed of this error, the emperor refuses to reduce the tax? What, then, should the minister do?'

His question sent a jolt of surprise through me. Koro Ha, worldly man that he was, certainly knew of the hunger and poverty that gripped the north of Nayen, where my uncle's rebellion still fought and to which my grandmother often alluded in her rants against the empire. Had he noticed some sign of my nocturnal lessons? Bags under my eyes and bruises on my arms? A glimpse of my grandmother and me slipping from the garden by moonlight? Some subversive undercurrent in my thinking, detected in the nuances of my essays and our conversations?

'The right and wrong of the emperor's actions are known only to the eternal divines,' I said, meeting his eye. 'Only they, in their fatherly relationship to the emperor, have the right to rebuke him. It would not be the role of the minister to do so, as it is not the role of a wife to rebel against her husband.'

Koro Ha lifted his chin and gave me a satisfied smile. He turned to my father and resumed his subordinate role. 'The boy's understanding is immaculate for his age.'

'Yes,' my father agreed. He patted the chair to his right and I sat and sipped tea with them, all the while struggling not to glare at Koro Ha. Then Father asked questions about other things: my mother, my reading in the classics, and history, for which Koro Ha said I had an aptitude. In this way he fulfilled his duty to monitor and lead our household, despite his long and frequent absences.

Father had shown me a wealth of fondness when I was younger. I had hazy, early-childhood memories, half formed and almost mythical, of riding on his shoulders through the garden of our estate under the warm summer sun. Of his whiskers tickling my cheek while he dandled me on his knee and told silly stories full of nonsense rhymes. But as his businesses had expanded, those happy afternoons had grown further apart, and with Koro Ha's arrival his affection had become a thing to be earned.

When we had finished the pot of tea, he dismissed us. Koro Ha and I bowed and backed out of his study. On the garden path, out of my father's sight, I fixed Koro Ha with a chilling stare.

'Oh, don't sulk, Wen Alder,' Koro Ha said. 'Your father was pleased with your answer, was he not?'

'I don't think he was pleased with your question,' I said. 'I certainly wasn't.'

'Is it the role of the student to be displeased with his teacher?'

'What if I'd said the minister should rebel against the emperor? Do you think you would still have a place here?'

'I would, most likely,' he said. 'I came very highly recommended. If you had answered poorly, your father would have been displeased, and I would have seen to it that you did not answer poorly again.'

I crossed my arms and let myself fall behind him. He folded his hands within the sleeves of his robe. Summer sunlight filtered through ginseng leaves to dapple the path with shadow. Birds chirruped in the trees. The stream that ran through our garden bubbled. The slap of a carp leaping for a water-walker struck a percussive note.

'Were you trying to embarrass me?' I asked.

Koro Ha shook his head. 'You will be asked similar questions all your life, Wen Alder, no matter how many times you prove yourself. Questions that test not only your learning but your loyalty. You will have the right education and the right name, and these things will help, but you have the wrong skin, the wrong hair, the wrong maternal line. I mean to help you succeed despite these impediments. Sometimes, the cost of success will be humiliation or a betrayal of your own heart. Your father understands this.'

I stormed past him, found my room, and locked myself inside for the rest of the afternoon. Grandmother had taught me to be proud of all the things Koro Ha presented as obstacles and flaws. More, I was certain that beneath them all I would find the secrets of magic, which ran in both my father and my mother's line. It was my inheritance, the tool I would use to secure my place of prominence and restore the prestige of my family. And beyond that, I remembered the stunning thunder-clap comprehension of the pattern of the world I had felt when my grandmother had snapped her fingers and conjured flame. Four years later, I still yearned for that feeling like a beggar yearns to fill his aching belly, haunted always by the memory of his last meal.

That night, Grandmother woke me with a tap on my window. I rose and dressed in trousers and a shirt of homespun cotton – simple clothes that let in the cool summer breeze – crept through the hallways and met her in the garden. We returned, as we always did, to the Temple of the Flame.

She continued our lessons that night with the tales of Nayen's first heroes, who ruled their petty kingdoms before the time of the Sun Kings. She traced the runes and had me read along to tales of Brittle Owl, who could not hunt or fight but who tricked a dragon into sharing the secret of written language; of Tawny Dog, who befriended a fox demon and learned to veer into the shape of a beast; of Iron Claw, who met the wolf gods in his dreams and, with their guidance, forged the disparate cities of Nayen into a kingdom that spanned the breadth of our island.

Compared to Koro Ha's lessons, Grandmother's were cap-tivating. Sienese literature, in my experience, was thick with moralism and analogy. In contrast, Nayeni tales were full of adventure, passion, and – most importantly – magic. One could often divine the ending of a Sienese narrative from a proper understanding of propriety and doctrine. The stories my grandmother told were suspenseful, twisting and turning in unexpected ways, full of grit and vigour. Nonetheless they felt hollow, a waste of time that only whetted my appetite for magic.

When the tale of Iron Claw was done, Grandmother stowed the books in the chest beside the altar and led me in practising the Iron Dance. We still used dowels instead of blunted iron, as an accidental bruise to the face or the hand could be explained more easily than a broken arm. The air reverberated with the clash and crack of our blows. I was becoming a young man, full of energy and wildness, and I revelled in the physical release, letting my mind focus only on the next sweep of her weapon while my arms and legs responded as though on their own.

We came away drenched in sweat. I nursed my usual smattering of bruises and Grandmother examined one of her own where I had clipped her elbow. She told me to sit on the edge of the altar and passed me a gourd of water. 'You're getting better,' she said breathlessly.

I grinned and puffed out my chest. Pride was another quality constrained by the structures of Sienese propriety. 'Someday soon I'll be better than you.'

'Oh really?' She grinned.

'Really!' I wiped my mouth and handed the gourd back to her. The web of pale scars on her hand stood out in the dark. 'And then you'll have to teach me magic, whether you want to or not.'

I expected a rebuke. Almost every night I begged her to teach me the most secret of her arts, pointing to some minor accomplishment as proof that I had earned the right. Always she rebuffed me. That night, though, she sipped from the gourd and studied me, as though taking my request seriously for the first time.

'You are not ready to learn,' she said eventually and set the gourd between us. Then, just as I was settling into familiar disappointment, she stood. 'But perhaps you are ready to witness.'

A flush of excitement bloomed in my chest and spread to the tips of my fingers and toes. I fought the urge to leap ahead of her as she led me out to the overgrown courtyard behind the Temple of the Flame. Ivy crawled over every surface and choked the fountain at the centre of the yard, which had once fed a now-dry streambed. A lonely pavilion stood beside the fountain. Grandmother knelt in its shadow and bade me kneel across from her, nothing but a vague silhouette beyond the dry streambed in the light of the dim crescent moon. 'Watch closely, Foolish Cur,' she said. 'I'll not show you again until you are ready to learn for yourself. With a head as thick and wool-stuffed as yours, the gods alone can say when that will be.'

A plan true to my name was forming in that thick, wool-stuffed head of mine. I remembered the rush of power I had felt when she'd kindled the hearth and named me: the burst of warmth through my body, the sharp awareness of reality, the elation of freedom. Though she had hidden her hand from me then, and hid herself in shadow now, I thought I could learn her magic by feel alone.

The scent of burnt cinnamon filled the air. My senses sharpened, making every paving stone, every line of grain in every piece of wood, and every snarl in the ivy seem infinite in complexity and importance. As I watched, power suffused my grandmother's bones, filling, warping, and changing her flesh. I shut my eyes and focused on the oiled-iron feel of the sorcery she worked and the changes it carved into the fabric of the world.

As the wake of her spell washed over me, my skin crawled and muscles clenched in rhythm with her transformation. When it ended, I felt a sudden chill, like being doused in cold water, and heard the flutter of wings.

I opened my eyes. An eagle hawk perched on the rotted brackets of the lonely pavilion. I could tell it was Grandmother, for I could trace the continuity of her power. An unknowing eye, though, would have seen only the bird.

I gazed up at her, awe filling me like an inheld breath. I half believed that she might be reading my mind or had felt my touch as I traced the pattern of her magic, for I did not know the limits of her powers. She watched me silently, then dropped to the earth and vanished into shadow.

The unfurling of her magic was faster than her veering had been. Things, after all, want to be what they are, and that is true of people more than anything else. After she had resumed her former shape, the burning smell and unsettling gravity of power clung to her like tobacco smoke.

'You've seen enough for today, boy,' she said. 'You're a mean whelp to ask so much of an old woman. My knees hurt. Carry me back to the house.'

Some days later, in the pavilion by the pond where we so often engaged in our lessons, Koro Ha and I revisited the Classic of Upright Belief, the foundational text of Sienese religion. Unlike my grandmother's stories, which shrouded their moralism in myth, Sien conveyed its spirituality as it conveyed all things: through aphorism and directive. The nearest thing to a god was the emperor, whose name never changed and who built the empire from the fractious Sienese kingdoms with the aid of the primordial divines. Before Sien, there was only chaos, from which civilisation had to be forged by the sages, the first Voices of the emperor.

When I was very young, I reconciled the two mythologies in which I was instructed – my grandmother's and Sien's – by conflating her wolf gods and the primordial divines. They had been the emperor's predecessors, neglected only because he had taken their place as a son must one day take the place of his father.

As I grew older, I came to understand more clearly that my grandmother's religion was not an eccentricity but a crime in the eyes of Sien. That her temple survived only because the Sienese had yet to find and destroy it. That her gods were not the divines who had once aided the emperor but his enemies.

That afternoon, I came across a passage by the sage Yu Carries-Fire in the Classic of Upright Belief: 'Where you find folk belief, know that it is crafted from naught but trembling awe of the celestial bodies, in ignorance of the forces of nature and in terror of the beasts of the field. Subsume whatever can be salvaged into upright belief; eradicate whatever breeds deviance. In this way, the ignorant can be brought to knowledge and the deviant into alignment with the will of the emperor.'

I set the book down. A question bubbled within me, seeking to be asked, but how would Koro Ha react? At twelve years old, I already thought myself clever and sought a way to craft the question to hide the source of my curiosity. 'I don't wish to accuse the great sage of inconsistency,' I said, 'but if folk religion is nothing but ignorant myth, how can any of it be salvaged?'

Koro Ha's eyes brightened, like coals stoked to flame. 'An interesting question,' he replied. 'Would you be satisfied if I answered that Yu Carries-Fire is concerned primarily with establishing social control of the uneducated masses and less with establishing pure spiritual practice?'

No, I would not be satisfied, as he had slipped around the hidden edge of my question. 'Yet he titled his treatise—'

'I know the title of the treatise, Alder,' Koro Ha said. 'Even the classics can be of double purpose. Religion is politics, is literature, is philosophy, and so on. The ability to perceive and elucidate the intertwining of the classics will be key to your success in the imperial examinations.' He tapped the next page of the book. 'Go on, now. Unless you think yourself prepared to put the text aside and write an essay unpacking its complexities?'

'I'm asking questions because I *don't* understand,' I said.

'All right, then,' Koro Ha said. 'Was there something more you wished to ask?'

I took a slow breath, as my grandmother had taught me to before we began the Iron Dance, and studied Koro Ha. As I did so, I reminded myself of a fact that I so often forgot: he was not truly Sienese, either. Despite his education and his mastery of imperial doctrine, his dark skin and tightly curled hair evidenced a childhood not unlike my own.

'My grandmother has been telling me stories,' I began.

'Ah,' Koro Ha said and set down his teacup. He folded his hands and leaned back, as though bracing himself for a blow. 'I wondered if – and when – we might have a conversation like this. What kinds of stories?'

I shrugged, trying to seem relaxed – ashamed at worst – yet hoping he could not see the anxiety roiling within me. Some of her stories would certainly merit eradication if Yu Carries-Fire had his way.

'Heroes and things,' I said. 'Adventure stories, mostly. But there are gods in them. Wolves that talk. Things like that.'

'And you enjoy these stories?'

'They are ...' I chose my next word carefully. *Fascinating* showed too much investment; *amusing*, too little to warrant wasting time with his question. '... strange, but intriguing.'

'And you are wondering if they ought to be subsumed, or eradicated?'

'They convey moral messages that are not always out of step with imperial doctrine,' I said, too quickly, too defensively. 'I am wondering if there might be any truth in them.'

Truth such as I had felt in my flesh and bones in the wake of my grandmother's power.

24

'You are wondering about magic,' Koro Ha said.

Ice ran down my spine, and Koro Ha's warm expression did little to thaw it.

'I remember such stories, Alder,' he went on. 'We had their like in Toa Alon, even though the empire ruled there with a harsher fist than here. There are others, too. Folk tales from the Girzan steppe, even from the Sienese heartland. Stories, it seems, always survive. You might even find books of them in the larger cities of the empire. Not particularly respectable reading, but not criminal either.'

'They're harmless, then?' I asked.

'I wouldn't say harmless. As we've established, literature is politics, and so on. But most who read them are not looking for those deeper layers.'

I took another deep breath, astonished that we were even having this conversation and hoping he wasn't weaving an elaborate trap.

'And magic?'

'Most people aren't looking for magic either,' he said. 'Some of the powers described in such legends may well exist – or may well have existed, once – but who can say what is fact and what is mere myth? At any rate, none in the empire save the Hands and Voices are granted such gifts.' He smiled widely. 'As I recall, you aspired to be the second-greatest sorcerer in the empire once. I thought that a childish fancy.'

I rankled at what I took for mockery. 'Are you saying I'm not capable?'

'Oh no, Alder. You are quite capable. But you have a long, long road ahead of you if magic is your goal.' He leaned forwards and tapped the next page. 'A road you'll never traverse if you cannot focus on your studies.'

*

That night, and many nights after, I lay awake recalling and contemplating the memory of my grandmother's power. Magic could reshape the world. Its power was undeniable. It needed no argument to bolster it, nor any faith to make it true. Regardless of whether I accepted Sienese doctrine or Nayeni myth, my grandmother would still be able to conjure flame and change her shape.

It was the only thing in the world that I yearned to understand for its own sake rather than because an authority had decided I must learn it. Once I had mastered it, it would be mine to do with as I would, bound neither to my father's dream of a restored Wen family nor to my grandmother's of a Nayen free of the empire.

The two competing branches of my family – to which, I felt, I owed an equal duty – could not be reconciled. To serve one would be to betray the other. But magic offered a way for me to escape that stifling contradiction, to carve out my own path through the world. I had endured my hunger for it these four years. How much longer would it be before the emperor chose me as a Hand or my grandmother deemed me ready to learn?

Too long, I decided.

The thinning strand of my patience lasted only until the next night that passed without a summons from my grandmother. When the moon was high and still I heard no tap at the window, I slipped out of the house and into the warm night.

Never had I come to the Temple of the Flame alone. The bared teeth of its guardian wolf gods menaced me. I avoided their gaze and stifled the thought that they might tell Grandmother I'd come without her. They were only stone, of course, but when a woman could become a hawk, was anything ever only itself?

I knelt where she had knelt in the courtyard, beside the pavilion and the dry streambed. I shut my eyes, steadied my breathing, and opened myself to the world. Crickets chirped and bullfrogs croaked in the courtyard around me. A breeze rustled through the bamboo grove nearby. The earth beneath my knees and feet was cool and wet. I breathed deeply and felt the faintest echo of the strange, oiled-iron sensation of my grandmother's magic. It was in the world around me, a constant ebb and flow of energy. One thing changing into another. One moment giving rise to the next. Shifting possibilities, resolving from moment to moment according to the pattern of the world. My body shivered in sympathy with the rhythm of that flow.

A thrill coursed through me, and suddenly I felt that I stood above and apart from the pattern of the world and everything in it, even my own body. All was mine to shape to my will, as though the world was a sheet of rice paper and all its objects and events a story being written. And I, hovering above, held the brush.

Without knowing what I was doing, I reached out – a grasping from somewhere deep at the core of me – and wrote my will into the world, mimicking the marks I had seen my grandmother make when she'd become an eagle hawk.

If Grandmother's magic was fine calligraphy, mine had all the sophistication of a child splashing in the mud.

Every muscle in my body seized. My mind collapsed into dread and panic, a marrow-deep certainty that I would die, as though I had flung myself over the edge of an abyss. I remember only a torrent of pain that dragged me, screaming, back into the twisted body crafted by my ill-formed spell. Limbs that did not know whether to be wing or hand, foot or talon. Hollow bones cracked and twisted by powerful muscles in need of a stronger skeleton. Glimpses of the overgrown path as I dragged myself back towards home.

How far I crawled on those broken limbs, I cannot say.

I came to my senses in my grandmother's arms, in my own room and my own body. Her face loomed above me, wan and drawn. She hugged me to her breast and, rocking back and forth, whispered gratitude to the gods. It was the most affection I had ever known from her.

'You stupid, stupid boy!' she hissed. 'I should never have shown you. But how did you— It shouldn't have been possible! Not yet, not without witch marks.'

I tried to apologise but my tongue stuck to the roof of my mouth. She released me and pressed a lukewarm cup of red tea into my hands. It was bitter and tasted of something medicinal, and I nearly coughed it up, but she made me finish it and soon I felt the warm infusion settling my roiling stomach and soothing the stiff pains that wracked my muscles and bones.

'You'll be deathly ill for a few days,' she said, pouring another cup. 'Deathly hungry, too, but your stomach won't take anything but tea and bland broth, so you'll have to suffer through it.'

'I'm sorry,' I blubbered, finding my voice. 'I just thought—'

'You didn't *think*,' she snapped. 'Your ambition and cleverness got the better of your thinking. Don't let it happen again.'

Despite her cold words, she sat with me while I wept and shuddered at the memories of the twisted creature I had been.

'I should have been more careful,' she muttered. 'I shouldn't have shown you. Gods! Not even your uncle was so sensitive to magic.' She looked to the window, where the moonlight had vanished into the full dark before dawn. 'I should go. Your mother and that tutor will be troubled enough by your sudden illness without wondering why I came to visit you in the dead of night.'

I clutched at her arm. She stared down at me, her face hardening. Despite the agonies of that night, what most tortured me was the fear that my foolishness had cost me what I wanted most: her secret knowledge and forbidden power. I was more desperate than ever to learn. Prior to that moment, my life had been hemmed in and driven forwards by my father and grandmother and their divergent designs, but for an instant I'd felt the pattern of all things, and my will had hovered above it, unbounded, able to shape the world at a whim. This first attempt had led to horror, but with training and time I was certain to master that power and understand the profound, heart-stirring truth at the core of it. My young mind had yet to meet a challenge it could not overcome.

'You'll still teach me?' I said, unable to hide the desperation in my voice.

She prised herself free of my hand. 'I've hardly a choice now, have I?'

3

Scars

All that first day of my recovery, while I drifted in and out of sleep, my mother lingered at my bedside, testing my fever with the back of her hand. It was more physical contact than we had shared since my early childhood, before I'd left her apartments for my own rooms in the eastern wing of the house, in accordance with Sienese custom. In the Sienese view, mothers and sons ought to be distant, as coddling left a young man ill prepared to manage his own household as a father – the emperor of his little realm. Propriety dictated that my mother should have sent page girls to deliver trays of tea and ginger candy and return with reports on my recovery. But my mother – as became clear to me in those days – was not Sienese.

Mother spent all of that first day and most of the next sitting beside me, and conspired with Grandmother to displace the Sienese cook who managed our kitchen. So instead of the rich fare I had been raised on, my grandmother prepared the same foods she had served my mother and uncle when they'd taken ill as children: a bland, slightly salty broth made with seaweed and dried fish; a light tea of wildflowers she had gathered herself from the forest around our estate; a few bites of glutinous rice and dried dates wrapped in bamboo leaves and then steamed

– Nayeni foods I had never eaten before but which my mother and grandmother trusted to make me well.

Koro Ha, meanwhile, was concerned less for my health and more for the damage a long period of convalescence might do to my education. Grandmother managed to fend him off for the first day, but on the second he argued his way past her defences and established a beachhead at my writing desk in the corner of the room. From there he launched salvos from the books of Sienese odes and poems, the classics of religion, and the various treatises on government and philosophy, forcing Mother to retreat. Being in a room alone – but for a sickly child – with a man other than her husband was a step beyond her bravery. One could stretch propriety only so far.

By the third day, Koro Ha had conquered me. I spent the rest of my convalescence studying, though my tutor's lessons were often interrupted by fainting spells that left me disorientated, as if my body had quite suddenly grown and no longer properly fitted my soul.

After six days, the Nayeni diet had cooled the fire in my bones, but I was still unable to stand. I had a fainting spell on the seventh day, and that night I heard my mother and my grandmother arguing, as they had so often when I was very young.

'What happened to him?' my mother demanded, her voice sharp with concern.

'It takes time to drive a foul wind from the body,' my grandmother replied. 'He's eating more, and the fever is broken—'

'He's dizzy and weak!' Mother cried, no doubt glaring as she went on: 'Whatever this is, it's beyond us.'

'It isn't. Just be patient.'

'Will you tell me, then?' Mother asked, loud enough for all the estate to hear. Then, quieter, but still full of anger: 'I let you mark him. I agreed that he should learn our stories. I said nothing about teaching him your witchcraft.'

'Your witchcraft, too, if you would have it.'

'*What. Happened. To. Him.*'

I had never heard such ferocity in my mother's voice, not even when my uncle had visited, unwanted and unannounced, eight years earlier. Neither had my grandmother, it seemed, for there was a long pause before she finally spoke. 'He dabbled in magic he shouldn't have been able to touch, let alone wield,' she said. 'Not even Harrow Fox—'

'Don't speak of my brother!' I heard a sharp intake of breath, then a long, slow exhalation, like that of someone preparing to perform the Iron Dance. When my mother spoke again, she was calm, poised, her voice a steady blade. 'He needs a doctor. I will send for one. And shut your mouth. If you don't like it, you are free to leave my house.'

'Tell him nothing,' my grandmother warned me on the morning of the eighth day of my recovery. 'Not of what we do in the temple, and especially not what caused this ... sickness, we should call it. If you must tell him something, just say something vague about a chill wind and the sniffles. Something a grandmother would treat with soup and tea.'

When I'd finished the tea she had brought, she collected the empty cups and bustled out of the room, muttering about woolheaded Sienese doctors and their random treatments, divined by nothing more than trial and error.

I had been examined before that day by Sienese doctors, who passed often through the nearby town of Ashen Clearing in their endless wanderings across the empire. At six years old, I'd contracted a pox that had afflicted the children there. A doctor had come to town, but my father tripled the doctor's usual fee to keep him on retainer in the guest room until I'd recovered. Ashen Clearing lost half a dozen children in his absence.

I do not remember that doctor clearly. Doctor Sho, however,

made a much more profound impression, with his knowing eyes and gnarled hands, both when he came to treat my botched veering and, later, when my thirst for secret knowledge brought me back into his company.

Doctor Sho's bare feet were calloused and cracked. A wild crop of hair hung gathered at the nape of his neck, and wisps of beard floated around a thin-lipped mouth. His eyes were bright and expressive, lacking the demureness expected in Sienese men, and the keen, knowing glint in them terrified me. If he deduced the cause of my illness, my grandmother's secrets would be revealed, my father and mother would be accused of harbouring a witch, and the Sienese would put us all to death.

He felt my pulse, pressing against my wrist. As he did so, I took deep breaths to slow my racing heart, hoping he wouldn't notice. He paused, pressed harder, then paused again. Then he murmured, jotted something on a scrap of paper, and opened the chest of drawers he had brought with him. Each drawer was no bigger than the palm of my hand, its fascia inscribed with the logogram for this herb or that mineral, and carvings of vines and forest creatures decorated the sides of the chest. Doctor Sho's fingers fluttered from drawer to drawer as he filled a series of paper sacks with pinches of various ingredients.

He placed the two largest sacks on my writing desk. 'These are herbal soups,' he said. 'Mix them with broth. Drink one tomorrow and one three days after. During those three days,' he continued, holding up two smaller sacks, 'drink this tea in the morning and this tea at night. On the second day, if you can't get out of bed, you'll need acupuncture and massage. Afterwards, if your stool smells like rot, send for me immediately. If you *can* get out of bed, go for a walk in the garden. On the fourth day, eat nothing in the morning, then meat and bread in the evening. After that, you should recover.'

All the while, he had been scribbling these instructions on

the sheet of paper he now handed to me. 'I'll explain this to your mother as well. If I don't hear from you, I'll return in six days for the other half of my payment.'

I looked at him in amazement. *All that from feeling my pulse?* The speed and certainty of his deductions were as astonishing as magic. I tried to think of something to say while he shut and locked his chest of drawers. Fearing that he must know the cause of my condition, and that my silence might confirm some suspicion, I summoned the courage to thank him but bit back the urge to ask what he had diagnosed.

'Keep your thanks,' he said. 'I'm being paid.' With that, he hoisted his chest onto his back, fastened the web of straps that held it in place, and donned his wide conical hat. At the threshold he looked over his shoulder and fixed me with a stare. 'You'll have worse than me to face if you dabble with such dangerous things again,' he warned, and left.

I followed his instructions dutifully, unwilling to risk the ire of a man who had seen through me with so little effort. Some of his medicines were cloying, others sour, and the herbal soups were as salty as the sea, but when I was able to rise on the second day, Grandmother muttered a grudging respect for the old doctor.

Koro Ha led me on a slow walk around the garden. At the Moon Bridge, my mother met us and, overcome with happiness to see me healthy again, gathered me into an embrace which violated every rule of propriety between mother and son.

Doctor Sho returned on the sixth day, examined me impassively, nodded once, collected a string of silver coins from my mother as payment, and left again without a word.

As soon as I could walk again, Koro Ha resumed our lessons in earnest. Though the imperial examinations would not be held for four more years, he seemed to believe that any day not spent studying would be a millstone around my neck. We spent our mornings reviewing the classics and dialectics and our afternoons practising calligraphy, composing essays, and writing poetry.

I lay awake most nights, listening for a tap at my window. It never came. Instead, I overheard many hushed arguments between my mother and my grandmother, their voices never as loud as they had been the night before Doctor Sho's arrival, so that I caught only a few muted words through the wood-and-paper walls. In my imagination, they must have been continuing the fight over my grandmother's lessons. Grandmother had promised to teach me magic, but my mother had been terrified by my illness and – I assumed – must have forbidden her from doing so.

This imagined conflict made me despise my mother. I still loved her, in that vague but potent way learned in infancy, but the sight of her had begun to annoy me. When she congratulated me on my successes with Koro Ha, her praise stung like nettles.

My feelings of alienation built and built until they overflowed from my waking mind into my subconscious, emerging in a horrible dream that returned me to that night in the forest when I had dragged my contorted body on twisted limbs, gasping for air with each attempt to scream, harried from every shadow by the stone eyes of the wolf gods.

I woke with a start, threw off my sweat-soaked blanket, and felt along the lines of my limbs to be sure they were human. When the hammering of my heart finally subsided, I heard a familiar tapping at my window.

'Foolish Cur!' my grandmother whispered from the other side of the oiled-paper screen. 'Meet me in the garden. We have much to discuss and only one night left to us.'

*

For the last time, we followed the pathway together through the forest to the Temple of the Flame, where Grandmother once again paused beside the statue of Okara. I waited anxiously, desperate to know why this would be our last night together and what she would teach me for my final lesson.

A sense of the interconnectedness of all things lingered within me. I had not reached for magic since the night I'd made myself an abomination, but my longing for mastery had only deepened. I realised that a single night would never be enough for her to teach me all I needed to learn. A thought that darkened my mood like a black cloud.

Finally, we reached the steps leading up to the temple. Grandmother sat and motioned for me to join her.

'I must go away,' she said at last. Her eyes took on a faraway look, as though gazing upon her destination. The wrinkles on her face and hands were deeper than I remembered. The glassiness of age had begun to creep in at the corners of her eyes.

'There is still much fighting in the North,' she went on. 'Your uncle Harrow Fox is caught up in it and cornered. I will go to him tomorrow.'

I knew my uncle only as a name, a reputation, and a bedraggled silhouette. Yet once or twice – when my studies with Koro Ha had hit a snarl and the imperial examinations had seemed to loom over me like some unconquerable monster – I had entertained a fantasy of slipping away from my father's estate, abandoning my duty to the Wen family, and making my way to join him in the mountains. Now my grandmother spoke of doing just that.

'Do *not* follow me,' she commanded, perhaps sensing my desire. 'You don't know enough to be of use. Read the books hidden here. Learn our histories. Teach your children. This will be your last lesson, and it is one I cannot leave you without.'

She entered the temple and returned with the obsidian knife

that she had used to name me. She extended her palm and I gave her my hand. Gently she pressed the tip of the knife to my naming scar.

I bit back a cry as she carved my hand with three curving lines that followed the creases of my palm. As she did, I felt a thrum of power, like a single heartbeat through the pattern of the world. In its wake, the sharpness of my senses dulled. I squeezed my eyes shut and felt for the ebb and flow of energy, the pattern of all things that I had apprehended in the moment before veering. All that remained was a sense of heat and power beneath the wounds my grandmother scored into my flesh. The absence of the pattern felt like an amputated limb and I stared at my grandmother, hurt and betrayed, trying to mask my panic while grasping desperately for a shred of the power I had held.

'These witch marks are the sign of our pact with the gods,' she said. 'Without them, you should never have been able to work magic. You tried to carve a figurine of jade and chose for your tool a woodcutter's sledge. If you'd tried to conjure flame, you likely would have burned the forest down.'

Her words, though meant to calm me, had the opposite effect. I did not understand what she had done, but I knew that the limitless freedom I had felt when first reaching for magic had been suddenly hemmed in, limited by this pact of which she spoke. Perhaps, as she had claimed, those limitations would protect me. But even if that were true, *she* had chosen that protection for me, as everything else in my life had been chosen for me. I wanted to scream, to seize her knife and carve away the marks she had made, in the hope that doing so would restore my freedom.

Yet if I were to learn magic – any magic at all – I needed her to teach me. Who else in my life could? And so, as I would so often in the years to come, I swallowed my anger, my frustrations, and my feelings of betrayal. I would glean what useful truths I could from her and use them to find my way back to the deeper power I had tasted and which, with a few strokes of her knife, she had taken away.

She poured clear alcohol over the wound and wrapped it in bandages till my hand was little more than a club of blood-stained cloth. This done, she entered the temple to replace the obsidian knife in its chest beside the altar with the books and scrolls that were the remnants of her culture. When she returned, I saw her hopes for me, and her fears, mingled and inseparable, written in the lines of her face.

'When you were born,' she said, breaking the silence, 'I fought the urge to hate you, as I still fight the urge to hate your mother. She was too young when the Sienese came. She forgets what they did to your grandfather. Or she never believed it. Harrow Fox, your uncle ... he remembers. When they came, it was with the promise of wealth and culture. Silks, opera, foreign delicacies. Wondrous weapons – rippled steel that could shatter our swords and grenades that could tear a palisade to tinder. These things they sold cheaply, for the payment they sought was not our silver but our souls.'

I nursed my hand but soon forgot my pain, lost in her words. Even the ache of her betrayal faded as I listened. Never had she spoken so much about herself, and certainly never about my grandfather.

Her fingers – calloused like a farmer's, or a soldier's – toyed with the hems of her sleeves as she went on. 'Your grandfather was the witch of our village temple, not me. I was the hostess of the common house. The people went to him to pray and came to me to drink and sing and hear the old stories. I was that, too – a storyteller.'

She shook her head and was silent for a moment while her gaze returned to the present moment and to me.

'What matters is this: the Sienese came. A few at first,

38

merchant adventurers – like your father – who travelled to the cities, then the towns, then the villages. They sought out things we took at first for harmless. Our stories. Our histories. Maps of our roads. Your grandfather spent many nights in the common house, answering their endless questions about our gods. He kept our magic secret, wise man that he was. Nayen was at war with itself in those days. Three rival lords all claimed the throne of the Sun King. Save the threat of conscription and burdensome taxes, we common folk cared little which of them won in the end. Yet the Sienese took an interest.

'Soon, more merchants came to our town, and soldiers with them, to defend their caravans. And we heard rumours that the Sienese no longer visited the north and west of our country, the territories claimed by our lord's rivals. They offered soldiers and their wondrous weapons and a swift end to the war, and our lord – may he burn forever – accepted. But of course, when his rivals had been put down, the Sienese legions were not finished with their conquest.'

Her shoulders rose and fell as she took a deep, steadying breath. 'Word spread of witches disappearing, of temples ransacked and burned. We made ready to leave but were too late. They came for your grandfather even as we shouldered our packs. We watched, Harrow Fox and I, while their sorcerers bound him in chains of light.' She swallowed, blinked, and took another breath. 'Rather than let them capture him, and with him his magic, he did what all witches of Nayen have done when cornered: he conjured a fire that filled the temple. It burned, with him in it, to the ground. Better to die than let the empire steal our secrets.' There was a hitch in her voice and she swallowed again. 'I gave birth to your mother three months later, in the common house of a village, far from our home, where I cut my own witch marks and tried to raise my children as their father would have wanted – wise, stupid man that he was.'

39

She rubbed her face with the heel of her hand and pressed on. 'They are liars, Foolish Cur. So, to survive, we became liars as well. I made a living mending nets, and Harrow Fox was a fisherman for a time, until the rebellion. Never have I felt such pride and terror as the day he joined them.' She gestured with the knife towards my bandaged hand. 'Until, perhaps, the day you worked magic without those marks. If you can, abstain from it. You've already tasted its power, and it is as alluring as strong drink. Worse, you are curious, and sensitive enough to learn on your own. Be careful. With those scars you won't make yourself an abomination again, but there are other powers just as dangerous and unwieldy. Do not seek them. And, at all costs, avoid discovery. If you become known as a witch, the Sienese will torture every secret they can from you before they let you die.'

She looked to the sky, where the stars were dimming and the moon descending. Dawn would break soon and end the last night of our lessons.

'I almost wish I hadn't taught you,' she muttered, and stood. I rose to follow her. She touched my shoulder and looked at the bloody bandages. 'Make up a story. Say you were whittling and the knife slipped.'

We walked in sombre silence and parted ways in the garden of the estate. She embraced me. My bloodied hand was caught awkwardly between us. I bit my tongue to keep from yelping and did not pull away.

A sudden fear of her leaving gripped me. She had been a pillar of my life, a window into half of my heritage, a teacher vital to my understanding of the world. My only means of learning magic, even if in a lessened form and limited by her fears for me.

'You don't have to go,' I said, my voice tight.

She smiled at me and, with rare tenderness, kissed the top of my head. 'Keep our ways alive,' she whispered, and then released me and walked swiftly to her wing of the women's apartments. I lingered in the garden until her silhouette disappeared behind the paper walls.

Instead of taking my grandmother's suggestion – for I had never whittled in my life – I broke one of the porcelain plates on my breakfast tray and smeared blood from my thumb on the shards. My mother's stewardess fussed over the damage and Koro Ha gave me a cursory scolding, but his real concern was the damage to my writing hand.

'You drop a plate, and now you may never write again!' One of his eyebrows twitched in frustration. 'What has been the point of all my effort if you cannot sit for the imperial examinations?'

More than wasted effort was at stake for Koro Ha. If I did well in the examinations, he could leverage that success into a position with a family of high station – perhaps even in the house of a Hand or a Voice. Many such families offered pensions and permanent quarters to tutors who guided their sons to success. If I could no longer write, any hope of such promotion and eventual retirement was lost to him.

'We will have to see how it heals,' he said at last. 'While we wait, we will dedicate ourselves to discourse and recitation.'

I was halfway through reciting the Classic of Streams and Valleys when an eagle hawk flew over the garden in a flash of auburn feathers. I faltered, the poetic words fading from my mind as I watched the bird disappear behind the forest canopy, wondering whether it was my grandmother, whether this would be the last time I would ever see her. Koro Ha made me start again, but my mind kept wandering and he released me from my lessons long before supper.

My grandmother was gone, and with her a path that my life might have taken. For all her encouragement to learn on my own, I knew that, without her to counterbalance them, Koro Ha and my father would lead me into their vision of my future. Any alternative I might have imagined would fade with time.

That night, I sat on my bed and examined my hand. True to my grandmother's word, the wounds had already healed. The blood staining the bandages was dry and dark, but the scars beneath them were pale and thin. They itched and burned when I flexed my hand, but there were no scabs to crack. Koro Ha would never believe I'd damaged it that morning.

I panicked. My mother and tutor would be looking for a jagged scar cut by broken porcelain, not these ritualistic markings! I couldn't break another plate – that would invite too many questions – and I kept no knife in my room. There were knives in the kitchens, but for the heir of the house to wander the servants' wing in the middle of the night would create gossip and rumour.

There was only one knife that I could use without drawing attention. I crept out into the garden and from there followed the familiar trails. The last time I had walked them alone had ended in disaster. There was no one to save me from any similar folly now that my grandmother was gone.

The wolf gods watched as I mounted the steps of the temple. Stone eyes regarded me with neither warmth nor rebuke. If they remembered the last time I had come alone, they did not show it.

I brushed my hand along the top of the altar. The fire my grandmother had conjured in its hearth still burned. The knife was where she had left it, lying with the books and scrolls of bamboo slats in the small chest beside the altar. Twice I had seen that obsidian blade used in the working of magic, but in that moment it was only a knife to me.

The grip was old leather, worn down to match knuckles more widely spaced than mine. I held it clumsily in my left hand and examined my right, deciding where to cut myself. The upper half of my palm – below the thumb and above the naming scar – was unmarked and seemed a likely place to have cut myself in a futile attempt to catch a shattering plate.

Gritting my teeth, I slashed open my palm, deep enough to suit my lie but not so deep as to damage the hand beyond repair. The wound was long and uneven, snaking from below my thumb to just below my middle finger, and I thought it likely to elicit a sympathetic wince from the most hardened and battle-scarred warrior. It certainly served to draw even my knowing eye away from the finer scars my grandmother had dealt. After rewrapping my hand in its old bandage, I returned the knife to its place and left the temple. As I did so, I felt the hairs on the back of my neck standing on end, but on turning around I saw only the stone eyes of the wolf gods, measuring me.

The next morning, Koro Ha panicked at the sight of fresh blood. He removed the bandage from my hand and rebound it in a poultice of herbs and mineral oil. If he noticed the ritual scars my grandmother had dealt, he said nothing. When he'd finished, he thrust a calligraphy brush into my left hand.

'I hope you enjoy writing, boy,' he said. 'You'll be doing a great deal of it in the days to come.'

4

Examination

Only the silence at night, when she ought to have been arguing with my mother, told of my grandmother's disappearance.
Father, Mother, and Koro Ha never mentioned it. Perhaps they
believed that, if we did not speak of her, the Sienese might
never learn that we had harboured her for so many years.

Over the next three years, I taught myself what I could of
magic, but the witch marks had made it smaller and weaker.
No longer did I hover above the world like a brush over blank
paper, free to write whatever I willed. Now, whenever I reached
for magic, I felt only the powers to conjure flame and change
my shape. Without my grandmother's guidance I dared go little
further than kindling a candle flame.

Is it any surprise that, as the examinations drew closer and
closer, I put her lessons from my mind? The only remaining
path towards mastery of magic lay in the unlikely possibility
that I might become Hand of the emperor.

If she ever learned that my thoughts had so much as drifted
in the direction of that possibility, let alone hoped for it – as
I did now – Grandmother's outrage would have burned hot
enough to put me in fear for my life. Yet after years of stag-
nation in my pursuit of magic, constrained by the witch marks
she had carved into my flesh before abandoning me to fight her

war, I cared little for what she might think, nor her hopes and intentions for me. When the time came for me to travel to the regional capital and take the imperial examinations, I had not been to the Temple of the Flame in more than a year.

My father made a point of being at home on the day before I was due to leave. He did not put me to the question, as he had so often in my youth, but instead led me to the small family shrine in the corner of our garden.

We swept the altars to the sages, polished their golden faces with rose oil, set incense to burn at their feet, and filled their table with fruits and sweet rice. This done, we knelt before the lacquered panel carved with the ancient names of our family's most notable members. Father invoked their aid and asked them to guide my tongue and brush during the examinations. I made my own venerations and asked Wen Broad-Oak to show me the path to becoming Hand of the emperor. When we stood, my father squeezed my shoulder – a warm touch, the sort I had not felt from him since my earliest memories.

'It's good that you're so ambitious,' he said, 'but it will take generations to rebuild our family's reputation. Your grand-parents – may they rest with our greatest ancestors – began it when they sold their pitiful farm to buy my first ship. I've done my part and seen you educated. Now it's your turn to do yours. All you need is a minor station, enough to hire a truly excellent tutor for your sons. Perhaps one of them, or one of your grand-sons, will reach such lofty heights.'

'Of course,' I said. 'But to quote the sage Traveller-on-the-Narrow-Way, "Is it not better to strive for the mountain-top than to settle in the foothills?"'

He grinned – to quote the sages was the sort of educated affectation he liked to see in me – and led me to the garden pavilion. That night we drank wine together for the first time. I did not tell him that his goals and mine were no longer the

45

same, that I would never be satisfied to be just a paving stone on the road to our family's restoration. I kept from him my resolve to press on until I reached the very top of the mountain, and my belief that only there did I have any hope of coming to understand the power I had wielded – power that had almost destroyed me.

In the morning, my father returned to his ships while Koro Ha and I set out for the regional capital. Though as a merchant my father travelled often, I had never left the small corner of the world where I was raised and found the prospect of travelling to the city of Eastern Fortress exciting. The journey, however, proved far from pleasant.

The Grand Highway that united Nayen from north to south still bore scars of the Sienese invasion. All during the three days of our journey, our palanquin bearers were forced to negotiate deep ruts and uneven cobbles. When I tried to read, the text bounced and shifted before my eyes. When Koro Ha practised the verbal components of the examinations, my teeth clicked together with every bump in the road. Once, I bit my tongue and tasted blood.

Late on the third day, our palanquin slowed to a crawl and I opened the window, expecting to find that we had arrived, but while we had passed through the city gates of Eastern Fortress, we had progressed little further. Our bearers now waded through an endless sea of young faces, some peering from other palanquin windows, others caked in the dust of the road.

Koro Ha sensed my anxiety. While our palanquin-bearers trudged through Eastern Fortress, he spun tales of the fine meals, opera performances, and tours of the city that would follow my examinations. I had never seen opera, nor tasted the foreign delicacies from the distant corners of the Empire, which he assured me would be available at the governor's banquet for successful candidates. His descriptions were a welcome distraction, but the gnawing in the pit of my stomach remained.

My father had arranged for us to stay with a business associate of his. Mr Yat was the owner of a copper mine whose goods Father's merchant fleet often carried to the Sienese mainland. He greeted us and instructed a steward to show us to our rooms, then to the household baths. When we were bathed and dressed, Mr Yat joined us in his modest courtyard for a meal of seared salmon in oyster sauce, braised greens, jasmine rice, and carrots fried in red pepper oil.

'I remember when Thistle, my second boy, sat the exams,' Mr Yat said, flashing a golden molar around a mouthful of fish. 'This was nine years ago. I took him to Centre Fortress myself to make sure he wouldn't shirk the bloody thing and waste his allowance on mainland luxuries. Poor boy nearly shat himself with nerves, but he passed. Now he's a scribe for some general in Toa Alon. Your father's the craftiest bastard I ever dealt with. If you've got half his brains – even if the other half's all muddled by Easterling blood – you'll pass.'

I chafed at the slur, but it would violate propriety to criticise my host. He poured plum wine for us that was sweet, mild, and a welcome distraction from my anxieties. I soon drained my cup. As Mr Yat moved to refill it, however, Koro Ha turned his own upside down and eyed mine meaningfully. 'You will need a clear head tomorrow,' he said.

'Let the boy have a little fun,' Mr Yat said, righting Koro Ha's cup and filling it. 'A relaxed mind is a nimble mind! I'm not sure which sage said that, but I'm sure one of them did.'

Koro Ha pushed the cup away. 'My apologies, Mr Yat. Thank you for your hospitality, but young Master Wen – muddled blood or no – will be more than a minor scribe to some far-flung general.' With that, he stood, bowed to our host, and looked at me expectantly. The wine was already going to my head, but I knew better than to disobey my tutor when he wore

47

that expression. Mr Yat mumbled about what a pleasure it was to help my father and wished me luck in my examinations, then poured himself another cup.

As we entered the reception hall of the guest wing, Koro Ha paused, and I feared that he meant to put me through my exercises one last time. Instead he picked up the brush case that my mother had given me to commemorate my taking the examinations. It was beautiful, layered in black lacquer and painted with alder branches. He held it out and I took it, feeling the same momentous weight I'd felt when my grandmother had named me.

'You will do us proud, Wen Alder,' Koro Ha said. 'I hope you sleep well.'

But that night I lay awake, recalling and reviewing the hundreds of discourses and aphorisms I'd committed to memory, fretting over the dozens of possible essay prompts, and wondering if any of the proctors would recognise the scars on my right hand for what they were. The little sleep I managed was fraught with nightmares. Though I longed to forget the night when I had wielded magic without the witch marks and veered into an abomination, my dreaming mind saw fit to dredge up memories of my long, tortured crawl along the overgrown path. In the nightmares I felt the stone eyes of the wolf gods as though they followed me through the woods. Their whispered words drifted from the shadows at the forest's edge.

'This one?'

'Unworthy.'

'Failure.'

I was into my fourth cup of black tea before Koro Ha woke. His gaze lingered on the bags under my eyes. What worse omen could he wake to see on the day of my examinations? I feared a reprimand or, worse, some half-hearted reassurance.

Instead, my tutor placed his hand on my shoulder and smiled.

'I think we all sleep terribly the night before. But it couldn't hurt to hope.'

Soon I was standing with the other candidates, who had gathered shoulder to shoulder on a marble plaza below the grand audience hall of the governor's palace. Banners fluttered from flag stands and fragrant smoke wafted from bronze incense burners arranged on the dais atop the stairway in front of us. Sweat soaked the silks of our robes and wilted the felt of our peaked caps.

The governor strode out between the twin pillars that framed the entrance to the audience hall, followed by his attendants. He too had dressed for the occasion in the peaked cap and flowing robes of a scholar, though two golden wings had been stitched to his sleeves and to the front of his cap, marking him as one who had earned the highest rank in the imperial examinations. Below the rim of his cap, a symbol had been marked on his forehead with what appeared to be silver ink. Even from afar, I recognised it immediately as the imperial tetragram: four logograms arranged in a square that together formed the emperor's never-changing name. As his dark gaze swung over me, I felt it linger for a moment, as though he scrutinised me personally. Did he see in my face some shadow of my notorious uncle? Without thinking, I held my breath, and when his gaze drifted on I heard others around me do the same.

'Young men of Nayen,' he called, his voice echoing from the walls of the courtyard, 'today you face the greatest honour and trial known to man. For the first time, the brightest young minds of your province shall be elevated to the illustrious civil service of our empire. And of those, one shall be raised to that highest station of all: the emperor's Hand.'

He held out his right palm, which bore scars depicting the same tetragram that he wore on his forehead. 'What is done with this hand is done in the emperor's never-changing name.

It is through a hand bearing this seal that the emperor performs his justice. Governors, generals, and scholars alone may bear it, and it is time for one of your own – from Nayen, the emperor's youngest adopted son – to be raised to such a station. One of you will leave sealed. Know this, and let it inspire you to excellence.'

The tetragram on his palm flashed silver. White fire curled around his fingertips. He closed his fist and the fire flashed bright as lightning, and then was gone. The young men around me cheered, for we were all accustomed to such displays at New Year festivals, and the sight of sorcery brought on feelings of celebration and excitement. Only I remained silent. I too had seen such displays, but never before had I been close enough to feel it as I had felt my grandmother's magic. When Grandmother had conjured flame, my skin flushed as with fever. When she had veered, every muscle in my body ached. The only commonalities between hers and the governor's sorcery were the phantom scent of burnt cinnamon and the sudden sharpness of my senses. His magic felt more abstract, but weightier, as though walls of stone had fallen from the sky to hem in the pattern of the world.

A scribe called my name, and then again, drawing my thoughts back to the mundane. I followed him along with seven other candidates, who chatted among themselves while I mulled over the sensation of the governor's sorcery.

'What a sight!' said the young man nearest to me. He grinned, dimpling freckled cheeks. His hair hung in red-brown ringlets that rolled out from beneath his cap. 'Soon enough one of us will have that power. What do you make of that, eh?'

Before I could answer, we arrived at a wide pavilion that overlooked a lotus pond. Eight writing desks had been arranged in an outward-facing ring. The scribe called out names and pointed to desks until we had each been assigned a station.

We settled in, arranging our inkstones and paperweights, and waited nervously for the proctors to arrive.

My hands were shaking. I took a deep breath to steady them and set about arranging my brushes and wetting my inkstone. The rhythmic scrape of grinding ink set my teeth on edge, as did the crinkling of the paper as I smoothed my composition scroll beneath twin weights. I dipped the weasel hair tip of my brush and was relieved to see that my fingers had stopped trembling, though I could still feel failure looming, tightening my chest and jumbling my thoughts.

We were instructed to begin our examinations by composing our pedigrees. For the next few hours, I would kneel in that pavilion and write a description of my lineage – with special attention paid to those like Wen Broad-Oak who had passed the imperial examinations – in demure language, a style meant to convey humility even as I boasted of my heritage.

My hand betrayed me. A trembling stirred my fingers, ruining the brushwork on a minor article. The awkward squiggle taunted me. It in no way changed the meaning of what I had written, but the proctors would be grading our handwriting as well as our composition.

I glanced around, mortified that I had stumbled immediately over such a familiar, simple feat that I had so often practised. Surely this failure had already sealed my fate. To go through with the rest of the examination would be a futile exercise. One of these other young men – so much more capable than I, who had destroyed my future with a slip of my nervous fingers – would become Hand of the emperor, earning the chance at freedom which would always be denied me.

A strangled cry sounded from elsewhere in the pavilion. A proctor, his expression as hard and sharp as an executioner's sword, swept across the pavilion like a typhoon. 'What is the meaning of this outburst?' he hissed.

Slowly, I peered over my shoulder. The proctor was looming over a candidate who sat with his head bowed to his chest, his shoulders shaking with choked-back sobs.

'Explain yourself!' the proctor said. The gentle swish of calligraphy brushes fell silent as we all attended the disruption.

'I ... I ...' the candidate sobbed. Then, without another word, he sprang to his feet and darted from the pavilion, his brushes, ink, and future abandoned.

The proctor swung his severe gaze around the room. 'Surely the rest of you have the mental fortitude to return to your task. Or must I make note that so many eyes drifted away from their own work, perhaps seeking inspiration in the writing of a neighbouring candidate?'

I did as instructed, heartened by the fact that at least I had not bolted in panic too, and focused on the blank space beside that offending article. The only way through was forwards.

I shut my eyes and focused first on my fingertips, then on the tendons and bones in my hands, then on the veins in my wrists. Moving up the arms to the elbows, then the shoulders, then the ribs. Finally, the heart. I listened to its beat, felt it slow. A centring exercise performed before the gods of Nayen at the beginning of the Iron Dance. I thought only of the next word, the next sentence, the next page. Soon I was swept up in the act of writing.

After a brief description of my father's business, I cleaned my brush and returned it to its case – a signal for one of the proctors to collect my scroll. A calmness settled over me as the swishing sounds of brushwork subsided and the other students finished their pedigrees. High overhead, above the garden, an eagle hawk cried.

For the rest of that week, as the examinations proceeded, I felt certain that I would fail and gradually abandoned any hope of being elevated to Hand of the emperor and being offered the chance to learn magic without secrecy or fear.

For the rest of the first day and the second, I composed essays and commentaries with haste, always finishing before the other candidates near me and always convinced that this was because I had neglected some key component of the prompt that had been obvious to everyone else. On the third and fourth days, during the verbal examinations, I paralysed myself with second-guessing. More than once I managed to spit out an answer only after the proctors had thrice repeated themselves.

On the fifth and final day of the examinations, we were taken one at a time to a small pavilion isolated from the rest of the garden by an arc of basalt columns to the north and a grove of bamboo to the south. When I arrived, two proctors were waiting, one of whom – a round-faced eunuch with the pinkish complexion of the southern Sienese – had officiated at one of my verbal examinations. Beside him sat a man I did not recognise, though the gold feathers embroidered on the hems of his sleeves marked him as having earned the first placement in his own examinations. He smiled at me through his wispy beard – which seemed to be a standard feature among scholars – and gestured for me to sit. As he did so, I saw the glimmer of a tetragram branded on his palm.

My right hand curled into a fist in the depth of my sleeve. It took every scrap of self-control to lower myself into the seat instead of bolting from the garden to try my luck in the mountains. Surely this Hand of the emperor could have no reason to pay special attention to me, unless he knew about my uncle, or my grandmother, or the marks carved into my flesh.

'Hello, Wen Alder,' said the proctor I'd recognised. 'Allow me to introduce Dow Usher, a Hand of the emperor recently dispatched to this province. He has asked to observe your final oral examination.'

I bowed deeply, nearly touching my forehead to the table. 'It is an honour, Hand Usher. May you know one thousand peaceful years, and the emperor ten thousand more.'

The sorcerer dipped his head in acknowledgement, then leaned back in his chair and folded his hands in his lap. Though he leaned in his seat like a daydreaming student, his eyes were bright, alert, and unblinking. 'You will do well, I'm sure,' he told me offhandedly, as though we were already close friends, and turned to the proctor. 'Begin, if you would.'

The proctor retrieved a scroll from his sleeve and began to unroll it. 'Young Master Wen,' he said. 'This portion of your examination concerns your command of literary analysis and imperial ideology. I will read a narrative, and you will be asked to evaluate it, first in its thematic meaning and literary merit, second in its value as literature to be disseminated throughout the empire.'

The proctor began to read, but all my attention was fixed on the Hand. I knew the rubric that the proctor would use, but by what metrics would Hand Usher evaluate me? I was convinced that he suspected me of something – practising forbidden magic, perhaps, or sympathy with my unsavoury relations – and that my answer would either confirm or refute his suspicions.

The proctor's story was a common didactic tale concerning a merchant, his wife, business interests far from home, long periods of separation followed by affairs, scandal, and so on. The analogies were not difficult to unravel if one understood imperial doctrine.

'Oof,' Hand Usher interjected just as I had begun to form an answer. 'Does anyone *really* care about the infidelity of mer-chants' wives?' He leaned towards me with a glint in his eye and the ghost of a smile. 'I've got a much better story in mind. One I'm sure you've never heard before. Master Proctor, if you will indulge me?'

'Of c-course, Hand Usher,' the proctor stammered. 'If I have offended you—'

'No offence at all,' Hand Usher assured him, 'only if I'm going to sit through this, I might as well enjoy myself. Are you ready, young Master Wen?'

My mind reeled as I tried to anticipate what sort of story Hand Usher had in mind. I took a deep breath to compose myself. 'I am ready,' I said.

'Excellent!' Hand Usher said. He clapped his hands together and began his tale.

This is the tale Hand Usher told.

Long ago, in a far-flung corner of the empire, there was born a pollical cat. This cat possessed a flexible dew claw, which he could use like a thumb. He was the favoured pet of the provincial magistrate and worked for his meals as a mouser.

But the cat was canny, as many beasts were in those days, and was dissatisfied with his menial role. For stimulation, he would listen to the lessons that the magistrate's son took from his tutor. The boy was indolent, and the cat often arrived at the correct answers first.

'How unjust it is that this boy will be an imperial official while I must waste my mind hunting mice,' the cat thought one day. 'If I were educated and sat for the examinations, I am certain that I would excel.'

With his flexible dew claw, the cat could grasp a stick as the boy grasped his brush, and by following along with the tutor's lessons he soon learned to write.

One day, the boy noticed the cat scrawling in the dirt and rose from his desk to watch.

'Focus, boy!' the tutor cried.

'But look! The cat's copied along,' the boy said.

55

The tutor scowled down at the cat, who swished his tail in defiance.

'It's only making scratches in the dirt,' the tutor said. 'It doesn't know what it writes.'

'But its handwriting is better than mine,' the boy said.

The tutor chased the cat away, then rubbed out the cat's writing with a sweep of his foot. 'A cat can never sit for the imperial examinations,' he said to the boy, 'but you will. By the sages, I'll see to it that you pass.'

The cat slunk away to a stand of bushes at the edge of the garden, where he crouched and glowered at the hateful tutor. 'What an injustice!' he yowled at the sky.

'What's all this yowling?' said a silky voice. In a flash of orange fur, a vixen leapt atop the garden wall. She showed her teeth and said, 'You are disturbing my afternoon nap.'

The cat, too incensed to be afraid, told the vixen what had happened. 'If I could sit for the exams, I would prove them all wrong,' he said. 'They would have to accept that cats, too, can serve the empire.'

'Ah,' said the vixen. 'But you *could*, with my help.'

The cat was wary and hunched up its back. Vixens were selfish beasts but with a magical gift: the skill to change one thing into something it's not.

'You have no reason to help me,' said the cat. 'What do you want?'

'A simple thing,' she said. 'When you have risen in the empire, you will arrange for me a marriage with a son of nobility. In exchange, I will alter your shape. But be warned! My spell will fail if you speak your true nature.'

The cat considered this. He planned to reveal himself as a cat, in the end, to prove that it was silly to educate only young men. But he could delay for a time, he reasoned, until he had fulfilled his part of the bargain.

'Very well,' he said. 'Make me a man!'

At once, a cinnamon-scented wind sent the cat tumbling over the ground. When he found his feet again, he stood not on the four paws of a cat but on the sandalled feet of a young nobleman. The vixen, too, had transformed, exchanging her orange fur for a bright robe of silk and her snout for a round, comely face.

With her depthless wiles, the vixen convinced the magistrate that she was the third wife of a distant, forgotten cousin, recently widowed and with nowhere to turn. She had brought her son – the cat – to seek refuge with their generous relative. By the end of a week, she had a place as the magistrate's concubine, and the cat became the companion and classmate of the magistrate's son.

The cat found companionship loathsome but a burden worth bearing for the sake of his goal. He threw himself into his books and his ink. Soon he had surpassed his classmate, earning a wealth of praise, while the magistrate's son earned nothing but shame. 'I have only been teaching your cousin a month,' the tutor would say, 'yet look how he surpasses you!'

When the date of the next imperial examinations was declared, the tutor registered the cat but not the son, who needed another three years to prepare. The cat felt a smug satisfaction at this. How embarrassed the tutor would be when he learned that his star pupil was, in truth, the cat whose calligraphy he had once dismissed! The cat felt the urge to reveal his true nature, but he remembered the vixen's warning and kept his mouth shut.

Finally, the first day of the examinations drew near. The cat and the household tutor travelled to the regional capital, where for five gruelling days the cat struggled alongside other hopeful young minds. In the end, not only did he pass but placed first among his peers.

Jubilant and vindicated, the cat waited in the governor's

garden to accept his commission. Now all he had to do was rise high enough to secure a noble marriage for the vixen. It would be foolish, after all, to reveal his true nature before making good on his end of their deal.

But the sight of the tetragram upon the governor's brow stirred the cat's ambition, for the governor was a Voice, and everything the governor saw and heard, the emperor would see and hear as well. Surely, the benevolent emperor would recognise the cat's ability, even if he revealed himself. It would satisfy him so much more to rise through the imperial ranks as what he truly was, not wearing the disguise the vixen had crafted.

The cat stood to accept his commission. He bowed thrice before the regional governor, as though he stood before the emperor himself.

'There is no need for such humility,' the Voice said. 'You have proven well your worth.'

The cat's heart thundered. Why waste time when his goal was at hand?

'If that is true, then it should not matter whether I am a man, as I seem to be, or a cat, as I truly am,' he said.

With a burst of cinnamon scent, the vixen's spell evaporated. The cat's robes pooled around his paws.

'By the sages, it's a demon!' one of the proctors cried.

The stink of fear filled the garden. The cat flattened its ears.

'No!' he cried. 'I can explain!'

But the Voice of the emperor heard only a cat's frantic yowl. With a wave of his hand he bound the cat in sorcerous light.

The governor's guards locked the cat in a cage in the far corner of the garden. As the door slammed and the lock clicked shut, the cat fell into a deep despair. His hours of study, his deal with the vixen, had all been for nothing.

'How will I get my noble husband now, cat?' the vixen said. Her amber eyes glowed atop the garden wall.

'Please, set me free,' the cat said, springing to his feet. 'We can try again! I will surely pass the exams a second time.'

'I think not,' the vixen said. 'It will never be enough to make you a man, for you want to be a cat doing man-things, which the world will not abide.' With that, she departed in an orange blur.

The cat was killed at dawn, its heart and pollical dew claw removed and sent off to be studied by scholars of demonology. The Voice of the emperor himself went to seize the magistrate's concubine, but the wily vixen was never found.

Hand Usher folded his hands and leaned back in his chair. A smile tugged at the corners of his mouth. 'What do you think of my tale, young Master Wen?'

The proctor watched us with a baffled expression. The story Hand Usher had told was highly unusual. It had more in common with folk tales and other fireside stories than high-Sienese literature.

I felt that I stood on the edge of a precipice. The results of my examination hinged upon my next words, I was sure. Whatever my standing had been, Hand Usher had diverted me from the ordinary course of evaluation, offering instead this single hurdle to be overcome. Why, then, make *this* tale that hurdle?

The story made little sense as an allegory for Sienese doctrine, but it reminded me of the strange thought experiments Koro Ha had often presented to me, and of his warning that my loyalty would always be tested simply because of my Nayeni heritage – tests that would have to be passed, without room for any doubt, if I were to be made Hand of the emperor. After all, the empire would never arm a potential enemy with so powerful a weapon as magic.

This was such a test, I realised. And with that realisation, the purpose of the story became clear.

'It should be spread to every corner of the empire,' I said. 'This is a story meant for children, to teach them a harsh truth of the world in plain terms. It has little poetic merit, but its themes are invaluable and easily grasped by those in danger of indulging conflicted loyalties. No provincial student should take the examinations without hearing it.'

The proctor snorted, clapped a hand over his mouth, and flushed with embarrassment.

Hand Usher's smile widened – only by the breadth of a hair, but enough.

'Proctor Lin, please record that young Master Wen has an impeccable grasp of imperial doctrine,' he said. 'Also note that he is a literary pragmatist with a keen sense of the tensions at play in the far-flung provinces of the empire. Affix my highest recommendation, as well as your own.'

The proctor's brow furrowed and his mouth gaped in confusion, but he made the notes as instructed. The Hand of the emperor stood, folded his hands in his sleeves, and bowed. 'I have high hopes for your future,' he said.

Some moments fix themselves in memory, to be recalled again and again throughout our lives. A breath of lavender perfume will always conjure my first deep romantic feeling, the thunderclap roar and burned-stone scent of chemical grenades my first true hardship. The night my grandmother named me, the night I first attempted to veer, and the night she carved me with witch marks were such moments. Hand Usher's smile, and his silhouette as he walked away, became another.

5

A Hanging Lantern

An invitation to attend a banquet at the governor's palace arrived at Mr Yat's house before I did. Nothing had been announced officially yet, and Koro Ha explained that the final rankings were still being tabulated. 'But outstanding students make themselves known,' he said while he read and reread my invitation with a glint of pride in his eye.

After Hand Usher's unusual test, I had expected to earn a high ranking. Still, it was a relief to see my name on an envelope bearing the governor's seal.

At dusk, a palanquin met Koro Ha and me at the gate to Mr Yat's modest courtyard. We had dressed in fine, colourful clothes, sharp cut and decorated with intricate embroidery. Koro Ha insisted that I wear my hair over my shoulders, as Hand Usher had done, reflecting the current fashion in the Sienese heartland. On our way to the governor's mansion, he brushed it aggressively to make it as straight as possible but left his own dark curls pinned beneath his scholar's cap.

Over the past five days, the atmosphere in the mansion had been solemn and subdued; now it was boisterous and overflowing with colour. Strings of paper lanterns hung between the gatehouse and reception hall, painting the marble tiles of the square in red and golden light. Bronze incense burners had been rolled out and placed along the edges of the garden, their heady scent mixing with the smells of plum wine and savoury delicacies.

A steward showed Koro Ha and me to our seats: mine towards the head of the long table with the other successful candidates, Koro Ha's at the foot with the proctors and other tutors. Small dishes of peanuts drizzled with vinegar and cabbage pickled with fiery peppers had already been laid out, and liquor and wine flowed freely.

'Hello again!' said the boy sitting to my right, flashing a broad grin. Freckles dotted his ruddy cheeks and his hair fell in auburn ringlets.

'Hello?' I replied, not recognising him.

'We sat next to each other during the opening ceremony,' he said. 'What good fortune that we both passed! I am Lu Clear-River.'

'Wen Alder,' I said, bowing slightly. I noticed immediately that his clothes were of courser cloth than mine and out of date with current trends. This, coupled with his complexion – more like my grandmother's than my own – made me wonder how he had come to sit for the examinations at all. I asked after his father's profession.

'Oh, he's only a farmer,' Lu Clear-River said. 'When I was a boy, our village took a collection from every household to educate the brightest child.' He gestured to himself and grinned. 'Their money wasn't wasted, eh?'

'Lucky you,' I said. 'Imagine if you had failed.'

'Ha! If I wasn't sitting here, I'd have probably thrown myself from a cliff by now.'

We laughed, and the tension that had been coiled within me for years finally unravelled. This was real. I had sat the examinations, and I had passed. A month from now, I might be learning magic as an apprentice Hand of the emperor.

62

'To not killing ourselves!' I said brightly and raised a cup of plum wine. A cheer went up among the other successful candidates – fifteen altogether – and we drank.

Course after course was brought out and laid upon the table, delicacies from across the empire. The fare was richer and more delicious than anything my father's kitchens had prepared, exotic and exciting to my limited but curious palate: braised eels in a thick sauce of sugar, soy, and salt; tubers thinly sliced and fried in chilli oil; roasted goat dripping with juices; fish served raw on a bed of pearl rice; pear wine so sweet it made honey seem sour; other liquors made from apples, plums, malted barley, sorghum, and even mares' milk.

Wondrous entertainments accompanied our meal. First an opera singer whose lilting voice drifted between the rafters, quietening our conversation as we sat and listened in rapt awe. Then dancers who trailed ribbons from their fingers and spun to the beat of hide drums and the twang of a zither. When they left the stage, they were replaced by a tall man dressed in a long cape of black felt on the outside and white silk on the inside. He wore a golden crown of many tines spreading outwards from his forehead like antlers, a red-and-yellow mask covering his face. He bowed deeply, letting his cape pool on the floor, black and white folding over each other in a rippling pattern.

'A Face Changer!' Clear-River whispered. 'My tutor told me about them. He saw them after passing his examinations in Centre Fortress. They only perform at the will of the emperor.'

The band began to play high, slow notes on their reed flutes and spike fiddles. The Face Changer took ponderous steps towards the front of the stage, flourishing his cloak and tilting his head with each step. The gilt on his crown flashed in the light of the stage lamps.

With a snap of silk, the Face Changer passed one hand over his mask, which vanished and was replaced by one of blue and silver, painted with the snarl of a foxbat. The audience gasped. It had been only a flash of colour, the wave of a hand, and the flutter of silk. Addled by wine, I wondered if the Face Changer wielded magic of some kind, but I felt neither a feverish flush nor sympathetic cramps, nor the heavy hammering-stone sensation of the governor's sorcery. Only a trick, then, though one so fast and well disguised that I could not begin to imagine what it might be.

The music increased in volume and speed, and the Face Changer's steps became quicker and more intricate. By the end of his display, he switched masks so quickly that I registered only one in three, the rest becoming a blur of shape and colour. Finally, the last mask vanished, leaving him bare-faced before us. He bowed deeply, then left the stage accompanied by applause that shook the hall long after he had gone.

The Face Changer was our final entertainment for the night, and after he had left a cadre of Nayen's scholarly elite joined us in the dining area. They proceeded around the table, welcoming us in turn into their community. First came the scribes – many of them little older than us – followed by the minor members of the bureaucracy, then the magistrates of rural townships, then the magistrates of Setting Sun Fortress and Seawall Fortress, the other two major cities of Nayen.

Finally, we were joined by the four magistrates who presided over Eastern Fortress itself. Each had jurisdiction over a quarter of the city, and each bore the imperial tetragram on his right hand. I breathed deeply to clear my head and focused on making a good impression. If I had not placed first in the examinations, employment in one of their offices was the next best thing I could hope for. If I proved myself, such an employer might take me on as an apprentice in sorcery someday.

One of these luminaries, Hand Jadestone, leaned close when he introduced himself. 'I heard a rumour about you,' he murmured in my ear. 'The servants whisper that Hand Usher administered part of your examination, yes?'

'It was nothing,' I dissembled, as Koro Ha had taught me to around my betters. 'Perhaps he was bored and sought entertainment in my poor performance.'

'What a wit!' Hand Jadestone said. 'Who is your tutor, boy?'

I nodded at Koro Ha. Hand Jadestone smiled conspiratorially, said that his nephew would soon begin his studies, and shuffled off towards my tutor. The other tutors watched with bulging eyes. Koro Ha nearly fainted at the Hand's approach.

Clear-River clapped me on the back. 'Don't forget us when you stand beside the Thousand-Armed Throne!'

I laughed modestly, even as I began to imagine that if I followed the golden path laid before me, those words might indeed prove prophetic.

The governor, Voice Golden-Finch, arrived at last, with Hand Usher close behind him. They bowed low to us, as though we were already esteemed servants of the emperor.

'At this time, I can announce that you fifteen have been judged adequate for civil service,' Voice Golden-Finch said. 'We must thank your tutors for the countless hours they have spent polishing your minds into bright jewels of civilisation.' With that he bowed again, this time at the foot of the table, and I and my fellow graduates followed his example. Koro Ha, beaming with pride, caught my eye.

'Some of you,' the governor went on, 'have lived until now as the poor sons of peasant farmers in this developing province. Know that, no matter where you came from, the road to Northern Capital and the foot of the Thousand-Armed Throne lies open to you if you work diligently and do not stray.'

We applauded, and the governor took a step back to make way for Hand Usher.

'They say that the patron beast of Nayen is the wolf,' Usher

65

began. 'Many kingdoms once warred in this land, like rival packs in a dark forest. Competition, as the philosopher Western-Hardship of the ascetic school wrote, breeds greatness in lesser men. Perhaps the warlike nature of your ancestors, distilled by centuries of strife, will produce great successes in the emperor's service. Perhaps. But remember, young scholars of Nayen, that you are not wolves any longer. You are hounds, brought to heel and trained by the empire in the one virtue that makes a hound an asset while a wolf is but a danger: loyalty.'

He paused. His eyes lingered on me, narrow and shrewd.

'Now,' he went on, his gaze finally breaking from mine. 'Let us remember the words of the sage and poet Sighing-Willow:

'*The victory road is paved in tears,*
'*The golden bridge is unforgiving,*
'*Your blood marks the path to journey's end,*
'*My friend, raise a cup of wine and rest!*'

We cheered, drank, and gorged ourselves. When the servants had cleared our dishes away, Voice Golden-Finch and Hand Usher bade us good night. They were followed shortly by the four magistrates of Eastern Fortress, and soon the party had diminished to just us fifteen candidates and our tutors.

Koro Ha approached me and touched me lightly on the shoulder. 'We should retire for the night, young Master Wen,' he said. 'You must present yourself with decorum when you receive your commission.'

'But I'm not tired,' I said.

'You are,' Koro Ha assured me. 'But the wine ...'

His voice became a droning hum that dissolved into the buzz of conversation and music around me, and I frowned down at the wine cup in my hand. I stood upon a golden path, close – so intoxicatingly close! – to a future as Hand of the emperor, to being schooled in magic, to having the power to reshape the world to my will.

66

I at least had the good sense to stand and lead Koro Ha to the corner of the room before speaking again.

'We are at a minimum the same rank, now,' I said. 'I am not a child to be told when he should sleep and eat and drink.'

'That is true,' Koro Ha admitted, straining to speak calmly, 'but I think now is a time for temperance.'

I was not too drunk to feel shame, but what shame I felt quickly blazed to anger. The room spun around Koro Ha as though he were the fulcrum of a great wheel.

'I don't agree,' I said. 'Tomorrow, I might become Hand of the emperor. Why should I care a whit for the wisdom of a mere *tutor*?'

A few of the other candidates nearby stopped talking to listen to our confrontation. I stalked back to my seat at the table and uncorked another bottle of pear wine. Koro Ha watched me for a moment, then left without another word.

'Alder, you must come with us!' exclaimed Lu Clear-River with a wide grin, clapping me on the back and forcing me to totter a few paces and wave an arm to keep my balance.

The main gate seemed to lurch back and forth above my head. Though the feast was over, Hu Yellow-Stone – a rotund and bombastic youth who had led a chorus of bawdy folk ballads – had invited Clear-River and me to continue our revels out in the city.

'I should go back to Mr Yat's,' I slurred.

Yellow-Stone rolled his eyes. Clear-River clasped me by the shoulders and shook his head. 'Alder, Alder, Alder. We're only going to be this young and handsome once.'

'My cousin says the singing girls in Eastern Fortress are the most beautiful in all Nayen,' Yellow-Stone said, patting the purse at his belt. We'd all been given thirty copper cash – a month's wages for a common labourer – at the end of the banquet. I had bundled mine into my left sleeve, where I could hold onto it and keep it from jangling. Even drunk, I had that much sense.

My new friends offered a temptation that my young, wine-soaked mind struggled to resist. The opera singer at the banquet had stirred me with her beauty and voice, and now Clear-River and Yellow-Stone filled my head with visions of the inner chamber, of lifted veils and robes cast upon the floor. My good sense at last collapsed beneath the weight of adolescent urges.

One of the gate guards – a noble soul, if ever I knew one – tried to convince us to wait for our palanquins. Yellow-Stone laughed and made a rude gesture, then draped one arm over Clear-River's shoulders, the other over mine, and led us out into the street.

Oil lamps threw flickering light across the cobblestones. Young men wandered in packs, meandering from drinking house to drinking house. I recognised many from the opening ceremony the previous day. They joked and shouted and boasted as they indulged for a single night, nursing the wounds left by shattered dreams. It was an atmosphere both manic and dour, incensed by alcohol fumes and oily smoke.

'This way,' Yellow-Stone said, pulling Clear-River and me along. 'The Butterfly House has the prettiest girls in all of Nayen!' He led us around a bend in the road, then down a side street where the lamps were spaced further apart and burned dimly.

'Aren't there any good places closer to the governor's mansion?' Clear-River asked.

'The Butterfly House is well hidden,' Yellow-Stone insisted. 'It adds to the allure! Just a bit further.' He peered into an alley-way where there were no lamps, only deep shadows and piled refuse. 'Or ... maybe we should have gone left back there?'

'Let's go back,' Clear-River said and tried to pull Yellow-Stone away from the alleyway. Instead, Yellow-Stone slumped forwards, like a man dead on his feet. Clear-River grunted as Yellow-Stone's weight settled on our shoulders. 'All that wine in his belly finally rushed to his head,' he muttered. 'Shit! I wasn't paying attention. Where in the bloody city are we?'

I looked for any street sign or landmark that might help to orientate me, and as I did so I saw three figures crossing the street towards us. One of them passed through the halo cast by a lone street lamp. Something glinted in his hand.

I tried to shout but panic had closed my throat. I pawed at Clear-River until he turned around. The figure with the knife approached us while his companions circled to our right and left, pincering us in the mouth of the alleyway.

'We couldn't help but hear that cash on your belt,' said the man with the knife, menacing Clear-River. 'Hand it over, and those fine silk robes, and maybe we'll be generous with your lives.'

The thought of returning naked and penniless to face Koro Ha, after all my bluster at the banquet, fanned my fear into outrage. The fingers of my left hand tightened around my purse, squeezing the copper cash inside into a heavy mass.

'Quickly now! Strip and drop your money!'

I dropped Yellow-Stone and darted forwards. Three steps of the Iron Dance closed the distance between me and the man with the knife. His blade flashed out; I ducked low and swung upward; my purse split his cheek like a cudgel. He collapsed, his nose spurting blood, as coins fountained from my torn purse.

A hand caught my right arm and wrenched it upwards behind me. I howled and pulled against my assailant, to no avail. Desperate, drunk, and hardly thinking, I reached for the only weapon I had.

A feverish heat coursed through me, burning away my drunkenness with the clarity born of magic. I conjured flame – a burst

69

of heat and light and the stink of seared flesh filled the air as the robber shrieked and let me go. I spun around in time to see two figures sprinting away, one trailing tongues of fire.

Clear-River stared at me, astonished. Or horrified.

'Let's get out of here!' I said, my voice quavering. Clear-River nodded, but his eyes lingered, full of questions. I avoided his gaze, unable to answer them.

We hauled Yellow-Stone to his feet. Somehow, he had slept through the entire attack, though a few sharp slaps to the side of his face woke him quickly enough.

'Bffwa!' he spluttered. 'Ah! Where am I? Oh, yes. The singing girls! Not much further—'

'Hang you and your singing girls!' Clear-River snapped. 'We're dragging you home, you drunkard.'

With Yellow-Stone's arms once again draped over our shoulders, we set off as quickly as we could. Every step made my stomach lurch – from drink, lingering terror, and the knowledge that with a word to Hand Usher or any one of our proctors – or anyone, really – Clear-River could divert the bright path laid before me to a prison cell, if not to the blade of an executioner's sword.

Yellow-Stone was not lucid enough to give us directions to wherever he was staying, so we deposited him in the cramped room that Clear-River and his tutor shared. Clear-River offered to walk back with me to Mr Yat's, and I accepted. As we left the inn, I grabbed his hand and pulled him close.

'I saved your life tonight,' I said firmly. 'If I hadn't been there, you and Yellow-Stone would be bleeding out in the street or kidnapped for a ransom your village could never pay. After I hit the first man, the other two ran. Nothing else happened. Do you understand?'

He shook his head, feigning confusion. 'Alder, you're forgetting. One of them knocked over a hanging lantern in his panic.'

I stared at him, as though a careful examination of his face might tell me whether he truly meant to keep my secret.

'That's how his clothes caught fire,' Clear-River went on. 'Don't you remember?'

I let go of him. 'Of course.' I managed a weak grin. 'Clumsy fool.'

'Lucky for Yellow-Stone and me you were there,' Clear-River said, and my chest tightened. 'How clever, to use your purse as a cudgel! They were true cowards if a half-drunk boy swinging a bag of coins was enough to scare them off.'

'Yes, cowards indeed,' I agreed. 'Well, my tutor will be up fretting. I can find my own way home. Farewell, Clear-River. I hope your name is high on the list tomorrow.'

He dipped his head in a half bow. 'I am sure that yours will be, Alder.'

At the end of the street, I glanced back. Clear-River stood in the doorway, watching me, and I felt my secret like a taut string between us.

Koro Ha had been right, of course. What a foolish thing I had done, getting drunk and venturing out into an unfamiliar city in the dead of night. He would be waiting up for me, and when he saw my filthy clothes and lack of purse he would know exactly what had happened. I expected a lecture that would last till dawn.

One of Mr Yat's stewards met me at the gatehouse and ushered me inside with an expression of pure relief. 'I feared something terrible had happened to you, Master Wen!' he said. 'I was just about to wake your tutor.'

'Koro Ha is asleep?' I said.

'He said he was tired after a long week. He asked to be roused two hours after dawn and suggested the same for you.'

The steward glanced at the window, where the faint light of sunrise already filtered through the screen.

'That will be fine,' I said.

I went up to bed and lay awake, listening to the house, letting my mind drift in the stillness and quiet. Koro Ha had gone to sleep. Was that a show of trust, despite his insistence that I leave the banquet with him? Or had his interest in my safety waned now that my education, and by extension our relationship as teacher and student, was at an end?

The steward returned to rouse me and I went down to breakfast, where Koro Ha raised an eyebrow as I took my seat. Servants brought trays of steamed pork buns and fresh cut fruit. My head ached and my stomach roiled. I asked for congee and soy milk.

'How was your night?' Koro Ha asked.

I took a bite of congee. It was bland but inoffensive and settled my stomach. Words bubbled up, tried to organise themselves and spill from my mouth, to tell him all that had happened the previous night. If there was a sympathetic ear in the world, it would be Koro Ha's. Or, at least, his ear *would* have been sympathetic, if I had not so coldly dismissed his advice and, in my drunkenness, jeopardised all that we had worked together to achieve.

'Koro Ha ...' I started, looking up from my congee.

He peered at me over the rim of his teacup. 'Yes?'

I paused. I could apologise, but would that be enough to mend the rift between us? I feared the inevitable reprimand, the further deepening of that rift if he reacted with a harsh word and I lashed out in turn. Whatever I had meant to say, it splashed and faded against my teeth.

'I never want to drink that much again,' I muttered instead.

Koro Ha sipped his tea. 'I suppose some lessons cannot be learned from tutors or from books,' he said, and left it at that.

6

Results

After a dozen cups of tea as dark and thick as ink, Koro Ha and I dressed in scholars' robes of black silk and regal cut, deepnecked, over shirts of white linen. Over his robes, Koro Ha wore the stole of his rank, stitched with his tetragram: four symbols arranged in a square. The first symbol was of a man kneeling over a writing desk and meant 'Scholar of the Second Degree'. Many of such rank were officials in regional government, yet Koro Ha had chosen to become a tutor.

The other three symbols were not true logograms but arrangements of the phonetic runes used to teach children how to read. Foreign names were often written in such symbols, though most scholars with such names chose to translate them into Sienese when creating their tetragrams. Koro Ha was a rare exception.

I'd never asked him about either of these eccentricities. It had always seemed impolite to pry into his past, but now I found myself wishing that I had. Once I'd received my commission, our relationship would change. If I, too, earned the Second Degree, we would be peers – brothers in scholarship. If I exceeded him and earned the First Degree, he would be obliged to answer any question I put to him, no matter how impolite.

Considering this, I was struck for the first time by how much my life was about to change. No longer would I be 'young

Master Wen', the son of a middling merchant; I would be a scholar, someone deserving of dignity and respect. And if Hand Usher chose me for his apprentice, I would become one of the most important men in the empire.

I shook my head to banish that lofty, foolish thought. Much as I longed to become Hand of the emperor, there must have been another candidate who had done better, who had not mangled an article in the first logogram of his pedigree. Who had not, just the night before, lit a man on fire.

Stewards met us at the gate and led us into the courtyard. We were seated just as we had been for the opening ceremony, yet I hesitated as the steward gestured to the open seat beside Clear-River, who had arrived before me. The tension between us had not faded, though I resolved to put on a good face.

'Good morning, Clear-River,' I said, taking my seat. 'Did you sleep well?'

He looked up with a welcoming smile. 'Alder! Good morning! I slept better than Yellow-Stone, at least. The poor fool woke up panicky as a startled fawn, screaming and demanding to know who I was and where I'd taken him. When he finally calmed down, he sprinted out of the inn and down the street. I hope he found his way home in time to dress for the ceremony.'

'It would serve him right if he didn't,' I said.

'Oh, don't be hard-hearted,' Clear-River said. 'The foolishness of youth led us all out into the streets, and only the miraculous intervention of the sages brought us home safely.' He smiled innocently, but his words drifted too close to the truth.

'That man stumbled into a lantern, remember?' I said.

Clear-River flicked the ends of his sleeves and harrumphed. 'You're no fun, you know?'

Before I could retort, we were interrupted by a clash of cymbals and the thrum of a zither. The proctors filed out from the reception hall onto the marble dais. Chrysanthemum blossoms drifted down from baskets upended on the balcony above them. Leading the procession were Voice Golden-Finch and Hand Usher, each with two tetragrams decorating their stoles of office. On the left they wore their personal seals, the first symbol showing a hand raised in salute to the logogram for *king* – enclosed within an open mouth in Voice Golden-Finch's case – while on the right, as on their bodies, they wore the emperor's never-changing name. Silver light streamed from the tetragram on the governor's forehead, and I felt the weight of his sorcery. The emperor himself, seeing through the eyes of his Voice, would witness our commissioning.

Clear-River leaned close to me and whispered, 'What did you think of the pollical cat story, Alder?'

Slowly, I faced him, schooling my expression into one of befuddlement.

'You weren't the only one to hear that tale,' Clear-River went on. 'There were three of us, but Hand Usher will choose only one. If it comes down to you and me, I think you should thank Hand Usher for the honour but politely refuse.'

'Oh?' I whispered back. 'How? No one in his right mind would refuse such an offer.'

'They'll find you out eventually, you know, even if I say nothing,' he continued as though I had not spoken. 'They say the emperor knows the thoughts of his Hands – their thoughts and all their secrets.' He fixed me with a stare, smiling all the while. 'If they catch you – and they *will* catch you – it'll be bad for the entire province. Do you think the empire will ever hold examinations in Nayen again if the first of our kind to become Hand of the emperor turns out to be a traitor?'

'I am *not* a traitor!'

'There were no hanging lanterns on that street. You betrayed the empire the moment you began to learn witchcraft and chose not to turn in your teacher. On the other hand, perhaps you're betraying that teacher by choosing to serve the empire.' He shrugged. 'Either way, you're betraying someone.'

My anger flared. He was right, of course. If I accepted an imperial commission, I would be setting myself against my grandmother. She had abandoned me, true enough, but I had not chosen the Sienese path because I doubted her tales of Sienese brutality and oppression, nor because I believed – as imperial doctrine would hold – that Sienese conquest was an enriching and civilising force in the world. Not even my own tutor believed as much, if Koro Ha's subtle questions that skirted the edges of treason were any evidence.

Choosing to serve the Sienese would be to discard all that my grandmother had risked her life to teach me, treating it as no more meaningful than dust. Yet service to the empire was the only path laid before me – certainly the only path that led towards magic.

I steeled myself against the guilt and shame Clear-River meant to stir in my heart and fixed my gaze on the dais before us. The servants hung a broad, elaborately embroidered scroll there on a golden stand but did not untie the ribbon that bound it. The governor and Hand Usher stepped to the edge of the dais while the musicians played one final, triumphal note.

'Best and brightest of this, the youngest province of our grand empire!' Voice Golden-Finch called out, his voice a nasal drone. 'Today we celebrate the successes of a few. We also remind the rest that the empire is generous with second chances.'

He went on to reassure us that those whose names were not written on the scroll would be welcome to sit for the next examinations in three years' time. Then, in the same droning tone, he launched into the encouraging tale of a man who failed the examinations three times in a row before finally passing and becoming a scholar of the Eastern Academy Quarter, the greatest body of learning in the empire.

His words buzzed in my ears, all but meaningless. My fingernails dug into the palms of my hands. I had no leverage over
Clear-River. Nothing to use against him if he threatened to
expose me.

'I saved your life,' I said, hoping to touch some shred of moral
feeling.

'You did,' Clear-River said, his smile growing wider. 'I could
have exposed you already, but I haven't yet because of that. I'm
offering to save yours in return. They'll execute you when they
learn your secret, and they'll learn it the moment they mark you
with the tetragram and the emperor peers into the shadowed
corners of your mind. If you're offered the apprenticeship,
refuse and I won't tell them anything.'

The governor swept his arm towards the scroll. 'With that,
let us unveil the results!'

The scroll unfurled. All but the first fifteen names were written in black ink. Fourteen were written in red. One name was
written in gold.

Clear-River's was the highest of the red names, just below
mine.

'They will know,' Clear-River whispered, 'and they will kill
you.'

The governor read the first of the red names. Yellow-Stone
– his hangover apparently forgotten – mounted the dais to receive the silk stole and silver medallion that were the symbols
of his commission. I looked over my shoulder and saw Koro Ha
beaming at me with pride. If I did what Clear-River wanted,
how could I explain my refusal to my tutor, or to my father, or
to anyone?

Thirteen years ago, the empire had searched our house for
the notorious bandit Harrow Fox. Perhaps thirteen years had
been long enough for that connection to fade beneath notice,
but refusing an apprenticeship with Hand Usher would draw

scrutiny towards my family. Even if we faced no punishment, who in the empire would trade with my father once it became known that he was married to the sister of a rebel leader?

The governor called out the seventh name.

'You're running out of time, Alder,' Clear-River hissed. 'Step aside.'

In the darkness of the forest, my grandmother had given me a taste of magic, but she had abandoned me. Now the empire itself had offered to teach me. I craved that knowledge more than prestige or power, more than the restoration of my family's reputation. Enough, I decided, to risk the threats of this ambitious, conniving peasant.

'No,' I said.

The governor called the twelfth name. Clear-River took a deep breath and shrugged. 'Well then, you prove yourself undeserving. What was the lesson of the pollical cat, if not that we should accept our place and not reach beyond the limit of our grasp? We'll see you at the execution grounds before long, I suspect.'

'Witchcraft hasn't been practised openly in Nayen since before we were born,' I said, tamping down my outrage. 'Does your village harbour a witch? Someone to appease the gods? Oh, you are too well educated to condone such things, but what of your parents? Turning me in will make you a suspect as well.'

'Hah!' Clear-River barked. A tutor seated nearby glared at him and he bowed his head in apology, then scowled at me. 'An empty threat, based on idle speculation. Besides, I need say nothing. The moment they mark your hand, the emperor will know.'

'That is nothing more than an empty rumour,' I said, projecting all the confidence I could muster. 'What would a farmer's son know about what transpires between the emperor and his Hands?'

'Even if the rumours are false, your right hand is marked, isn't it?' He leaned close and whispered, 'They cut you when they gave you witchcraft, didn't they? Hand Usher has fought witches. He'll recognise those scars. You *have* to refuse, Alder, or you'll die.'

But there was a flaw in his reasoning. I remembered my grandmother's tale of my grandfather, of his death by his own conjured flame. If every witch in Nayen would sooner die than be captured, and succeeded in self-destruction when cornered, then the exact pattern of scars that marked a witch would still be secret from the empire, just as Nayeni magic was secret.

There was a very real chance, however slight, that Hand Usher wouldn't recognise my scars. That no Hand of the emperor even could.

'Perhaps,' I said, and matched Clear-River's stare. 'Nevertheless.' His eyes widened at the coldness of my voice and I pressed on, leaning towards him: 'It was a hanging lantern. Nothing more.'

The governor called Clear-River's name. He blinked as though awakening from a dream, then scurried to the dais. Did a whispered accusation flit between him and Hand Usher as he bowed to receive his stole? No matter, I decided. It would be his word against mine. My pedigree was better. I had placed higher. But my scars and my parentage would add weight to his accusation.

Clear-River returned to his seat, sat stiffly, and stared straight ahead.

'Finally, we are pleased to welcome the first Hand of the emperor to rise from Nayen,' the governor announced. 'Wen Alder, son of Wen Rosewood, descendant of the great general Wen Broad-Oak, who was himself Hand of the emperor.'

Every eye in the courtyard sought me out as I walked to the dais with all the confidence I could muster. On reaching it, I bowed thrice: first to the governor, then to Hand Usher, and finally to the crowd below. Koro Ha's face shone like the sun. Clear-River's eyes were hooded and unreadable.

'By your exemplary performance, you have risen above your fellows,' the governor said. Light still rippled from his forehead, and I felt the weight of the sorcery that bound his mind to the emperor's and gave him the power to speak with the authority of empire. 'Hand Usher has, in his generosity, selected you to be his apprentice. From him you will learn the canon of sorcery, and with his guidance you will begin to lend your substantial talents to the administration and defence of the empire.'

Hand Usher stepped forwards, bearing a seal cast from gold and decorated with coiled lion serpents. 'This seal will mark you with power and privilege,' he said ostentatiously, his voice showing none of the coy, playful man who had told the tale of the pollical cat. Yet the corner of his mouth quirked upwards as he went on: 'You will bear the never-changing name of the emperor, the key to the canon of sorcery. Offer your palm to receive this honour.'

The fingers of my right hand curled into a fist. I imagined Clear-River watching from below, expecting my downfall the moment I showed Hand Usher my scars.

At the same time, a new worry struck me: the marks my grandmother had carved had changed the feel of magic, constraining it. What might happen if those marks were overwritten with the imperial tetragram? I knew the danger of meddling blindly with magic. I looked Hand Usher in the eye, made my expression as open and honest as I could, and offered my left palm.

Hand Usher's smile faded.

'What are you doing?' he hissed. 'It must be your right hand.'

'I can write with my left,' I assured him.

His lips parted in confusion. He looked to the governor. I pressed on.

'Your Excellencies, why are Hands of the emperor marked

on the right palm, if not because it is the hand with which they write? They compose edicts and administer justice with the brush, just as they defend the empire with sorcery. It is the palm that holds the brush which should be marked, to lend the Hand's actions the authority of the emperor's name.'

I hoped that Hand Usher might see resonance between my unconventional thinking and his own.

'And you write with your left?' he said.

'I do,' I affirmed.

Hand Usher faced the proctors, who knelt in neat rows on the edges of the stage. My stomach clenched.

'Which of you administered the essay portion of Master Wen's examination?' he asked. Three proctors raised their hands. Hand Usher waved towards the youngest of the three. 'You, tell me. With which hand did Master Wen hold his brush?'

The young proctor studied me carefully. 'Your Excellency, I do not recall any of the candidates using their left hands.'

'It would have stood out if one had, yes?' Hand Usher said. 'Not something you would have overlooked?'

'Quite unusual, Your Excellency.'

'Thank you.'

The young proctor bowed. Hand Usher turned back to me, his eyes bright with suspicion. I kept my expression impassive, still offering my left hand. Murmurs rose from the otherwise placid crowd.

'You!' barked Hand Usher, pointing at the next proctor, another old scholar with another wispy beard and balding head. 'Did Master Wen use his right or his left hand?'

The proctor cleared his throat. 'I would not tolerate any deviation from ritual and code such as a young man composing with his left hand, for, as the great moral philosopher Hu Finch-in-Rushes wrote—'

'Thank you, Proctor,' said Hand Usher.

The old proctor cleared his throat indignantly, then settled back on his haunches. Hand Usher took another step forwards. I could smell his breath, redolent of tea and spices and meat. My mind was racing yet empty, like the centre of a storm.

'You!' Hand Usher's voice was rising. He pointed to the third proctor. 'Same question.'

The third proctor looked at me severely. 'He used his right.'

'Thank you!' Hand Usher bowed quickly to the proctors, then whirled back to face me. 'Will you challenge the testimony of these three, who watched your examinations like a hawk watches a field mouse?'

Silence held while the crowd swallowed their murmurs.

'No, Your Excellency,' I said. 'I did not say that I wrote my examinations with my left hand, only that I can and do use it, and that it is better suited to the emperor's service.'

'The story grows! You can write with both hands, then? A rare talent.'

'Not a talent but a skill,' I said with a bow. 'One taught to me by my tutor, through long hours of practice.'

'Why would your tutor waste time on such a novelty?'

'So that I might serve the emperor even if I should lose one of my hands, as I so nearly did as a child.'

Hand Usher's expression shifted, ever so slightly, from incredulous anger to piqued curiosity. 'Explain.'

'When I was a boy, a poorly made plate shattered in my right hand,' I said. 'Unwilling to let me lie fallow while it healed, my generous and long-suffering tutor devoted himself to teaching me to use my left. The injury made him realise that in this chaotic world there would be value in the ability to continue one's work even after losing so dear an appendage as a writing hand. After my injury healed, he made me write every exercise twice over, once with my right hand and once with my left, until even my own father could not discern which had written.'

New murmurs rose from the crowd. I wondered what Koro Ha was thinking. Likely he was cursing me as a braggart and a fool.

'It is my duty to give the emperor the best I have to offer,' I went on. 'Given the choice between my hale, unmarred left hand or my disfigured right, I offer my left.'

'What a ridiculous story!' Voice Golden-Finch exclaimed, flicking his sleeves in irritation. 'The right hand is the natural tool for writing, the left the tool for pillowing the elbow of the writing arm. Every treatise on calligraphy agrees.'

'It may be strange,' Hand Usher said, 'but it demonstrates a rare quality.'

'What quality?' demanded the governor. 'It demonstrates only deviance!'

'When the family dines together, is it not proper that the son offer the best morsels to his father? Is it not proper to pour out the first pot of tea – bitter as it often is – rather than serving it to guests? Master Wen shows that kind of respect.' The ghost of a smile returned to Hand Usher's face. '*If* this story is true.'

'It is, Your Excellency,' I said. 'My tutor can corroborate.'

'So can my eyes.' Hand Usher clamped his hand around my right wrist and pulled me off balance. I stifled a yelp as he yanked back my sleeve and exposed my right hand, examining my palm closely. I was certain that he would declare me a traitor, a witch in hiding. Did I have the fortitude to conjure flame, to destroy myself upon the dais, rather than let the empire steal the secrets my grandfather had died to defend?

Hand Usher waved to one of the servants. 'Bring paper, brush, and ink,' he commanded, 'and Master Wen's compositions.'

He released me. Servants scurried into the reception hall and returned with a writing table. Hand Usher bade me kneel. One of the proctors produced a lacquered case that had been sealed with wax and stamped with my name.

'The first document in this file is your pedigree,' Hand Usher said, brushing his fingers along the top of the case. 'You will reproduce it with your left hand. If what you say is true then I should see no difference between the calligraphy you wrote six days ago and what you write today.'

The servants prepared the table. An ink stick and a grinding stone, brushes, a pitcher of water – tools I had used all my life. I fought a tremor in my hand as I dripped water onto the stone and began grinding ink. My fingers slipped on the brush, as though holding one were not the most familiar thing in the world.

Hand Usher folded his hands into his sleeves and I began to write. I focused on the page, on each line of each logogram, and my brushwork regained familiar, practised ease, forming words I had written countless times. The hairs of the brush slid smoothly along the page, paused, then straightened as I lifted it from the final article.

Hand Usher peered over my shoulder. His breath quickened as he read. He gestured to the servant who had carried the sealed case that held my compositions. Wax cracked, hinges swung open, paper rustled, and I heard a single, sharp exhalation.

'My apologies, Master Wen,' he said. 'I should never have doubted one who has demonstrated excellence by every measure.' He tossed the first pedigree I had written – complete with the flawed first article that I'd been convinced would cause me to fail my examinations – onto the ground, then folded the one I had just composed and placed it within the case. 'You are correct to offer your left hand. It is better than your right.'

He knelt on the other side of the writing desk and smiled – with a furrowed brow, true, but it was a smile nonetheless – and bowed to me, never taking his eyes from mine.

'You will be a worthy if curious apprentice,' he remarked. And with that he retrieved the seal of the emperor's name, took my left hand, turned it palm up, and said, 'Wen Alder, I seal you and name you Hand of the emperor.'

7

Recognition

The next day, I prepared to return home to thank my parents, celebrate my success, bid them farewell, and collect my belongings before returning to live and study with Hand Usher at the governor's estate. Before I left, however, Hand Usher offered me two warnings.

'Magic leaves a wake through the pattern of the world, like a boat on a placid lake,' he said. 'You will begin to feel such wakes bubbling beneath the surface of your awareness. *Do not reach for them.* You are not yet ready. If you tried to wield magic, you would be as dangerous to yourself and others as a toddler with a broadsword.'

I had felt these wakes since I was eight years old, but the tetragram had brought with it something new: a font of power. It was less a spring than a geyser, in fact, and I began to feel the rush and pulse of it the moment the golden seal had struck my flesh.

'Second, I must warn you that, though you have succeeded at the imperial examinations, failure is not beyond you. You have been given power because we believe you are worthy of it, but if you prove yourself unworthy, it will be taken from you. The cost of failure will be your left hand and exile to a far-flung corner of the empire. You are fortunate indeed that you can write with both.'

As he spoke, a chill ran through me at the incongruity between his words and his mild expression. I bowed, thanked him for the warning, and mounted the palanquin that would take me home for the last time for many years to come.

Imperial couriers travelled across the empire bearing word of the results of the first examinations to be held in Nayen. Only days after Koro Ha and I had returned home, my father arrived in our wake. He beamed with pride as he clasped my shoulders and shouted orders at our stewards and servants to begin preparations for a banquet.

'I shouldn't have doubted you for a moment, Alder,' he said. 'As soon as I heard, I sold off what I could of my cargo – at a bare fraction of the price I'd have commanded in Northern Capital, I'll have you know – and set sail for home.' He marvelled at the tetragram written on my left palm in glittering silver. 'To think, my son ... Hand of the emperor!'

I wondered whether he would have rushed home if I had not so vastly exceeded his expectations. He released me, then whirled towards Koro Ha and embraced him, crowing that the ten years he'd spent paying my tutor's salary had all been worth it.

My mother cried quiet, happy tears. She praised my successes, but her eyes darted away from my tetragram. She had heard the same rumours that Clear-River had used to threaten me and knew as well about my grandmother's lessons. I wanted to reassure her – I felt no eyes peering through my own, nor any prying presence in my thoughts, only the flow of a new fountain of power – but she had never openly acknowledged my Nayeni heritage, let alone the magic her mother wielded. There were things we both wanted to say but could not, and after she had congratulated me an awkward silence festered between us.

I spent the next several days packing while my father's friends and business associates slowly filled our estate near to bursting.

Not a single room went empty, and Father boasted that the common house in the nearby village of Ashen Clearing had been all but commandeered by those guests who arrived too late to claim space within our home. The day before I was due to return to Eastern Fortress and begin my apprenticeship, our servants – with help from a few young Nayeni girls hired in from the village – laid out long tables in the garden, with seats and place settings for five dozen guests. My father emptied the cellar of its casks and dusty bottles and hired women from the village to weave a wreath of wildflowers, its centrepiece my name picked out in yellow chrysanthemums as brilliant as gold.

At noon, our guests took their seats, filling our quiet estate with clamour and conversation. My father seated me at a table, alone, atop a dais beside the garden pavilion. He roved through the crowd, leading the guests one at a time to the pavilion, where each one smiled, dipped his or her head, and marvelled at the silver lines on my palm while Father said, 'I would like you to meet my son, Hand Alder!'

The faces and names of these strangers slipped from my mind as soon as Father led them away towards a table piled high with sugar-dusted cakes shaped like hands and stamped with the imperial tetragram. I searched the crowded tables for Koro Ha – or even Mr Yat, whom I knew, at least, though we were not friendly. I saw neither. While I recognised the incredible expense my father had gone to in organising the celebration, as a demonstration of his affection, I felt alone and used – not celebrated, in fact, but displayed like a jewel in his treasury.

Perhaps if I perceived my achievement as he did – as a valuable first step in the restoration of our family's reputation – I would not have been so disgusted at being so displayed. Yet I saw becoming Hand of the emperor only as a means to the end of magic, one that – as Hand Usher had warned me – shackled me with its own expectations and constraints. Things I could endure a while longer, now that the promise of magic was nearer than it had ever been before. Once I had mastered it, however, I had no intention of dedicating myself to the furthering of my father's ambitions, nor to the advancement of the empire or my grandmother's rebellion.

While I accepted deferential bows and congratulations and pressed the hands of strangers – putting on a gracious mask over my simmering frustration – I felt a renewal of resolve. As soon as I had mastered magic well enough to do so, I would grasp the freedom it offered and use it to shape a third path.

Dusk had settled over the garden by the time the last introductions were made. Bottles and casks were breached in the light of a hundred hanging lanterns, each decorated with the imperial tetragram in golden ink. My father had quizzed me on the dishes served at the reception for successful candidates so that he could serve the same menu. Of course, our kitchens paled in comparison to Voice Golden-Finch's, and I flushed with embarrassment as I put aside a plate of undercooked eel. I tried to drown my misery in drink, which only made me more miserable, which compelled me to drink further. By the time my father, all pride and grandiose gesticulations, presented me with a lacquer panel inscribed with our family pedigree, with my name added at the end in bold, eye-catching lines, I was thoroughly drunk.

I smiled and bobbed my head, trying to cast my mind back to the first time I had studied those names with Koro Ha. There was Wen Broad-Oak, my exemplar, whose accomplishments first seeded my mind with the notion that I might one day wield magic. That seven-year-old boy would have been thrilled to see his name so proudly displayed alongside those venerable ancestors. And I did feel a twinge of pride, but it was overshadowed by my desire for the night to be over so that I might return to Hand Usher and begin my apprenticeship.

There were other small rituals meant to celebrate me but which only deepened my embarrassment. I was made to stand and recite quotations from the sages from memory. My father brought out transcriptions of my examination essays and bade me read them – which I did, until I glanced up and saw that those of our guests who were not engaged in quiet conversation were staring at me glassy-eyed, bored and uncomprehending.

These were not the literati I had dined with in Eastern Fortress. These were my father's friends: merchants and local landowners – wealthy but least important to the health of the empire, by Traveller-on-the-Narrow-Way's reckoning, hailing from this backwoods region of Nayen where my father had put down roots only because he could cheaply build an impressive estate. I looked for my father and saw him seated with some other merchant, their heads bent close, speaking over me while I read.

My embarrassment curdled to disgust and I stopped reading in the middle of a sentence, whereupon my father roused the crowd into half-hearted applause before returning to his conversation. I sat there on the dais and finished my drink, then stood and retreated to my rooms without a word.

On the way, I found Koro Ha at last, standing on the bank of the garden's shallow pond, a pipe in one hand and a wine cup in the other. The cacophony of the party reached us as a muted echo and the pond was lit only by moonlight. Koro Ha had not seen me yet, and I watched him as he gazed out over the pond, sipped his wine, breathed slowly through the stem of his pipe, and blew a ring of smoke. He had never smoked before. Or had he, and kept it secret from his student?

At last he turned, starting as he saw me.

'Alder!' he exclaimed, then broke into a cough and covered his mouth. When he had recovered, he palmed the bowl of his pipe and held it low, perhaps hoping I had not seen it. 'Your father has gone to all this expense and trouble for you. You should be there.'

'Not for me,' I said. 'I'm only his excuse to show off. He's been making the rounds, tying up business connections while I've been entertaining the crowd by reading my examination essays.'

I reached for the pipe. Koro Ha raised his eyebrows. Before, he would never have condoned my indulgence in such a vice. Now, he could hardly refuse me, Hand of the emperor that I was.

'You find that insulting,' Koro Ha said matter-of-factly and handed over the pipe.

'I do,' I said. 'But perhaps I shouldn't. My father isn't well educated. None of those men are.'

I put the pipe stem to my lips, inhaled, and spluttered as the acrid smoke filled my lungs. Koro Ha covered his mouth and hid his laughter by clearing his throat. I coughed, spat, and thrust the pipe back into Koro Ha's hand.

'Educated or not, he is still your father,' Koro Ha said. 'You know the first aphorisms. You know what you owe him.'

'My rank has changed things,' I said. 'I'm Hand of the emperor now. What does that make me, if not his elder brother in the great hierarchy of empire?'

Koro Ha sighed and offered me his wine cup. I drank. It was mild and mixed with water, and it soothed the burning in my throat.

'You are ambitious, Alder, and have made good on your ambition,' Koro Ha said, 'but try to enjoy your successes as they come. The eye trained always on the next bend in the path never sees the beauty of the forest.'

'Which sage was that?'

He smiled. 'Koro Ha.'

I laughed and returned his cup. 'Sound wisdom, then, from a reliable source.'

'Oh, I don't know about that,' he replied. 'I am only a tutor, and you are Hand of the emperor, soon to be schooled in secret knowledge and sorcerous arts.'

'Yet I have you to thank for my successes,' I said. 'Without your guidance, I would be little more than the foolish son of a simple merchant.'

'Not at all,' Koro Ha said. 'An artisan's work is only as good as his raw material. As Traveller-on-the-Narrow-Way put it, "A great carving is equal only to the quality of the jade."'

His words filled my chest and sank into my stomach. All my life I had struggled to meet Koro Ha's standards. He had pushed me to do better, disciplined me for my mistakes, chastised me for my foolishness. Never had he given me such a compliment.

Here, at the end of our time together, as I was about to lose a man to whom I was closer than my own father, I longed to knit our minds and hearts together. I wanted to be sure he would understand all that he had meant to me, my frustrations as well as my gratitude, before I went on to my apprenticeship and he to his next student. Yet I still felt the rift I had hewn between us in my drunken stupidity.

Already I had cut myself off forever from one pillar of my childhood. My grandmother had abandoned me first, but what had Koro Ha done to me, that I should treat him as I had? Whatever harshness he had shown me, it had been motivated by genuine concern and genuine belief that success in the imperial examinations would be my best chance for a good, prosperous life in the empire. Yes, he had been paid to educate me, but he might have done so callously and less carefully. The tale of the pollical cat would have been little more than nonsense, after all, if not for his effort to prepare me for the suspicion that the tint of my skin and curl of my hair would provoke.

These thoughts swirled with the wine and rose to the base of my skull, where a strange, painful pressure built and built, seeking some eloquent means of release – a means that proved elusive while we stood in an awkward, straining silence.

Bleed it. I would not let a lack of eloquence rob me of this last chance to apologise to Koro Ha. Not when he had treated me with more dignity and kindness than anyone I knew.

'I'm sorry,' I blurted.

He paused, the wine cup at his lips, and furrowed his brow. When he said nothing, I pressed on.

'I treated you badly at the governor's banquet,' I said, letting the words tumble out one after the other, afraid that if I hesitated I might lose my nerve. 'You were right. I was drunk, and I did foolish things that nearly cost us both everything. I shouldn't have dismissed your advice, and certainly not just because I placed more highly than you in the examinations.'

Uncomfortable silence settled again between us. Koro Ha studied me, his expression slowly softening.

'It's all right, Alder,' he said gently. 'I was young and foolish once, too.'

'It isn't,' I protested. 'You're my teacher. You saw the best in me. And in return I treated you like a lowly servant and flouted your advice.'

'You did, and I forgive you.' He smiled and put the stem of his pipe to his mouth. 'You will have other teachers, Alder. I know they will see what I have seen. Now, have another drink with me. There's yet more of your father's party to endure.'

II

—

Apprentice

8

First Lessons

I moved into the guest house in the eastern region of Voice Golden-Finch's garden, which had been given to Hand Usher for the duration of his posting in Nayen. Our rooms overlooked an artificial lake where kingfishers nested in a tall porous stone and often dived to pluck minnows from the water. To the south were the bamboo groves and artificial cliffs that had been the backdrop of the imperial examinations. Grassy fields modelled on the Girzan steppe sprawled to the north, where the governor's sons, Oriole and Pinion, took daily riding lessons. The western part of the garden was the smallest, a flat expanse of sand dotted with standing stones where the Voice raked meditative patterns. At the garden's heart was the expansive house of the governor and his family, closed even to Hand Usher and me without invitation.

Hand Usher wasted no time in beginning my lessons. He bade me study maps till I could trace the borders of every province and identify their value to the empire: Nayen, a mountainous island shielding the empire's eastern coast; Toa Alon, a gold-rich land with jungles that crawled over the marble foothills of the Pillars of the Gods, the mountains that formed the southern edge of Sien. To the north, vast plains for horse and cattle, stretching on and on into tundra where Girzan tribes still roamed. And in the west, the Batir Waste and the oasis city of An-Zabat, the bridge between Sien and distant lands, source of foreign luxuries but troubled by the intractable windcallers. And the heartland, full of forested hills rich with sulphur and rolling plains of wheat and millet.

When I had mastered the maps, Hand Usher presented me with economic puzzles. As Koro Ha had trained my mind in the structures of classical allusion and sophisticated language, Hand Usher taught me the logic and tactics of trade: how to manipulate lines of credit, to sell surplus that overflowed the storehouses, to balance tax and tariff to encourage desired trade and discourage the superfluous.

'You have a head for this,' he told me one day after reviewing my work. 'I will put in a good word for you at the Bureau of Economy. Perhaps, when you finish your apprenticeship, you might cut your teeth as a minister of trade in some far-flung city.'

I failed to mask my disappointment. The ghostly smile he so often wore appeared on his lips. 'You don't like that idea?'

'It isn't my place to comment,' I said.

Hand Usher dismissed that thought with a wave of his hand. 'Alder, you're a Hand of the emperor. There are fewer than a thousand people in Sien who outrank you.'

'But you are my superior,' I said. 'Whatever you think is best, I will do.'

'Well, I think it best that you tell me how you feel about becoming a minister of trade.'

This was new. None of my father, my grandmother, nor Koro Ha had ever asked me how I felt about their designs for my life. The slight smile on Hand Usher's lips did not touch his eyes and made his expression quite impossible to read.

'I thought my responsibilities as Hand of the emperor would be ...' I sought the right word '... more unique.'

'Unique in what sense?' Was that a hint of laughter in his voice?

For two months I had struggled to ignore the tetragram on my palm and the depths of new power it had opened to me. I had trusted that Hand Usher would begin to teach me sorcery when the time was right. Now he taunted me with the mundane. Had I been too careful? How was a person supposed to react when given power for the first time?

'We alone among the emperor's servants wield sorcery,' I said. 'I had thought to use it, not to hold some bureaucratic office that any successful candidate could fill.'

'There it is!' Hand Usher exclaimed, then stood from the table in our shared common room. 'Come, Alder. I want to show you something.'

Baffled, but not about to protest when I seemed at last to be making progress towards the knowledge I desired, I followed Hand Usher without a word. He led me along the curving path that circled the artificial lake. The smells of hay, manure, and horse sweat met us as we rounded the pine-shrouded hill on the northern shore. The governor's sons were there with their horsemanship instructor, putting a young stallion through its paces.

Hand Usher gestured towards the horse. 'I present, for your consideration, the world.'

Oriole, the elder of the two boys, goaded the horse from a trot into a canter, and I looked at Hand Usher sceptically.

'Not literally, of course,' Hand Usher said, 'but like that young stallion, the world is full of energy. It lunges about this way and that, never standing still. Left to its own devices, it will bolt, all that pent-up energy culminating in naught but chaos and destruction.'

The stallion whickered and reared. Oriole twisted his body and pulled on the reins, bringing the horse back under his control.

'Whoever holds the reins can give that energy focus and

direction,' Usher went on. 'Of course, the world is a many-headed beast with many sets of reins. Military might. Trade and economy. Culture. Social structure. Magic. And there are many pairs of hands reaching for those many reins – so many that the world does not know which way to run, and we are left with just as much chaos as if the beast were to rule itself.

'History is the story of many kings and many gods, all grasping for the reins of the world, pulling it this way and that, and letting the weak be trampled beneath the chaos wrought by their contest. The promise of the empire is the promise of order. One king. One god. One emperor. And us, his many Hands, grasping the reins on his behalf.'

'And that is why I must learn economics?' I asked.

'Among many other things,' he replied, the playfulness returning to his voice. 'For example, horseback riding.'

Without waiting for me to react, he set off across the field, trailing the hem of his robe through the muddy grass. I rushed after him, biting back my frustration.

Though Oriole was of a similar age to me, I had not spent much time with him in my first months as Hand Usher's apprentice. While I had buried my nose in books about geography and economics, Oriole practised archery, swordsmanship, and wrestling with the men of his father's household guard – when he was not on horseback, that was. What few books I had seen him reading were biographies of great generals, treatises on leadership and tactics, and, most frequently, romantic accounts of Sien's mythic age of heroes.

When he saw Hand Usher and me crossing the field, Oriole brought his stallion to a walk beside me. 'Ah, our esteemed guest has stepped out into the sunlight,' he said. 'How can we serve you, young Hand of the emperor?'

There was mockery in his voice, but I was unsure whether to take it as good-natured ribbing or a genuine insult.

'Greetings, young Master Oriole,' Hand Usher said. 'I was wondering if you might help me with something. Hand Alder, you see, has never ridden a horse – something which must be rectified.'

'Father rides when he leads his soldiers,' Oriole said thoughtfully, 'but I thought most Hands were carried to battle in palanquins and fought in silken robes.'

Hand Usher laughed, but I felt a stab of offence. 'We are more than just scholars,' I said, 'as Hand Usher and I were just discussing.'

'Indeed. We must be whatever the emperor needs, scholar or soldier,' Hand Usher observed sagely. He was still smiling, though, which only deepened my annoyance.

Oriole studied me up and down. 'Well, you're no horseman. Not yet, anyway. I'll start you on a pony.'

With that, Hand Usher bade us a good afternoon and Oriole took my education in horsemanship in hand. He did indeed start me out on a pony, a grey-maned gelding called Wheat. The old horse stood placidly while Oriole showed me how to brush him down, but when the time came to put on the saddle and tack, the beast snorted and wriggled. I jumped at such sudden motion from a creature easily five times my size, and Oriole laughed.

'A bit more intimidating than a stack of books, eh?' he said.

Ignoring Oriole, I hauled myself onto Wheat's back and gripped the reins. The horse snorted, tossed his head, and started walking of his own accord. I gripped the reins and saddle horn in panic and tried not to think of falling off.

'Relax!' Oriole said. 'As stiff as you're sitting, it's no wonder he wants nothing to do with you.'

'How am I supposed to relax when he squirms like this?'

'Take a deep breath and let him walk,' Oriole advised. 'Just for a start, until you get used to being up there.'

Feeling utterly helpless, I loosened my grip. Wheat took a few more steps but soon settled, blowing through his nostrils and eyeing the grass as though pretending I wasn't sitting on his back.

'Now try to stay up there without getting all tense,' Oriole said. He took charge of Wheat's reins and guided the gelding along at a slow walk. He spoke gently to the horse and reminded me from time to time to straighten my back, loosen my muscles, and stop worrying so much. Less than an hour had passed when my legs and lower back began to ache.

'That's enough,' I said. 'Let me down.'

'Giving up already?' Oriole said.

'Hand Usher was only joking.'

'Was he? I can never tell when that man means what he says.'

'Why would he want me to learn horseback riding?'

'How should I know? You're his apprentice. Maybe he thinks you'll be going to war soon.'

'Or it's a joke.'

Oriole grinned up at me. 'If I were you, I wouldn't take that chance.'

I hated to admit it but Oriole was right. Whatever Hand Usher's reasons, this was the task he had given me. If I went against his wishes ... I flexed my left hand and tried not to think of the second warning he'd given to me on the day he had marked me and made me his apprentice: that failure would mean the loss of my hand, along with my place in the empire.

Wheat carried me in circles until the sun began to set. Oriole helped me down and suppressed a laugh when I groaned.

'You laugh at a Hand of the emperor?' I snapped at him, fighting the need to massage the stiffness from my thighs. 'Any failure of mine reflects upon you, you realise. Hand Usher might have some right to waste my time, but you do not.'

His sharp eyes narrowed. 'Very well,' he said. 'I'll take care of Wheat, if you feel brushing down your horse is beneath the dignity of your station.'

I felt the sting in his words but had no desire to deepen my humiliation by trading barbs with the spoiled, idiot son of a nobleman. I turned to go.

'And you may want a pillow for your seat at dinner,' he called after me.

I glared at him, swallowed a cutting retort, and hobbled away.

After two weeks, I was fed up. What little progress I was making hardly seemed worth the suffering. I could guide Wheat at a walk but tensed up as soon as the gelding began to trot. I fell at least once a day and Oriole seemed to find it impossible to help me to my feet without some sarcastic quip.

'Cheer up, Hand Alder,' he said on one such occasion as I hauled myself back into the saddle. 'There's no shame in falling off your horse. True, a Girzan five-year-old could outride you, but you'd have them well in hand when the time came for a poetry contest.'

'Better fingers calloused by a writing brush than an arse calloused by the saddle,' I muttered. 'They do not consider one's ability to ride a horse during the imperial examinations.'

'And is that the measure of something's worth?' Oriole said, his voice suddenly cold. 'Whether or not it's part of the exams?'

He spoke as though I had offended him, which only stoked my anger. He had subjected me – his elder brother, by way of my station, in the grand hierarchy of empire – to near-constant mockery. That *he* should take offence at *my* treating him in kind, as though he were deserving of more respect and dignity than me, was not only absurd but, I felt, the most egregious of all his offences.

I endured the rest of the lesson in silence, letting my anger burn down to hard, smouldering coals. He said little, only pointing out a few small flaws in my posture, or the position of my feet in the stirrups, or my handling of the reins. He seemed to pick out every small flaw in my riding, as though trying to prove his superiority. When we finished, I dismounted and tossed him the reins.

'Brush down the horse for me,' I said. 'I have business with Hand Usher.'

He stared at the reins in his hand. 'You'll have to learn how to care for a mount sooner or later.'

'Not today,' I said and turned to leave, muttering under my breath, 'and not from you.'

I sought out Hand Usher and found him sipping sorghum wine and practising calligraphy. Dozens of sheets of rice paper littered his room. He had written the same logogram on each one, an archaic form of the word *horse* in a sweeping, loose style.

He looked up when I entered the room and bade me sit across from him. I had to move a stack of pages to find the seat cushion.

'How go your lessons with Oriole?' he said.

Without waiting for me to answer, he dipped his brush and pressed it to a fresh sheet, then with a single, smooth motion scrawled the logogram he had been practising. He held the sheet up to the light of his lamp, grimaced, and tossed it aside.

'Oriole and I do not get along,' I said, swallowing the words *intolerable* and *lout*. 'I think my time learning horsemanship would be more productive with a different instructor.'

'More productive or more pleasant?' he asked, reaching for another sheet of paper.

'If my training were more pleasant,' I replied, 'I might be able to better focus and learn more quickly, instead of being distracted by constant annoyances.'

'Hmm.' Hand Usher selected a fresh sheet and spread it open

on the desk, pinning it in place with two slate paperweights. 'Whom would you prefer?'

'The governor has a Girzan nomad to train his sons.'

'Ah, yes. Yul Pekora.' The paper rustled as Hand Usher smoothed it flat. He reached for his brush. 'The cavalry commander for the province of Nayen. Doesn't it seem indulgent to waste the commander's time?'

I wanted to point to the sheets piled up around me, to show that Hand Usher seemed to take no issue with wasted time, but I kept my hand in my lap. He put brush to paper, wrote the logogram, and discarded it as swiftly as the last.

'Nevertheless,' I said, 'Oriole and I do not get along.'

'And you fault Oriole with this?' Hand Usher said, smoothing yet another sheet of paper.

'Of course I do!' I snapped. 'He shows me nothing but contempt.'

'And what do you show *him*?'

Hand Usher wrote the logogram, set his brush aside, and held the sheet up to the light. I had no answer for his question. Thinking back, I had been cold and aloof with Oriole. But could anyone fault me? He had begun our interaction with open mockery.

'Do you know why handwriting is assessed as part of the imperial examination?' he asked, still studying his scrawled horse.

'It reflects the character of the writer,' I answered.

'It reflects *temperament*,' he corrected me. 'To quote the sage Rushes-in-Water, "The energy present in the body and the mind in the moment of writing is reflected in the brush stroke." By a close examination of a handwriting sample – and a proper understanding of the context in which that writing sample was composed – one can deduce a great deal about the personality and attitudes of an individual. People are far worse at regulating their handwriting than they are their facial expressions, tone of voice, and even body language. Yet masterful calligraphers learn such deft control of the brush that they can convey whatever temperament they wish. For instance, I have been trying to capture your particular stew of anxieties in this logogram for *horse*.'

He offered the sheet to me. To my eye, the lines were just the same as the others he had drawn. They were loose and quick and did not read to me like *anxiety* at all. Certainly, I saw nothing in the logogram that reflected what I felt.

Hand Usher snatched the sheet back. 'Pfa! It's still not right.' He tossed it aside and reached for another blank sheet. 'It must be *perfect*, you understand.'

'How was it flawed?' I asked, bewildered and grasping for whatever lesson Hand Usher was trying to teach.

'Precisely!' Hand Usher dipped his brush. 'Like all the others, it was technically proficient in every way, but it lacked a certain undefinable quality. The same thing hangs about you, Alder – the sense that your outward excellence hides some secret flaw. The guardedness that makes you so boring to drink with.' He wrote another logogram, then threw up his hands in frustration. 'This horse? I could drink with this horse and enjoy myself thoroughly.'

I was already on edge, and his sudden talk of secrets nearly made me panic. What did Hand Usher suspect my hidden flaw might be?

'If I have disappointed you in some way—'

'You are careful, Alder, and that is commendable,' Hand Usher said, 'but you must also be *human*. Now, if you will excuse me, I need to drink more and think less if I'm ever going to get this calligraphy right.'

I retreated, conscious of my every gesture and expression and how they might be interpreted.

In the darkness and privacy of my room I collapsed onto the

bed and flexed my right hand, feeling the tug of flesh against old scars. From our first interaction, Hand Usher had been toying with me. The tale of the pollical cat had cut through to the heart of my anxieties, and he had told it after knowing me for a smattering of minutes. I could not help but perceive everything he said or did or asked of me as a series of esoteric tests steeped in obtuse metaphor. But while the tale of the cat had been as clear to me as water, his motivation for insisting that I learn horsemanship from Oriole was as opaque as stone.

A careful sifting of his words yielded no insight. Maybe something to do with sorcery? All of this had sprung from my finally asking to learn it. But I knew imperial sorcery only by the wake it left in the world – not nearly well enough to decipher whatever coded message Hand Usher meant for me.

I recalled the night when I had overstepped the bounds of my grandmother's teaching and been left a twisted wreck of flesh and bone. But I was older now and had some experience of magic – enough, I hoped, to touch this new power without it overwhelming me.

I glanced down at the by-now-familiar tetragram on my left palm: four logograms – axe, scroll, crown, and scale – arranged into a square, all bounded by a thick wall: together, the emperor's never-changing name. They seemed written in silver thread, and magic ever rushed beneath them. Cautiously, I dipped into that river of magic and hoped for a flash of insight.

Power swept through me, potent but constrained, as though someone had come before me and carved channels in stone through which magic now flowed like a river of mercury. It filled the channels and battered at the floodgates, threatening to overflow.

With a gasp, I withdrew. Magic drained out of me and left me with the impression of a promise unkept. The feeling slowly faded and left new understanding in its wake.

I reached again for sorcery. It rushed in, again threatening to overflow the channels in stone – yet it did not; the channels contained it. And as I held that power, I saw that it was no threat to me.

Magic without pact or canon was wild and unwieldy. On that dark night so many years ago, when my foolish experiment turned my body into a twisted ruin, it had overwhelmed me the moment I'd reached for it. The scars my grandmother had carved into my right hand provided a measure of control, but never enough to make me feel *safe* reaching for power.

Witchcraft, I now saw, was a dangerous bargain with an untamed power, the wolf that follows at the heels of a hunter: docile only as long as it is regularly fed. Sorcery was mastery, domestication. It bound magic with bit, bridle, and reins.

I let the power drain out of me, this time with a measure of satisfaction. This, then, was the purpose of my learning horsemanship – to understand that, though powerful, sorcery was constrained and therefore safe.

Though I felt pleased with myself for solving Hand Usher's puzzle, the answer left me as disappointed as I had been on the day my grandmother had given me my witch marks. Imperial sorcery was just as constrained as witchcraft, if not more so. Yet where else in the world could I learn anything of magic?

Surely the emperor himself had mastered it in the way I sought, and used that mastery to forge his empire. There had to be clues in the imperial canon, however deeply buried, that could guide me back to that limitless, freeing, terrifying power I had once wielded. I would learn imperial sorcery, with all its constraints, and apply what I could to witchcraft. And in so doing, I would begin to build my own theory of magic, to make my own path through the world.

But why had Hand Usher wanted me to learn all of this from

Oriole? And what had he meant when he said that I needed to learn how to be human?

It occurred to me then that some lessons might be best delivered bluntly rather than couched in metaphor.

9

Two Cups and a Game of Stones

The central house where the governor and his family lived was an estate within an estate, a courtyard house in the classical Sienese style. A low, square wall separated this innermost courtyard from the rest of the garden. The private residences of the governor and his family were built with their backs against this wall, their faces turned inward to the private garden of the family, the heart-within-the-heart of the governor's estate, symbolising the very centre of the empire itself. At all hours, two of the governor's household guard flanked the gate that joined this inner compound and the outside world. The guards watched my approach with hard eyes under the flickering lamp-light and the steep brims of their helmets.

'I'm to meet with Master Oriole,' I said, offering one of the two bottles I had brought with me. 'When I went to fetch these, I thought of what a shame it is that we young men can spend our evening drinking when you fine soldiers are left in the dark and cold with such dry throats.'

One of the guards took the bottle and studied the label. It was a rough but potent sorghum liquor that my father had preferred. The guard grunted, passed the bottle to his companion, and opened the gate. 'Many thanks, Hand Alder,' he said. 'Enjoy your evening.'

Everything in the governor's private compound was of finer provenance than my father's, of course – the house built from cedarwood, the steps from marble, and the carp in the courtyard pond – deep as some lakes – were as long as I was tall – but it was all arranged along familiar lines. And sure enough, Oriole's rooms were in the eastern wing of the house, just as mine had been.

Lamplight flickered beneath Oriole's door. I hesitated for a few dozen breaths. There would be awkwardness at first, I was sure, but I planned on only a few drinks, then a bit of friendly conversation. Enough to improve our relations and make my lessons in horsemanship bearable. What young man would refuse a few cups of liquor? I knocked and heard the rustle of paper and the squeak of a chair sliding across a tile floor.

'One moment!' Oriole called out. Then, likely thinking he could not be heard through the door, he muttered: 'About time. I asked for tea when the sun was still out!'

He opened the door in rumpled clothes with ink stains on his fingers. 'Hand Alder!' He stared at me, his eyebrows twitching with the effort of trying to reconcile my presence at his door with our simmering dislike for one another.

'Oriole,' I said with a slight bob of the head. I lifted the bottle and shook it. 'May I come in?'

'Ah.' He glanced over his shoulder to a writing desk littered with books. 'I mean, of course. Just ... well, I wasn't expecting you.'

As I stood in the doorway, what little confidence I had felt in my plan gradually drained out of the soles of my feet. This was the sort of thing people did to seem friendly, wasn't it?

'I didn't mean to impose,' I said.

'Of course you didn't,' he muttered. 'Just like you didn't when you moved into my house and conscripted me into teaching you how to ride.'

'That was Hand Usher's imposition, and upon me as well as you,' I bristled. 'I can make an appointment and come back later if you're too busy at the moment.'

'Who am I to turn away a Hand of the emperor?' he said.

I stared at him, not certain if he was being serious or throwing my status back in my face.

I ignored my bruised pride and shook the bottle again.

'Let's at least have a few drinks,' I said. 'Perhaps discuss our mutual frustrations with my mentor.'

Whether he meant it as an accusation of arrogance or not, it was true that to decline my invitation without very good reason would mark him a poor host in his father's house, and could even be seen as an insult to the emperor himself. In the end, that ingrained social pressure – and perhaps the promise of a heady drink at the end of what seemed a long evening – won out over his dislike for me. He reached for the bottle before opening the door wider to let me in.

'I knew Hands of the emperor could feel magic being done nearby,' he said, 'but I didn't know you lot could sense students in distress as well.'

I followed him into the room. He pushed the books to one corner of the writing desk and thumped the bottle down.

'I've got cups around here somewhere,' he said, rummaging through his bookshelf, which held far more knick-knacks than books. Eventually, he drew a mismatched pair of cups – one white porcelain, the other rough terracotta in the Girzan style – from behind a small bronze horse and a lacquer mask depicting the face of Lin Twelve-Ox, a hero out of ancient legend and the subject of several famous plays.

'Don't let me interrupt you,' I said, still taken aback to have found him studying. As we were of a similar age, by rights he should have taken the imperial examinations with me, yet I had not met him until I'd moved into the governor's estate.

He followed my gaze to the writing desk, his expression stiffening to mask his embarrassment. After a moment, though, it collapsed into a sheepish smile. 'I could use the break, to be honest.'

'My way of thanking you for your help,' I said, gesturing to the bottle. He opened it, filled the cups, and offered me the porcelain one.

'Cheers, then.'

I tried not to grimace at the bite of the liquor against the back of my throat.

Oriole hissed through his teeth. 'Oof. You've a taste for the rough stuff.'

'Not really,' I admitted. 'I thought you might.'

'I'm glad you have such a high opinion of me!' He shook the bottle. 'Shame to let it go to waste, though.'

I offered my cup. The second drink didn't bite as hard as the first. Oriole offered me the chair, sat on the edge of his bed, and dragged a trunk between us to serve as a table.

'I don't know how much more of this I can drink for its own sake,' Oriole said. 'If we're going to drain this bottle, we'll need to find a pretence. A drinking game or something.'

Oh no. My goal was certainly *not* to drain that bottle.

'We don't necessarily *need*—'

'I've got it!' Oriole sprang to his feet, rummaged around on his bookshelf, and retrieved a wooden box, decorated on the top with a pattern of tiny, equally spaced dots. It held two lidded bowls of small stones, one set white, the other black.

'Ever play Stones before?' Oriole said.

I had not. The rules of the game were simple, and Oriole quickly explained them to me. The goal of the game was to have more stones on the board than your opponent. Each player placed one stone per turn and could remove opposing stones by surrounding them with their own.

'Let's play, but let's add one extra rule,' he said, offering me the bowl of white stones. 'For every five stones you capture, you have to take a drink.'

I tensed, unsure. That sounded like *quite* a lot of drinking.

'All right,' I said slowly, promising myself that, no matter how drunk I got, I would not follow Oriole out into the city, no matter what adventure he might promise.

'Shit!' Oriole said as I closed a trap and captured six of his stones. 'Oh, bleed it. Well, at least you have to drink.'

He poured for me and I drained my cup, stifled a hiccup, and nodded for him to take his turn. The game had started quickly, but its inner complexities quickly became apparent and our progress slowed as our strategic senses became increasingly dulled by the alcohol. Oriole had a significant lead – which meant he was also significantly more drunk than I was – but I was laying the groundwork for a comeback.

'Of course, opportunity often distracts from danger,' Oriole said. He held a stone poised above the board and grinned, his eyes sharp and knowing even through the haze of intoxication. The stone completed a long, sinewy loop of black that jutted into my territory.

'How did I miss that?' I blurted.

Oriole picked up the seventeen stones he had captured, then reached for the bottle. 'You may outsmart me in most of the ways that matter, O Hand of the emperor, but I'm a sneaky bastard when it comes to Stones.'

I was already frustrated by the blow he had dealt me in the game, and his bitterness rankled me. 'There's no need to be an ass about it, Oriole.'

'I'm just surprised that I'm beating you.' He drained his cup and refilled it. 'We're not all blessed with talent, Alder.'

'What are you talking about?' The liquor had made me belligerent, and I remembered Clear-River's jealousy, and his threats. 'You didn't even sit the examinations!'

'Oh, but I did!' Oriole slammed his hand down on the trunk between us. Stones jumped from the board and clattered onto the floor. 'I sat them, and I failed them. But what does it matter, eh? It's not as though I *need* an imperial commission. My father offered to finance a business for me, and meanwhile our tutor has shifted his focus to Pinion. It seems the younger brother must defer to the elder, unless the elder brother proves himself a dunce.'

I looked to the books on Oriole's desk, hastily shunted out of the way to make room for liquor and cups. 'You're planning to retake it,' I said.

'Of course I am!' Oriole snapped. He stared at the ruin of our game, then leaned over to pick up the fallen stones. 'We're not all born geniuses, able to pass the fucking thing on our first try, raised from lowly birth to the heights of prestige and power. Some of us are born with bloody expectations around our necks and spend our whole lives trying to live up to them.'

He tossed a handful of stones back onto the board. 'Hell. None of this is your fault. We should be friends. Or I should show you deference, at least. But every time I look at you, I picture you on the stage with Hand Usher, living a dream that will never come true for me.'

I looked at him, astonished. *Oriole* wanted to be Hand of the emperor? Burly, straightforward Oriole, who preferred mythic romances to the literary classics? It was hard for me to imagine what his reason might be, other than the glory of the achievement itself.

But of course, his father was Voice of the emperor. Realisation struck, and I found myself wondering at his pedigree. How would I have reacted if I had failed, and then the personification of my failure was brought to live in my home? I knelt to help him gather the rest of the stones.

'I'm sorry,' I said.

He paused. 'What for?'

'I know what it's like to live under heavy expectations,' I said. 'My father was only a merchant, but he spent most of his small fortune on hiring my tutor. And there were ... other pressures. I can only imagine it was worse for you.'

Oriole slumped back into his chair and started sorting the stones into their respective bowls. 'You can imagine, but I doubt your imagination would do it justice. I'm the first eldest son in ten generations to fail the examinations. All their names in the family record are followed by "Placed rank blah-blah-blah on the first attempt". Not all became Hands or Voices, but my father did, like my grandfather and great-grandfather before him. And now I'll be a piddling merchant – a mere footnote in my brother's pedigree – when I should have been a general.'

'No, you won't,' I assured him. 'You'll retake it.'

Oriole tossed the last stone into its bowl. 'That's the plan. Every three years, until I pass it or I die. I'm beginning to think death is the more likely outcome, though. Especially without a tutor.'

'I'll tutor you,' I said.

The tension between us, which had been easing as we gathered the stones and spoke of our fathers, suddenly snapped back. Oriole scrutinised me, as though searching my face for some trick or a sign of mockery.

'Think of it as a way of balancing things between us,' I said. 'You help me with horsemanship; I'll help you with the examinations. That way we'll be equal.'

It occurred to me as I said this how little equality I had known. My every relationship was constrained by rank and deference to the dichotomies that existed between husband and wife, father and son, elder and younger brother.

Did Oriole, too, long for a refuge from propriety in a freer, more equitable friendship? More importantly – and more worryingly – did he see the potential of having such a friendship with me?

'I don't want to waste your time,' he muttered.

'I want to help you,' I said firmly, and though I wanted to bite back my next thought, I took the risk of voicing it. 'And it won't be a waste. I half suspect this is why Hand Usher wanted you to start teaching me horsemanship.'

'So that you would end up tutoring me?'

'So that we would become friends.'

He seemed puzzled, but his expression slowly warmed. 'I never understand what that man is thinking.'

'Me neither, most of the time. But we're not going to unpack the mysteries of Usher's mind tonight.' I passed him his bowl of stones. 'There's liquor left in that bottle, and I'm finally getting the hang of this game.'

10

The Canon of Sorcery

Weeks later, Hand Usher came to watch my riding lesson, un-announced. The lesson was nearly at an end – I had brought Wheat down to a gentle trot around the field to warm him down – but the old gelding had energy left in him and I seized the chance to show Hand Usher what I had learned.

I prodded Wheat up to a canter, then pushed myself up off the saddle till I was half-standing in the stirrups. Wheat took the cue to gallop. It felt almost natural, now, to ride the rhythms of his pumping muscles and churning hooves. We circled the field twice before I reined him to a trot, then to a stop beside Hand Usher and Oriole.

'See?' Oriole said. 'As I said, it's like he was born on horse-back.'

Hand Usher stroked Wheat's neck. 'Well done, Oriole. And thank you. If it's not too much to ask, would you take Wheat back to the stables for us? I've a lesson of my own to teach today.'

Oriole took Wheat's reins and flashed a grin at me. 'I've finally got Alder to start brushing and unsaddling him, but I suppose one day without doing his chores can't hurt.'

I rolled my eyes but returned the grin, elated that I'd finally passed Hand Usher's test. While he led the horse away, I made a mental note to buy Oriole a bottle of fine rice wine – something we could actually enjoy together without resorting to a drinking game – to thank him for his long-suffering help.

It was impossible to mask my excitement. My reading in economics, history, and politics had continued, but Hand Usher had taken a hands-off approach. He assigned books for me to read, and occasionally initiated discussion about them, but he never engaged in lengthy dialectic as Koro Ha had done, nor did he task me with written compositions. Now he would give instruction in person rather than handing me a book – which meant, I hoped, that he would finally begin to teach me magic.

A path of cobblestones worked in spiralling patterns, evoking the flow of a river through deadly rapids, led us around the artificial lake near the guest house. A narrow pier jutted out over the water to a small pavilion nestled behind the great porous stone at the centre of the lake, hiding it from the rest of the garden. Brightly feathered songbirds flitted in wicker cages that hung from the eaves.

'You and Oriole are getting along,' he said. 'That's good.'

Not a word about my horsemanship, which confirmed what I had suspected about the true purpose of the lesson. Were all Hands of the emperor subjected to such roundabout apprenticeships, I wondered, or only those who studied with Hand Usher?

'I know you've been dabbling with sorcery,' he said, studying an eagle hawk that had built a nest in the hollows of the stone. 'I've felt the wake of your power in the night. You do nothing with it, which is wise, but you cannot resist the urge.'

While his aloofness made him doubly difficult to read, I was sure that his words were another test. 'Is it not wise to examine the horse and tack before mounting?' I asked.

Hand Usher flashed his ghost of a smile. 'That almost sounds like a quotation from a sage.'

'Would it have been better to shirk from sorcery in fear?' I pressed.

'Not better,' he replied after a pause. 'Maybe safer, but you have been chosen for power and must accustom yourself to it.'

He beckoned me to join him at the railing. A breeze off the lake stirred our robes and the wisps of his beard. I smelled burnt cinnamon. A liquid shiver ran down my spine. He opened his right hand over the water, his palm facing the sky. A rolling wake, or the ripple from a heavy stone dropped into a pond, unfurled from the tetragram branded there. The silvered lines on Hand Usher's palm flickered into flames, and those flames coalesced into a sphere like opalescent glass.

At last I would learn to wield and understand this power that I had longed for since childhood. And not in the moon-shadowed ruin of an abandoned temple from an outlawed witch but in the governor's own garden, from a Hand of the emperor. Excitement swept through me, along with the heady sensation of magic. I gripped the railing to keep my feet.

'This is sorcery in its purest form,' Hand Usher said. 'Potential itself. The threads from which the ancient gods wove the world – or so myth and legend tell. Just as they tell of the heroes and tyrants who swore fealty to those gods, who doled out paltry fragments of power in return, and whose wars plunged the world into chaos. Chaos the empire was forged to prevent.'

He shut his fist. The sphere vanished, and with it the ripples of elation, the keenness of eye and mind.

'Reach for that power,' Hand Usher said. 'I know that you know how.'

My right hand curled tighter against the railing. Again, I reminded myself that this was not forbidden, that Hand Usher meant, really and truly, to share with me the secret for which I had always thirsted.

I held my left hand out over the water and touched the power that churned always beneath those shimmering lines. The songs of the birds around us became as delicate as crystal; their feathers shone like stars. Before, I had touched magic only in the dark of night, shut within an ancient temple or my private rooms. Even then, to look at the world while wielding magic was to see its every detail, in all beauty and all ugliness, amplified a thousandfold. Beneath the bright midday sun, all the world became as though refracted through a lens of light itself.

'You must remember to breathe, Alder,' Hand Usher advised.

I gasped, filling my neglected lungs, yet my voice was still breathless. 'What do I do now?'

'Do you feel the channels?' Hand Usher asked.

I nodded. They were all around me, patterns imposed on the magic I held by a force outside myself. The stone channels, by which the emperor had domesticated this world-shaping power. They bent and turned around each other, and I dwelt at the heart of that maze.

The churn and flow of energy surged around me, just as it had done so in the Temple of the Flame. But now, the impregnable walls of the canon created a space within those shifting possibilities, a maze to bind my will and my use of magic.

'Move into the first channel,' Hand Usher said.

Confusion gave way to understanding. The channels fed one into the next, I now perceived, like locks in a canal. As the mind moves from thought to thought, I moved into the first channel. My tetragram began to shine, then to flicker.

'This is the sorcery of transmission, the first power in the canon of sorcery,' Hand Usher said. 'With it the emperor built the rest of the canon, capturing and containing powers granted by the gods to conscript mortalkind into their ceaseless wars. That is the purpose of Sien's slow conquest of the world – to subject these powers to mortal mastery. And, in so doing, to free humankind from the tyranny of the gods.'

Sorcery poured from my tetragram and out into the world, forming an opalescent sphere that hovered in my hand. I felt the weight of it like an inheld breath, like the apprehensive moment before a difficult decision.

'By transmission, all our power is delivered unto us, sent from the emperor to his Voices, and from them to his Hands,' Hand Usher said.

'How do I use it?' I asked.

'Release that sorcery and attend mine,' Hand Usher said.

I retreated from the first channel and felt relief as the magic trickled out of me. Sorcery – at least, this first kind of sorcery – was a burden to hold, not the unfettered joy and wonder I had known in the moment before my first, failed veering.

'We cannot wield transmission,' Hand Usher said. 'Only the emperor may control it, for with it any Hand or Voice might shape a competing canon of his own. There must only be one. One canon, one emperor, for only then may chaos be averted. But the rest of the canon is ours to command.'

Now that I understood the maze of channels, I was able to follow the motion of Hand Usher's will when he reached for sorcery. This time he did not linger in the first channel but pressed on into the second. I gasped as sensation washed through me – another breath of cinnamon, the warmth of sun-flushed skin, a chill wind in my lungs.

Lightning flashed from Hand Usher's tetragram. Steam billowed where it speared into the lake. The Hand closed his fist.

'Once, the Girzan horse lords howled prayers to their many-winged storm gods and hurled bolts of holy lightning down upon their enemies,' Hand Usher said. 'Magic we now wield as battle sorcery, the first of the six sorceries – other than transmission – that comprise the canon.'

It was a simple thing to emulate him, to move from the first channel into the second. I splayed my fingers and battle sorcery poured from me.

There were subtleties of form and timing by which Hand Usher hurled darts of lightning or held a blade of iridescent light, but the limitations of the canon were clear. The spell had already been cast; the Hand only gave it direction.

The excitement that had been bubbling in my veins flattened and left me feeling leaden and hollow. A lump filled my throat and pressure built behind my eyes, like I was a toddling child with a scraped knee. Hand Usher spoke of rivers, of herds, of ever-present lightning and the whorl of stars – all metaphors. It took all my attention and will to stand quietly and pretend to listen, to keep from lashing out in anger or collapsing in a weeping, defeated puddle. There was nothing I could learn from him – nothing *true*. Nothing with the weight and meaning I had felt when I had touched magic in its purer form, unconstrained by the canon of sorcery, unbounded even by witchcraft.

I had come so far from that horrible night on the overgrown path, yet I had made no real progress at all. All Hand Usher told me in that first lecture, I already knew – that every creature, every stone, every drop of water is but a painting that captures a single moment in the eternal exchange of energies that is the pattern of the world. It was this pattern that I had felt when I had knelt in the Temple of the Flame and tried to copy my grandmother's magic. Magic – in all its forms – breaks that natural pattern and imposes one of its own.

But we Hands of the emperor did not reshape the pattern to our own design. We could only choose where and when to impose the emperor's will, transmitted through his canon.

I closed my fist, squeezed until I felt my fingernails bite flesh, pressed my frustrations into the meat of my palm. I longed for understanding and mastery of magic – of the pattern itself, and of the inscrutable, wonderful, terrifying power I had touched that night at the temple. Mastery that the canon had been designed to deny me. If I damaged the mark, desecrating the symbol of the emperor's power, could I free myself from those limitations? Begin to learn, again, the deeper magic that had offered the promise of a third path and a future of my own making?

A drop of blood dripped from my fist. I relaxed my hand. There could be no retreating to the past, no making other choices that might lead me into the mountains with my grandmother and my uncle. I would grit my teeth, press on, and hope to learn deeper truths through the fog of Hand Usher's teaching.

The next day, we returned to the lakeside pavilion. Hand Usher brought along a basket of stones of varying shapes and sizes.

'That,' he said, pointing to the placid surface of the lake, 'is the pattern of the world, flowing according to its own laws and logic, undisturbed.'

He selected a stone and tossed it into the water, then gestured to the ripples that rolled out from where the stone had struck towards the bulrushes near the shore.

'The stone was a spell,' he said. 'See how it disturbs the waters? The ripples are not the stone itself but only the evidence of its passing. You are a reed. See how the ripples move them?'

He then threw more stones, of different shapes, into different parts of the lake and bade me note how some ripples were larger, others smaller, some close together and others further apart, and how the bulrushes bent and swayed differently depending on the ripples that reached them.

'Each spell leaves a different wake in the world,' he said. 'Your tetragram – in addition to granting you the canon – gives you the ability to sense those wakes. When you become a master at reading them, you can know what magic an enemy wields and how to react accordingly, even before the spell strikes you. By following them to their source, you can find the one who cast the spell.'

'As long as the stone falls near enough,' I noted and threw a small stone to the far side of the lake. Its ripples died well before they reached the reeds.

This, coupled with the sorcery of transmission, must have born the rumour with which Clear-River had threatened me. The emperor could not see into the minds of his Hands, as he could when he communed with his Voices, but he did convey the canon of sorcery to us. Perhaps he always felt the wake of the canon's use, no matter how distant.

I asked Hand Usher about this. He hefted another stone and held it out to me. 'You are the hand, he is the mind, and the Voices are the muscles and meridians that bind you together,' he replied. 'If I have decided not to throw this stone but instead to give it to you, is it possible for my hand to disobey me?'

I stared at him, wondering if I would ever receive a clear answer to any of my questions.

'If it did, you might want to call a doctor,' I said.

'Ha! But the empire is nothing if not healthy, and sorcery is its life blood. Now, let us turn to a practical lesson.' He handed me the stone, then set off towards the centre of the garden. 'Stay here until you feel the wake of my sorcery.'

'And then what?' I asked.

He smiled that ghost of a smile. 'Come and find me.'

Half an hour later, I felt the chill in my lungs and flush on my skin that told of battle sorcery. It took me until long after dark to find him, sitting in a servant's closet with a book and a candle, lightning playing across his fingertips. At first, I had little to go on but the strengthening of the sensation as I drew closer to him, or its weakening if I wandered in the wrong direction, but as we repeated the exercise again and again over the following days I learned to read the ripples through the pattern of the world like a map. Some mornings I would wake with a feverish flush and a cold wind in my chest, and he would already be gone, hiding somewhere in the estate, and later the city, holding a spell – more powerful the further he ventured – and waiting for me to find him.

Once, after six months of such practice, I followed the wake of his spell beyond the city walls. At dusk I found him in an abandoned field, though at first sight I thought him a blazing star fallen from the sky. Arcs of lightning spilled from his chest, his back, his shoulders, burning furrows in the earth and leaving behind steaming streaks of glass. I came as close as I dared. Still, my body pulsed with heat, and my lungs felt like blocks of ice. It was the most brilliant and terrifying display I had witnessed since watching my grandmother become an eagle hawk.

He saw me and released the spell. The last bolt of lightning fizzled out with a hiss and crack. The sensation of its wake faded and left me feeling both reassured and threatened. The canon of sorcery would not give me the knowledge and mastery to wield magic according to my own will, but I could no longer question the power I would wield as Hand. The same power that would be levelled against me if the secret marks carved into my right palm were discovered.

'Well done,' Hand Usher said and strode past me, back towards Eastern Fortress. 'You're as sure-nosed as a huntsman's hound and ready for your next lesson.'

The more familiar I became with the canon of sorcery, the more I theorised about witchcraft and about the deeper power I had felt that first night, before the witch marks, when magic had seemed to fill the world around me, waiting only for the motion of my will. My growing understanding of the canon's limitations had helped me to see my grandmother in a new light. Her witch marks had constrained my power, yes, but not nearly as rigidly as the canon. And it seemed that no one in the world – save perhaps the emperor himself – wielded magic without some mediating limitation, whether from an ancient pact or the designs of empire.

I had begun to forgive Grandmother, for the witch marks if not for her abandonment, and longed for the opportunity to delve into the magic of her people, to find its boundaries and search them as I had searched the structures of the canon for any remnant scrap of mastery. But I could not risk experimenting. Hand Usher lived in the room next to mine, close enough to feel the wake of a conjured candle flame.

Autumn was upon us when Hand Usher began to teach me the next sorcery in the canon. Once again we stood on the shore of the lake, where lotus pods jutted stripped of their petals. Hand Usher held a songbird that had been mauled by one of the cats that roamed the governor's estate, its blue feathers bright against the yellow silk that swaddled it. It lay still, dosed with a drop of poppy oil, but breathed in quick, agitated gasps.

'Left alone, the bird will die,' Hand Usher said. 'It has lost too much blood, and its body cannot recover quickly enough to survive. But with the sorcery of healing, we can speed that process and save its life.'

He spread his hand over the bird and moved into the third channel. The same glassy flames burned from his tetragram, but this time the wake I felt through the world was gentler than that of battle sorcery: a wash of calmness, a softening of colours and muting of sound, and a sensation like the first sip of tea on a chill winter morning.

The bird's wound knit itself. Its breathing eased. New feathers sprouted around its scar. Hand Usher placed it in one of the cages hanging from the eaves of the pavilion, where a teacup of sunflower seeds and millet waited. The bird set upon the food with quick jabs of its beak, as though it had not been on the edge of death just a moment ago.

'This sorcery only supplements the body's capacity to heal,' Hand Usher explained. 'If the body is too weak – as in the old or very ill – the healing may strain it unto death. And though the danger of the wound has passed, the bird must eat to replenish its strength or else starve.'

Here, in the sorcery of healing, I saw the hint of an answer to one of my oldest questions: how had my grandmother undone my greatest mistake? I, too, had been left weak and on the edge of death. Only Doctor Sho's medicines had restored my strength. Seeing the bird hale again, my curiosity overcame my self-control.

'I do not mean to offend, Hand Usher,' I said, 'but … this sorcery seems miraculous. Battle sorcery was easier to comprehend. But this? What are the limits? If I were to cut off one of the bird's legs, could that leg be regrown through sorcery? Or perhaps a new leg grafted in place of the old? Could we deceive the body and graft on a second set of legs, or wings?'

I felt the scrutiny of Hand Usher's gaze and knew that I had overstepped. 'Better, and more compassionate, to ask why we Hands do not dedicate ourselves to roaming the country, mending wounds and reviving the sick,' he admonished. 'But the answer is the same: the emperor has a purpose in mind for us, just as he has a purpose in mind for healing sorcery. Perhaps the barbarian gods and their worshippers could do the things you describe, but the limits of sorcery are bound by the emperor's will, and the emperor does not will such abuses of nature.'

What of my lessons in horsemanship? What of my friendship with Oriole? Was I not meant to learn that there is a place for easing the reins, a need at times to step outside convention? Perhaps Hand Usher had introduced the idea that boundaries might acceptably be stretched only to see whether I would break them. Was I even now failing the most important of all his tests?

'I seek knowledge only that it might enable me to better serve the emperor,' I said.

'Your curiosity is an asset to you, Alder, but when an answer is given you must learn to accept it,' Hand Usher replied. 'Let that be your lesson for today. When you have learned it, we will return to sorcery.'

I felt my frustration with Hand Usher as a tension in my back and shoulders, a tightness in my stomach. I longed for my grandmother, or for Koro Ha – for a teacher who would say what he meant and who had not begun our relationship with a threat.

As dusk settled over the estate, I sought out Oriole. We often took meals together, eating between rounds of Stones or while I quizzed him on the Sienese classics. That night I had no appetite for scholarship or games, but if I went to sulk in my rooms my ill feelings would only fester.

'Ah, Alder!' Oriole greeted me. 'Good timing. I just finished this essay and could use some—'

'Tomorrow, I promise,' I told him. His room had taken on a permanent reconfiguration to accommodate our friendship. The bed had been moved against one wall to make room for two chairs and a table always ready with the Stones board, the bottle I had bought him for his help, and our mismatched pair of cups. I poured myself a drink.

Oriole put away his writing tools and joined me at the table. I handed him the bowl of black stones and made my first move. The click of stone against board set my teeth on edge.

'You look like a hornet flew up your robe,' Oriole said.

'Make your move,' I said, more harshly than I'd intended.

Oriole put up his hands as though I'd threatened to strike

him. 'If it's none of my business, fine, but I've never seen you so agitated.'

How could I explain myself to Oriole? He knew something of my contorted home life, bounded by a rigorous education that left no time for games like Stones, though I had said nothing of magic or my grandmother's lessons.

Oriole placed his stone. 'What is it, Alder? You're learning sorcery, aren't you? Or has Usher put some absurd new hurdle in your path?'

I placed my next stone, glaring at the board. How much could I tell him? I knew his own frustrations with his father, the examinations, and the structures of Sienese society. Could he hear mine, without seeing through them to those parts of my mind first cultivated by my grandmother?

'I'll send for food,' he said, and stood. I realised then that I needed to speak my mind, to be heard and understood honestly by another. To feel a little less alone in a world where the boundaries of my bifurcated upbringing had left me isolated. Whom could I trust with such thoughts, if not Oriole?

'I'm beginning to think Hand Usher's eccentricities are not an intentional teaching style,' I said.

Oriole settled back into his chair, food forgotten for the time being.

'Pinion and I had a bet on when you'd finally get fed up with him,' he said. 'I won, of course. Pinion thought you'd snap a month ago.'

'I thought he wanted me to arrive at the correct conclusions on my own, rather than just giving them to me,' I said. 'Now I think he's just parroting the same circuitous nonsense he heard from his own teacher. Worse, it isn't only an unwillingness to discuss sensitive questions, or ignorance; he seems totally incurious about the answers!'

I described my lesson in the sorcery of healing and Hand

Usher's blanket dismissal of my questions, though I chose not to mention the memories the lesson had evoked. Oriole was my friend, but he was still Sienese, and the son of a Voice. He would neither understand nor forgive certain of my secrets.

'Maybe sorcery just *can't* do the things you described,' Oriole said. 'It might be as simple as that.'

'Why wouldn't it be able to?' I asked. 'Nothing I suggested seems to deviate from what he showed me, only to apply it in different ways.'

'Maybe it's possible, but the emperor doesn't give you those powers.'

'Well then, why doesn't he?' I said, disappointed that Oriole didn't seem to grasp my deeper frustration.

'You may as well ask why imperial doctrine exists,' Oriole said, 'or why the classics are featured on the imperial examinations but not the mythic romances – much more interesting stories, by the way, and just as meaningful.'

'The examinations can't cover everything,' I said, 'else you'd need an entire lifetime to study for them.'

'Sorcery is the same, isn't it?' Oriole said. 'You have to learn how to use it before you can serve the emperor as his Hand. Sorcery is just like everything else in Sien – curated. That which is best and most useful to the empire is elevated over things like adventure stories or grafting extra wings onto birds or whatever.'

I felt the urge to push back on that point, using Oriole himself as an example. He had been left out of that curation when he failed the imperial examinations, after all. Did that mean he was not useful to the empire? But I bit my tongue. There was no need to hurt him simply to get my point across.

'This is bigger than books,' I said instead. 'This is about the power to reshape the world itself. Why would the empire cut itself off from any benefit or use that magic might possibly provide?'

Oriole paused and studied me. He placed a stone and leaned back in his chair. 'Maybe there are parts of the world the empire doesn't want reshaped,' he said. 'Or maybe it isn't your place to reshape them.'

His words reminded me of the story of the pollical cat and Hand Usher's first and most important lesson: that if I wanted to survive in the service of the empire, I needed to know what I was.

And what was I? The emperor's Hand. The agent of his will. Entitled to no knowledge or power beyond that which the emperor deigned to give me.

The next day, after I'd nursed my hangover with millet gruel, black tea, and fried dough, I returned to Hand Usher in the pavilion behind the porous stone. Mist curled between the songbird cages and caught the sunlight, imbuing the pavilion with a golden glow. Hand Usher looked up from the book he was reading. I did not take my seat beside him but knelt on the wooden floor.

'Are you ready to learn, Hand Alder?' he said.

'I have been a fool,' I said. 'Are there any in the empire whose place it is to know the things I have asked?'

The ghost of a smile flickered across Hand Usher's face. 'The emperor, of course, and his Voices.'

'Only them?' I asked, dejected. I had been the first Hand from Nayen. What were the odds that I would be the first Voice as well?

'There are some in the Imperial Academy,' Hand Usher said, and hope welled within me. 'Researchers who serve the emperor by analysing new magics recovered from conquered provinces.'

'Then I will do all I can to one day join them,' I said.

'A worthy goal,' Hand Usher replied, 'and one well suited to your temperament. But first, you must master the six sorceries. Let us return to your lessons.'

As the sun burned away the mist, I practised the sorcery of healing, restoring a torn ginseng leaf still on the tree, then the broken foot of a captured mouse, then a cut that Hand Usher inflicted on his own finger.

I learned the sorcery of healing more slowly than I had mastered battle sorcery. It was not as simple as it had at first appeared. Some wounds – cuts, bruises, hairline fractures – could be restored with a direct application of sorcery. More complex injuries and ailments required a defter hand and deeper knowledge of medicine and anatomy.

After a third songbird died in my care, Hand Usher bade me focus on mastering the natural sciences before we progressed any further. Months passed, and then a year, while I returned to that easiest and most comfortable task: devouring books. Meanwhile I continued to tutor Oriole, who improved noticeably from week to week and month to month, until I was certain he would pass the imperial examinations when he next sat them.

Altogether I spent two years of my life in the garden of Voice Golden-Finch, learning from Hand Usher and befriending Oriole, a time I recall with mingled fondness, heartbreak, and frustration. A time that came to an end when the rebellion simmering in the north of Nayen at last boiled over and the governor sent me to war.

II

Strategy and Tactics

In the early spring of my nineteenth year, word of an uprising in the north of Nayen reached Eastern Fortress. Nayeni bandits had come down from their mountain holdfasts to attack imperial patrols and raise their flags in the towns and villages that dotted the foothills. Shortly after this news reached us, Voice Golden-Finch sent a letter written in the formal calligraphy of his office, sealed with his personal tetragram and delivered by his steward to my rooms, naming me second in command of a company of soldiers that would be sent to drive the emboldened rebels back into hiding – or exterminate them, if possible. Along with the order came a summons to his audience hall that afternoon.

My mind reeled. *I* was being put in *command*? And of a force that would be fighting Nayeni, at that? Was this the same group of bandits, I wondered with a pang of dread, led by my uncle? The rebellion my grandmother had gone to join?

But that had been seven years ago. They might not even still be alive.

At any rate, I felt wildly unprepared to lead fighting men. I had read tactics – the Classic of Battle and the Treatise on Logistical Analysis were required texts for the imperial examinations – but I had no practical military experience. The only martial training I'd had was in the Nayeni Iron Dance – which I had not practised in years – and my games of Stones with Oriole, which had at least fostered strategic thinking and taught a facsimile of battle tactics. Of course, he still won four of every five games we played.

No matter. Prepared or not, I had been given orders by a Voice, which bore a weight of command second only to orders from the emperor himself. I could only trust that Voice Golden-Finch would explain when I answered his summons.

As I walked across the garden, dressed in my finest clothes and my scholar's cap, my stomach churned. I felt wildly out of my depth yet unable to admit it, unable to tell Voice Golden-Finch – and, by proxy, the emperor – that I was unfit for the task they had given me. My inner turmoil so absorbed me that I nearly bowled over Oriole on the path.

'Alder!' he yelped, catching me by the arms and steadying me. His clouded expression deepened as he saw the nervousness in my eyes and the sweat on my brow. 'Again, you get the thing I've always wanted,' he scowled and all but shoved me away before stalking off along the path, his posture written in jagged, furious lines.

'Oriole!' I called after him, hurrying to match his pace. 'You heard, then. You must know I don't want command. I never wanted it. If we could trade places – you off to war, and me staying here to study for the exams – you know I would in the space of a breath. You're better suited to it. You've read all the romances, the tactics manuals, every treatise on every battle—'

'It doesn't matter,' he said, glaring down at the cobblestones. 'I failed the examinations.'

'But you won't this time,' I assured him. 'The next examinations are a year away. In fact, it's good that you won't be going away to war. You'll have a whole year to keep preparing. Keep your studies up, and you'll—'

'I'm not you, Alder,' he said and halted suddenly, his breathing harsh, his hands balled into tight fists, his sharp eyes full of anger. 'And I'm sick of pretending that I could be if I just tried hard enough.'

There were more words to be said, anger to be vented at how the world had erected barricades between him and everything he wanted, everything he ought to have inherited. Yet words had never been Oriole's gift.

My heart ached as I tried to bridge the gap between us. 'You don't have to be me, Oriole,' I said.

'Yes I do!' he snapped, as harsh as he had ever been before our rivalry had blossomed into friendship. 'To be anything of value, I do. I have to be you, with your books and your ink and your quotations from the sages.'

I sensed in his words an echo of my own longing for a third path, carried since childhood. Was that, too, something we could share? It was a risky arena for conversation, fraught with the treasonous aspects of my upbringing, secrets I still held dear. Yet I believed that I could trust Oriole – if no one else – with such feelings, if not the reasons for them. And I found, to my surprise, that easing Oriole's burden would be worth the risk of exposing those parts of myself most hidden and dangerous.

'No, you don't,' I told him. 'You have a great deal to offer, even without an imperial commission. Your father imagines you as either a Hand of the emperor or a trifling merchant – either a success in his eyes or a total failure. But you could be something else, Oriole. Find a third way through the world. Your own way. Something you and your family can be proud of. It will take imagination, certainly, but together we can—'

'What do you mean *together*?' he scoffed. 'You speak as though you've had to find this "third way" yourself, but when has the path to success and prestige ever been anything but clear and sparkling for you, Alder? I don't think you intend to mock me, but this feels like a joke. Don't speak to me of it again.'

'There are things about me you don't know,' I snapped. 'Which of us has had an easier life, do you think? The one who studied twelve hours a day for ten years to earn a place in this palace, or the one who was born here?'

The muscles in his jaw pulsed, yet he swallowed his anger and strode off, leaving me standing on the path, feeling hollowed out. Though this strange assignment might yield an opportunity to win renown and advance towards my goal of a placement in the academy, I found it nothing but a source of heartache for the wedge it had driven between Oriole and me.

Oriole was right. The odds that he would become Hand after having failed the examinations the first time were as slender as a strand of silk. Passing would prove enough of a challenge – though one I believed he could surmount. Placing first was a near impossibility.

But not every officer in the imperial army was a Hand or a Voice of the emperor. Generals were, but even battalion commanders might be ordinary men without sorcery. If he passed, and distinguished himself in battle while still young, Oriole could easily enter the military career he dreamed of. Not a third path, exactly, but a detour leading back to the path he longed for.

I turned back towards the audience hall, now with an agenda of my own.

The last time I had been in Voice Golden-Finch's audience hall, it had been furnished and decorated for the banquet to celebrate the success of the candidates who had passed the examinations. Now, in place of long tables, chairs, and festive lanterns, the hall was a vast, open space furnished with oil lamps, bronze incense burners, and tall lacquered panels depicting scenes of filial piety from the Classic of Family Relations. There was a single high-backed chair upon which Voice Golden-Finch sat, dressed in black silks stitched with a repeating pattern of yellow feathers. A cap with the same decoration rested high on his head, leaving his brow uncovered, along with the tetragram branded there in silver lines. Hand Usher stood to his right and inclined his head to greet me.

I knelt before Voice Golden-Finch and touched my forehead to the tiled floor.

'Rise, Hand Alder,' the Voice said, 'and accept your orders.'

'I will, Your Eminence,' I said. 'But before I do, in utmost humility I must ask why I have been chosen for this lofty role. I am as yet proficient in only two of the six sorceries. I have no experience of leading men into battle, and my education in the arts of war has been cursory at best.'

'You have been given this task precisely so that you might amend those last two deficiencies,' Voice Golden-Finch said. 'A Hand of the emperor is many things, but he is first and foremost a weapon. Ordinarily, no Hand would be needed to bring these bandits to heel – rebels, they call themselves – but reports indicate that they have witches wielding barbarous magic among them.'

Panic seized my throat. Barbarous witches, like my uncle and grandmother. If they led this rebellion, and were captured, my grandmother at least would recognise me. Would she reveal our family ties to the empire to avenge my betrayal of all she had tried to teach me? If she did, I would find myself shackled and kneeling beside her on the executioner's field.

Of course, I could never let Hand Usher learn that I feared such a possibility. I swallowed my panic and focused on Golden-Finch's words.

'Hand Usher has volunteered his services,' the Voice went on, 'and requested that you accompany him, both as his apprentice and his lieutenant.'

I looked up, expecting to see Hand Usher's ghostly smile. Instead, he fixed me with a harsh, disappointed glare. 'I hope that your trepidation is genuine humility and not cowardice,' he said.

'I was recalling the lesson of the pollical cat,' I said. 'I accept that as a sorcerer I will have to fight, and that I will have to learn to command. I am not yet a commander, Hand Usher, yet you ask me to assume the role of one, when a man better suited to it might serve instead.'

'Oh?' Usher's mouth twitched. 'Whom?'

'Master Oriole,' I said, and watched the ghostly smile bloom on Usher's lips.

'Ha!' Voice Golden-Finch flicked out the ends of his sleeves. 'The fool couldn't even place in the examinations, yet you suggest he should be elevated above you, a *Hand*?'

'His passion is for the arts of war,' I said. 'He has memorised every book of strategy and every tactical treatise. If I am suited to be a commander, he must be twice over.'

'My son's fanciful obsessions are his *weakness*, Hand Alder,' Voice Golden-Finch retorted.

'Even if he is better suited in some ways, you are a Hand and he is not,' Hand Usher cut in. 'You *will* command armies, beginning with this one, and no one unmarked by the emperor's tetragram can ever hold station equal to or above you.'

I considered that for a moment. 'Then I would bring him as my advisor,' I said.

'An *advisor*?' Golden-Finch sneered. 'A *scholarly* role, for a boy who spent his youth shirking his studies?'

'Yes,' I said. 'Or a tutor, if you prefer. He will teach me the arts of war as he taught me horsemanship.'

'This is absurd,' the Voice said. 'Oriole will have a merchant fleet, and a steward to manage it for him. *That* is the only role suited to frivolous men with minds interested only in romantic heroism and vain amusement. He has tarnished our family enough without polluting your campaign with his useless advice, likely leading men to their deaths in the process!'

'I think myself just as likely to lead men to their deaths,' I argued. 'If he fails in this, you will have lost little. If he succeeds, he will return in triumph. Give him this chance, Your Eminence, to remove the stain on your family legacy.'

Voice Golden-Finch glared at me where I still knelt on the tile floor. I had not only questioned his wisdom in giving me command; I had suggested that I understood his son better than he did – a direct subversion of his fatherly authority.

'Are all Nayeni so brazen?' he said at last. 'First, with your ambidextrous stunt on the day you became Hand. Now, with this.' He shifted his gaze to Hand Usher. 'Well? Will you have my fool of a son along for this little war?'

'It is a Hand's prerogative to choose his own staff,' Hand Usher said and shrugged. 'If Alder believes that Oriole will be of use, then we will bring him with us.'

I touched my forehead to the floor once more. 'Thank you,' I said with genuine, deep gratitude. 'I am sure he will be an asset.'

'Yes, well, let's get on with it,' Golden-Finch said. 'And stand up, Hand. You're embarrassing yourself.'

As Voice Golden-Finch laid out the parameters of our campaign, my mind drifted to the future, to how excited and grateful Oriole would be when I told him that he would, after all, have his chance at glory. I too was grateful that I would have him to guide me through the uncertainties of my first command, with the fresh wound in our friendship mended.

We set out from Eastern Fortress with a company of 3000 Sienese soldiers. Our men – many of whom were veterans of similar campaigns deployed to quash other small uprisings – seemed to think that we would be back to the estate by the start of typhoon season in late summer, when walls of wind and water dashed themselves against the northern and western shores of the island. We were facing only bandits, after all.

Oriole spoke of the campaign with excitement. Finally, he would see battle at first hand. He would be like the heroes of the mythic romances he loved so much who fought in the emperor's first wars of conquest to unite the kingdoms of Sien a thousand years ago: clever Su White-Knife, who tricked the king of Twin Mountain into surrendering to a force of 300 men, or mighty Lin Twelve-Ox, who led from the front lines and fought with a spear as broad as the trunk of an oak.

'I can't understand why you're so uninterested in the romances, Alder,' he said. We were riding at the head of our column through the flatlands just north of Eastern Fortress. He had caught my eyes glazing over while he launched into the tale of Ren Kingfisher, who could read terrain and weather as if they were logograms. 'I've had my head buried in the literary classics for the last two years, and they're dry as old bones. Out here, in the fresh air, I feel like a hero of old.'

'Alder's mind latches onto his two great fascinations in life, his career and magic,' Hand Usher broke in from his place just ahead of us. 'The canon of sorcery would not be created until after those first conquests, when the empire turned its eye on the Girzan steppe. If any of your heroes had sorcery, Alder might find reason to pay attention.'

'I'm more than a bundle of ambitions,' I retorted, annoyed by Usher's ribbing. 'The mythic romances might be exciting and inspiring, but as I did not grow up reading them I'll never be as attached to them as you are.'

'What stories did you grow up with, then?' Oriole asked.

The stories my grandmother had told me in the Temple of

the Flame bubbled up from a neglected corner of my mind, of Brittle Owl, Tawny Dog, and Iron Claw, each with exploits of their own to rival the heroes of the empire's founding. I was a Sienese Hand, but the myths of my childhood were Nayeni. I felt the urge to share them with Oriole – as he had shared the stories that had formed him – to reveal a facet of myself I had long kept hidden from Koro Ha, from my own father, and now from everyone in my life, lest I be accused of sympathy for the rebellion, a crime tantamount to treason. Instead, I returned those stories to the dusty corners of my mind. I hoped someday to trust Oriole well enough to share them with him, along with at least a shadow of the truth of my bifurcated childhood, but I would never trust those tales with Hand Usher.

'The classics,' I said at last, bitterly. 'I told you, my childhood left little time for anything but study.'

As we ventured into the Nayeni highlands, our expedition fell prey to that most nefarious enemy of all armies: logistics.

Even accounting for the difficulty of moving 3000 men and all the sundry necessities of war, the journey from Eastern Fortress to Setting Sun Fortress – the largest city in northern Nayen, which would serve as the staging ground for our attack on the bandit force – should have taken three weeks. We had anticipated ruts and shattered cobbles – the scars of conquest borne by all the highways of Nayen – and found plenty of both, as well as mountain roads overgrown with ferns and brambles or eroded by wind, rain, and decades of neglect. Along with these obstacles, however, splintered wheels and broken axles slowed our wagons, and a dozen men were killed and a dozen more injured when a bridge collapsed while we were crossing it. A month and a half passed before we arrived.

While the men pitched camp outside the walls of Setting Sun Fortress, Usher, Oriole, and I occupied the guest rooms of the city magistrate. After enjoying our first decent meal since leaving the governor's estate, we reviewed the numerous and lengthy reports that the magistrate and his scouts had been keeping on the enemy.

'They march beneath the banner of Frothing Wolf,' Hand Usher said with a note of surprise. 'I'd have thought she'd be long dead by now.'

'Who is she?' I asked, feeling a breath of relief that these bandits were not led by my uncle, Harrow Fox. An end, at last, to the lingering worry that I might encounter him or my grandmother during this expedition.

'A witch,' Oriole said, looking up from the compact Stones board he had brought along. I had beaten him at camp the night before and he'd been itching for a rematch all day. 'One of the leaders of the Nayeni who fought on, long after their kings and cities had surrendered.'

'This must be her last attempt at rebellion before old age cripples her,' Usher said, setting that report aside and taking up the next. 'Though it is not surprising she would meet with some success recruiting here. The fighting went on longest in the North, and many of these Nayeni never truly accepted imperial rule.'

We carried on studying the reports. Most described raids on small villages in the foothills and valleys by bandits armed with ploughshares beaten into spearpoints, woodsmen's axes, hunting bows, and other weapons improvised from farming tools. The reports grew repetitive and Oriole and I made a game of reading them by placing stones on our game board each time we finished with a document. While we did so, Hand Usher unrolled a map of the surrounding area and began marking each raided village.

'What do you two make of this?' he asked, studying the strange pattern of the bandits' movements. Oriole and I looked up from our Stones board, the game having reached a point of tension while Oriole played into a trap I had laid, distracting us from the reports we ought to have been reading. The pattern of raids seemed haphazard to me. The bandits would attack one village while ignoring its neighbours, before moving on to sack an entire valley indiscriminately.

'Is there any difference between the villages?' I said. 'Maybe they're passing over targets that are impoverished. Why bother raiding somewhere with nothing worth taking?'

Hand Usher stroked the wisps of his beard. 'We could ask the magistrate for tax records to confirm, but the wealthier villages would also be the best defended.'

'It isn't that,' Oriole said. He leaned across the table, his eyes sharp and bright with realisation. 'In *The Conquest of the Western Kingdoms*, Lin Twelve-Ox stood before the gate of Clay River Fortress and offered to move on, killing no one, destroying nothing, if only the people would swear fealty to the emperor. The city chose to resist, so he killed every man, woman, child, and beast within, then burned the city to the ground and salted its fields. After that, all but the foolhardiest of the Western kings surrendered at the sight of his banner.'

'You think Frothing Wolf is emulating an ancient Sienese hero?' Usher asked him.

Oriole shook his head. 'I doubt she's ever heard of Lin Twelve-Ox, but just because a village hasn't been sacked doesn't mean she's neglected to capture it.'

'The magistrate's scouts report that the head men of those villages are loyal to the empire,' I noted.

Oriole shrugged, obviously relishing the fact that he had come to this strategic insight before either of the two Hands in his company. 'They may well be. She may have struck a deal with the people directly, going around the head men, extracting promises of support, or a promise to rise up when the time was right.'

'And, O wise advisor, when do you think that will be?' Usher asked, offering his ghostly smile – for the first time I had seen – to someone other than me.

Oriole studied the pattern of raided villages, furrowed his brow, chewed his lip, and then, as confident as if he were placing the winning piece in a game of Stones, jabbed his finger at the map. 'Iron Town,' he said.

'Why?' I asked, searching my memory for everything I knew of that small blot on the map. 'There used to be a mine there, once the main source of iron for the north of Nayen, but it's played out now. It has a garrison, forges, a stone wall—'

'One that held against a Sienese legion for two years,' Usher said.

'Exactly.' Oriole looked up from the map. 'Iron Town is a symbol. If Frothing Wolf can capture it, and hold it, not only will she have access to the means to better equip her fighters, she will have retaken one of the last strongholds to fall during the conquest. She'll be able to rally the villages loyal to her, and we'll have a true rebellion to contend with instead of a few hundred bandits.'

Usher ran his fingers through his beard, considering Oriole's words. His reasoning seemed sound to me, but I was far from certain. Of the three of us, only Usher had ever waged war.

'Well, Alder,' Usher said at last. 'I had my doubts, but this advisor of yours seems worth having along after all.'

Oriole grinned as if Usher had just named him Hand of the emperor. I felt a swell of pride – on behalf of my friend, and at Usher's compliment – but with it a painful and unexpected resentment. It was one thing to recognise that Oriole was better suited to the arts of war than I was, but it was another to watch him make insights that had escaped me, to have my own weaknesses highlighted by his strengths. I reminded myself this was why I had brought him along, and that I could learn, and that strategy and tactics had never been of interest to me before.

'Now,' Usher went on. 'How should we respond?'

'We go to Iron Town,' I said, trying to anticipate Oriole's answer. 'Our forces outnumber Frothing Wolf's. We can defend the stronghold easily.'

'We can,' Usher said. 'But if she has taken it before we arrive, we'll have to lay siege, and at the onset of typhoon season.'

'So what are our other options?' I asked, chastened. 'Wait out the typhoons here and attack in late summer?'

'If we let her take Iron Town, her army will grow,' Oriole noted, his voice laced with worry. 'We might be in for a long siege, stretching into the autumn, even the winter.'

And perhaps even next spring and summer, when the imperial examinations would be held again in Eastern Fortress. If this adventure cost Oriole his chance to retake them, he would not have another opportunity for three more years. By then he would be twenty-three. Young men who chased the examinations at that age – especially those with wealth and prospects, who did not need to pass them to find success – were derided as wastrels at best and outright fools at worst.

'Oriole is right,' I said. 'To quote the sage Traveller-on-the-Narrow-Way, "It is best to catch the fallen stone before it dislodges a rockslide." We should strike fast. We might reach Iron Town before Frothing Wolf does. If not, it will be easier to uproot her before the villages send rebel reinforcements.'

Oriole nodded and gave me a grateful look. 'We might even pin her against the walls while she still lays siege.'

'Or, if luck turns against us, we might be delayed on the road again, or the typhoons might come early and our own forces will be harried by weather when we arrive,' Usher objected. 'If we wait, we can send word to your father and have reinforcements of our own on their way by the time we march on Iron Town.'

Usher folded his hands and rocked back on his heels, his relaxed posture at odds with the gravity of the decision before us.

'If we move now, we have a chance to end things quickly,' I pressed. 'If we wait, we cede Iron Town to her. I say we take the chance. Though, of course, you are commander.'

'I am,' Usher said. 'But I think you are right. Tomorrow we rest and resupply, and send a report to Voice Golden-Finch informing him of our plan and our possible need for aid. The day after, we march for Iron Town and hope the weather and fortune favour us.'

Plainly relieved, Oriole returned his attention to our game, his gaze sweeping the board. I suppressed the urge to gloat while I waited for him to make his move. In three turns, I would have control of the board. His gaze lingered on the subtle angles of attack I had been building towards his territory, then looked up with a gleam in his eye.

'Seems I'll have to stop handicapping myself,' he said.

With that, he clicked a stone onto the board in a move I would never have anticipated and which, at first, seemed entirely arbitrary – until I thought ahead and realised that, with that single stone, he had reversed my trap entirely.

Usher chuckled at my baffled expression and glanced at our game. 'Well, young Master Oriole,' he said. 'Let us hope the rebellion's plans are frustrated so easily.'

12

Iron Town

Our banners hung heavy, soaked and dripping, hardly stirred by the wind that whistled through the evergreens and whipped at our cloaks. The walls of Iron Town appeared before us out of the falling rain. The gate was shut and barred. A banner of coarse cloth stitched with a red wolf on a black field hung from its lonely guard tower. Buried latrines, abandoned tent pegs, and the old coals of camp fires littered the clearing around the walls.

Usher, Oriole, and I huddled beneath the boughs of an old oak, soothing our horses and shivering. Soldiers bustled around us, unloading carts to build a camp atop what Frothing Wolf's forces had left behind. The squelch of boots in the mud mingled with the ring of hammers and the hiss of knives as the soldiers sliced stalks of bamboo into pointed stakes and began trying to construct palisades on the uneven terrain.

'If not for the rains and that bloody mudslide, we could have pinned them against the walls,' Hand Usher complained, slouching beneath his cloak and peering through the runnels of water that fell from the wide brim of his conical hat. A muscle above his jaw pulsed as he studied the gate.

'The reports put their numbers between three and five hundred, while we still have nearly three thousand,' I said. 'We can destroy the gates with chemical grenades while you and I rake the battlements and towers with lightning. Our men are tired, but we can still overwhelm the enemy.'

'We need more information,' Oriole said. 'That gate doesn't look damaged to me. If the people of Iron Town let them in, we might be facing not only Frothing Wolf and her bandits but the townspeople as well. This could become a bloodbath.'

A stone settled in my stomach. I was Hand of the emperor, but the thought of killing hundreds of ordinary people whose only crime was conceding to an attacking force left my mouth dry.

'Not unlike Lin Twelve-Ox at Clay River Fortress,' Usher said. 'Slaughter is so much less appealing in reality, isn't it, Oriole?'

Oriole set his jaw and stared Usher down. The Hand went on miserably studying the stone walls that stood between us and our quarry.

'At any rate, I need to eat,' Usher said at last. 'And a fire. Until we know more, we can't make a decision.'

Rain hammered at the canvas roof of Hand Usher's command tent while we huddled inside over bowls of millet gruel and dried fish, a dish that looked like paper pulp, smelled like brine, and tasted like the sacred food of the divines after days without a hot meal.

While we ate, Hand Usher unrolled a small map of Iron Town and the surrounding countryside on his camp table, placing a small token carved with a wolf's head behind the walls.

'The rebels are here,' he said, 'however many of them there are.'

In front of the gates he set a stack of twelve copper cash, and as he spoke he arranged the coins into an arch. 'This is us. Three thousand soldiers in squadrons of fifty. If we'd arrived in good weather, with a healthy supply train and the full contingent we brought from Eastern Fortress two months ago, we could have surrounded them and squeezed with crossbow volleys, grenades, and bursts of battle sorcery.'

He tapped his fingernail against the last of the coins, then bent that finger and braced it against his thumb.

'But there were mudslides on the way.'

The coin tumbled across the table and rolled to a stop against my bowl. Again, Hand Usher braced his finger.

'The typhoons and mountain roads have made our supply train unreliable.'

A second coin clinked against the first.

'And a quarter of our men are sick or injured.'

He flicked another coin, then drummed his fingers on the map. Heat rose to my face and I curled my hands into fists. Oriole slapped the table top, making the coins jump and rattle, then crossed his arms and glared at the map like it was a Stones board and he had just lost half of his pieces.

'This is my fault,' I said. 'If I hadn't urged quick action—'

'You are my subordinate,' Usher said. 'Any blame lies with me, but I say we acted reasonably. Aggressively, yes, but the typhoons came early. The gods of Nayen have come to Frothing Wolf's defence, it seems.'

'Those gates are strong, but not strong enough to survive grenades and battle sorcery,' Oriole said, his expression turning dour.

'The thought of slaughter sits ill in all our stomachs, I'm sure,' Usher said. 'It may be necessary; it may not. There is certainly a logic to punishing the people of Iron Town for opening their gates to the rebellion, but that is not our purpose.' He tapped the wooden token behind the town's walls. 'Frothing Wolf should have died or been captured in the conquest. That she survives to wage this petty rebellion is an embarrassment. Without her, I doubt these malcontents would have done more than rob a few merchants' wagons. She is a thorn in the empire's side, and our objective – more than anything else – is to remove her.'

'And if we assault the gates, breach them, and put the town to the sword, she may well escape, unless we can be sure to shoot down every bird that flies over the walls,' I observed, rubbing my right thumb along the scarred ridges on my palm.

'The witches of Nayen have slipped the empire's grasp so many times, often leaving their soldiers behind to die,' Usher noted. 'A witch on the wing might be tracked by the wake her magic leaves in the world, but it fades the further away she flies. It is a hard thing to shoot an eagle hawk from the air, even with battle sorcery.'

'She knew the empire would send troops,' Oriole said. 'She'll be ready for a siege, though she may know she can't win one. The symbol of holding Iron Town through the winter might be enough of a victory to suit her purposes – another story adding to her legend. A recruiting tool next time she – or her successor – stirs up these mountain peasants and tries their hand at war.'

'So what do we do?' I said.

'Give her the siege she wants,' Oriole said. 'And while we do, find a way to reach her, and kill her, before she panics and flees.' He tapped an area of the map to the south-west of the town wall. 'There are old mine shafts here. They might go beneath the town wall, they might not. If they don't, we could start tunnelling north and pop out like moles in the town square.'

Usher stroked the wisps of his beard. 'It's worth investigating.'

Oriole grinned. The plan he had outlined – using an overlooked part of the terrain to surprise and corner the enemy – was just the sort of strategy that the mythic hero Su White-Knife would have used – or so I had come to understand from Oriole's constant retelling of those tales during our journey north. At this point, certain fragments of the romances had lodged themselves permanently in my mind, occupying space that might have been better used for ... well, almost anything else.

'I'd like to see the shafts for myself,' Oriole said. 'The better to advise you and Hand Alder on their usefulness, of course.'

Usher offered Oriole his ghostly smile. 'Naturally. Tomorrow evening, you will take a scout detachment with you, on foot, and report your findings. Now, we should be to our beds.'

Oriole stood, bowed to Hand Usher, and left the tent. I rose to follow him, but Usher stopped me at the tent flap.

'You saw the value in him, and that is commendable,' he said, 'but it is inauspicious to fall into the shadow of one's advisors. You are Hand of the emperor, Alder, and my second in command, yet you wither and let Oriole and me devise all our strategies.'

Embarrassment prickled down the meridian lines of my arms and legs and tightened my throat. 'I told you,' I said. 'I'm not suited to war.'

'Nevertheless, you must learn to be a warrior,' Usher said. He gestured towards my left hand. 'That is a weapon, and you have been trusted to wield it.'

I thought of the Iron Dance, the pads of my fingers – now smooth – where I had once worn callouses, the bruises that had blossomed on my thighs and along my ribs, the ache in my muscles after a long night sparring with my grandmother. She had tried to teach me war. It had never interested me as anything but a way to prove myself to her and earn lessons in magic.

So, too, I perceived the siege of Iron Town. If I had to serve this military purpose to earn a place in the Imperial Academy, among those who dedicated their lives to understanding the deep powers of the world, then I would, though my mind would never leap to the next tactical angle the way Oriole's did.

'Of course, Hand Usher,' I said and left his tent.

Oriole was waiting for me outside, the hood of his cloak thrown up to shield him from the rain. 'What was that about?' he asked.

'I am his apprentice,' I said, brushing past him and making for my tent. 'We have things to discuss that don't concern you.'

'Right,' he said, falling into step behind me. 'Well, how about a quick game to close out the night? We haven't had a chance to play since Setting Sun Fortress, and you almost had me—'

'I think we should do as the Hand says and get some sleep.'

'Oh,' he said. Then, after a pause: 'Well then, I'll see how the men are settling in. Good night, Alder.'

'Good night,' I said without looking at him, and lay awake until long after, listening to the rain.

The downpour had faded to a drizzle by morning, but the dark, churning clouds above warned of torrents yet to come, so we made what use we could of the mild weather. Usher put me in charge of entrenching our position and surrounding the town while Oriole spent the day selecting a company of scouts and planning the expedition he would lead to the mine shafts that evening. I was grateful for the opportunity to prove myself without direct competition.

My ignorance soon showed itself, however. We had enough men to surround Iron Town loosely but too few to maintain a siege without palisades and patrol lines. Our soldiers' efforts to establish both had been confounded by the mountainous terrain, too uneven and unwieldy for building and made muddy and treacherous by a week of heavy rainfall. I rode from entrenchment to entrenchment, making suggestions, but always the squadron captains gently contradicted me. Yes, a palisade would shield the tents from any archers on the walls, but given how the water pooled at the bottom of the slope, any digging might dislodge the entire escarpment. Better and simpler, and less effort, to place the tents further away and risk extending the patrol line by a few dozen paces.

After the third such conversation, I resigned myself to approving whatever plans the captains had already devised, though I made them explain their reasoning and pretended to evaluate, consider, and decide. I felt foolish, but it would be more foolish to risk the lives of my soldiers by ignoring the advice of men with more experience, if lesser rank.

Late in the afternoon, on my way back towards our main camp in front of Iron Town's gate, I bumped into Usher, who praised the fortifications whose construction I had overseen. After wrestling with guilt, shame, and frustration, I confessed that I had done nothing at all, only approved whatever plans were presented to me, a confession which prompted Usher's ghostly smile and a nod of approval.

'Not every commander need be as clever as Su White-Knife,' he said. 'Most ought to do little more than ensure discipline and compose strategy. Who will know better where to build the latrines than the men who must use them?'

The sun had begun to set and the forest was filled with shadows and the thrumming songs of nightjars by the time Usher and I reached the main camp. Oriole and his scouts were making ready to leave, dressed in dark clothes with branches tied to their hoods and shoulders, armed only with short swords and hunting bows. Better, after all, to slip away from any Nayeni they encountered than to engage and give away our interest in the mine shafts.

Oriole greeted us with a half bow. 'We're off, then. We'll be back before sunrise, whether those mines will be of any use or no.'

'Take care,' Usher said. 'The enemy may have their own scouts in these woods.'

'Of course,' Oriole replied with a hint of excitement. 'Any creature we see might be a witch in disguise.'

'Perhaps it would be prudent to take Hand Alder with you, in that case,' Usher said thoughtfully. 'He will feel the wake of any witchcraft and be able to warn you.'

Oriole looked at me. 'He's welcome to come, if you can spare him.'

Usher shrugged. 'I leave it up to him.'

Was this another test? Why lecture me the night before on the importance of establishing myself as a commander, of stepping outside Oriole's shadow, only to send me along as his subordinate – for what else would I be, when the plan was his and I was along only as a precaution that felt far from necessary?

'Do Hands of the emperor often go on scouting missions?' I asked. 'If any of the birds in their nests or the beasts in their dens were witches in disguise, Usher or I would have felt them already. It is your plan, Oriole. I'll not intrude on your glory.'

Oriole frowned as though wondering if he should be offended. A needle of guilt prodded at me, but I ignored it. Such boundaries needed to be established, if only to meet Hand Usher's expectations. Our friendship would survive, I was sure.

'All right, then,' he said and nodded to his sergeant. 'We'll be off.'

'We look forward to your report,' I replied and rode on.

That night, while I lay on my cot and watched the shadows play on the wall of my tent by the light of the sentry fire, my mind swam with the frustrations and indignities of the day. Not going with Oriole had been the right choice, I was sure. Our roles needed to be defined. He was my advisor and a soldier, so it was proper for him to gather intelligence, while it was my role to receive what information he learned and decide how it ought to be used.

At last sleep crept up on me and pulled low the lids of my eyes. It delivered me to the path before the Temple of the Flame, to that awful night my mind loved to revisit when I felt contorted and afraid. This time, though, I was not trapped in the abominable body my ill-cast magic had made. I was myself, hale and whole. Strangest of all, my left hand was marked with the glittering silver lines of the tetragram. As I looked at the mark I felt a gnawing guilt, as though I had betrayed a secret or brought a contaminant into a sacred space.

The forest around me seemed real, the leaves sharp, the bark rough, the breeze cool as it rustled through the canopy and gently brushed my cheek. An owl cried. A fox yowled, then scurried through the underbrush. The moon and stars were out in their fullness. The stone eyes of Okara – youngest and cleverest of the wolf gods – burned with an awful fire as they studied me. They alone seemed the stuff of nightmares.

'You waste your attention on him,' rumbled a low voice from Ateri's jaws. She stood sentinel between her children, as I remembered her, yet something was strange about the carving. There were new patterns in the fur around her neck, like raised hackles – like fear.

'He could have been a witch of the old sort,' said another voice, masculine but thin, and Okara's eyes flashed. 'Am I a fool, that I would let Tenet possess such a weapon and pay no mind?'

'He is bound by pact, now,' growled Ateri. 'He is no different from any of Tenet's other tools.'

'Perhaps,' Okara said. 'Yet he returns here, to the night he touched the pattern, unmediated. To the night he revealed himself, when all our eyes should have fixed upon him. He might be as a coin tossed onto a Stones board, scattering the pieces, disrupting the rhythm of play.'

'A game in which no player has made a move in a thousand years.'

'Tenet has made moves.'

'His little conquests?' Ateri scoffed. 'He will rule over mortals, for we denied him the dominion he desired. Let him. What care wolves for the lives of ants?'

'Ants who once worshipped us, as fewer and fewer do each day. You underestimate Tenet, as you underestimate this one.'

I realised with the slow, sleepy rhythm of dreaming thought that I was this coin, this weapon, this *witch of the old sort*.

'What do you mean?' I said, a strange panic setting in. These were the wolf gods of Nayen, and they were talking – about me. 'And who is Tenet?'

Okara's eyes flashed again. 'You see?' he said.

Ateri snarled, and I felt a sudden cramping in my arms, my legs, down my back, across my chest. Every muscle spasmed, as if twisting me into something other than what I was, and at the same moment my head swam with the scent of burnt cinnamon.

'You must realise what you are,' Okara said—

—and I woke, drenched in sweat, my limbs quivering and cramping. A groan bubbled in my throat as the dream shattered into shock and pain. Then another cramp seized me, weaker than the last and radiating from my left shoulder, which – my sleepy mind noted, piecing the puzzle together – was pointed towards Iron Town.

These were no mere cramps. My body was detecting a wake of magic, the like of which I had not felt since my childhood. Somewhere in Iron Town, a witch had veered.

I scrambled from my cot, threw my cloak over my shoulders, and ran to find Usher. I found him outside his tent, standing in his bedclothes, staring at the walls of Iron Town, his eyes glittering in the moonlight.

'You felt it!' I panted.

There was another faint breath of cinnamon, and then a flush of warmth spread up from my toes and over my shins. The witch had conjured fire. This was no Nayeni scout arriving and returning to human form; someone fought in Iron Town.

No, *beneath* it. I followed the angle of the wake, as I had done when seeking Usher in the garden back at Voice Golden-Finch's estate. It led not only towards the walls but downwards.

'Oriole!' I breathed.

'We don't know that,' Usher said.

'They were found,' I said. 'What else could it be?'

'We can't *know*,' Usher shot back. 'Not yet.'

'Usher, he's fighting a *witch*,' I said. 'If we hurry, we can—'

'Nothing of strategic significance has changed,' Usher said. 'Even if what you fear is true, it means only that Frothing Wolf will be more on her guard.'

'You value killing her over saving Oriole's life?' I asked, stunned.

'I do.'

We waited in silence – for another wake of magic, for Usher to say more to put me at ease, to assure me that we would do whatever we could to save my friend.

'We will know tomorrow,' Usher said, 'whether or not the scouting party returns.' And with that he returned to his tent.

Dawn broke with no sign of Oriole or any of his men. I had not slept again after feeling the wake of witchcraft and would have lingered in the main camp all day, waiting for any word of Oriole's fate, but Usher insisted that I walk along the siege line and monitor the progress of our fortifications.

I made the round as quickly as I could, approving whatever my captains proposed with hardly a moment's hesitation. It didn't matter how well entrenched we were, or how porous our sentry lines. Oriole might have been killed, and my mind could do nothing but fret over that possibility.

He had to be alive. Either he had escaped or he'd been

captured. It seemed inconceivable that he had been struck down in a burst of flame, to die screaming, or that a veered witch with wolf's jaws had torn out his throat. Nevertheless, I imagined such scenes in all their awful detail, though I refused to believe them. I *couldn't* believe them. Not when my last words to him had been so callous.

Guilt snapped at my heels. If not for me, he would be safe at home in Eastern Fortress, studying for his examinations. If I had gone with him to explore the mines, I might have felt some small wake of magic, given him enough warning to run before the witch attacked.

As I approached the main camp, I heard shouts and saw soldiers milling about in excited conversation. A fire lit in my veins. I kicked my horse to a trot and picked my way as quickly as I dared through the camp.

I found Usher at the medical tent, standing over a soldier whose right arm had been bandaged and hung in a sling. The man had been speaking but fell silent as I dropped from the saddle and tossed my reins to a sentry.

'What happened?' I demanded, first of Usher, then of the wounded man. 'Where is Oriole?'

The soldier looked to Usher, who gestured for him to speak.

'They took us by surprise,' he said. 'We followed the mine shafts north, towards the town. Then another tunnel – newer, freshly dug – forked off from the main shaft towards the east. A few of us wanted to go back – we'd found what we set out to – but Master Oriole wanted to press on, to gauge where in the town the tunnels would open. So that's what we did. We were careful with our lanterns, keeping their hoods drawn shut but for a sliver ...' He took a deep breath, grimaced, and rubbed his bandaged shoulder. 'Something gave us away. A boar charged out of the darkness, gored two of us, then changed into a woman and filled the tunnel with fire and I ... I ran.'

'You did the right thing,' Usher told him. 'The information you brought back is valuable, and at any rate your sword arm was badly burned. There is no shame in survival.'

The soldier nodded, but the haunted expression did not leave his face.

'And Master Oriole?' I asked, throat dry and head swimming. 'Did you see him die?'

'No,' the soldier said. 'The whole tunnel was filled with fire.'

'You made it out alive. He might have too,' I said and turned to Usher. 'If we attack, we can save him.'

'Or Frothing Wolf will kill him along with any other prisoners before fleeing,' Usher said. 'Assuming he still lives.'

'I won't assume he's dead!'

'I assume nothing,' Usher replied tersely, 'but our priority must be to eliminate Frothing Wolf.'

'Then *I'll* kill her.' A chill ran through me as I realised what I had said. Yet, even as my thoughts reeled with fear for Oriole, a plan had formed in the dark corners of my mind.

Usher's gaze narrowed. 'How?'

I pulled up my sleeve to show the reddish tint of my skin. 'I am half Nayeni. I look like one of them. I can talk my way into Iron Town, find Oriole, then find Frothing Wolf and kill her with battle sorcery. When you feel the wake of my magic, you can attack the town. We can save Oriole's life!'

Usher took a deep breath. 'You speak their language?'

'My grandmother taught me,' I said, only realising then that I had revealed more than I intended. Before, Usher had known nothing of my illicit education, but now I had given him a hint – assuming he had the presence of mind to note it.

He nodded slowly, his fingers playing at the wisps of his beard. 'And when they see your tetragram?'

'Give me a bandage,' I snapped at one of the medics. He handed me a length of linen.

'You see?' I said as I wound the bandage around my left hand and wrist. 'I'll dress as a peasant and claim I've come to join them. I can go through the mines.'

'This is reckless, Alder,' Usher protested. 'If you are caught—'

'Frothing Wolf will likely escape,' I said, 'but I can fight my way out while you rush in. Do you have a better plan?'

He sighed. 'No,' he admitted. 'Not yet.'

'Then I leave at dusk.'

I decided to approach from the south. There were villages in that direction, several of which had not yet been raided, and it was plausible that someone from one of them might have visited Iron Town before and known about the mine shafts. At any rate, such a story felt more likely than my stumbling upon the mines by sheer happenstance.

Dressed in a tattered cloak, mud-stained trousers, an old shirt, and a pair of peasant's sandals, I made my way through the undergrowth, swinging far south and west and circling back towards the entrance to the mines, my path lit by the narrow beam of a battered lantern. In the gloom of dusk and the constant drizzle of the rain, I navigated by topography and sense of direction, though the latter was confounded by the churning of my stomach and the pulse of blood in my ears.

After doubling back twice, I at last found the rutted road that the scout had told me would lead to the mines, and began to trudge uphill, rehearsing again and again the story that would, I hoped, see me past the guards. Once past them, I would find Oriole. Only then would I seek out Frothing Wolf and kill her, though the prospect terrified me – I had never killed before. When she was dead, I would return to Oriole and protect him while Usher and our forces breached the wall.

The mouth of the mine opened in the face of a cliff, the rutted path its unfurled tongue, the wooden supports its jagged teeth. I sought silhouettes in the shadows of the nearby trees and the dark recess of the mine, yet saw none. Neither did my muscles cramp in the wake of a veered witch lurking in the boughs above. If there were guards, they had concealed themselves further in.

The floor of the shaft angled downwards, but without reference to trees or sky I had only my sense of weight to tell me that I was descending. My racing heart and the creeping sense of terror that clutched at my limbs distorted my sense of time. How long I walked, I cannot say, only that I laughed with relief at the sight of freshly wounded earth and the branching tunnel the surviving scout had mentioned.

This was it, then. If my presence had not yet been noted by the Nayeni, it soon would be if I pressed on any further. One last time I recalled the lie I would tell, going over in my head the Nayeni words I would need. That language was dull to me, and heavy, like rusted steel too long sheathed.

With a deep breath – as though to begin the Iron Dance – I entered the tunnel. It was narrow and cramped, and the uneven floor sloped uphill. The air was thick, heavy, and hot. I imagined the Nayeni bandits trudging single file, armed and armoured. Had they too fought down panic while they crept along down here, or had the prospect of battle focused their fear into fury? I found it better to imagine them like me, feeling small and terrified of the weight of earth piled above their heads and of the danger they would find at the tunnel's end.

A breeze wafted over me. The promise of the surface and fresh air was a relief – until I caught the scent it carried: scorched flesh and blood. The stench of recent death.

The light of my lantern swept across a blackened mass, curled like a man in pain. Then a skull, with strips of charred flesh clinging to the orbits. I took a sharp breath and gagged, yet could not tear my gaze from the corpses as I pressed on, skirting wide around them. Was Oriole there, reduced to nothing but a pile of gristle and bones?

'Show your hands!' a voice barked from the darkness in Nayeni. 'Unless you want to join the dead.'

Startled, I dropped the lantern. It clattered and rolled behind me, coming to rest with its hood jostled open. The pool of light touched the man ahead of me, glinting off the head of an arrow aimed towards my heart and bathing his eyes in shadow. I held up my hands and spoke around a thick tongue and dry mouth.

'M-my name is Nimble Cat,' I stuttered. 'I heard about the rebellion and came to join you.'

'Turn around!' commanded another voice.

I did so, and the moment my back was turned I heard movement, then felt a sharp blow to the backs of my legs. With a grunt I fell to my knees. Rough hands grabbed my elbows and wrenched my arms behind my back.

'Toad, lookit his palm,' the second voice said.

Had the bandage slipped, or been torn? I fought the urge to crane my neck and look, even as a rough cord tightened around my wrists.

'He's fire-named,' the second voice went on, with notes of reverence and surprise. 'And witch-carved. Who are you?'

I cursed myself for a fool. All my precautions and I had overlooked this most obvious thing – the Sienese had never recognised my witch marks, but Nayeni rebels in service to a witch surely would.

'You must have keen eyes, to see such thin scars in this darkness,' I said, scrambling to build new layers to my lie. It wasn't impossible that a village child might have been brought up to be a witch, though it stood to reason that Frothing Wolf would know of any who still dwelt in the north of Nayen.

'Who carved you?' the first voice snapped.

'M-my grandmother! Sh-she was a temple witch before the

Sienese came. Her great regret was that she did not get to fight them – a regret I'll not die with, as she did.'

Shouldn't the arrival of another witch, no matter how unexpected, have been cause for celebration? Yet the cord around my wrist only tightened further, and when it was tied the soldiers hauled me to my feet, spun me around, and shoved me further into the tunnel – which told me something unexpected: not all witches of Nayen were allies.

The tunnel, which had been gradually sloping upwards, became suddenly steeper. It ended in a ladder, which I had to climb like a steep staircase, boosted from below by one of my captors. We emerged in an alleyway just inside the southern wall, where three more guards waited. One of them – a young woman – was armed only with a dagger at her hip. Toad nodded to her in deference, but her sharp, dark eyes never left me.

'What've you found, Toad?' she asked. 'Another imperial bastard for my sister to bleed for information?'

I suppressed a mingled jolt of relief and dread. They had a prisoner. Oriole, I hoped, even if he was being tortured. Better in agony than already dead.

'He says he's a witch,' Toad said.

The young woman's eyes widened. 'Well, well,' she murmured, then stepped behind me, grabbed my right hand, and twisted it roughly. Her finger brushed the thick scar I had carved in the heel of my thumb. 'Whoever carved you did a shoddy job,' she said. 'What's your name, boy?'

'Nimble Cat.'

'Mine's Burning Dog,' she said. 'Daughter of Frothing Wolf. You've come to Iron Town why? Looking for a glorious death?'

I told her the story I'd constructed. She seemed to weigh it, and at last let go of my hand before rounding on Toad.

'What are you lingering for?' she demanded. 'A Sienese battalion might be marching up our arses.'

Toad bobbed his head and slunk back into the tunnel.

'Please,' I said. 'When I heard that Frothing Wolf had taken Iron Town, I felt my grandmother's spirit pulling me to join you.'

'Your grandmother, eh?' Burning Dog said. 'What did you say her name was?'

Words died in my throat. How well would the truth serve me? I had no idea what relationship existed – if any – between Frothing Wolf and my uncle and grandmother.

'What?' Burning Dog said, stepping close to me. 'Can't remember?'

She gave me no chance to answer before punching me in the stomach. I crumpled around her fist and gagged for breath. She knelt over me, grabbing a handful of my hair, and pulling my head off the ground. I fought for breath.

'Those sloppy witch marks wouldn't convince a drunken fool,' she said. 'Try to come up with a more convincing story before I see you again.'

Two of Burning Dog's guards hauled me to my feet and half-carried me, sore and gasping, through the streets of Iron Town. Every wall they led me past had been etched with sword strokes or pierced with arrows. Those buildings that were not scarred were burned down to skeletal ruins. Piles of corpses blocked alleyways, some partly burned, filling the air with a sickening stench.

Almost as sickening was the state of Iron Town's denizens. Wraith-thin children, their eyes bright and feverish in deep sockets, hid from patrolling soldiers in the ruins of burned-out homes. Those men and women who had not been given weapons worked into the night, dragging corpses or building makeshift barricades in the streets, moving with sluggish exhaustion.

These people had already endured one siege. How long could

they survive another, I wondered, moments before Burning Dog's soldiers threw me into a cramped, empty hovel and slammed the door.

Night was falling, and without a lamp or a candle the darkness of the room was impenetrable. At first, I dared to hope that they had taken me to wherever they were keeping Oriole, but it quickly became clear that I was alone.

So much for clever Alder, who had talked his way past the suspicions of Hand Usher and Voice Golden-Finch. Burning Dog had seen through me in half a heartbeat. Conflicts unknown to the empire – or, at least, to me – divided the witches of Nayen, it seemed. Enough for Burning Dog to see the arrival of an unexpected witch not as a boon but with suspicion.

I managed to roll over and lever myself into a sitting position against the wall, where I sat, fretting as the night wore on. In my haste, Hand Usher and I had not agreed on a firm timeline, and I wondered how long he would wait for me before attacking. Worse, Oriole had already been in rebel hands for an entire day. How much longer did he have, either before he succumbed to their tortures or they grew tired of prying at him and slit his throat?

Two courses presented themselves. I had sorcery and witchcraft at my disposal. It would be a simple thing to free myself. Less simple to fight my way through Iron Town, knowing neither where Oriole was kept nor how many witches I might face. And as soon as I reached for battle sorcery within the walls, Frothing Wolf would panic and retreat, likely ordering her prisoners killed as she fled.

The second option was to wait. To come up with a better story, as Burning Dog had instructed. To try to talk my way into an audience with Frothing Wolf. Or, at the very least, to find out where Oriole was being kept and tortured.

All that long night I tried to devise a convincing and

compelling lie, a reason for Burning Dog to bring me – a stranger, claiming to be a witch and therefore dangerous – into her mother's presence. But I was exhausted, and terrified, and worried for my friend. Every falsehood I began to spin fell apart the moment I considered it with any scrutiny. When I had talked my way past Hand Usher's suspicions after my examinations, I had done so with a version of the truth, with a story based on facts that could be supported with evidence. My scars. Koro Ha's lessons in ambidexterity. The flawed first article of my pedigree.

I needed that kind of lie. A bending of the truth.

I heard voices on the other side of the door, one of them Burning Dog's. I was out of time. A key turned in the lock and the door swung open, letting in the cool light of early morning.

'Sleep well?' Burning Dog asked, looming above me. 'Or did you spend all night weaving another flimsy lie?'

The best lies anchor themselves in irrefutable facts. They draw their strength from that which cannot be denied, lending all that is false about them the facade of truth. And what could be more undeniable than magic?

I moved into the second channel of the canon. For a moment, lightning flashed from my fingertips, the spell so slight and the wake so thin that I doubted anyone but Burning Dog and I had felt it. Only enough to cut my bonds. I stood while the smoking cords sloughed from my wrists and pooled on the ground behind me. Burning Dog backed away, conjuring fire, staring wide-eyed as I stepped towards her with my palms raised in a gesture of surrender. I offered my most disarming smile and conjured a breath of flame, to show that I was, indeed, a witch.

'My name is Foolish Cur, grandson of Broken Limb, nephew of Harrow Fox, known to the Sienese as Wen Alder,' I said. 'You may have heard of me.'

13

Frothing Wolf

Burning Dog led me to the modest magistrate's hall near Iron Town's central square, tongues of fire flickering at her fingertips, ready to turn me to ash the moment she felt the first stirrings of battle sorcery. More guards stood beside columns which once had born the tetragram of the minor magistrate who ruled in Iron Town. Someone had scored away the magistrate's tetragram, leaving only a few glimmers of gold paint between deep gouges in the wood. In its place, a black banner stitched with a red wolf hung above the lintel. With frantic hope, I wondered whether the magistrate's hall also served as Iron Town's jail, as many did in rural places.

We passed through the gate and along a winding path through a meagre garden. As I followed Burning Dog, my gaze swept between stands of bamboo and low artificial hills, seeking guards, iron bars, manacles – any sign of prisoners – but I saw nothing of the sort.

The path ended in a short staircase that led up to a wide, open room, like a modest imitation of Voice Golden-Finch's reception hall. A set of lacquer panels lay on the floor, cracked and scored by fire. Landscape paintings had been torn from the walls and fed to the lone brazier. What remained of the velvet upholstery on the magistrate's chair, which lay hacked and gouged on the floor, was stained dark with blood. Where it ought to have stood, a simple table had been set out and arrayed with maps of the town. Around the table, in modest chairs, sat three Nayeni. Foremost among them was an iron-haired woman, her face as harshly angled as Burning Dog's, with a red wolf stitched to the collar of her shirt.

Their conversation faded at our approach. Frothing Wolf looked up. Her eyes seemed to flay me open, as though with a look she could unravel my every attempt at deception. After a dozen heartbeats, she looked at her daughter. 'Did Frigid Cub relieve you?' she asked.

'She's with the prisoner,' Burning Dog replied, 'who's proven a resilient bastard, despite the softness of wealth and noble breeding.'

Who else could that describe but Oriole? How badly had he been injured when the Nayeni attacked? What had they done to him that he should prove *resilient*? Most importantly, where were they keeping him?

'If Frigid Cub is with the prisoner, and you're here, then what witch guards the tunnel?' Frothing Wolf said, her voice harsh as an icy wind.

'No one, but—'

'But *nothing*, daughter!' Frothing Wolf snarled. 'Do you think those boys with their bows and arrows could so much as delay a Hand of the emperor tearing through that tunnel with a flick of his finger and a bolt of lightning?'

An itch worked its way up my left arm. All I had to do was reach for the pulsing geyser of power that had been with me since I'd become Hand of the emperor, move into the second channel of the canon, and point my finger. I did not know the full limits of Frothing Wolf's power – I had learned so little of witchcraft before my grandmother had left – but I doubted she could veer and flee before lightning tore her apart.

But if I killed her, every witch in Iron Town would feel the wake of my sorcery, as would Hand Usher, who would take it as his cue to assault the gates. Chaos would erupt.

I forced myself to wait. I still had no idea where to find Oriole, knowing only that he was being tortured. I might be able to find him in time to defend him while the battle raged around us, but then again I might not. This witch Frigid Cub might kill him the moment I struck her mother down and Hand Usher tore through the gates. Fear of that possibility stayed my hand.

'Then send a runner with orders for Frigid Cub to guard the tunnel,' Burning Dog said. 'I've brought you something more interesting – and more dangerous – than a Sienese princeling playing soldier.'

Silence held between the three of us while Frothing Wolf searched my face.

'You look like him,' she said at last. A cruel smile played at the corners of her lips. 'Your uncle, Harrow Fox. Don't look so surprised. We once fought side by side, before ambition rooted in his skull and turned him against me. I'd heard the rumour that Broken Limb had made a witch of her mongrel grandson, and that he had in turn betrayed us to serve the empire. I'd hoped it wasn't true.'

An impulse to hurl lightning and fire and burn her out of the world surged through me. To be done with the siege of Iron Town, along with this treacherous conversation.

Frothing Wolf gestured for me to approach her. 'Show me the tetragram.'

My fingers were steady, to my great surprise, as I unwound the bandage that covered my left hand. She leaned over the table and, when the first glimmers of silver-lined flesh showed through, took a single, sharp breath.

'You see, Mother?' Burning Dog said.

'Quiet, child,' Frothing Wolf said – but she did not tell

Burning Dog to leave. Two witches together stood a chance of overcoming a Hand of the emperor. Again, she searched my face, this time looking not for my uncle's features but for answers. 'The only reason I haven't killed you is because you're Broken Limb's grandson. Much as I would like to believe her shamed by your treason, she is a canny woman. I think it no accident that she spent so much time in hiding with your mother, and that you've now appeared wearing both witch marks and the tetragram.'

'My grandmother took a lesson from the emperor's grand strategy,' I said. 'He steals the magics of those he conquers and gives them to his Hands. She saw in my father's ambition for me a chance to steal from the emperor in turn. To have a sorcerer of her own.'

I hoped she was unaware that, without the emperor's transmission to his Voices, and thence to his Hands, I would have no access to the canon of sorcery. Her ignorance would hold the seams of my deception.

'I have been apprenticed to Hand Usher these last two years,' I went on. 'We were sent to put down your rebellion, and I saw a chance to defect. I had hoped my grandmother might be with you.'

'Yet you hid yourself, at first,' Frothing Wolf said.

'War can fracture even those with common goals,' I said. 'You and my uncle both aspire to the Sun King's throne, but only one of you can unite Nayen as he did. I was unsure that I could trust you, or your daughter. Until she gave me no choice.'

Burning Dog snarled at that, but I ignored her and pressed on. I could see sparks of belief in Frothing Wolf's eyes. I only needed to stoke them to flame.

'Nayen is my home,' I said, and felt a strange pain swelling in my chest, clutching at my throat. 'The Nayeni are my people. Better to fight alongside you – even if you and my grandmother

169

are rivals – than against you on behalf of the emperor, who murdered my grandfather, hunts my uncle, and reduced my mother to a mewling coward.'

The best lies are strengthened by a foundation of truth, I told myself again. That was all. I was no traitor, though once I might have been. I served the emperor. But the thought felt flimsy, scrawled hastily on paper, where what I had said to Frothing Wolf felt carved in stone. Did some part of me, long suppressed, wish to follow my grandmother's path? Or was this thought born only of panic, my mind sealing the lie with false conviction, trying to give Frothing Wolf as little cause as possible for doubt?

She chewed her lip as she weighed my lie. By revealing myself as Broken Limb's grandson, I had made myself at once dangerous to her and a possible ally. After all, if I served the empire, why would I invent this convoluted lie rather than strike her down at the first opportunity? And what risk would be more worthwhile than stealing her enemy's greatest weapon?

Could she sense the uncertainty within me? Would she call out the lie or see it for truth?

The sound of boot heels on the stairs and the creaking hinges of the gate tore her gaze away from me. I followed her eyes to see a woman I at first took for Burning Dog. The structure of her face was similar, but her hair was cropped shorter and a hooked scar cut a pale line through her left cheek.

The sister. Frigid Cub. Who had been torturing their prisoner. At the sight of her, my swirling thoughts settled into clear purpose. Whatever I might say, whoever my family might be, I was here to rescue Oriole.

'Who's this?' Frigid Cub demanded. I saw her eyes widen in shock at the sight of my tetragram, then her gaze flicked to her mother.

'Broken Limb's grandson,' Frothing Wolf said. 'He is

defecting, he claims. The product of one of his grandmother's many schemes. How fares the prisoner?'

'He's lost consciousness again,' Frigid Cub said, 'and I've not been able to revive him.'

Burning Dog spat a curse. 'You enjoy that work too much.'

'Your sister is right,' Frothing Wolf said. 'We need him to *speak*, not just bleed.'

Frigid Cub shrugged. I bit down outrage and fear. Here was a chance to find Oriole, but if I showed too much interest in his wellbeing, I risked giving myself away.

'When the empire sees fit to dig information from a prisoner, a Hand is always present,' I said. 'Their healing magic permits for much more devious tortures, without exhausting the subject too quickly.'

'Are you offering to help?' Frigid Cub asked. She seemed to consider. 'You *were* with the imperials. You might know the man.'

I shrugged. 'He is my enemy now, whatever he was to me before.'

The moment he was safe, I would burn them both to ash.

Frothing Wolf waved a hand dismissively. 'What could he know that you do not, Hand of the emperor? You must be privy to their plans.'

'I am.' My stomach churned. 'The broader strategy, at least. I can tell you that their objective is not to take Iron Town, only to kill you and your daughters. They believe the rebellion will die without you. I *can* tell you that there might be assassins slinking past your walls at night – that Hand Usher won't attack until he is sure he has you cornered, or already dead. But I am not privy to every tactical decision. And, to be honest, I think Hand Usher has always doubted my loyalty. I doubt he's told me all of his plans.'

'We caught the prisoner creeping in the tunnels,' Burning

Dog said. 'He and his men were dressed like scouts, but they might have been assassins. Or spies.'

'Perhaps,' Frothing Wolf said, considering. I dared not press the issue.

'I am no expert in torture,' I said, turning to Frigid Cub, 'but if you need my help, it is offered.'

'I'll keep that in mind,' she replied curtly and turned to leave. 'By the way, shouldn't you be guarding that pit, *sister*?'

Burning Dog glowered at her back. When her sister had left, she gestured at me and asked, 'What of him?'

'Go to your task, daughter,' Frothing Wolf commanded. 'I will see to our new ... ally.'

Frothing Wolf claimed that I was now her guest – had even given me a room in a wing of the magistrate's hall and a meal of thin gruel – but wherever I went, a cadre of guards was always close behind, their weapons all but prodding at my back. She bade me accompany her while she surveyed the town's defences. I thought it a strange demonstration of trust in me but took it as a sign that my gamble had worked and she had accepted my lie.

I had already seen the desperate state of Iron Town's people. Now I was no longer gasping for breath and had the time to study the scene around me, it became clear that, whatever Frothing Wolf's original intent in attacking the town, she would never hold it through the winter. Or, if she did, it would be by starving the populace to feed her soldiers, who already looked haggard and hungry. Frothing Wolf's own angular features had been thinned and tightened for want of food.

I had hoped her rounds would include the prison where Oriole was being kept, giving me a chance to kill her and free him all at once. Instead, she donned a helmet, handed me one of my own, and led me onto the battlements, where Nayeni archers harassed the Sienese forces below, launching arrows that either buried themselves in trees or fell to the earth long before reaching their targets. The Sienese made no effort to return fire; even their iron-banded crossbows lacked the range to strike the top of Iron Town's walls at such a distance. Frothing Wolf studied the patrol lines I had overseen only the previous day.

'What do you think of our chances, Foolish Cur?' she asked. 'You know the status of our enemy, the weight of men and resources the empire has brought against us. How long can they maintain their siege?'

'Longer than we can defend against it,' I replied. 'They will starve us out long before winter ends, and eat well, as long as their supply lines hold.'

She spat over the wall, then turned her back on the Sienese and pointed towards the town. 'Look there. Do you see those towers, near the garrison yard?'

I followed the line of her arm. Two mounds of earth rose near the northern wall – grain silos, which should have held enough millet to feed Iron Town's population through the winter. My eye drifted past them, to the garrison itself. The walls around its yard were two-thirds as high as those that defended Iron Town. From our vantage point, I could see into the yard, where I saw prisoners bound to stakes – the survivors of the Sienese garrison.

And Oriole. I could not see him, but where else would he be held?

'Do you know what the Sienese did the moment we emerged from the tunnel?' Frothing Wolf went on. 'They opened their silos, doused their grain with lamp oil, and put it to the torch. Do you know what we did, the moment we had control of the town?'

I shook my head, unable to tear my gaze from the garrison yard, searching for any evidence that Oriole was being held there. If I found it, I could kill Frothing Wolf now, run to the yard, and protect him while Hand Usher stormed the town.

But I had to be certain.

Suddenly I realised that Frothing Wolf was waiting for me to speak, and that my silence and fascination with the garrison yard might be cause for suspicion. I forced myself to look away. 'What did you do?' I asked.

'We gave a ration from our own supplies to every family in Iron Town,' she said.

'That was kind of you,' I said. 'But stupid, if your aim is to win this battle.'

'You think we should have let the people starve? Or that we should have fled the moment this Sienese army appeared, knowing that we could never hold the town against them?' She shook her head and grinned. 'Some battles aren't meant to be won, Foolish Cur. Some battles we fight only to remind the enemy that we still exist, and that we can still hurt them.'

'And to remind the people of the empire's cruelty,' I added. 'To stoke their hatred, before they accustom themselves to Sienese rule.'

'That too,' Frothing Wolf said, returning her attention to the Sienese encampment. 'Now tell me, Foolish Cur, which tent is Hand Usher's?'

That gave me pause. 'He is well guarded,' I said.

'As am I,' she replied. 'Yet he sends his assassins. Mine, I think, are just as capable.'

I pointed to a tent in the Sienese camp – not to Usher's, though, but to mine. 'There. Though he is often out surveying the fortifications.'

Frothing Wolf patted my shoulder, then led me back to the stairs. 'Your guards will escort you back to your room. Hopefully tomorrow morning we can toast Hand Usher's death, which may well buy us the time we need to make this siege more than a statement.'

For the rest of the day, I paced the small room Frothing Wolf had given me. Now I knew where to look for Oriole, and I might have fought my way to him through the town, but what if I was wrong? I had no way to investigate the garrison yard openly without arousing suspicion. And Frothing Wolf's assassins might discover that I had lied about the location of Hand Usher's tent and inform her on their return. Then I would have no choice but to kill her and hope that Oriole was still alive somewhere.

I waited for nightfall, and then – as though I was not under guard and had the freedom of the town – opened the door to my room and stepped into the hall. The two soldiers flanking it tensed and reached for their swords. I put up my hands and smiled sheepishly.

'I need the latrine,' I said. 'Care to show me the way?'

'You have a chamber pot,' one said.

'And which of you two will empty it? I'd rather not spend the night sleeping next to my own shit. Or is that how Frothing Wolf treats her allies?'

'Someone's been living too long in imperial palaces,' the other guard said to his companion.

I crossed my arms, felt my heart thundering, and tried to devise a secondary plan if this one failed. 'Just take me to an alleyway or something,' I said. 'And quickly.'

The first guard rolled his eyes but seemed to relax and led the way.

'Thank you,' I said and followed him while the second fell into step behind me.

We left the magistrate's hall and turned into a nearby alleyway, abandoned and reeking with an acrid tang. It was dark but for the distant light of a brazier in the street behind us.

'Nearest thing to a latrine we've got,' the guard ahead of me said. 'Now just don't expect us to look away while—'

In two steps of the Iron Dance, I crouched, stepped backwards, and threw an elbow into the throat of the guard behind me. He pawed at his neck and collapsed while my left hand found the hilt of his sword and pulled it free. The guard ahead whirled and drew his own sword, but not quickly enough. With another step, I stabbed at his eye, the socket crunching like breaking porcelain, and with a rattling gasp he fell lifeless to the filthy ground. I left the sword lodged in his skull.

The other guard's face had purpled above his crushed throat. He watched me with bloodshot, bulging eyes, and my stomach gave a sickening lurch as the life went out of him with a final, ragged spasm. I tried not to look at the brains and blood soaking the earth.

With a shuddering breath I steeled myself and set off from the alleyway towards the garrison yard. The guards' corpses would be found before long, and the shroud of my deceptions would quickly unravel. I had only until then to find Oriole.

The four guards at the garrison door eyed me with suspicion as I approached, doing my best to seem unhurried, thankful for the drizzle which had washed my victims' blood from my face.

'Frigid Cub asked for my help with an interrogation,' I said before any of them could speak. 'There is a prisoner on the verge of death, she said, who might have held back valuable information despite her efforts.'

'And how are you meant to help?' asked one. 'Are you some kind of doctor?'

'Surely you were told about me,' I said and showed the palm of my left hand. All four tensed at the sight of my tetragram. 'Foolish Cur,' I continued, 'the witch who was for a time Hand of the emperor and stole Sienese magic for the rebellion.'

The lie cut through them, tempered by truth. Why else would a Hand of the emperor approach them and reveal himself, rather than burn them all to ash with battle sorcery? They waved me through without another word.

The yard where Iron Town's garrison would drill and assemble was a tiled square no wider than 100 paces. The tiles were worn and poorly maintained, with shoots of grass sprouting between them. Some bore fresh bloodstains – evidence, perhaps, of the garrison's last stand against Frothing Wolf's forces. Or of torture.

The dozen survivors of the garrison had been bound at wrist, elbow, and knee and made to sit in rows. My eyes swept over them in the torchlight, hoping to see Oriole but failing to find him, until my gaze settled on a post driven into the ground in the far corner of the yard. A young man slouched there, naked, mottled with bruises, his hair lank with drizzle, fingers broken and blackened, limbs wrenched at painful angles. He was held upright only by the shackles around his wrists.

At first, I did not recognise him – the Oriole I knew, whom I had last seen full of excitement and vigour, ready for his first taste of war – had nothing in common with this broken, disfigured wreck. But I knew with a sickening certainty that it was him.

Suddenly the horror of the violence I'd seen and committed over the last two days, combined with little sleep and less food – all of it caught up with me. I felt weak, terrified, and – absurdly – desperate for Doctor Sho, whose medicines had nursed me back from brokenness and could do the same for Oriole.

He was still breathing. Short, shallow breaths that gurgled past his lips and rattled in his lungs. By the look of his bruises, most of his ribs had been broken. His lungs, his stomach, even his intestines might have been punctured by those cracked and splintered bones.

'Oriole,' I whispered, cupping his face in my hands, desperate for his eyes to open, to hear his voice. 'It's Alder. I'm here. Everything will be all right.'

He answered only with laboured breathing, muted by the drumming of the rain and the creak of his chains.

'Oriole, say something,' I said, my voice growing frantic. 'Open your eyes. Blink if it hurts too much to speak.'

No response. If he did hear my voice, it was through too dense a fog of pain.

Healing sorcery requires direction. If I poured it into him without knowing what I wished to heal, his body – weak as it was – would go into shock, like the songbirds that had died in my care. But he might die of his injuries anyway, before I could even attempt to undo the ruin Frigid Cub had worked. Better to do what I could to stabilise him, then get him out of Iron Town, where Hand Usher and I could take the time required to heal him properly. I reached through the canon and put my hand to his chest.

'So, you do know him.'

I leapt to my feet and spun to face whoever had spoken, and in the same moment felt the cramping wake of veering. A dark, feathered blur flew over my head. When I turned to face it, Frigid Cub knelt behind Oriole, a knife in one hand pressed to the side of his neck.

'Frigid Cub,' I said, my mind searching for some lie, some line of attack, something to move that knife away from Oriole's throat. 'Your mother sent me. She wanted to make sure—'

'No, she didn't,' Frigid Cub said. 'She's had either Burning Dog or me watch your room since she left you. I followed you from the alleyway. I was ... curious to see what you'd do, and why you sneaked into Iron Town, if not to kill Mother.'

The tip of her knife dug into Oriole's skin. A line of fresh blood trickled down his neck, cutting a rivulet through the dried gore caked to his chest. I lurched forwards, fought to get myself under control. Could I put a spear of lightning through her face without hitting Oriole? It was possible – I had seen Hand Usher perform more difficult feats with battle sorcery – but fear stayed my hand.

'So, who is he to you?' Frigid Cub asked. 'What makes him so valuable you'd risk your life, and a chance to kill the notorious Frothing Wolf, to save him?'

'He's the governor's son,' I said.

She shook her head. 'You're a Hand of the emperor, which makes you more valuable than him, even if he comes from a good family. Come now, Foolish Cur,' she said and pushed the knife deeper into Oriole's neck, drawing a thicker runnel of blood. 'Be honest.'

A moan bubbled from Oriole's lips. I moved into the second channel and hurled a bolt of lightning into the ground, shattering tiles and stirring the other prisoners into a terrified storm of yelling.

'Your mother will have felt that,' I said. 'She will come, fearing for your life, and when she steps through that gate I will spear her through the heart.'

'No, she won't,' Frigid Cub said, her eyes hardening. She flexed her jaw, the scar beside her mouth rippling. 'She'll flee and fight another day, because your facade has crumbled now and the threat to her life is real.'

'What a mother,' I snarled. 'Willing to abandon her own daughter. I am good at lying, Frigid Cub. Much better than you. Let me take him and leave Iron Town and I will let you, your mother, and your sister live.'

'Didn't she tell you, Foolish Cur?' Frigid Cub said, tensing. 'The point of our fight isn't to win, and certainly not to preserve our own lives. The point is to prove that the empire, and its servants, can still be hurt.'

'Wait!' I blurted. 'Don't kill him. He's my friend.'

Frigid Cub's smile was slow and cruel. 'Finally, a sliver of the truth,' she said, and opened Oriole's throat.

Disbelief struck like an arrow. Frigid Cub lunged towards me, and the wake of her sorcery washed over me like the heat of a fever.

I opened my hand. Lightning speared through the cloud of flame she conjured and hurled her to the ground. A second pulse of battle sorcery blasted the tiles beneath her apart. The third incinerated her to a cracked, charred ruin.

The howling in my head drowned out thoughts of my mission to kill Frothing Wolf, of the siege, of anything but the gaping wound in Oriole's neck and the blood pooling at his feet. With Frigid Cub's knife I smashed the lock that held his shackles closed, then, cradling him, lowered him to the ground. His skin was warm but he was motionless, unbreathing.

'No ... no,' I stammered, and reached for the third channel of the canon.

Oriole's pallid flesh looked almost hale through the muting of my senses in the wake of my healing sorcery. I held my tetragram above his throat and willed that awful wound to close. A part of me remembered songbirds dying in my hands and urged caution. Another part, which saw the blood on the tiles, on Oriole's chest, and pulsing from his throat, knew that caution was pointless.

A crack like thunder sounded from the southern wall – the first explosion in the staccato percussion of Sienese grenades. I felt the chill in my lungs and the warmth on my skin in the wake of Hand Usher's conjured lightning. He had felt my warning to Frigid Cub and the wakes of our battle and attacked at last.

Too late.

I reached deeper into the canon of sorcery, drawing all I could from the third channel. It swept through me like frothing rapids, dragging me under, submerging my senses till the world became a smear of colour and a slurry of muted sound and texture. I pressed my hand to Oriole's wound – as though closing that small distance of empty air might make the difference – and poured magic into him.

His heart had stopped. His wounds remained.

I dredged for every scrap of power but foundered against the stone wall of the canon, the border of the magic the emperor permitted his servants to wield. I hammered against it, a desperate scream ripping from my throat. As a child, when I first touched sorcery, I had encountered no such boundary. My will had hovered above the pattern of the world. Reality had been mine to rewrite, mine to shape. Knitting Oriole's wounds – even the wounds of a corpse – and setting his heart beating, his lungs pumping, would have been a small thing with such power. But the canon could do nothing beyond the emperor's designs. And the emperor did not share my wish to save Oriole's life.

But I had other magic.

Grasping for a strand of hope, I reached for my grandmother's witchcraft – my grandmother, who had knitted me back together the night I made myself an abomination.

I felt the heat of fire, the ache and cramp of veering. Nothing else. No secret witchcraft of healing.

How had she done it? Desperation became a howling anger. I knew too little! I'd been denied every opportunity to truly *learn*. Hemmed in and limited by the designs of others, cut off from the power that could have saved my friend.

Despair dug a hollow within me. All I could do was force more and more healing magic into him, like pouring water into a depthless void. The world blurred till there was nothing left but Oriole, his wounds, and the pitiful magic I continued to wield, hoping against hope that his wounds would knit, his bruises fade, his lungs fill, and his heart beat again.

'Alder,' said a familiar voice, muted and softened as though it flowed through water. I felt a hand on my shoulder, then another cradled the side of my face and pulled my gaze away from Oriole. Hand Usher stared into my eyes. Even smeared and distorted, I saw panic on his face.

'Let go, Alder,' Hand Usher urged. 'He's dead.'

His words shattered against my disbelieving mind. I pulled away, reached for Oriole, threw myself against the walls of the canon, knowing I could never break through. Hurling myself again and again regardless. Oriole's only hope, and mine, lay beyond, in the deeper power I had touched before my world was narrowed by pact and canon.

'Alder!'

I was deaf to him. And so he found another way to reach me.

Even muted by the wake of my own desperate magic, I felt his sorcery. A heavy wake, like a caught breath and a weight on my shoulders, not unlike transmission. Lights flashed in the corners of my eyes. A tightness gripped my arms and legs, forcing my hands to my sides and my knees together. I collapsed beside Oriole. Yet still I tried to work some impossible magic beyond the canon, only now my will felt slow, as though it were a leaden, senseless limb.

'*Stop*, Alder!' Usher's voice was a harsh, unimpeachable command. 'There is nothing to be done for him.'

Only then did it become true to me. As I came to my senses, I saw the flickering ropes of iridescent light that bound my arms and legs. I stared at them, dumbfounded. The wake of Usher's sorcery winked out of existence, my bonds with it.

'Alder.' Usher knelt and reached for me. 'You're all right now.'

'What ... What did you do to me?' I asked, my voice a thin quaver.

His face hardened, if only for an instant. 'What you were

doing was dangerous. The dead cannot be restored, Alder. You would have only killed yourself.'

'What did you *do*?' I repeated.

'I employed a sorcery you'll learn in time,' he said and pulled me to my feet. 'For now, tell me what happened here.'

I tried to steady myself and managed to keep my feet, but as my eyes drifted back towards Oriole a spasm shook me. My empty stomach retched.

'You did everything you could,' Usher said, holding my shoulders to help me keep my feet.

'No,' I said, prising myself away from him, my grief catching flame, burning to anger. '*No*, we didn't. We could have attacked this morning. We could have saved him!'

Usher's face hardened, but he did not answer my accusation. His eyes sought the charred remains of Frigid Cub, lying on broken tiles in a puddle of mud and ash.

'Is that … ?'

'Her daughter,' I said. 'I don't know where Frothing Wolf is. There is another daughter, likely defending the tunnel.'

Hand Usher had the tact and presence of mind not to show any reaction to my failure. His gaze returned to Oriole and a flicker of grief crossed his face.

'We could have saved him,' I said again.

He opened his mouth, as though to respond, then closed it. The falling rain mixed with Oriole's blood, which flowed away in red, slick ribbons.

'I will deal with Frothing Wolf if she is still in Iron Town,' he said and gestured towards the rest of the prisoners – the former imperial garrison. Half a dozen soldiers moved among them, prising open shackles with the tips of their daggers. 'Lead these men to our camp,' he commanded. 'There is still fighting, but the Nayeni will surrender without their witches.'

'We could have—'

'We *could* have,' Usher said firmly. 'but we did not. And you and I will have to live with that mistake.'

'That *mistake*?' My voice hitched. 'Our *mistake* cost Oriole his life. Cost dozens of men their lives—'

'There is always death in war.'

'What war?' I was shouting now, my anger finding vent in raw-voiced words. 'This was no war! This was just a few hundred malcontents holding a town already on the brink of starvation, who we might have forced to surrender *the day we arrived*! Frothing Wolf would have escaped, but she escaped anyway. And Oriole would still be alive.'

'And what action did you take to save him, these two days you have spent in the company of our enemies?' Usher snapped.

I steadied myself, felt an itching in my witch marks. One shield of lies had shattered in my battle with Frigid Cub. Time again to take up the other.

'Do you honestly think they would let a peasant volunteer, suddenly arrived – during a siege! – stand guard over their most valuable prisoner?' I demanded. 'They gave me a posting on the wall. I abandoned it the first chance I had, killed two men who tried to question me, and reached Oriole's side while he still lived, only to watch Frigid Cub cut his throat. Which is more than can be said of you.'

His face hardened. I could only hope my impudence made my half-truths more convincing, spoken as they were without the veils of deference and propriety. 'Your grief is understandable,' he said at last, coolly, 'and I will overlook this disrespect. But you will do as you have been ordered, Hand Alder.'

With that he left the garrison yard, leaving me to stand numbly, staring at the roiling clouds, waiting for my men to finish freeing the other prisoners. Soon afterwards, I felt wakes of fire and battle sorcery, then a cramping in my shoulders. Usher had found Burning Dog or Frothing Wolf, who had veered and escaped in turn. To my surprise, the thought filled me with bitter satisfaction. Though Frothing Wolf might survive and remain a thorn in the empire's side, her uprising had cost her one daughter and a defeat that would tarnish her legend. And Usher, despite his callousness, had been unable to kill her.

There was a horrible justice in these warriors circling each other without end, meting out petty wounds, slowly bleeding each other dry, but always failing to deal a killing blow. If only they could do battle alone, isolated from the pattern of the world. Somewhere that their war would not leave towns besieged and starving. Where the romantic tales of wars long past could never trick the young into seeking glory, only to drag them down into death.

14

Grief and Translation

Those few of our soldiers who died were buried with all honours in Iron Town's graveyard. The Nayeni were burned. Usher bade our medics prepare Oriole's corpse for a long journey in the heat of summer. The wagon that bore his corpse smelled of salt and sand and cedar. They had done something to preserve him. What, I did not wish to know.

The early typhoons passed and the sky cleared. Usher and I and the bulk of our force left Iron Town, hoping to be out of the mountains before the next storm cycle struck. All told, we were two weeks in Iron Town. Two weeks that left me hollowed out and broken-hearted. Sick of war, already, after my first taste.

Usher and I spoke little during the journey back to Eastern Fortress. We conversed mildly, talking of the weather – so much more amenable than the storms which had delayed our march to Iron Town – or discussing where to camp each night. Neither of us mentioned Oriole, though his absence left a notable emptiness and always his wagon followed at the back of our column, draped in a cloth of funerary white that bore his father's tetragram. Neither did we speak of my outburst in the garrison yard, nor the binding sorcery Usher had used against me. What ties there were between us felt raw and recently torn. Iron Town had been meant as a stepping stone, one of many on the path to the Imperial Academy. Instead, it had cost me my friend and my teacher, and left me more hopeless than I had ever been.

At the end of midsummer, when the typhoons again began to rain upon Nayen, we at last arrived at Eastern Fortress. Messengers had been sent ahead and preparations already made for Oriole's funeral. His wagon now smelled less of spices, and the men tasked with tending to it had taken to covering their mouths and noses in scented cloths.

Nevertheless, when Voice Golden-Finch met us at the gate of the governor's citadel, dressed all in white, his head and beard shaved in mourning, he threw himself across the wagon. Sobs shook him and he pressed the lines of the tetragram upon his brow to the funerary cloth, which was soaked and heavy with rain.

'My son,' he moaned. 'Oh, my foolish son.'

He stood and his eyes swept over me, with a flash that I took for hatred, before settling on Usher.

'We will have words, you and I,' he said.

Usher bowed. 'As soon as your son is returned to the earth and the period of mourning has ended, I will—'

'No,' Voice Golden-Finch said, his voice hoarse. 'We will speak now. And then we will bury him.'

At his gesture, several of his guards took the reins of the mules who had been pulling Oriole's wagon and led it away. Voice Golden-Finch gestured for Hand Usher to follow him. Neither of them so much as acknowledged me as they walked away. Left alone, I instructed a steward to unload my belongings and bring them to my rooms, then sought out the secluded pavilion behind the porous stone where Usher had taught so many of my lessons.

My path there led past the grassy field where Oriole had taught me to ride, where a stablehand – his arm wrapped in white cloth to show that the household was in mourning – now put a young stallion through its paces.

When I reached the pavilion, I sat and watched the king-fishers dive for their meals, undisturbed by the gentle rain. In that quiet place, alone, alienated in a garden that had been my home these last few years, the hollow within me filled suddenly, like the spillway below a broken dam.

I had lost Oriole. I had lost everything. I wept and, perhaps unconsciously seeking the most comforting of memories, thought of my mother, sitting beside my bed as no Sienese mother should have done, feeding me sticky rice and bland broth.

I wished I could return to that moment, with a mother and grandmother to care for me in my weakness. And in that wish, I felt for the first time the terrible isolation of adulthood.

Two days later, Voice Golden-Finch led the household in Oriole's funeral procession. He and Oriole's brother, Pinion, had stood vigil the previous night, composing poems in his memory and carving them into the bare wood of the coffin. At dawn, servants carried the casket out of the inner courtyard, and Voice Golden-Finch and Pinion followed behind. After them, shrouded in layered veils of heavy white gauze, came his mother, along with the other women of the house, wailing and shaking, leaning upon one another for support, exhibiting the stricken affectations expected of Sienese women shattered by grief. Usher and I followed side by side without speaking. Behind us, professional mourners howled and tore their garments while a troubadour played a flute song like the keening of ghosts.

We walked through the garden, its trees and pavilions papered over with prayers for the departed, until we reached the plot Voice Golden-Finch had chosen for Oriole's burial.

Servants had dug a chamber out of a hillside topped by a young plum tree. The coffin was placed within and the servants piled earth to cover it. This done, Voice Golden-Finch took up the first of the 100 white bricks that would mark his son's grave. He weighed it in his hand and looked up at the plum tree, its branches dark with leaves but not yet blossoming.

'In the Classic of Living and Dying, Traveller-on-the-Narrow-Way writes that all of life is but a temporary emergence from the great pattern of the world. That we should mourn the dead, but only as we mourn the end of a song or the close of a dance. He goes on to write, "As a cresting wave must return to the body of the sea, so the dead return to the pattern." So it is with my son, Oriole, my first born.'

He placed his brick, the cornerstone of a gate that would mark Oriole's passage from life into death. Pinion placed the next, his mother the next, and then the other mourners came up one by one to place theirs. I longed to take one up, to participate in this ritual of closure, but when he had spoken Voice Golden-Finch's eyes had rested on me for a moment, and I felt such shame that I dared not step forwards.

Usher, too, hesitated. Only when Voice Golden-Finch himself handed Usher a brick did he step forwards and place it. Then, perhaps following his father's example, Pinion did the same for me.

It hurt me to look at the boy, three years Oriole's junior but so like him in every way, with the same dark hair and pale skin. A narrower nose, but the same hard jaw and sharp, clever eyes. 'Take it,' he insisted, pressing the brick into my hands when I hesitated. 'However things ended, you were a friend to him.'

His kindness threatened to break my composure, but I took a deep breath and accepted the white, rough brick, and forgiveness with it. I placed it on the left-hand column and stepped away.

When the last of the mourners had laid their bricks, Voice Golden-Finch led the procession to his audience hall, where they would eat a simple feast in celebration of Oriole's life. I lingered behind and watched the servants finish building the small waist-high gate, mortaring it, sealing Oriole's coffin in the ground, where the raw wood would slowly decay and return his body to the earth and the pattern of the world.

While Voice Golden-Finch shut himself away to mourn his son, Hand Usher assumed the governor's duties. He sent couriers to me bearing documents and ledgers from the Office of Trade and instructed me to flag anything unusual or note-worthy for his attention. I performed the task to the best of my ability, relishing the occasions when I saw some flaw in trade policy, and could spend hours distracted from my grief while I composed arguments and wrote memoranda in support of my suggested changes.

Grief always crept back in, the moment I put away my brushes.

My studies in magic had not resumed. I wondered if they ever would, and whether I truly wanted them to. Sorcery had not been able to save Oriole. In truth, every step I had thought would lead me towards greater power and greater mastery – my witch marks, my tetragram – had further constrained me. Only the Imperial Academy, where I could pursue my curiosity to the limit, promised any kind of true understanding of magic. But to get there, I would have to prove myself as Hand of the emperor. As a weapon in fruitless wars, like the one that had cost Oriole his life.

I spent much of the autumn and winter after Iron Town alone in a pavilion that overlooked Oriole's grave, spending my free time reading the mythic romances that he had loved. As winter neared its end, delicate white blossoms flecked with red and yellow bloomed in the plum tree that grew above the grave. Everything else had withered and had yet to sprout anew when Hand Usher at last came to visit me there. We had seen little of each other since Iron Town, and the wound that had been ripped open between us there had been allowed to fester. He joined me with a pot of jasmine tea and filled two cups.

'You have done well these last months,' he said, offering me a cup. 'As I said, you have a head for economics.'

I set down my book but did not take the cup he offered. He placed the cup on the table and folded his hands.

'Voice Golden-Finch and I have been discussing your situation and seeking the advice of the emperor,' he said. 'Together we have decided that you should finish your apprenticeship in sorcery away from Nayen.'

I was unnerved to hear that Usher and Voice Golden-Finch had brought my failure to the emperor's attention, discussing me across the leagues between Nayen and Northern Capital through the canon of transmission. And they had decided that I should be reassigned. Had Usher stood up for me? More troubling, would the academy ever be open to a Hand whose teacher had rejected him? I was lucky, I supposed, that he had not cut off my left hand as punishment for my failure.

'Where will you send me?' I asked.

In answer, he retrieved three small books from the pocket of his robe. One was bound in leather, its spine stamped with a strange linear script I did not recognise. The second was an ordinary cloth-bound volume entitled *The Trade Language of the An-Zabati: A Primer*. The third was an old book of wooden slats, its title, *Folklore and Legends of the Batir Waste*, rendered in archaic logograms.

'There will be a position for a minister of trade opening soon in the city of An-Zabat, on the western edge of the empire,' Usher said while I examined the books.

'You would name me a minister?' I said, looking up from the primer. 'I am only an apprentice. I know only two of the channels of the canon, and—'

'In the last few months, you have thrice found flaws in Nayen's trade ministry, and the new policies you have proposed have all been implemented and deemed successful,' Usher interrupted. 'Your instruction in the canon will continue in An-Zabat, under the tutelage of the Hands stationed there. An-Zabat is the centre of trade in the West, and as such it is a nexus for all manner of strange knowledge and foreign science. A place that will surely fascinate you.'

'Usher, I … This isn't a punishment for my failure in Iron Town?'

His face softened as I had never seen it. 'There are many paths through the world a Hand of the emperor might take,' he said. 'Many uses for us within the grand project of empire. War is but one of those. You have taken your first steps along two such paths – one towards military leadership, the other towards a more bureaucratic, ministerial role. I think we all agree you're much better suited to the latter.'

'I thought perhaps this was the Voice's way of sending me far away,' I said, some of my trepidation fading. 'After what happened at Iron Town. To his son.'

Usher laughed. 'It may well be that he agreed to my suggestion for that very reason, but this placement in An-Zabat was my idea, not his. This truly is the best next step on your path to the academy. If you distinguish yourself, you will command the emperor's attention and earn the place you desire.'

He gestured to the books on the table between us. 'An-Zabat is far from here, and a newly conquered territory. Many of its people do not yet speak Sienese. With these, you can learn something of their language and culture before you arrive.'

I looked again at the books, and at Usher's face, so open and expressive – at least, in affectation. I had never seen him so kindly, and I thought back to our return from Iron Town, to Voice Golden-Finch's sharp, hateful glare. If the governor had agreed to this assignment, there must be some hidden thorn upon which I was meant to prick myself. Or perhaps it was enough that reassignment would remove me from Golden-Finch's sight, his house, and his province.

Yet I was unwilling to pry. Hand Usher and I both knew, I was certain, that Iron Town had destroyed whatever working relationship had existed between us. I would leave Nayen not because the empire wanted me for a minister of trade but because I had alienated my teacher.

'Very well,' I said, picking up the books he had brought me. At least I would no longer be pressed into life as a soldier, balancing life and death on the scales of strategy. 'When do I leave?'

Hand Usher's final task as my teacher would be to present me to the emperor in Northern Capital – in person, at the foot of the Thousand-Armed Throne – and secure my commission as minister of trade. But he could not undertake this task until Voice Golden-Finch completed the period of mourning for his son and resumed his duties as governor. During that time I drifted like a ghost through the governor's gardens, haunting my apartments or the pavilion overlooking Oriole's grave, and set my mind to my new assignment.

At first, the An-Zabati tongue baffled me. Unlike the logograms and Nayeni runes I knew, its writing system used symbols that represented single sounds rather than complete ideas. But once I'd accustomed myself to this difference and had grappled long enough with An-Zabati's unfamiliar grammar and syntax to make effective if rudimentary use of them, acquisition of the language became mainly a matter of expanding my vocabulary.

For the rest of the winter, I dug into the three books Usher had given me. The one written in An-Zabati turned out to be the original from which the book of folklore had been translated. I composed my own translations to practise the nuances of the language and lost myself in tales of desert demons, clan disputes, and the oft-angered god of the sky.

Most fascinating to me was the tale of Naphena, the most revered goddess of the An-Zabati. She was nothing like the gods of Nayen, who took the form of beasts and gave nothing to their followers without extracting a price in blood and worship. Neither was she like the emperor – remote, powerful, and demanding of deference – though both were human, at least in form. Naphena's defining act was one of self-sacrifice. When year upon year of drought left the Batir grassland a barren waste, she gave her life to reshape the pattern of the world and create an oasis that the people named *An* for water, *Za* for rest, and *Bat* for the land beneath the endless sky.

She had rewritten the world, making water where there was none – a miracle, as the An-Zabati told it, or a primal, deeper magic unconstrained by pact or canon. If her power was able to make an oasis in wasted lands, perhaps it could have pulled a man back from the mouth of the grave.

If only she still lived and could teach me.

The chill winds of winter gave way to the clear skies of early spring. Voice Golden-Finch resumed his duties and Hand Usher informed me that we would leave Nayen in a month's time, once preparations for the imperial examinations were complete. Propriety demanded that I spend some time at home to bid my parents farewell before undertaking such a long and treacherous journey.

On the morning of the day I was to depart, I paid a visit to Oriole's grave. When I arrived, the last blossoms of winter were decorating the branches of the plum tree. Pinion stood beneath them, still wearing his white mourning stole, sweeping the dust and fallen leaves from the lintel of the small gate. I hesitated, reluctant to interrupt, but Pinion must have heard my approach for he turned and, on seeing me, bobbed his head in welcome.

'Hand Alder,' he said. 'I thought you might have left already.' Though his face was so eerily like his brother's, Pinion held himself with a seriousness more akin to my tutor Koro Ha. He set the broom down and gestured for me to join him.

'I don't want to intrude,' I said.

'You aren't,' he said. 'As I told you, you were his friend. In truth, he was closer to you than to me in his last years.'

'Yet I am the reason he is dead,' I said.

Pinion furrowed his brow at that. 'Nevertheless,' he said and stepped to the side.

Feeling somewhat embarrassed – he had not corrected me, after all – I could not reject his invitation. I stood beside him and ran my fingers along the bevelled edges of the lintel, where Oriole's name had been carved, feeling the roughness of the bricks.

'I don't think he would blame you,' Pinion said at last. 'I remember seeing him just before you left for Iron Town. He was happier than he'd been in years. I'm sure he would thank you if he could, even after how badly things went.'

'You're wrong,' I said, and felt something well up within me, as black and heavy as ink. 'You didn't see how he suffered.'

'And you are forgetting what it meant to him,' Pinion said.

I could think of no answer to that. We stood in silence, listening to the breeze through the branches of the plum tree, watching the sparrows of early spring build their nests.

'He wanted to serve the empire and make Father proud more than anything,' Pinion said. 'You gave him the chance to prove himself. I hope I can find such a friend, if I fail the examinations.' There was a bitter note in his voice, and I remembered my own examinations – the pressure to perform, the certainty that I would fail.

'I'm sure you will succeed,' I said.

'I wish I didn't have to,' he said abruptly, his bitterness blossoming into anger. 'Oriole wanted to be Hand of the emperor. I've never wanted that. What's worse is, I can't even say anymore what I would do instead. When I was younger I loved to paint, but was that only a childish fancy, or something I might have done if Oriole had succeeded and I had been allowed to fade into his shadow.' He breathed deeply and shut his eyes. 'I ought not to be telling you all of this. Only ...' He trailed off.

I considered whether to let the conversation die or to share my own frustrations and make myself vulnerable, as he had. Here was a chance to sow the seeds of a new friendship, to show Pinion that he was not alone in his doubts.

'I can't say, either,' I said at last. 'The examinations were the path my father chose for me. I tried to be a good son, and I did well – well enough to find myself on a new path, at least, though it turned out to be even more constrained. But such is the nature of life in the empire. So many choices are made for us.'

'The son must always suborn his will to the father,' Pinion said wryly. 'And the emperor is father of all.'

'What can we do but do what seems right?' I asked. 'Does it seem right to you, to take your brother's place and become Hand of the emperor?'

'It does,' he replied. 'But is that because it *is*, or is it only because that's the path every logogram of imperial doctrine would bid me walk?'

'A good question,' I said.

'What about you? Does going to An-Zabat seem right to you?'

At first, I thought to say no, that An-Zabat, like Iron Town, had been chosen for me. Then I remembered the story of Naphena and her oasis, a miracle wrought from magic. Naphena herself had died in the crafting of her spell, but she might have left a legacy, or at least some clue as to how she had performed such a miracle. The thought sent a thrill of excitement and anticipation through me for the first time since Iron Town.

'It does,' I said. 'But only because I have found my own reasons to press on.'

'Well,' Pinion said and smiled. 'Farewell, Alder. May both our paths be as golden as they seem.'

With that, he took the broom and left me alone by Oriole's grave, where I imagined the wonders I would see in An-Zabat: its mighty domes and soaring towers; its new people, neither Sienese nor Nayeni; and its oasis, birthed by magic – a clue, I dared to dream, to the mystery I had sought to unravel throughout my entire life.

My father spent the whole of my short visit home indoctrinating me in his various business interests, insisting that I keep an eye out for merchants selling wares from the western lands beyond the Waste – olives, muslin, a certain violet dye – with which he could turn a high profit, and to keep an eye out for buyers of silk and cinnabar. I listened and looked over his charts and books of accounts, but reminded him that I would be minister of trade and could not be seen to interfere to the benefit of my own family.

He pursed his lips and waved his hand in dismissal. 'All that moralism was well and good for the examinations, but why would fathers spend so much on tutors if not as an investment?' he said. 'You're going to be an imperial bureaucrat. Corruption is expected!'

I chose not to respond to this statement, which only deepened the divide between us.

In truth, I was not sure what I had hoped for from this visit home. Comfort, perhaps. A brief return to the simplicities of my early childhood, before Koro Ha, before I was fire-named, when life was little more than a meandering journey from one amusement to the next, free of complex questions, pressures, and grief. Interrupted only by the occasional anomaly, such as my uncle's unannounced visit and the soldiers who had come in search of him.

But I found that I could not put down the burdens I carried. However much I longed for a simpler past, the future would come for me. As my departure for An-Zabat drew near, my anxiety conjured old recurring nightmares – the steps of the temple, my twisted flesh and brittle bones, the blazing eyes of the wolf gods watching from every forest shadow. Dreams no less terrifying for their familiarity.

And if I was honest with myself, the past had never been simple. After Iron Town, all that I had suppressed of my grandmother's lessons had been stirred back up, left to float around in the confines of my skull, agitating questions I had long thought settled.

The rebellion had killed Oriole, my only friend, but neither of us would have been put in the path of violence if not for the emperor's need to tighten his grip on Nayen. Worse, the magic the empire offered me – the very thing that had enticed me away from my grandmother's path and into the emperor's service – had failed to save Oriole's life. What was the point in learning a magic so constrained, so useless, when I needed to reshape the world most?

The nightmares continued, now delivering me to that blood-soaked courtyard as often as to the Temple of the Flame. I took to avoiding sleep and wandering my father's gardens at night until exhaustion finally dragged me to bed for a few dreamless hours before sunrise.

On one such meandering walk, my feet carried me to the garden gate, then to the foot of the path that led to the Temple of the Flame. New weeds had sprouted there between broken roof tiles. The stone wolves were less menacing than they had been a decade ago and appeared half as tall, yet when I walked past them I felt a tingling down the back of my neck, as though they were tracking me with their eyes. I ignored the feeling. They were only stone, no matter that in my nightmares their eyes were flame and they spoke with human tongues.

In the temple hall there were paw prints in the dust – made by a fox, perhaps, or a mountain dog – but no sign of human visitors. The flame in the altar's heart had gone out; its stone surface was cool beneath my fingers.

Treasonous nostalgia dredged up pleasant memories of the place. My grandmother had known me like no other person in the world. I could never share the side of myself that was cultivated here, beneath the buckling eaves and faded murals, on the swollen wood of the floor, with anyone else. Even Oriole had known only a fragment of me. Could I go on presenting only a curated version of myself forever, living an identity tailored to the needs and pressures of empire?

For a torturous moment I wished that Grandmother had taken me with her when she'd gone north to join the rebellion.

Like the taste of a delicacy melting on the tongue, or the sound of a fading note, the feeling passed. Her path would not have led me to freedom either, only to a different set of limitations, different shackles for my power and my future. She may have cared for me and done the best she could for me, but she understood as little about me as Hand Usher and could give me even less.

I felt a need to find a souvenir of this, my final visit to the Temple of the Flame – a reminder that I had once wielded magic freely without witch marks or the canon, and that I might someday do so again.

I thought at once – as though the thought were forced upon me by an outside power – of the chest beside the altar. The books were still there, but they were conspicuous and would be difficult to hide. But beneath them, swaddled in a bolt of cloth, I found the obsidian knife. I picked it up and felt the heft of it, marvelling that this small, primitive weapon had dealt me so much grief. It was perfect – a memento meaningless to anyone not inducted into the rites of witchcraft yet rich in meaning for me.

On the way back to my rooms, I was surprised to see a figure dressed in a wispy robe beneath a heavy shawl, holding a lantern that cast a halo of light in the midnight dark of the garden.

'I heard you wandering the grounds,' my mother said. Her gaze drifted to the forest behind me. 'I thought you had put such things behind you.'

'I couldn't sleep,' I told her, struck by an odd shame as if I was a child caught sneaking sweets from the kitchens. I tucked the obsidian knife up my sleeve.

'Alder, there is something I have been meaning to say to you,' she said hesitantly, 'but there was never a good time. We were always ... well ... Sienese mothers so rarely have a chance to be alone with their sons.'

'Save when they're sick,' I noted.

She smiled at that, but her expression quickly regained its gravity.

'I know what your grandmother taught you,' she said. 'She taught my brother, too, and dragged him into her desperate, vengeful war against the empire. And ... well, you have seen what that war is like now. She is a madwoman, Alder. You must forget everything she told you – her stories, her magic, all of it.'

'Even that the empire killed your father?' I said softly.

My mother had been practising the poise and demureness

expected of Sienese wives all her life, and her flicker of anger was quickly doused. 'Especially that,' she said firmly. 'I'm sure you have heard that the emperor knows the thoughts of his Hands.'

In that moment, every unkind assumption I'd had about her seemed vindicated. I thought of the other Nayeni women I had met – Grandmother, Frothing Wolf, her daughters. My mother was so much weaker than them, so much more fearful.

'Which of us is Hand of the emperor?' I said. 'Which of us would know the truth of what the emperor does and does not do?'

'No rumour so oft repeated is truly baseless,' she replied. 'You think little of me – I see it in your face – but you have no idea what I have done to keep you safe in a world that should have killed us. An-Zabat is a long way from Nayen. That's a good thing. It will give you a chance to forget everything she taught you.'

'Mother, I wield sorcery and command armies. Who in the empire is safer?' I smiled, showing a warmth I did not feel, and strode past her. 'Good night, Mother. We both should get some sleep.'

Back in my rooms, I stowed the obsidian knife in an old brush case, sealed the latch with wax, and hid it at the bottom of the black trunk that carried a transcript of my examination essays, a collection of the sages' writings that Koro Ha had given me, and the books from Hand Usher on An-Zabati language and culture. Despite my mother's warnings, my visit to the Temple of the Flame seemed to have the desired effect, and my sleep that night, and for many nights after, was untroubled by anxious dreams. Instead, I dreamed of the wonders awaiting me in the west, by way of an audience with the emperor, in An-Zabat and of the academy, where, if Hand Usher could be believed, some scholars still studied the deeper truths of magic. If there was a third path towards magic and freedom to be found, I would seek it there. And I would swallow my growing distaste for the empire long enough to find it.

III

Hand of the Emperor

15

The Thousand-Armed Throne

Two months later, Hand Usher and I disembarked from the warship *Winds of Great Fortune* at the city of River Wall, on the north coast of the River Sien. After spending the night in a local magistrate's house, the next day we boarded the *Golden Barge*, a luxurious river boat that ferried the emperor's servants to Northern Capital. The *Barge*'s cedar planks were stained deep red and every oar was scored with gold filigree. The captain and crew of the ship were the most decorated veterans in the Imperial Navy. The oarsmen, they informed me, were peasants conscripted for a year's service to the emperor.

Such press-ganging had yet to come to Nayen. Here, though, in the heart of the empire, no one dared revolt.

Though the river was slow-moving, the oarsmen propelled us swiftly and we made brisk time. As we travelled, I drank in my first sights of inland Sien. I had grown up in a land of mountains, hills, and forests, of shadows and creatures lurking in the dark. The country we were travelling through was as flat as an ink-stone by comparison. The few hills were gentle and rolling and blanketed in wheat, maize, and sunflowers. We passed sprawling settlements that I took for major towns. Hand Usher laughed and told me they were villages, with 20,000 souls at most.

The city was fringed by a forest of buildings that grew denser as we travelled northwards. Then, like a mountain range appearing on the horizon, we caught our first sight of the city wall. It stretched to the east and west, seemingly without end, the soldiers that walked its battlements little more than silhouetted specks against the blue sky. We passed between off-set guard towers, each mounted with a ballista designed to hurl grenades large enough to shatter any warship, then beneath the vast arch of the Southern River Fortress gate. The wedged spikes of its portcullis were as wide as two men abreast.

I imagined we would reach the Eternal Citadel – the emperor's palace – by nightfall, but the city sprawled on and on. Mooring docks jutted haphazardly into the river like the broken teeth of a tavern brawler. Fishermen threw nets from the piers and hauled in as much filth as fish. Other ships of the Imperial Navy slipped past broad merchant barges and pleasure yachts bedecked in gold that trailed ribbons of silk and peacock feathers. On land, a cacophonous jumble of carts, livestock, market stalls, rickshaws, palanquins, beggars, and guard patrols jostled past each other on streets that meandered through the urban landscape like the threads of a spider's web. The private gardens of wealthy urbanites decorated the landscape with rare flecks of green.

'Every soul in Nayen could be housed in a quarter of this city,' Hand Usher said. He stroked his neck – clean-shaven, for even he would not appear slovenly before the emperor. 'You get used to the smell eventually.'

Not until noon on our second day in the city did we see the palace. Its sweeping roofs rose above the urban sprawl like waves of liquid gold. We turned onto a canal that led through another gate faced in marble and carved with sea drakes, into the emperor's personal harbour. The captain of the *Golden Barge* flew Hand Usher's banner, and by the time the boarding plank was lowered a palanquin was waiting on the pier to receive us.

While we were carried to our guest house, Hand Usher explained the maze of walls and buildings we navigated. The Eternal Citadel itself was a city within a city, as large as Iron Town and populated by the families of the emperor, his Voices, and his Fist, his personal guard of 1000 elite soldiers. Usher pointed out the spire of the Imperial Academy's observatory tower in the distance, and I felt a renewal of my ambition. One day I would have a place there, away from the complexities of politics and the horrors of war, free to puzzle over the great riddles of the world, magic foremost among them.

The palanquin delivered us to the Gatehouse Garden, which outshone even the opulence of Voice Golden-Finch's estate. Small houses, pavilions, and gazebos had been built to blend into a landscape of sapphire ponds, emerald foliage, and striking artificial cliffs. Tawny deer, peacocks, and all manner of songbirds wandered the garden as though in the wild. The smell of late summer blossoms and incense mingled in the air, and even the servants wore silk and velvet.

Only empire could produce such opulence. Power flowed out from the Thousand-Armed Throne, and wealth – seized in conquest and tribute – flowed back from every corner of the world. I was impressed but could not help but wonder how many people had died as Oriole had died, in the mud and the rain. Their lives – and the lives of the conquered – were the cost of this luxury.

Hand Usher had justified Sienese conquest as an ideological war against chaos, an effort to unite humanity against the primordial gods. How did he feel, knowing that the wealth that decorated this garden for the emperor's guests might have armed a dozen legions? He surveyed it all without expression, and I dared not ask.

*

'Remember to breathe,' Hand Usher said. 'And don't lock your knees.'

We sat on marble benches in the antechamber of the emperor's throne room along with a dozen others, all awaiting our audiences. I was a fidgeting mess, plucking at the vast sleeves of the court robe Hand Usher had given me, running my fingers along the ridged spine of the book of translated poetry I had completed while studying the An-Zabati tongue, which I would present to the emperor in thanks for my commission.

Hand Usher and Voice Golden-Finch had not recognised my witch's scars, but the emperor was nearly a god. I could feel the magic that radiated from him already, a weighty mountain asserting itself against the natural flow of the pattern. A familiar fear, long tamped down, bubbled within me.

Another young man rose from the bench across the room, scurried to the broad entryway, and vomited onto the marble stairs. I felt an immediate solidarity with him.

'See?' Hand Usher whispered. 'A few nerves are perfectly normal. All you need to do is say, "I, your servant, humbly present this gift to the emperor and accept his commission to the province of An-Zabat." Someone will take the book from you. The emperor may have a few questions, and then we'll be dismissed. Simple.' He spoke with casual confidence, but the tips of his fingers played at the hems of his sleeves like a child waiting for an audience with his father, and his eyes darted towards the grand door at every creaking hinge and echoing footstep.

My fingers curled around the book in my lap. The blue silk that swaddled it was soft against my scars. What worth, I wondered, could a thousand-year-old sorcerer, ruler of the known world and venerated for generations as a living god, find in a simple book of translated poetry? But it was the gesture that mattered, of course, to symbolise that all my labours were but a gift to be laid at the emperor's feet. And presenting a gift of such a humble book was, in truth, not what troubled me. There was nothing simple about bearing secrets into the presence of the divine.

A steward called my name. Hand Usher and I followed him. Our feet echoed on the marble floor as we entered the throne room through vast doors plated in bronze. Incense wafted between columns of fragrant cedar and up to wreathe the vaulted ceiling like mist. Lamp stands filled the room with a flickering glow. The ministers of the imperial court lingered silently among the columns, and behind them loomed fifty of the emperor's Fist – his personal guard.

On a dais at the far end of the hall, the emperor sat on his throne. The seat was formed of folded legs of burnished gold, his backrest a waist and torso. Eyes with whites of pearl and pupils of jet watched over the court and seemed to study some distant, divine horizon. From the shoulders of the throne sprouted its 1000 arms, arrayed in layers like the feathers of an eagle's wings, reaching outwards and upwards to cover the entire wall. A tetragram worked in silver filigree glimmered in the palm of each hand. Which one, I wondered in a moment of awe, represented me?

Three ribbons – two red and one yellow – had been laid on the floor. We knelt and bowed our foreheads to each red ribbon and counted thirty heartbeats before rising again. At the yellow ribbon, we waited with backs bent and faces low for the emperor's permission to rise.

The weight of his presence gripped my bones and filled my mouth with ashes. Never had I felt magic like this. I had thought to see the sorcery of transmission – for even now he worked that spell, conveying the canon throughout the empire – as streamers of light, or hovering globes, or an argent halo. There was only the emperor, his throne, and the depthless wake of sorcery, as heavy as all the oceans of the world.

His voice boomed out from the throne. 'Lift your eyes, Hands Usher and Alder, and look upon your emperor.'

I did as instructed. The red silk of his robe showed in crimson patches through gold and silver embroidery so dense that one image bled into another. He wore a crown fashioned after the antlers of a lion serpent. A gold thread had been woven between the brow tines, and from it hung strings of jade beads polished to shine like green stars. They swung gently at the touch of his breath.

'You seek our blessing,' the emperor said.

'We do, Your Majesty,' Hand Usher said.

A servant appeared from beside the emperor, a beautiful youth so delicately featured as to seem ageless. He paused in front of me and waited.

'I, ah, I, your humble servant,' I began, extending my arms towards the youth. 'I present this gift to the emperor and accept, ah, humbly, your commission to the province of An-Zabat, Your Majesty.'

The servant took the book from me and disappeared into the shadows behind the throne.

'We accept this gift and wish you a safe journey,' the emperor said. 'May you carry the light of civilisation to the far corners of the world.'

We backed away from the throne, bowing again at the red ribbons. A steward led us to a side exit and out into the garden. After the heady smoke of the throne room, the fresh air and sunlight gave the feeling of waking from a dream.

'Well done, Alder,' Hand Usher said, clapping me on the back.

I shrugged out from under his hand. 'Don't mock me.'

'I wasn't. The first time I met the emperor, I fainted right there on the first red ribbon. Now, will you have a farewell drink with me? I must return to Nayen, and you have your own path to follow.'

'He didn't even read my book,' I muttered, but I followed Hand Usher back to our rooms, where we spent the night drinking and talking – associates now, no longer master and student. I hoped that the governor of An-Zabat, Voice Rill, and his subordinate Hands would be more straightforward teachers.

After we opened our second bottle of plum wine, Usher paused, cup in hand. 'Oriole would be proud,' he said suddenly, with a crack in his usual mask of ironic detachment. There was no hint of that ghostly smile.

A lump formed in my throat as I raised my own glass. 'To his memory,' I said.

'And to your future,' Usher said. 'To the wonders and challenges that await in An-Zabat. May you return wiser and more worldly.'

As the night wore on, I realised that I would miss Hand Usher. Though our relationship had soured, he had been a part of the brightest years of my life, the languid days in Voice Golden-Finch's garden, full of learning and companionship, before the horror of Iron Town. Days I still recall with fondness, no matter how time and war may have darkened the memory.

16

The City of Water and Wind

The obelisks of An-Zabat stood like pillars holding up the blue
dome of the sky, glimmering with silver filigree that mimicked
the patterns the wind writes on desert dunes. Red banners bearing the emperor's tetragram hung from each, a reminder to the
city's people, who had conquered both desert and sky, that they
had been conquered in turn.

I had seen the wonders of Northern Capital, sailed canals
across the great plains of western Sien, and crossed the deserts
of the Batir Waste by windship, and I thought myself worldly
after so many weeks of travel, but even the Thousand-Armed
Throne paled in comparison to the obelisks.

Crewmen struck all but the steering sail as the windship
coasted on its runner blades into the elevated harbour. The
ship's windcaller breathed deeply and planted his feet wide. I
tried – and failed, not for the first time – to comprehend the
magic he wielded. It was brisk and subtle, like a cool breeze on
the back of my neck that left little wake in the pattern of the
world. A slight ripple like light on fractured glass ran along
the whorled tattoos that covered his arms. He pushed the wind
up and around into the steering sail to turn the ship about. It
coasted into place, facing out towards the rolling dunes.

Over the fifteen days of our journey, I had watched the

windcaller closely. The An-Zabati had shrugged off the empire's every attempt to add their magic to the canon, which only deepened my desire to learn it. I knew it would not be the true, unbridled power I had felt before my grandmother had marked me, yet I nursed a hope that deeper understanding could be learned from the magics that Hand Usher would call *primitive*, and which I knew to be just as powerful as the canon itself. Hopefully there would be opportunities to indulge my curiosity – and to investigate An-Zabat's goddess, and her miracle – after I had begun my work as minister of trade.

Any such magic would likely be as constrained as witchcraft, I knew, and would not offer me mastery. Yet I was thirsty for any knowledge that lay beyond the limits of the canon. Any deeper truth I might learn was a paving stone on that third path through the world that I would build for myself, first to the academy and then beyond, to true freedom.

A palanquin carried me through the city towards the imperial citadel, whose broad sandstone walls competed with the obelisks for dominance of the skyline. Every few blocks we passed a ruin blasted apart by chemical grenades or a structure scarred by battle sorcery. The people were strange to me, bronze-skinned and light-haired, and though I had studied their language the snatched phrases I heard fluttered past my ears, as meaningless as the wingbeats of a moth. Stranger still were the dromedaries that pulled carts or carried bundles on their humped backs. They seemed to me creatures from outlandish mythology.

At the heart of the city, in the shadow of the citadel, we passed the Blessed Oasis. A statue of Naphena, the city's patron, giver of rain and spring water, stood at the heart of the square. She had been carved in sandstone and plated with silver, and in her arms she held an urn bedecked with rubies and sapphires. A quartet of guards – two men and two women, all wearing long, curved blades on their hips and with whorled tattoos upon their arms – stood nearby, almost as still as the statue, as though they were in fact a part of the sculpture. They would remain motionless like that, I suspected, until the moment someone dared to desecrate it. Water that sparkled as brightly as the jewels cascaded from the urn to splash in the basin at the goddess's feet. Children played there in the clear, cool shallows. The miracle was not Naphena's statue itself but the wealth of water here, in the middle of this parched and wasted land. I felt for some remnant of the magic she had worked hundreds of years ago but could identify only the brisk wakes of windcalling from the harbour.

A vast bazaar filled the square around Naphena, a feast of sound, colour, and life. Merchants hawked all manner of goods imported from the empire and the western lands: shimmering silks and brightly feathered birds, intricate clockwork devices, spices, and luxurious wines. Tumblers and magicians performed between the stalls to thunderous applause and a rain of coin.

The largest crowd surrounded a woman who spun and leapt in stunning arcs, all the while sending a pair of silver-embroidered scarves fluttering from hand to hand. A by-now-familiar chill ran down the back of my neck as she tossed the air to make her scarves dance and flutter. I watched her for a dozen heart-beats, trying to trace the wake her magic left in the world. The windcallers, it seemed, used their magic for more than war and windships.

As we drew closer to the great stone gate of the citadel, I saw that the walls bore the fractal scoring left by battle sorcery, along with other scars that looked as though they'd been gouged by great blades that had been deflected by the stone. Outward-facing ballistae threatened the city from newly built towers at the four corners of the citadel wall, and guards patrolled the battlements carrying heavy crossbows and wearing bandoleers of grenades.

I turned away from them. They reminded me too much of Iron Town. I needed to focus on the present and on the future, not on old wounds better left behind in Nayen.

Winding canals flowed through the citadel courtyard, feeding shallow ponds. Pink-plumed herons imported from southern Sien waded among the lilies. Pavilions built of imported wood dotted a sculpted landscape of grassy hills, bamboo groves, and porous limestone boulders dredged from distant lakes. After traversing the Batir Waste and the dusty, crowded streets, finding a garden from the Sienese heartland in the middle of An-Zabat was surreal.

As I stepped down from my palanquin, a thin steward approached me. 'Welcome, Your Excellency, Hand Alder,' he said, bowing deeply. 'I am called Jhin, your humble steward for your tenure in An-Zabat. The servants will bear your luggage to your rooms. Excellencies Hand Cinder, Hand Alabaster, and His Eminence Voice Rill await you.' Jhin was tall, slight, and dark. He reminded me of Koro Ha, in fact, and I felt a wave of nostalgia for my old tutor.

'Where do you hail from, Jhin?' I asked as he led me deeper into the garden.

The steward dipped his head. 'We are all servants of the emperor and citizens of his empire, Your Excellency.'

'Yes, but we all come from somewhere,' I said, feeling flustered but not entirely certain why. 'I can tell just by looking at you that you're not Sienese, just as anyone could tell at a glance that I hail from Nayen.'

Jhin's deference never faltered. 'Toa Alon has been long a province of the empire,' he said. 'We do not think of these things the way you seem to in Nayen.'

I recalled Koro Ha's warning, early in my education, that my allegiance would be questioned again and again, and decided to press the issue no further. What had happened in Toa Alon, I wondered, to make its people so cautious about showing their loyalty?

We soon arrived at the Pavilion of Soaring Verse, where three men lounged on couches around a narrow artificial stream that spiralled across the floor. An-Zabati servant boys waved fans of peacock feathers there while others filled cups with mild plum wine, then floated them on paper rafts down the stream. The lounging officials plucked the cups from the water to sip at their leisure.

'Welcome to An-Zabat, Hand Alder,' Voice Rill greeted me as I lowered myself to a fourth couch. He was older than Voice Golden-Finch had been, and the imperial tetragram on his forehead shone from among sun-darkened wrinkles. 'You must be tired from your journey, but you are welcome to join us while Jhin and the servants see to your luggage. We have been composing poetry in turns. A bit of idleness in the heat of the afternoon.'

'Not that there is much demand for court poetry in An-Zabat,' Hand Cinder observed. His dark blue robes were embroidered with a design resembling plates of armour. He grinned at the third man. 'I suppose one must keep the dream of a more sophisticated posting alive, eh, young Alabaster?'

Hand Alabaster adjusted his brass spectacles and tossed his long, silk-smooth hair over his shoulder. 'I can, Hand Cinder, but I fear An-Zabat may be the apex of your capacity.'

Cinder's grin broke into a guffaw. He waggled a finger at Alabaster. 'Watch out for this one, Hand Alder. You'll find no crueller wit in this city.'

'I believe it was Alabaster's turn to recite, was it not?' Rill said, reining in the conversation.

Alabaster shot Cinder a baleful look, then straightened his back and assumed an aloof, performative posture. While he gathered his thoughts, Voice Rill described the rules of their contest, explaining that each man took a turn composing and reciting a poem. If the others approved of the composition, they would take the next cup to float by on the artificial stream. If they judged the poem banal, clumsy, or otherwise unsuccessful, they would let the cup pass.

It seemed odd that all the imperial sorcerers in An-Zabat would spend an afternoon drinking, but I told myself that they were making a minor festival of my arrival and that I should be flattered. Besides, it would be imprudent to begin such important relationships with criticisms of their drinking habits.

A paper fan snapped open in Hand Alabaster's fingers. At this cue, the servants prepared the cups and paper rafts. He began his recitation.

> '*Three herons leap from their pool, taking flight.*
> *Broad wings flash silver in the sun.*
> *My hand skips across the page, smearing ink.*
> *I dip my brush and think of home.*'

He snapped the fan shut and Voice Rill plucked a cup from the stream. I reached for one as well. The poem was derivative of the classics but nonetheless evocative.

'Ha! I win!' Hand Cinder declared. 'He took the cup with his right hand! You owe me, Alabaster. The "Left-Handed Easterling", my arse!'

I looked between the two of them, feeling conspicuous. Hand Alabaster rolled his eyes at Cinder, then smiled at me apologetically. 'You are somewhat notorious, being the first Nayeni to rise to Hand of the emperor,' he said. 'We were sent your pedigree, along with the announcement of your commission and a few ... other notes. Cinder and I had a small wager about whether or not you were truly left-handed, or if that was only a nickname, considering the ... unusual placement of your tetragram.'

'Nayeni on my mother's side,' I said, trying to sound flippant while stifling mixed embarrassment and anger. I had travelled the entire breadth of the empire only to find a derogatory nickname waiting for me. 'And, to settle the wager, I am ambidextrous. My tutor saw to that after an injury in my youth.' I showed him the scars on my right hand. 'A plate shattered in my hand. Was that part of the story left out? Perhaps abandoned somewhere around Northern Capital?'

'I fought in Nayen, you know,' Hand Cinder went on as though I had not spoken. 'Aren't there still skirmishes with bandits in the highlands? Ha! Voice Golden-Finch and Hand Usher have bungled that province, haven't they?'

'No mere bandits,' I said, then bit back a sharp word and fought down thoughts of Oriole.

'Hand Cinder, you did not take a cup,' Voice Rill said.

Cinder baulked at the sudden change of subject. 'Of course not! It was his third composition about homesickness in a row.'

'You oppose the theme?' Alabaster asked, peering over the rim of his glasses.

'Yes,' Cinder said. He plucked at the embroidery on his sleeve. 'And the imagery was overwrought.'

Alabaster looked to Rill for support.

'I thought it was lovely, Alabaster,' Rill said. 'Hand Alder, would you like to recite next?'

'Ha! Yes,' Cinder said. 'Let's hear what the Easterling can do.'

Twice now Cinder had insulted me. I breathed deeply and grasped for composure. The servants had already prepared the next batch of paper boats. Cinder, Alabaster, and Rill were growing impatient. I blurted:

'Sweet plum trickles from the bottle lip ...'

My mouth hung open. Was I a child, deriving images from whatever was happening around me? The servants studied me as they poured, wondering if I had finished. I grasped for the next phrase, for something congenial, impressive without being showy, and classical without being derivative. And quickly! Cinder drummed his fingers on the table. I pressed on.

> *'Hearth fire warms our frigid bones.*
> *New companions on the mountain road.*
> *Come and sit and share my wine.'*

To my astonishment, they all took cups. Alabaster swirled his for a moment, considering. 'The rhythm was a little odd,' he muttered, then drank.

We passed the rest of the afternoon drinking and criticising each other's poetry. By the end, I felt comfortable enough to let my cup pass the third time Hand Cinder compared the spears of the Sienese legions to a crescent moon, and later when Voice Rill drunkenly stammered a pastoral verse about butterflies. At nightfall, servants brought a meal of traditional Sienese dishes: fire-pepper beef, wheat noodles with wood-ear mushrooms, and young cabbage stir-fried in garlic, all made from ingredients imported from the heartland, no doubt at vast expense. I ate, then excused myself. Jhin showed me to my rooms, which were as spacious as my father's reception hall.

Perhaps it was Hand Cinder's repeated use of the pejorative 'Easterling', or perhaps it was simple homesickness and vertigo at having been suddenly thrust into a new place and a new role. Or perhaps it was something deeper, the perpetual sense of dislocation that had dogged me since my conflicted upbringing, agitated by Cinder's thoughtless cruelty. Regardless, in the privacy of my quarters I felt the urge to practise the Iron Dance that night, something I had not done since before taking the examinations. Uninhibited after several bottles of liquor, I fell into the first forms without thinking.

After a dozen steps, I reached the part of the dance – a strike with my elbow, a forward lunge – that I had used to kill the guards in Iron Town. I let my arms fall slack. What was I doing, clinging to the traditions of Oriole's killers?

A spike of fear struck me and I checked the seals on my luggage. Nothing seemed to have been disturbed, but I had to be certain. I unpacked the volumes of the sages' writings that Koro Ha had given me, then searched through layers of documents and scrolls until I found the brush case in which I had hidden my grandmother's knife. Only when I saw that the wax seal on its latch was still intact could I relax.

My heartbeat slowed as I repacked everything, resealed the trunk, and flopped onto my bed. I told myself I was exhausted after a long journey and a few too many cups of wine. That was all this was. Drunken foolishness.

I lay awake for some time, that word – *Easterling* – winding its way through my mind. And just as sleep took me, I realised that, of the three sorcerers, Hand Cinder would most likely be tasked with my instruction in the canon.

17

Minister of Trade

The next morning, I sought out Voice Rill as soon as my head stopped pounding and my stomach settled. I found him in the Gazing Upon Lilies Pavilion, which stood in the centre of the largest pond in the citadel. Ribbons of light like mercury wafted from Voice Rill's forehead, leaving behind them the familiar heavy wake of transmission. I waited on the bridge to the pavilion until the light and wake faded as Rill finished his daily communication with the emperor.

'You impressed Hand Alabaster last night,' Rill said when I joined him. 'That is not an easy thing to do.'

I thanked him and could not help but add, 'There is a reason I was given this posting at such a young age.'

Voice Rill stroked his shaved cheeks. The tetragram on his forehead glimmered like the surface of the pond. 'Indeed. And you will go far, I think,' he said. 'You have the same eager face I wore when I was a young Hand. I first served in Toa Alon, you know – ah, perhaps you don't; it has been a province of the empire so long there is hardly reason to draw its borders on the newer maps. A beautiful country, full of lush mountains and temples built of wondrously carved stone. Gorgeous flora and fauna – some more dangerous than beautiful, though. Famous healers as well, the Toa Aloni. No longer, of course ...' He trailed off and peered out over the waters.

'I am eager to begin my work,' I said, 'and to resume my training. I had only begun to master the canon under Hand Usher. Perhaps, if he has time, Hand Alabaster could—'

'You will master the canon in due time, Hand Alder,' Voice Rill said. 'This province places heavy demands upon us. Your duties as minister of trade must come first.'

'Of course,' I replied.

My role, Voice Rill explained, would entail the setting and collection of tariffs and taxes, the monitoring of weights and measures, the management of mineral rights to the Batir Waste, and – most importantly – maintaining the tenuous relationship between the windcallers and the Sienese merchants who relied upon their windships.

'The Waste devours caravans,' Rill explained as he led me to the secluded Wind Through Grass Pavilion, which would be my office. 'Out of every three soldiers who marched from Sien to conquer this city, two died of thirst. Without the windcallers, there can be no trade in An-Zabat.'

Here, at least, was an anchor for my curiosity. To do my duty well, I would have to learn as much as possible about the windcallers and their magic – including the goddess's miracle.

'Naturally, all of this will be done through intermediaries,' Voice Rill continued. 'There is a robust bureaucracy in An-Zabat, and the merchants work closely with our subordinate ministers. We are fortunate in that we can do most of our duty from this garden, though Cinder chafes at the quantity of paperwork.'

'Surely there are some tasks better done in person out in the city,' I broke in, grasping for some legitimate excuse to wander beyond the walls. 'Meetings with the windcallers or other important An-Zabati, for example.'

Rill chuckled softly. 'You are a Hand of the emperor now,

Alder. Any An-Zabati you might wish to speak with should be summoned *here*. To go to *them* would be to belittle your office – a grave violation of propriety. No, what little business you must conduct in person will be done within this garden.'

It was a disappointing revelation, but I refused to let it dampen my mood. One question nagged at me, however – innocent enough, it seemed to me, and one that Voice Rill could answer.

'I do not mean to seem insolent,' I said, 'but why are the windcallers allowed to use their magic? In every other part of the empire – except for the rebellious north of Nayen – native magic has been added to the canon or eradicated. Hand Usher spoke of the emperor's mission to free humanity from the chaos of old gods and older superstition and bring all under his guiding rule. Is that not our purpose here?'

Voice Rill paused on the path, his eyes narrowing. The tetragram on his forehead, too, seemed to study me, as though the emperor himself had heard my question. I remembered Clear-River's threats and my mother's warnings, and it occurred to me that, while the emperor may not know the thoughts of his Hands, he surely knew the minds of his Voices. I wondered if I had offended him – Rill, the emperor, or both – and readied an apology.

'An-Zabat is unsustainable without trade,' Voice Rill said slowly. 'There is a green belt watered by the oasis, and a few crops grow there, but the city long ago swelled beyond its ability to feed itself. We have tried the ordinary methods to induct the magic of the windcallers into our canon – capturing and interrogating practitioners, and so on. No windships sailed to or from An-Zabat for a year, and the city nearly starved. We will have their secrets one day, but for the time being you will negotiate with them.'

'I will not fail the empire,' I said, cowed by the severity of his words.

Rill nodded, his expression softening. 'We do not expect you to.'

The Wind Through Grass Pavilion bulged with books and documents. Landscape paintings of southern Sien's verdant mountains hung in every wall space free of shelves and cabinets. A desk stood beneath the north-facing window, which looked out onto a dense bamboo grove that offered shade and privacy. The desk's few accoutrements included a bell for calling the servants, heavy jade paperweights engraved with a pattern of crawling vines, and a slate bowl for grinding ink. The smell of paper and old incense hung in the air and reminded me of my lessons with Koro Ha.

My own private academy, I mused.

I hesitated as the weight of my responsibilities as minister of trade, at last made real by this mountain of ledgers and books, settled on my shoulders. The life and prosperity of a city – and a significant share of the imperial economy – had been thrust into my hands with only a modicum of ceremony. There was nothing to do but get to work and hope that Hand Usher had not set me up only to mock my failure.

As I dug my way through the shelves, squinting at impressively minuscule handwriting and coughing at the dust that puffed from pages left undisturbed for years, I began to grasp An-Zabat's economic situation. Almost all of the city's income came from luxury items crossing the Batir Waste. The windships ferried ivory and furs from the frozen North, palm oil, dyes, and spices from the West, and jade, silks, and grain from the empire across the desert sea. They all made port in An-Zabat, to rest, resupply with food and water, and exchange goods. It was a lucrative business for investors and speculators, and the taxes collected in An-Zabat were triple the empire's total revenues from Nayen.

I stood at the centre of that financial whirlwind and had to keep it spinning – indeed, I had to make it spin faster and more expansively, if I could – and it spun only by the good grace of the windcallers. The empire had conquered An-Zabat, but the windcallers ruled the city's purse and food supply.

If I managed my task well, especially if I found some way to break the windcallers' monopoly, the emperor would be unable to refuse me admission to the Imperial Academy or even a Voicehood. At the very least I would become known as more than the Left-Handed Easterling. None of these possibilities offered escape from the constraints of the canon and empire, but all were paving stones on the path in their own ways – lofty goals, and ones I would never achieve if I let far-off futures distract me from the task at hand. Patience and diligence would be key to my success as a bureaucrat, and every opportunity to prove my worth, no matter how tedious, offered another step towards freedom.

I opened another ledger, spluttered and waved away a cloud of dust, and continued my work.

There was a knock at my door. I looked up from the ledgers, bleary-eyed, and wondered at the darkness in my room. I had been working past sundown, so engrossed that I had forgotten to light a lamp. Another knock roused me from my chair. I stepped carefully around the pile of ledgers I had already reviewed – higher than my knees now, but still little more than an anthill beside the mountain of volumes that burdened the shelves.

A moment of despair rooted me to the floor. If that was all the progress I had made in a long, unbroken afternoon of work, it would take me—

A third knock spared me the agony of calculation.

Jhin bowed as I opened the door. A cool breeze wafted in

after him, and I realised that my office had become not only dark but stuffy with dust, sweat, and stale air. I'd entirely forgotten to open the window.

'Ah ... Your Excellency,' Jhin said. 'I apologise for the disturbance.'

'Not at all,' I replied. My stomach gurgled and I flushed. 'Pardon me. I seem to have forgotten to eat.'

'Your dedication is admirable,' Jhin said. 'Hand Alabaster sent a message inviting you to dine with him in the Golden Fortune Pavilion this evening, but a meal could be sent to your rooms if you—'

'I would be happy to join him,' I said, eager for a reprieve from the dusty room.

'Of course, Your Excellency.' Jhin bowed again, turned smartly on his heel, and led the way.

Standing stones lined the path to a high cliff built from basalt columns brought by windship from western Sien. The Golden Fortune Pavilion, where Alabaster kept his offices, was nestled beneath the cliff. The up-curved eaves of its roof were decorated with golden medallions bearing the logograms for good luck and wealth. Incense wafted from one of the windows, mingling with the rich aroma of the meal Hand Alabaster's servants had prepared.

Alabaster rose to greet me. His office was arranged much as mine was, with over-stuffed shelves sprawling across the walls. The art in between described solemn, melancholy scenes: jagged cliffs emerging out of fog, the wintry branches of a cherry tree. We settled into our seats. A servant followed me in and filled the teapot between us from a steaming kettle.

'What do you think of your new home?' Hand Alabaster asked when the servant had left.

'The little I saw of it on the way from the harbour intrigued me,' I told him, 'though I must admit I'm daunted somewhat by the complexity of my responsibilities.' I was hopeful that I might have stumbled upon an opportunity to go out into the city. The notion of sneaking out on my own had struck me once or twice, though I could not be sure that my placement in An-Zabat was not yet another convoluted test. But if I were on official business and accompanied by another Hand, no one could accuse me of breaching propriety. 'Perhaps you and I could arrange to venture out together. You could give me a tour, help me understand our subjects more fully in order to better govern them. As minister of culture, you surely know the city as well as anyone.'

Alabaster frowned over the rim of his teacup. 'I meant the garden, Hand Alder,' he said. 'You strike me as a literary sort. More so than Cinder, certainly. I have put a great deal of effort into the garden – one of my primary duties. When our first crop of students come to sit the examinations, I want them to feel that they have stepped into the heart of Sien.'

Embarrassed, and frustrated to have been thwarted once more in my desire to see An-Zabat directly rather than glimpsed over the walls of a garden, I sipped my tea while I composed my thoughts. 'The gardens in Nayen reflect the mountainous landscape of the island, with natural slopes and pools preserved rather than artificial ones constructed, though Voice Golden-Finch certainly spared no expense in adding flourishes to suit his taste. This design adheres more to classical forms, which seems fitting to your purposes.'

Alabaster pushed his spectacles up the bridge of his nose. 'Would you have me make a garden out of sand and rocks?'

'Your method is clearly suited to An-Zabat,' I said, realising that I had offended him.

A pair of servants brought trays of food – pork hand pies, noodles in oyster sauce, and stir-fried greens and garlic. Alabaster picked absently at his meal. My stomach grumbled, but I waited for him to begin eating, respecting his role as host and mine as guest.

'I want us to be friends, Alder,' he said at last. 'Voice Rill is a respectable man, but the gulf of rank between us is too wide for friendship. Cinder and I can work together, but he is a militant brute.'

'Gladly, Alabaster,' I said, thinking of Oriole. My time in An-Zabat would be busy but need not be lonely. 'In fact, I had hoped you might continue my training in sorcery, though for the time being our friendship may be limited to shared meals. Dealing with the windcallers seems no easy task.'

Alabaster waved dismissively and filled my cup. 'No easy task, but not one to occupy much of your time. There is nothing to be done. They are a stubborn, incorrigible lot.'

He patted his brow with a handkerchief, then straightened his spectacles and gazed out of the window. 'Enough talk of this infernal province. Tell me about yourself, Alder. We should know each other if we are to be friends.'

After a month in An-Zabat, I began to craft policy. I levied new taxes on grain imports and dedicated the income to building and filling new imperial silos. A strategic reserve, I called it. A defence against any future attempt by the windcallers to close the ports and starve the city.

As Voice Rill had said, this work was done through paperwork and intermediaries. Each morning I woke to find a stack of reports on my desk. At the end of each week these were joined by a ledger totalling weekly imports and exports. I wrote instructions to my various subordinates in the Port Authority, Office of Weights and Measures, and Ministry of Revenue, stamped them with my personal seal – a parting gift from Hand Usher – and gave them to Jhin, who in turn gave them to couriers to deliver throughout the city. I never met with these subordinates. Voice Rill insisted that such a meeting was unnecessary.

'This is not a barbarian kingdom, where your ministers obey because of the force of your personality,' Voice Rill told me when I expressed my misgivings. 'Who you are, and who they are, ought not to factor into your relationship. You are their older brother within the imperial bureaucracy. It is their duty to obey.'

Alabaster and I continued our companionable meetings, always in either his office or in the Abundant Nectar Banqueting Hall, where a cloud of hummingbirds fluttered among hanging baskets of fluted snapdragons.

After a few weeks he began to show me excerpts of the letters he'd received from his betrothed. 'Do her lines seem perfunctory to you?' he would ask, handing me a poem she had composed. I always reassured him, but as I had never been romantically involved myself I felt out of my depth.

By the end of my second month in An-Zabat, my work had fallen into a consistent rhythm, and I found that my responsibilities in maintaining the day-to-day operations of my ministry were less demanding than I had anticipated. The usual reports and orders to my subordinates consumed my mornings, but most days I'd finished my work by mid-afternoon. An-Zabat was a thriving port, yet the business that crossed my desk barely changed from week to week.

Then one day, three weeks after I had created the strategic reserve, I received an unusual letter in my stack of correspondence. It was written in a steady but unpractised hand – by someone who had learned to write logograms in adulthood, I surmised. Further, it bore no stamped tetragram to identify its author. The short message itself, written in clipped, terse phrases, was direct and lacked any of the subtleties expected in official imperial correspondence.

Honoured Minister, it read. *The tax you have levied is unacceptable to us. It must be rescinded. Do not forget what happens when the empire overreaches in An-Zabat.* It was signed by a dozen names I did not recognise, written in phonetic runes.

I rang the bell on my desk to summon Jhin, who also did not recognise the names. 'My assumption would be that they are wealthy shipowners or merchants, or perhaps windcallers themselves,' he concluded, adding nothing that had not yet occurred to me.

In Nayen, we had received similar protests from time to time. They could often be resolved by a few cursory meetings, minor gifts, and simple gestures – salving the wound to the pocket-book by cultivating the injured party's sense of self-importance. I sent off a flurry of instructions to my subordinates, ordering them to identify the signatories to the petition and to do their best to placate them without giving them what they wanted, and then asked Jhin to bring my lunch.

My meal was interrupted by a familiar chill in my lungs and flush on my skin – the wake of battle sorcery – followed by the hiss and crack of lightning. Jhin refilled the cup of tea that I had spilled. 'It is only Hand Cinder at drills,' he reassured me.

Intrigued, I abandoned my half-finished meal and followed the sound to an archery range where I had seen members of the guard at practice. I found Cinder racing back and forth across the archers' line. The iron scales of his armour flashed in the sun as he leapt into the air and lashed out with a cracking whip of battle sorcery. A dummy burst apart and scattered smouldering straw across the range.

He paused at my approach. 'Hand Alder! Have you dug yourself free of the day's paperwork?'

'What remains is hardly urgent,' I said. 'I felt a wake of sorcery in the garden and couldn't contain my curiosity.'

'Rill and Alabaster forget that we're soldiers first.' The whip disappeared with a snap as he relaxed his hand. 'I spend free afternoons here, if not in the company of my lovely wife. When did you last practise sorcery?'

'Not for a year,' I admitted, thinking of Oriole on the blood-soaked ground. 'More, actually. In truth, my training in sorcery is incomplete. Hand Usher thought it best that I begin my work here in An-Zabat and suggested that one of you might teach me.'

'Well, even a neglected blade can be sharpened,' he said, then gestured towards the target dummies. 'Show me what you can do.'

The canon was still there, where I had left it the last time I'd reached for it, in Iron Town. A maze of canals transmitting – and constraining – the power to rewrite the pattern of the world. The scent of cinnamon rose as power surged through me, followed by the warmth and then the chill of battle sorcery's wake. Lightning crackled from the tetragram on my palm and blasted a dummy in half.

I held steady in the channel to shape a blade that hissed from my hand. Thin slices of straw arms and legs arced through the air. I imagined Frothing Wolf and Burning Dog's faces on the hessian heads of the dummies as the current of violence pulled me along. The scent of ozone and charred straw hung over the archery range. Sweat soaked my scholar's robes.

'Sorcery comes as naturally to you as poetry, it seems,' Cinder said and squeezed my shoulder. 'If all Easterlings are so gifted, it's no surprise the rebels have claimed a foothold in your homeland. The fourth channel is binding sorcery, and after that, shielding. I might find some time to teach you, if—'

'Thank you, Hand Cinder, but I should focus on my duties as minister,' I said, feeling a churning disquiet in my gut.

Cinder studied me, his confusion evident. 'I thought you intended to continue your education in the canon,' he said. 'I promise you, Rill and Alabaster will be far worse teachers than I.'

'I'm sure,' I said, and – as politely as I could – stepped backwards and out from under his hand. 'Only this display has reminded me how badly out of practice I am, and how much there is yet for me to learn. I should practise on my own for a while, I think, before burdening you with my ignorance.'

Cinder seemed to be formulating a response, but I did not give him time to voice it. I thanked him for his time and left him there. I wanted to learn, but not from him, and not the canon. Reaching for it again had only reminded me of its limitations. The emperor was not interested in giving his Hands knowledge or understanding, only the tools to do his bidding, even when that meant leaving a friend in the grip of death.

Hand Alabaster was no better company. His endless melancholy over his distant betrothed grew exhausting, and I began to suspect that he whiled away his days composing verse for her and doing little else. As minister of culture, he ought to have been preparing An-Zabat to hold its first imperial examinations, but when I visited his office I saw only small packages of correspondence – less than a tenth of the meagre pile I dealt with each day.

One evening, while he read and reread a lovelorn couplet, my frayed patience finally snapped. 'How many tutors have you brought to An-Zabat?' I asked him.

He peered over the top of his spectacles. 'Excuse me?'

'Are there any promising students you expect to sit for the first examinations? Have you arranged for proctors to be sent from Sien?'

'These provincial barbarians will never rival the scholars of Sien,' he replied. 'What does it matter whether there are examinations in this wretched city?'

'Nayen was once such a province,' I noted sharply, feeling heat rising in my face. Alabaster had been kind to me, but did he, like Cinder, think of me only as an Easterling, albeit one with enough literary sensibility to amuse and distract him?

Alabaster shrugged and said, 'It still is.'

I left without a word. He did not call after me, nor did he ever apologise, and I lost any hope of finding companionship in An-Zabat.

18

The Dancer

I continued to do my duty, but my life became stagnant and repetitive, punctuated only by solitary walks through the garden that served only to deepen my misery rather than lift it. The bamboo groves and shimmering ponds consumed preposterous quantities of water that might have been used to expand the city's green belts and weaken the windcallers' grip. More, An-Zabat's eternal summer robbed the garden of the seasons and their rhythm of new growth and decay, stripping it of the dynamic complexity that defined the pattern of the world. How was the empire served by this poor simulacrum of the Sienese heartland?

The monotony was broken at last by Jhin's frantic knock at my office door one bright morning, when I had just begun to work through the ledger on my desk.

'I hate to trouble you, Your Excellency.' Jhin's voice trembled with urgency beyond the closed door. 'There is ... ah ... a disturbance at the citadel gate.'

I opened the door to find Jhin dabbing sweat from his forehead, eyes wide and worried. 'Well?' I said.

'The windcallers – their leaders, that is, or at least those claiming to lead them – they are here,' Jhin said. 'At the gate. In force. Demanding an audience with you – or, rather, with the minister of trade. They did not ask for—'

'Did they give a reason?'

'No, Your Excellency.'

I brushed past Jhin, my mind full of questions, my heart pumping with excitement for the first time in what felt like months. The windcallers had most fascinated me, but I had been unable to spend more than a disappointingly scant amount of time studying them. Now they had come and demanded to see me. It would be negligent, I considered, to deny them an audience, a breach of propriety not to do my duty as their elder brother in the vast family of empire and receive them with all hospitality.

Jhin fell into step behind me. 'Voice Rill and the other Hands have also been notified,' he said, and I quickened my pace in order to reach the gate before Rill intercepted me with a speech about the importance of allowing the imperial bureaucracy to serve its function. Jhin kept pace, muttering under his quickening breath.

I took the stairs to the battlements two at a time and shouldered my way through a crowd of a dozen guards, their hands drifting towards their quivers or their bandoleers of grenades. On the plaza below, arrayed in an arc before the gate, stood six An-Zabati: four men, their burly arms inked with whorled tattoos, and two women. One of the women wore a sword at her hip. The other surprised me more, for I recognised her immediately by her short-cropped ringlets and the silvered scarf draped across her shoulders.

'Are you the one we seek?' said one of the men, old and grey-haired but with a voice that boomed to the top of the battlement as easily as across the deck of a windship. He spoke Sienese, thickly accented.

'I am Hand Alder, minister of trade to An-Zabat,' I shouted back, my voice like a reed flute in comparison.

The grey-haired windcaller nodded. 'I am Katiz. We should speak. I am happy to do so here, if I must.'

As he finished speaking, I heard the clank of armoured foot-steps on the stairs behind me. Hand Cinder appeared on the battlement, arrayed in glittering scale. He studied me, arched an eyebrow, and crossed his arms, apparently satisfied to spectate, unless my bungling tipped this political incident into violence.

A crowd had begun to gather, peering cautiously from the mouths of alleyways and the doorways and windows of nearby homes. Not the most conducive audience to a sensitive conver-sation about economy and politics, which I was sure this would become.

'My steward will escort you to the audience hall,' I said. 'I will meet you there.'

Again, Katiz nodded.

'Your Excellency, this is—' Jhin protested.

'Jhin, if you would be so kind,' I said, again brushing past him, and Hand Cinder, to mount the stairs.

'Good luck, Alder,' Cinder said, then shouted: 'You heard the Hand! Get that gate open! And I want an honour guard with the steward. Move your arses!'

The guards sprang into motion while I hurried as fast as dignity would allow towards the audience hall at the centre of the citadel. Only moments after I had taken my seat on one of the four chairs atop the hall's dais and draped my stole of office around my neck, the windcallers arrived, led by a fidgety Jhin and flanked by a dozen soldiers, their hands on the hilts of their swords.

'I'm sorry, I must insist, before you enter the presence of the Hand—' Jhin said.

'No!' the sword-bearing An-Zabati woman blurted in Sienese. Then, to Katiz, she went on in An-Zabati: 'I will not let you walk into the den of our enemy unguarded!'

'And I would not expect you to,' I interjected in An-Zabati. The windcallers all paused in their stride to hear me speak their language.

The younger woman – the dancer I had seen when I first arrived in the city – burst out laughing. 'He speaks like he has a mouthful of sand!' she said in her own tongue. 'But at least he *has* learned to speak. It is good for rulers to know what their subjects say, yes?'

Jhin, uncomprehending, looked from the sword-bearer to me, his face pleading.

'It's all right, Jhin,' I said. 'Have these guards wait outside. I have the canon for my defence. And I doubt these people have come to the citadel to instigate bloodshed. They know that would only cost us all, and the people of this city the most.'

Jhin hesitated, then bowed and led the guards – fingers still twitching at their weapons – out into the garden, to lurk nearby in case this audience did, indeed, spark sudden violence. The windcallers fanned out before me, standing with crossed arms and impatient postures, unaccustomed to the formalities of court.

'Now then,' I began, again speaking An-Zabati and attempting an aloof posture even as my pulse hammered in my ears. 'Tell me your concerns, that the empire might address them.'

The dancer covered her mouth. 'Please,' she said in Sienese, stifling laughter. 'We like that you have learned the tongue of the Waste, but we all speak the tongue of the conquerors better, I think.'

'Our concern *is* the empire,' Katiz put in.

'What, in particular?' I asked, speaking Sienese as the dancer had requested, though that stifled laugh had chafed.

'You have made a new tax,' Katiz said. 'Grain. You fill silos with it. Do you think we cannot see what you are doing? Do you think we do not understand why?'

I recalled the letter I had received some weeks ago, under-signed by unknown names. 'I received your petition,' I said. 'Were you unsatisfied by the efforts taken to ease your concerns?'

'What efforts?' Katiz said. 'The tax must be rescinded.'

'It is a common practice to keep a grain reserve,' I said, and silently resolved to send out reprimands to the bureaucrats I had tasked with solving this problem, and possibly a demotion or two. 'Such a reserve protects against disruption of the food supply by famine, war, drought—'

'Drought?' the dancer said, that lilt of laughter still in her voice. 'I can see how you might forget, coddled as you are in this garden behind your walls, but it does not rain in An-Zabat.'

'I meant a drought in the heartland,' I said, fighting to maintain a diplomatic tone. 'In which case, the strategic reserve will stabilise the price of grain, while it lasts, and keep the poor of this city from starving.'

'If there is a drought in the east, we will buy from the west,' Katiz said. 'So it has always been. Let us be honest with each other. It is not for the sake of the poor that you do this; it is so that the next time you pluck windcallers from the harbour, chain them in your dungeons, and do all you can to strip their power from them, we will not be able to fight back as we once did.'

'You will not be able to starve the city, you mean,' I said sharply. 'I must protect against any disruption in the food supply. My concern is for the people of An-Zabat.'

'The people of An-Zabat!' the dancer said. 'What do you know of them? What have you seen of their lives? They do not fear starvation – they fear *you*. Come out into the city and I will show you the people of An-Zabat.'

Heat rose in my face. She had struck too close to my own shame, my own frustration with the garden. She was right, of course, yet my isolation from their lives was not my fault but another limitation in my life forced upon me. I wanted to tell her of Voice Rill's prohibitions, to argue against the accusation of indolence she implied, but I dared not so openly violate propriety while holding an audience.

'You are bold to threaten one who could order your death,' I said, venting my frustrations in a somewhat less productive way.

The sword-bearer's hand fell to her weapon. I felt a chill down my spine in the wake of windcalling, though the air in the hall was still.

'Oh?' the dancer shot back. 'Are you so desperate to see how long your *strategic reserve* will last?'

'Atar, enough,' Katiz cut in. 'Shazir, take your hand off your sword. We are not here to start a war but to maintain peace.'

'And how do you suggest we do that?' I asked.

'You created the problem,' Katiz said. 'You must solve it.'

I considered that, and my options, and arrived at a solution. 'I cannot give up the strategic reserve entirely,' I said. 'Regardless of what you think, it does serve a benevolent purpose, one key to the stability of this city – a bulwark against any number of possible tragedies.'

'And we cannot allow you to have it,' Katiz said.

I thought for a moment. 'Then I will give it to you,' I said.

The windcallers exchanged baffled glances.

'Consider it a gesture of good faith,' I said. 'I am genuine in my desire to help the people of An-Zabat and to ensure the prosperity of this city. I will continue to levy the tax on grain, and my agents will continue to fill the silos, but you will be in charge of defending and distributing that reserve.'

They held a brief, whispered conference. I leaned back in my chair, watched them, and thought through the explanation for my actions that I would offer to Voice Rill.

'I say this is a trap,' Shazir muttered in An-Zabati, loud enough for me to hear. Katiz chided her and they resumed their hushed conversation. All the while, the dancer – Atar – stared at me, her emerald eyes bright with curiosity.

'You are not Sienese,' she said suddenly. 'Where do you hail from?'

'My mother was Nayeni.' I showed the palm of my left hand. 'Whatever my parentage, I am Hand of the emperor, am I not?'

'Perhaps,' she said. 'But this is not something they would do. You think differently, Nayeni, with wisdom the empire lacks.'

'And who are you to stand with these masters of trade and magic and negotiate with me?' I said. 'I saw you dancing for coin in the bazaar.'

She answered with a smile and my heart stuttered. 'As I said, Nayeni, you know very little of An-Zabat.'

'Very well,' Katiz announced, turning away from the other windcallers and back towards me. 'It is a good compromise, though we will not tolerate any interference in our distribution from the silos. We may see fit to use this reserve in ways the empire would not consider.'

'Very well,' I said, dragging my gaze from Atar, feeling a little dizzy and a little insulted and *very* interested in seeing her dance again. 'As long as my bookkeepers are kept informed of how much goes into the reserve and how much is distributed.'

Katiz nodded and put out his hand, his first two fingers slightly bent. 'It is agreed, then.'

I stepped down from the dais and took his outstretched fingers with my own. Atar quirked an eyebrow. I could almost hear her say, *You speak our language. Of course you know something of our customs.*

Their business done, the windcallers left the audience hall. Atar was the last to go, and at the threshold she glanced over her shoulder, as if to invite me for a third time out into her city. She left the scent of lavender in her wake.

No sooner had the windcallers left than Voice Rill summoned me to the Gazing Upon Lilies Pavilion. As before, the light of transmission flickered from his brow. This time, he bade me approach before severing the mental tie between himself and the emperor.

'Your creativity is boundless,' Voice Rill said. 'You must forgive your superiors, who sometimes fail to grasp the intricacies of such strategy. Would you please explain why you have given away our best defence against the windcallers – one that you devised, I might add?'

I bowed, for I spoke not only to the Voice but to the emperor himself. 'Imagine if conflict between the empire and the windcallers breaks out into open war. What will they do then?'

'Close the ports,' Voice Rill replied. 'Starve the city. As they did in the past.'

'Indeed,' I agreed. 'At which point Hand Cinder might lead the garrison out to seize the silos we have been so dutifully filling. The fighting will cost us, yes, but the windcallers cannot hope to defend the silos against our legions. They will have no choice but to abandon the strategic reserve, and we will capture it, in which case it will have served its original purpose.'

'Or they could put the silos to the flame,' Rill said.

'They could,' I said. 'But think of the people, Voice Rill. It is one thing to stand behind the windcallers when they refuse to sail until their captured fellows are released. It is another to watch them burn perfectly good grain while their children wail and their cheeks grow hollow with hunger. If the windcallers burn the strategic reserve ... well, the citadel larder and the garrison are always kept well stocked, are they not? We will hide behind these walls while the very flame that lights the silos ignites the rage of the An-Zabati, and they will side with us. Let us see how long the windcallers can hold out against the hatred of their own people.'

'You have given them their own undoing,' Voice Rill said. A troubled expression crossed his face, as though he had found some fault with my plan, but it resolved into a placid smile.

'Well done, Hand Alder. I am glad we were not mistaken in giving you this responsibility.'

I bowed, for I heard in his words an echo of the emperor, and then excused myself. I should have felt satisfaction as I walked back to my office to resume the day's paperwork – which would now include the official orders transferring control of the silos to Katiz and his windcallers. Instead I was needled all that day by the feeling that I had overlooked something. Something in Voice Rill's expression, or in the political situation of the city. And the dancer's words lingered in the back of my mind – *you know very little of An-Zabat* – and with it her invitation, and the curve of her neck.

By the end of the next day, those lingering words had become a constant echo against the walls of my skull, taunting me while I plodded through the day's paperwork and wandered the gardens, seeking something to occupy my mind and chase away the lingering disquiet the windcallers' visit had stirred.

While wandering, I spied a group of porters bearing crates of various supplies, arriving by a servants' gate in the wall of the garden, and was struck by a bolt of inspiration. Here was a way out into the city which did not require Voice Rill's permission. Dozens of people must pass through it each day, I reasoned, not only to bring supplies into the garden but also to deliver the correspondence that travelled in a constant stream between us ministers and our subordinates. Getting back into the garden might prove more difficult, of course, but as I returned to my rooms a plan had already begun to form. First, I summoned Jhin.

'I would like some clothing in the An-Zabati style,' I said when he answered my summons, doing my best to hide my excitement beneath a cool, mildly annoyed detachment.

'Might I ask why, Your Excellency?' he said.

'They seem better suited to this climate than these robes,' I told him, flicking out my sleeves. 'My rooms become stifling in the heat of the day.'

'I see.' Jhin dipped his head slightly. 'I can assure you, Your Excellency, that while An-Zabati clothes are indeed well suited to the desert, the wardrobe I have selected for you is made of the finest silk and tailored not only to this climate but to the dignity of your office.'

'The embroidery itches as well,' I said. 'I'm not used to all this gold and silver thread, you know. Must I always dress as though I might receive the emperor himself at any moment? No, a plain kaftan will do.'

Jhin blinked, his composure beginning to crack. 'You would dress like a servant, Your Excellency?'

I sighed, seasoning my voice with just a hint of exasperation. 'Put a few lines of red or silver or what have you on the cuffs, if you must.'

'Your Excellency, I—'

'As my steward, your task is to bring me what I require, is it not?' I said. 'My discomfort distracts me from my work, which slows the business of the empire. Now, if you would be so kind? The sooner I am able to dress in something that breathes a little better, the sooner I can review these new import taxes.'

After another moment of hesitation, he bowed and departed, returning that evening with a bundle in his arms and a mildly defeated expression.

That night I hardly slept, yet I rose with the dawn of the desert sun to dress myself in the kaftan Jhin had brought me and venture, at last, out into the city. So giddy was I that I nearly forgot to take one of the unopened reports from my desk – still bound in its scroll case and with the wax seal of whoever had sent it to me intact. It was vital to my return; a sealed message for Hand Alder would be my ticket back through the servants' gate at the end of the day.

I had the presence of mind to snatch a pair of workmen's gloves on my way, pilfered from an unlocked storeroom full of gardeners' tools. The common people of An-Zabat were unlikely to know my face, but they would certainly recognise the tetragram from the banners that fluttered up on their obelisks. I completed the disguise by pulling my hair into a tight bun, a peasants' hairstyle that would deflect the recognition of any gate guard or servant who had seen my face before but who would never believe that I might so debase myself.

Sure enough, the two guards at the servants' gate let me pass without as much as a second glance, though my heart thundered against my ribs while I pulled the gate open and stepped through into an alleyway already echoing with the sounds of the city.

After the quiet seclusion of the garden, An-Zabat nearly overwhelmed me. Heat radiated from the packed earth of the crowded streets. Raised voices haggled over prices. Crowds cheered for performers. As I neared the oasis, the roar of cascading water from Naphena's urn rose above the cacophony, and the air filled with the smells of dry-spiced meats, the tang of oil and salt and sugar, of herds and sweat and excrement.

I began my immersion into An-Zabati culture with a survey of the food stalls scattered throughout the oasis bazaar. First, lamb dry-rubbed with black pepper and fire-roasted till juices dripped down the skewer. Then a cup of brined olives that stung my nose. As I moved from stall to stall, I soaked in the sights of the bazaar – men haggling over bolts of cloth, a fruit seller glaring at a nearby pack of bedraggled children, a tumbler juggling knives in flashing arcs while a thin-limbed monkey scampered between the onlookers, holding out a basket that was slowly filling with coins.

For a time I stood in Naphena's shadow, studying the statue. It was nearly as tall as the glittering obelisks that towered over the city, rising, it seemed, from every crossroads. If the waters of the Blessed Oasis were indeed the product of some ancient and wonderous magic, Naphena's fountain should have left a wake to rival the emperor's own. Yet the statue and the pool left no wake at all.

I nursed my disappointment with a bag of honey-candied dates and resumed my wander through the bazaar, hoping that some insight into the puzzle of the oasis would strike while my mind was distracted, until I felt a sudden, brisk chill on the back of my neck. I turned towards it and saw a ripple in the air like light on glass and the flash of silken scarves glimmering in the sun.

Atar, the dancer.

Power flowed from spiral tattoos on the backs of her fingers. As her hands twirled, she wove the wind like the threads of a tapestry, making the scarves swim through the air as though of their own accord. While I watched her, two preposterous, thrilling thoughts occurred to me. First, that she was a person I could learn from, genuinely *learn*, outside the rigid structures of the canon. The second thought arrived as a jolt through my chest as she spun, throwing her hair across the slope of her neck, and met my gaze.

Her emerald eyes widened in astonishment, and her next few movements held a stiffness born of confusion and surprise, but she found again the rhythm of her dance. She followed it to the last step, then bowed to wild applause and a rain of coin that filled the basket at her feet.

All the while, her gaze never left me.

If I had been able to pull myself away, what might have happened differently? How might the world have failed to change?

She gathered up her basket and her audience dispersed to rejoin the market crowd. She crossed the river of bodies as gracefully as she'd danced and came over to stand beside me, her head cocked and eyes narrowed.

'Minister of Trade,' she greeted me in Sienese and jangled the basket of coins. 'Did you linger to collect your tax from this poor street performer?'

'I hoped for some hint of why a street performer might stand beside the windcallers and treat with the empire,' I replied in An-Zabati.

She laughed, a sound that left a wake through me like magic.

'As I said, there is much you do not know,' she said, following me into her own tongue. 'I must confess, I did not expect you to accept my invitation.'

'We are both more than we appear,' I said. 'And, as you have so rightly pointed out, I have much to learn of An-Zabat. Would you care to teach me?'

'You think I have nothing better to do than give you a tour?' she said, glaring as though I had offered some grave insult.

I stammered, trying to think of a retort, put off balance by her sudden shift in tone and by the strange, anxious wonder she evoked in me. Seeing my discomfort, she laughed again, then turned on her heel and set off into the city.

'Come, then,' she said. 'Few of the deeper truths of An-Zabat can be found in this bazaar.'

Atar led me through a maze of alleyways and narrow streets, deeper into the city. Soon the houses we passed bore the old scars of conquest: the jagged burns of battle sorcery, mud bricks torn by an errant sword, a building shattered by chemical grenades. Human waste ran in the gutters. There were still crowds, but all the life seemed to have gone out of the people we saw. They walked with hunched backs or huddled in doorways with bottles and pipes that trailed a sweet blue smoke. Atar pressed a few coins into the hands of beggars and urchin children. She did nothing to hide the wealth she had carried from the bazaar and showed no fear of robbery.

For my part, I constantly fought the urge to glance about me, wary of hidden knives. With a backward glance I spotted a pair of bulky figures draped in white kaftans, with swords hanging from their hips. My first glimpse of them sent a spike of fear through my heart, dressed and armed as they were in the An-Zabati style. Accomplices of Atar's, perhaps, here to seize the chance to kidnap a Hand of the emperor and hold him for political ransom. Or mere brigands, spotting me as an outsider in their city, ready to pounce the moment I stepped into some secluded alleyway.

But a second glance revealed tell-tale signs that at once assuaged my fear and filled me with a new, different paranoia. Beneath their hoods, their faces were Sienese, and they walked with the familiar gait and bearing of Sienese infantrymen. Guards from the citadel, then, who had tailed me since my departure. They followed closer now, likely feeling the same nervousness I did.

Clearly, I had not been as successful in my subterfuge as I had thought. Had Voice Rill sent them, or Jhin? A steward had some command of the household guard, after all. Regardless, an awkward conversation with one or the other would be waiting for me when I returned, and there was little I could do about my unwanted escort now.

'There was poverty here before,' Atar said, pulling my attention back to the city around me, 'but An-Zabat was not broken like this. These people had steady work, even if only as labourers. Only the windcallers can live as they did before.'

I paused in the mouth of an alleyway and watched a child kneeling on hands and knees, staring hawk-like at a refuse pile. A tawny rodent darted from the pile. The child snatched at it, but the rodent slipped his grasp and darted away.

'I've seen the ledgers,' I said, forcing my eyes away from the pitiful child. 'An-Zabat is a thriving port. More money flows through this city than any other province of the empire.'

'An apt description,' she said. 'It flows through, as water flows through the canals from the Blessed Oasis, but very little leaks out and trickles down. After the conquest, trading rights were stripped from the local merchants and given to their Sienese rivals. An-Zabati windcallers ferry goods to and from the city, An-Zabati middlemen buy and sell them in the bazaar, and the fortunate few make a living, but it is the Sienese who profit, who amass the wealth born of all that labour. And all around them, the city is dying.'

We went on and witnessed scene after scene of desperation and suffering. Youths clawing at each other over a scrap of dried meat. Fathers tearing bread into thin pieces which they handed to their children, keeping nothing for themselves. Gaunt mothers clutching babes who watched us with hollow eyes.

I had seen such things in Iron Town, but that had been a place besieged, its suffering an artefact of chaos and war. Which of my subordinates should have written that, despite the fortunes that changed hands in the Barge Bazaar, children starved not an hour's walk away?

I should have known. I had seen the ledgers, the names of the importers and exporters who owned the goods that moved through An-Zabat. Sienese names.

'I'm sorry,' I said.

She cocked her head. 'For what?'

'For whatever part I have played in this suffering.'

'You are minister of trade,' she said. 'You stand at the centre of it.'

Her words stung and made me flush.

'The empire gives you your task and you perform it, *Hand of the emperor*,' she went on. 'This is what you agreed when you accepted your position here. Did you not know the nature, and consequences, of your work?'

Guilt gnawed at me and I recalled the Classic of Wealth and

Labour, in which Traveller-on-the-Narrow-Way wrote that a merchant is no better than a bandit if his wealth does not elevate the farmers and craftsmen who are the backbone of the empire. What was I doing as minister of trade, collecting tariffs and taxes to pay for the garden I lived in and the luxuries of the Eternal Citadel, if not hoarding wealth that could have fed these children?

I had spent the bulk of my life cloistered in relative wealth, first in my father's gardens, then at Voice Golden-Finch's, and now in the imperial citadel of An-Zabat. I had known of poverty, of course, but in a world where anyone could improve their lot through success in the imperial examinations, it was easy to ignore. But what hope would these desperate children have to compete against those like Pinion and me, whose entire lives were devoted to study, whose fathers hired skilled tutors, who never had to spend an afternoon sifting through rubble and refuse to find their next meal?

I remembered Lu Clear-River, now with sympathy I had never felt before. It must have seemed a cruel joke that he, a peasant's son, should struggle to the heights of Sienese society only to be kept from the highest position by the son of a wealthy merchant.

'Is it any surprise that many in this city hate the empire?' Atar said suddenly, drawing me back to the present. We stood in an empty square that might once have housed a market. Now it was only a field of dust and ruin, barren and dark in the deepening twilight.

'You speak as though we alone are to blame for their suffering,' I said. Something within me refused to accept such a one-sided history. 'As you said, there has always been poverty. Before the empire, was An-Zabat ruled by benevolent kings willing to empty their storehouses to feed the poor? And what of the windcallers? They continue to grow fat from trade, and their struggle against the empire closed the ports for a year. How does that help a starving child?'

'Many have died in the struggle,' she said, her voice hardening, 'but their deaths were *naphnet*, and they knew this. They were willing to die for a greater cause. If the empire supplants the windcallers, that will be the end of us all.'

'A story that serves the windcallers,' I said, furrowing my brow at this word, *naphnet*, which I had not encountered before. Its meaning was clear enough – a reference to the goddess and the sacrifice she had made to create the oasis.

'A story based in truth,' she said. 'The windcallers travel far, Nayeni. They have seen what happens when your empire closes its fist.'

Her gaze drifted, fixed onto something behind me, and hardened. 'You have helped the people by giving up your silos,' she said. 'That was well done, and that kindness is the only reason I offer you these truths, for I think there is some chance you might listen. There is more I would show you, if you wish to see. Meet me at the bazaar, two nights from now, at dusk. And come alone.'

She crossed the empty square, then headed down another narrow street. The sun had set by now, and the city seemed painted in black and purple ink. When she had vanished from sight, I turned and saw the white, shapeless forms of my unwanted escort, lurking at the edges of the square, the only figures in sight.

I sighed and waved for them to join me. 'I hope you paid attention to the turnings,' I said. 'I've no idea where we are.'

19

Firecaller

The next two days passed as slowly and heavily as an over-burdened barge. My morning paperwork had never been more simplistic or routine, though I now read it with a more know-ing eye and saw the signs of Sienese prosperity and An-Zabati destitution that I should have noted all along. Two thoughts occupied my mind, circling round each other: excitement for my reunion with Atar and a fretful question – how would Voice Rill react to my venture out into the city?

Just after noon on the second day, I had my answer.

He came to me, this time, which was enough cause for con-cern on its own. I was finishing my day's work, and beginning to plot my evening escape from the citadel, when I heard Jhin's excited, pleading voice. Then the door swung open and Voice Rill stepped through.

'Hand Alder,' Voice Rill said, a beatific smile on his face and his hands folded into the sleeves of his robe. 'I heard from gossiping soldiers that you spent a day exploring the city in the company of a dancing girl. How is it that I am hearing this second hand and not from you, when it is such an … uncom-mon activity?'

So, Jhin had sent the guards who followed me after all. That, or Rill wanted to obfuscate the degree to which he kept an eye on me. If the latter, what did it mean that he had waited two days for this confrontation?

'I thought it beneath your notice,' I said, summoning the justification I had rehearsed. 'Surely I am not the first minister of trade to take an interest in the daily lives and marketplaces of the people he governs? The dancer offered to give me a tour of the city and I accepted.'

'A tour that included less-than-savoury locales?' Rill pressed.

'It did,' I admitted. 'But as Traveller-on-the-Narrow-Way wrote, "The most objectionable of truths carries beauty to the honest man." I want to craft policies that will make this city thrive as it never has before, Voice Rill. I cannot repair flaws and bolster weaknesses that I do not see.'

'That may be,' Rill said, 'but we had previously discussed your venturing into the city and I made myself *very* clear.'

'I did not venture out officially as minister of trade or Hand of the emperor,' I said. 'There was no damage done to the prestige of my office. No violation of propriety. I only went out and saw the city for myself to better understand it.'

'The reports of your subordinates are insufficient?' Rill said. 'Then fire them. Find better ones.'

'There are things I might notice that any subordinate might not,' I said firmly. 'I was given this post, Voice Rill. I must be allowed to fulfil its duties to the best of my ability, and that means seeking out the information I require. I cannot do my work while hamstrung, and if you mean to so restrict me, I fear there may be no path forwards but for me to tender my resignation and seek a position elsewhere in the empire, if only to preserve my own reputation.'

He stared at me, perhaps wondering if I was bluffing – a question I pondered as well while I met his stare, hoping my face betrayed no sign of my racing heartbeat. If I did, indeed, resign, there was a very real risk that the path to the academy might be forever closed. I might be condemned to a life in some far-flung but peaceable corner of the Sienese heartland, mediating trade disputes, never given cause to wield magic, let alone wrestle with its depths for mastery.

'I expect to be kept *informed*,' Rill said, and relief washed through me. 'I should not be learning of your doings, whatever they may be, by way of rumour. You are young, and new to your post, and energetic – which is an admirable quality. I trust that I will be notified before you take any similar action in future?'

'Of course,' I assured him. 'If you will allow it, I intend to return tonight. There are sides to the city that only emerge after dark, my guide tells me. I would see those.'

Voice Rill's brow crinkled, though the lines of his forehead did not touch the tetragram branded there. 'She may be luring you, Hand Alder. It is a common tactic, often effective against young men such as yourself.'

'She may be,' I answered, somewhat embarrassed to have my attraction to Atar brought up so frankly. 'But I will keep my wits about me. And if things go badly awry, I am more than able to defend myself.'

'And you will have guards, of course.'

'If you insist, Voice Rill,' I said carefully. 'Those who accompanied me before were … less than subtle, and I worry that the city reshapes itself to their presence. I want to see the city as it is, left to its own devices.'

'Was this your guide's idea?' Rill asked thoughtfully.

'She suggested it,' I admitted, 'but I agreed.'

'Travelling the streets at night, in the company of a woman …' He breathed a heavy sigh, shook his head, and refreshed his smile. 'Unorthodox, to say the least. Bordering on a violation of propriety. I trust you will hide your tetragram, to avoid rumours of a minister's dalliance with a dancing girl?'

Heat rose in my cheeks. 'Of course,' I said. 'And—'

Voice Rill waved a hand. 'Whether it *is* a dalliance – as Alabaster thinks it must be – or not, you've no need to explain yourself to me. I was young once, long ago – hard to believe though that may be. And I think that there is value in seeing things first hand, not only by way of reports and ledgers. So, very well. You may conduct this … research, if that is what it is. Who knows?' His voice took on a conspiratorial tone. 'The girl may fall for *you*, and perhaps she has her own secrets. The windcallers, I am sure, spend time among such women. She may know things of value to the empire.'

'She may,' I said. 'Thank you, Voice Rill. I will keep you informed of any such discoveries.'

The rest of the afternoon passed in an excited flurry. At dusk I donned my peasant's clothes, pulled on my gloves, and told Jhin not to expect my return until morning.

Atar sat on the rim of the Blessed Oasis, her basket of coins in her lap. Her face brightened, and I felt a thrill at its brightening, when she spotted me through the thinning crowd.

'I was about to leave without you,' she said.

'A Hand of the emperor is never late,' I told her. 'In fact, you should be honoured that I've come out to meet you, rather than summoning you to the audience hall.'

'If you did, I would not come,' she replied and slipped down from the rim of the fountain with a jangle of coins and a bounce of curls. She peered through the crowd behind me and smiled when she was satisfied that no guards lurked in my wake. 'Well. We have an appointment to keep.'

Our winding path led to an obelisk that rose from the roof of a broad two-storey building. A brazier in the plaza in front of the building threw deep shadows across its scarred sandstone walls, which showed signs of hasty repair. A tall, broad-shouldered silhouette stood guard at the door. I did not recognise her until she drew the tulwar at her hip.

'Put that away, Shazir,' Atar said.

'Are you sun-addled, winddancer?' Shazir asked, pointedly *not* putting her sword away. 'He is Hand of the emperor! We stood in his audience hall not two weeks ago! Why is he in your company?'

'He is more than that,' Atar said. 'He asked to be shown the truths of our city, and he came alone. Nothing he will see tonight is secret or forbidden.'

'No,' Shazir said, 'but it is *ours*.'

'He should see the good he has done,' Atar argued. 'And he should see what stands to be lost if his empire kills An-Zabat, as it has killed all else it has conquered.' She placed the back of her hand on the flat of Shazir's blade and pushed it aside. 'At the very least, he is the winddancer's guest. You are a blade-of-the-wind. War is yours, but the dance is mine.'

Shazir's expression soured, but she stepped aside, sheathing her weapon, and I felt a coil of tension unwind in my shoulders. Atar's company was thrilling, and exploring An-Zabat was more stimulating than anything I had done since coming to the city, but I had not for a moment forgotten that I was among people with every reason to hate the empire, protected only by Atar's influence, my own prowess, and the threat of imperial retribution for any harm that might befall me.

The interior of the building was spacious and open, a single vaulted hall with stairs leading up to balconies and smaller rooms, and lit by lamps in sconces that ran up the four corners of the hall. Several dozen people huddled around low tables while twenty or thirty more stood in a line along one wall. At the head of the line, an old man ladled thin soup into wooden bowls. The pale shape of a woman marked the wall behind him, indicating where a statue had once stood. A few women dressed in simple robes dyed the blue of sky and spring water oversaw the line and offered coins to some of the more desperate-seeming patrons.

'This was once a temple to our goddess,' Atar explained. 'Not every obelisk rises from such a place, but many do. When the empire fought the windcallers, they stripped this place of all its finery.'

It was nothing like the Temple of the Flame, but when I looked at the silhouette on the wall and the high, vaulted ceiling, I felt the same knee-weakening awe that had struck me on the first night my grandmother had led me into the forest, when I'd first come face to face with the wolf gods.

'I have read the story of Naphena,' I said. 'She is not like the gods of Nayen. They are wild, dangerous, and cruel as often as kind.'

'She was a woman before she was a goddess,' Atar said. 'A woman gifted with great power that threatened the gods, and so they forbade her to use it. Yet she taught us what she could, and in her final act gave us this city, and ascended to stand rival to the gods who once hated her.'

'She made the oasis, did she not?' I noted. 'It's a fascinating thing. Clearly magic, but it leaves no wake in the world.'

'Fascinating indeed,' she agreed with a lilt of amusement. 'Katiz, windcaller and master of a dozen ships – as well as the patron of this place – feeds the poor here in honour of Naphena, and has been doing so for many years. Of course, the portions are slightly larger than usual lately, thanks to your granaries.'

Atar approached one of the blue-clad priestesses, who took her basket of earnings and disappeared up a stairwell, and I realised that Katiz had outflanked me. If the windcallers had cause to close the city and burn the silos, the people would blame the empire, not those who had been feeding them all along. I thought myself clever, but Atar was right: I knew very little of An-Zabat.

Strangely, I did not find these thoughts troubling. I felt only the familiar, mild sting of having lost a game of Stones to a skilled opponent. A bittersweet sting, reminding me of nights spent over a Stones board with wine and a pair of mismatched cups.

'You are smiling,' Atar said. 'Has the hard heart of an imperial minister been touched by this show of charity?'

'My intention was always to help the people. I am glad Katiz has done just that,' I said, and meant it.

Atar studied me curiously. 'There is more to see, Nayeni. You asked who I was to stand side by side with the windcallers and treat with you. Would you like that question answered?'

'I would,' I said.

She nodded and led me from the temple, then down another alleyway that ended in a heavy brass door set into what looked like a squat sandstone block. Beyond the door, stairs led downwards. Atar took a lantern from a wall sconce and descended.

'What is this?' I asked, lingering in the mouth of the stairway.

'You do not fear the dead, do you?' she called back, her voice echoing.

The light from her lantern hardly pierced the shadows around us. Where it did, skulls, carved or real – it was impossible to tell in the dark – peered out from recesses in the walls. I quickened my steps to keep close to Atar, and to put space between myself and the shadows.

We walked until my feet began to ache and my sense of time became distended. At last, after what felt like hours, our path ended in another brass door, which opened onto the crisp, dry air of a desert night. We stood above a sandstone canyon that echoed with the rhythm of reed pipe, sitar, and drum. A glow on the eastern horizon lit the silhouetted obelisks of An-Zabat.

Below us, in the light of a full moon and a sky brilliant with stars, men and women had formed a ring around a lone figure who leapt and spun to the music.

'This is the Valley of Rulers,' Atar said, 'where the old kings of An-Zabat dwell.'

The walls of the valley were speckled with round stone doors without handles. Atar led me down to the gathering, where the dancer was returning to the circle and another was taking his place.

Katiz approached us. He recognised me with a flicker of concern across his otherwise stolid face.

'New feet for the dance,' Atar said.

'The imperial minister of trade?' Katiz asked.

'You know the good he has done,' Atar said.

The windcaller regarded me, stroking his thick beard, the colour of straw at the ends, fading to silver around his mouth.

'The empire is devious,' he said. 'Do you trust him?'

'Not entirely,' Atar replied. I felt a pang of hurt and stifled it for its foolishness. 'But the dance is my dominion, as your ships are yours, and I would show it to him.'

He put up his hands in surrender. 'Very well,' he said. 'But all who come to the circle must dance.'

'He will dance,' Atar assured him.

With a last, lingering look, the windcaller returned to his place in the circle. The woman in the centre leapt in a flash of bangles.

Atar took my wrist – I shivered, and not just from the coolness of her hand or the desert night air – and people made space for us in the circle. 'You can dance, can you not?'

'That seems like something we ought to have discussed earlier,' I said, hardly thinking, distracted by the leaping woman, the hand on my wrist, the smell of honey and lavender and salt.

Atar stared at me, mouth open halfway between shock and bemusement. 'Are you saying you cannot?'

I gestured to myself with an acrobat's flourish. 'Do I look like the sort of man who dances?'

Atar laughed, and I grinned like a fool. 'Why yes, Nayeni, you do.'

The woman in the circle landed with a jangle of bracelets, then returned to her place. The man to her left stepped out to take his turn. He drew a tulwar much like the one Shazir carried, then began his dance, a whirling, lashing spin around the edge of the ring.

'He is a blade-of-the-wind – a warrior windshaper, like Shazir,' Atar informed me. 'The one before him was a merchant.'

'They're not all windshapers?' I said, considering that term. There was only one word for An-Zabati magic in Sienese, for only one use of that magic was of interest to the empire.

'Many are. Most are not. Those who can guide the wind lead the dance, but there are as many dances as there are walks of life, for the wind moves us all.' There was a proud tilt to her chin. 'It is my task to know every dance, and to teach them.'

The blade-of-the-wind landed with a low sweep. The sand where his sword passed shifted, swirled by a gust that flowed from its edge and sent the brisk wake of windcalling down my spine.

He changed places with the next dancer, a young house-keeper. She was thin, and I wondered how well the larders of her house were stocked, yet she danced with grace and energy. A shepherdess followed her, then a farmer – a rare and re-spected profession in An-Zabat – then a windcaller from a ship at harbour, and so on. Each dance was unique, and Atar told me that each one had been passed down through generations.

'Before Naphena made the Blessed Oasis, our people roved the Waste in tribes,' she said. 'When two tribes met, they would dance beneath the moon and share water, and in this way come to know and trust one another. Once, every soul in An-Zabat knew their dance, and would come to share it at least once a year, but it is difficult to care about such lofty things when your stomach churns and your head aches from hunger.'

The next dancer dived out onto the sand. He tucked and rolled, then sprung up and dived again like a porpoise leaping from wave to wave.

'Who is he?' I asked.

'A glassblower,' Atar said. 'It is said that the first glass was made by a great serpent that dwells in the sun. The glassblowers do well, now, for the Sienese covet their work.' She gestured towards the tombs built into the walls of the valley. 'Before you came, we were ruled by interlopers from the West. Before them, by merchant princes who paid tribute to the horse tribes of the North. Before them, there was someone else with spears and soldiers. Rulers come and go, but the wind, the goddess, and her people will remain.'

A truism that would not hold if the empire succeeded in adding windcalling to the canon, breaking the windcallers' monopoly, I considered. My thoughts were interrupted by the man to my right, who finished his dance, returned to the circle, and clapped me on the shoulder.

'Your turn,' Atar said. 'Show us your dance, Nayeni. Show us what you are.'

Every eye in the circle fixed on me. Despite my earlier jest, the first steps came slowly, but movements trained deep into muscle and bone are not easily forgotten. I shut my eyes and recalled the Temple of the Flame, my grandmother correcting the angle of my arms, the arch of my back and knee. My hands curled into fists, wanting for the rattan dowels I had used in place of swords.

The Iron Dance had nothing of the wind. It did not whirl

or spin around the circle like the dances of the An-Zabati, but it too carried the legacy of a people who resisted imperial rule. And maybe here, among the An-Zabati, I could find the first steps of a new path, one not chosen for me. One that might lead to the secret of Naphena's blessing and the deeper truths of magic I had always longed to know.

For that to happen, Atar needed to see me for what I truly was – more than a minister of trade, a Hand of the emperor, a servant of Sien. More than I had shown to anyone, even Oriole.

The windcallers would not betray me. They would benefit from the presence of a renegade in the citadel. And we were far from the city. The wake of my magic would fade long before it reached Voice Rill.

Still, there was danger in what I did, and there was a moment of hesitation. Of fear that I had overlooked something. That I gambled too much, in this. A presentiment, perhaps – faint, not strong enough to dissuade me from my course. Not when I turned my head and caught a glimpse of Atar's eyes while she watched me dance and saw possibility reflected there – both magical and mundane.

It is a great strength of the young, this willingness to shoulder risk. It can also be our greatest weakness.

Arcs of heat and light and a breath of cinnamon trailed from my fists as I moved through the Iron Dance, burning away the cloth of my gloves and leaving my hands – one witch-carved, one marked by the empire – uncovered. Gasps erupted from the crowd. The drums faltered. My steps, however, did not, for I had never danced to drums.

I came to the last steps, the final downward blow. The fire gathered at the tips of my fingers splashed and rolled across the ground. The drums rumbled to a stop.

'Firecaller ...'

The cheer began slowly, like the first pulses of high tide.

'Firecaller! Firecaller! Firecaller!'

The chant became a wave, rolling and crashing over me as I walked – flushed and astonished at what I had done, and at their reaction – to my place in the circle.

'Firecaller!'

Atar smiled, took my right hand, and leaned to my ear. 'So, you *are* more than you seemed. You have a story to tell, I think. Later. It is my turn now.'

And Atar, who knew every dance of An-Zabat, gave a performance that outshone mine as the sun outshines the stars.

When all who had come had danced, Katiz stepped into the centre of the circle and held aloft a wide brass bowl, decorated in swirls of silver filigree much like those that decorated the obelisks and the statue of Naphena in the Blessed Oasis. 'A cool wind promised water!' he cried.

The gathering answered, 'All things flow to An-Zabat!'

He knelt and dug a shallow basin. Within it he placed the bowl, so that only its lip showed above the sand. He looked up at me, his hands hesitating over the empty bowl. There was danger in my presence, even if I had revealed my own forbidden magic. Some quiet calculation transpired behind his eyes, weighing the risk that I might still betray them, that this was all some elaborate scheme on behalf of the empire. Finally, he offered me a shallow nod – a small gesture of trust, preceding a revelation to match the weight of the secrets I had shared.

Power rippled from him and into the bowl, then down deep into the earth. It was not the wake of windshaping – which I knew well by now – but had the same cool, refreshing texture. A trickle of water seeped into the bottom of the bowl. People began to join Katiz in the centre of the circle. One by one they cupped their hands and drank.

'Do not look so surprised,' Atar said. 'There is air in the water and water in the air, is there not?'

What Atar took for surprise was instead sudden, astonishing realisation. The subtle magic woven into the blade-of-the-wind's performance and the familiar silver filigree on Katiz's bowl together answered a question that had gently nagged at me since my first sight of the Blessed Oasis.

I turned towards the distant glow of An-Zabat. There, running down its obelisks and deep beneath the city, I saw magic, like a gentle breeze across a calm, clear pond. The wake of Naphena's miracle was not an intrusion but a necessary thread – the source, in fact, of the interplay of energies between the oasis, the green belt, and the people of the city. Only now, knowing what to look for, could I feel the wake of that old and ancient power anchored to the obelisks and the statue, keeping An-Zabat alive.

'Come, Firecaller,' Atar said and took me by the hand. 'It is our turn to drink.'

20

To Shape the Wind

'I brought rice gruel and ginseng tea.'

A tray clattered on my bedside table. Jhin crossed the room and threw open the curtain covering my window.

'I'm not hungover,' I complained, blinking against the late-morning light.

'You did not return to your bed until dawn,' Jhin pointed out. 'For the third time this month.'

Over the past few weeks, Jhin had grown increasingly impertinent, treating me like a self-indulgent child and not as his elder brother in the great family of the empire. Intellectually, I had become suspicious of notions like propriety and hierarchical deference, particularly after seeing how they helped to insulate the Sienese rulers of An-Zabat from the struggles of the common people. A strict adherence to propriety, after all, would have denied me any opportunity to see the things I had seen in the city. Yet after a childhood and career marinating in notions of who ought to treat whom in such-and-such a way, his tone rankled.

'I've been doing research in the city,' I told him. 'Observing its economy first hand, to better craft policy, as Voice Rill and I discussed.'

'Oh?' Jhin said, while he set about preparing my meal. 'And has this research been fruitful?'

'I've seen children hunting rats. Mothers and fathers starving themselves to be sure that each of their children had at least a morsel.'

'Children hunt rats in many cities, Your Excellency.'

I tried to keep my tone level even as I gave in to my annoyance with him – and, more profoundly, with the structures of empire he seemed determined to defend. 'Did not the sage Traveller-on-the-Narrow-Way write, "The man whose riches were borne on the backs of the wretched, and the thief who enriches himself with the wealth of others: they are alike and should be scorned alike"? What of the empire, then? What of ...' I waved a hand at my silk sheets, the fine art on my walls, the jade and gold and marble ornaments throughout the room. 'What of all of this? How am I any better than a thief for living in such luxury while children starve?'

My words hung in the air, and I realised how absurd what I had said would sound to him. It would have seemed absurd to me, too, but for Iron Town and for Atar. And for my grandmother, who showed me a second way of looking at the world when I was too young to understand the value of that gift.

His mouth drew into a line. When he spoke, there was a note of warning there that I had not heard in his voice before. 'Why am I your steward and not dead like so many other urchins of Sor Cala, the City of Stone, where I was born? Paths were laid before us, Your Excellency. Not every path is the same, and not every path ends well, but all we can do is follow them as duty and propriety demand. This is a thing hard learned in Toa Alon.'

A common enough defence for the hypocrisies of empire, but not one that I was willing to hear. Oriole's path had led him to death in the mud at Iron Town, but that end had not been inevitable. As every decaying leaf and growing tree helps to shape the pattern of the world, so every human act shapes the paths that we all might follow. And those in power, like Voices of the emperor, or ministers of trade, can shape those paths with a motion of their will. I would not forge blindly ahead, as I had done when I brought Oriole to Iron Town, without a thought for the harm I might be doing to those around me.

'You are exhausted from your late night, Your Excellency,' Jhin said. 'I suggest you take the day and get some rest.'

I took his advice, but that night I went out again into the city, where once more I met Atar. I told her of my unorthodox upbringing, divided between my grandmother's lessons and my Sienese education, and she in turn taught me more of An-Zabat and its people. Of course, what I longed most to understand was its magic.

'How did Naphena make the oasis?' I enquired as we walked the streets by night. Atar, as winddancer, was well known and well respected in all corners of the city – taverns where the desperate found a night of relief in wine; harbourside alleys where those with naught to sell but their own flesh found custom. Atar moved through them all, sharing coin and kindness in equal measure, and no matter where we ventured, we were never far from the shadow of an obelisk.

'It was a miracle,' she replied, 'a working of magic in defiance of the gods.'

'Yes,' I said, 'but how? Is it the same as your cistern bowls, only on a much grander scale? And how does the spell go on, centuries after her death?'

Atar seemed bemused by my question. Our conversations had grown increasingly complex as I became comfortable, if not entirely fluent, with the An-Zabati tongue, able to ask about concepts that she had shied away from discussing in Sienese for want of words with the right depth of meaning.

'You may as well ask why the sun rises, or the winds stir the desert sands, or why it never rains on the Waste,' she said. 'She rewrote the very laws of nature in this place and fixed her will in the stone of the obelisks. She made the world other than it was.'

I studied the obelisk that loomed above us. Old sandstone, weathered by wind, but the silver filigree was bright and untarnished, as though it had been created that morning. Now that I understood the magic in the obelisks, I could feel its wake – a subtle chill down my arms, evidence that the pattern was not as it would otherwise have been.

'When I was a child, I worked magic without being taught,' I said. 'My grandmother had not marked me yet, but I was able to sense the ripples of her magic and to reach for power. I felt that every possibility was open to me. I've been trying to understand that feeling for my entire life.' I gestured to the obelisk. 'This is the first thing I have seen that comes close to the magnitude of power I felt.'

I did not mention the emperor himself, whose perpetual transmission of sorcery to his Voices and Hands was a mountain jutting up through the pattern of the world. The obelisks were a wonder, but they did not shake my bones and fill my heart with terror and awe.

Atar rubbed her forearms, where she wore the spiralling tattoos that were the mark of her magic. 'You speak of a thing we encounter from time to time – children able to feel the ripples of windshaping. Always they are chosen for windcallers, or blades-of-the-wind, and marked from a young age. To wield magic without the marks is to tread on ground the gods defend with jealousy. That is why Naphena created our pact, so that we might have power sheltered from divine wrath.'

'In my grandmother's stories, the gods themselves gave the Nayeni witches their marks,' I said.

Atar considered this. 'Perhaps your gods are kinder than ours

– still jealous, but willing to share some scraps of their power. In the desert, we know that the sky and the sands are at best indifferent, and at worst want our deaths.'

I thought of the wolf gods, their snarling faces and their fiery eyes, which had long studied me from the dark corners of my nightmares. No longer, thankfully. Not since that last visit to the Temple of the Flame.

'I don't think they are,' I said. 'Maybe the witches of Nayen had a benefactor like Naphena, but one we have forgotten.'

'Perhaps,' Atar mused. 'But if that is true, then it fills me with a deep sadness. We must not forget those who worked to better the world. Come now, Firecaller. There is much else to show you.'

The following months passed in a flurry. By day I continued tracking tariffs and tax records, adjusting rates of exchange and monitoring the flow of goods in and out of the city, as I had always done. On the last day of each week, I slipped away from the citadel.

Atar told me of her childhood as the daughter of windshaper parents. Her father had lost his life fighting the empire. Her mother, badly wounded and malnourished, had succumbed to an illness not long after, and at fourteen years old Atar found herself an orphan and responsible for her ten-year-old brother. Though her mother had begun to teach her to shape the wind, she had no ship, and in the chaos of the imperial crackdown on the windcallers, and the windcallers' uprising in response, she had found herself alone and on the streets.

'I knew my own dance,' Atar told me, 'and I had learned others by watching at the Valley of Rulers. It was a way for a young girl to feed herself, and by the time Katiz recognised me in the bazaar, I had garnered something of a following in the city. He convinced Falma – the winddancer before me – to accept me as an apprentice. When she returned to the sand, I assumed her duties.'

'Where is your brother now?' I asked.

She looked to the horizon. 'Not long after I began to dance in the bazaar, I returned one day to find him missing. Despite Katiz's help, I have yet to find him. Perhaps, hungry and desperate, he ran off to join the crew of a windship. Perhaps he met his death at the edge of a bandit's knife or an imperial spear. Who can say?'

We began to visit the Valley of Rulers on our own, and Atar taught me to dance like an An-Zabati scribe, then like a merchant. She would show me the steps and laugh when I inevitably floundered in my attempts to follow her. 'We will make a dancer of you yet, Firecaller,' she would say, smiling, and correct the bend of my knee or the line of my arm with a gentle touch. More than once I fought the urge to make mistakes on purpose, to see her bemused smile and to give her an excuse to stand close.

On my third full moon at the circle, I performed the Soldiers' Dance to much applause. After, while we walked back to the catacombs with only the moon and stars for lanterns, I asked her to teach me to dance like a windcaller.

She paused on the sandstone path. 'That secret is not mine to share,' she said, then went on with a gentle smile: 'Do not despair, Firecaller. I will help you earn it.'

As we neared the brass door that led back to the city, the moonlight lit in the curls of her hair. She looked back at me, and her eyes seemed deep and infinite, as though all the answers I had longed for my entire life might dwell within their depths.

My chest filled with fire and I acted without thinking, following an urge that seemed to strike from far beyond me. My hand found hers and pulled her towards me. She stiffened instantly – which doused the fire within me and shattered a half-formed hope. Of course she did not want me as I wanted her. Though we may have become friends, and though I had shared secrets that could see me killed, I was still minister of trade, Hand of the emperor.

I was more than Sienese, but Sienese nonetheless.

I let go. The silver of my tetragram glimmered in the dark.

'I'm sorry,' I muttered, stumbling to find words that would repair the damage I had so impulsively caused. 'I thought—'

'Thought what, Firecaller?' she said abruptly. 'That I could forget who you are? Some of us have learned to master our desires. They can so often lead us into danger and deceit.'

'No, I just ...' Again, words escaped me, as they never did usually – not at Iron Town, not when Hand Usher nearly uncovered my secret even as he elevated me to Hand of the emperor. Lies had come easily, all my life. The truth – for I would offer her nothing less – hurt so much more to form.

'Since I was an infant, other people have had plans for me,' I said at last. 'My grandmother meant for me to resist the Sienese. My father wanted me to advance our station in the empire. When my grandmother left, I had no path but the one that led to the imperial examinations and Hand Usher, who made me Hand of the emperor.'

'You could have refused.'

'Could I?' I replied sharply, hearing an echo of Clear-River's ultimatum in her words. I took a deep breath and spoke again, determined to keep my voice calm and measured despite the anger welling within me. Atar was not its focus. 'My grandmother disappeared one night, gone to join the rebellion, with hardly a word to me, let alone an offer to join her. What was I to do? Venture into the north on my own, to be captured by bandits and ransomed back to my father? As long as I lived in his house, or in the house of Voice Golden-Finch, there was no room for me to decide what I wanted to be. Only now have I found anything like such freedom.'

'And now that you have freedom,' she said, 'what will you choose?'

'I want to stay here. With you.'

'Oh? You would sacrifice comfort, prestige, and power to fight for a land not your own? Why?'

'I want to fight by your side,' I said.

She faced the city skyline, punctuated by obelisks silhouetted against the stars and the broad sweep of the desert sky. 'You have given aid to the poor of our city,' she said, 'and for that I thank you. And I thank you for your tales of Nayen, for the broader sense I carry of the world, and for the knowledge that we are not alone in our struggle against the empire. But you were always a guest here, Firecaller.'

'Yet I have never felt more at home,' I said.

'Truly?' she said and held my gaze for a long moment, and I dared to hope, though my heart ached and thundered. 'I have seen the desire in your eyes, as I have seen it in the eyes of many other men. And I will admit, I feel an echo of it. But this thing you want ...' Her voice became soft and sad, but there was a current of anger in the hard set of her shoulders. 'Do you think I would be a Sienese wife, locked away in the depths of your estate?'

'Of course not! I—'

Her eyes narrowed and I swallowed my words. 'Then would you have me leave my people to fight in Nayen?' she went on. 'Or would you abandon yours and crew a windship? Do you truly love me, Firecaller, or do you love the idea of a third path, neither Sienese nor Nayeni?'

I wanted to argue, to mount a defence of my feelings as I would answer a question of Sienese doctrine, but the divide between us would not be bridged by argument. She waited for my answer, and when I met her with nothing but silence, she left me there. I waited till she had disappeared beyond the brass door to the tunnels beneath An-Zabat. Only then did I go on, following the echo of her steps through the catacombs, grasping for words that might convey my heart – words I failed to find, while her last echoing footstep faded and I emerged in the pre-dawn dark, alone.

That night I revisited every moment Atar and I had spent together, sifting for any strand of hope I could cling to. A glance. A lingering touch of her hand. The press of her shoulder against mine while we stood in the circle and waited for our turns to dance.

The next day I buried myself in mercantile reports, trying to numb my heart with ledgers and over-steeped tea. As I was finishing for the day and staring down the spectre of another long, sleepless night, Hand Cinder paid a visit to the Wind Through Grass Pavilion. Jhin had hardly announced him before he strutted into the room, taking it in with a blithe sweep of his gaze.

'I haven't seen much of you these past months,' he said, planting himself in one of my reading chairs.

'My duties have kept me occupied,' I said distractedly.

He nodded sagely. 'I heard about that. A few new taxes, a "strategic reserve", which for some reason you saw fit to hand over to the windcallers.'

I felt a chill, but Cinder was too dense to have seen through me completely. 'People in the city are starving,' I said. 'Full bellies are less prone to violent revolt.'

'People in every city are starving,' Cinder argued. 'But I suppose an Easterling would understand revolt. Anyway, you never finished your training in the canon. Isn't it about time to correct that?'

I no longer had any desire to study the canon, nor to fight for an empire that might sacrifice me, just as it had sacrificed Oriole – an empire that, by the very proclamations of its sages, acted cruelly in pursuit of little more than ostentatious gardens and gilt palaces, leaving ruin and starvation in its wake.

Yet this visit had been sudden and unannounced, and Cinder was obviously suspicious.

'You are right,' I said. 'I could use a reprieve from paperwork.'

He clapped me on the back and led the way to the archery range. The targets, I saw, were different today. The straw dummies had been dressed in the vests and loose trousers common in An-Zabat, and their heads painted with long noses and curled hair – poor caricatures of the people we ruled.

'A nice touch, eh?' Cinder said. 'I had the servants put them together this morning.'

'It seems a waste of fabric and time,' I said carefully.

Cinder shrugged. 'Perhaps, but it amuses me.'

I stifled a flare of anger. *Are not the people of An-Zabat the emperor's children? How is this a fulfilment of your duties to them, your younger siblings in the great family of empire?*

But this was a test. I sensed it, and though I did not know the rubric, I knew that to find any but the most superficial flaws in this *amusement* would mean failure.

'Very well,' I said. 'We must all take what joys from life we can, however simple.'

I opened my left hand and reached for the second channel. The first dummy burst apart in a rain of smouldering wood and cloth.

Cinder barked a laugh. 'Such enthusiasm!' he exclaimed. 'But we're not here to practise battle sorcery. It is time to advance your mastery of the canon. Close your eyes, breathe deeply, and reach for the third channel.'

What followed was an afternoon of absurdity and frustration

as I tried to master binding sorcery. It had a heavy, unwieldy feel, like a weight on my shoulders, and no matter how I tried to shape it, the ropes of light I threw at the dummies always faded with a moment's lapse of concentration. Whenever I asked a question, Cinder guffawed, slapped me on the back, and told me I would figure it out eventually with enough practice, like he did. It was satisfying, I suppose, to realise that Hand Usher was not the worst teacher in the empire.

After a few futile hours, Cinder suggested that I continue practising on my own and told me to inform him when I could hold the bonds for a count of thirty. 'Until then, any of the subtleties I could teach will be lost on you,' he said dismissively.

He left, and I made a good-faith effort but soon left the archery range and returned to my paperwork. On completing it, I sent Jhin to ask Hand Alabaster if he would be willing to meet me in the Abundant Nectar Hall for a meal that evening. Cinder's visit had reminded me of the need to maintain my ties with the citadel, regardless of how my colleagues annoyed or disgusted me. If I meant to forge my own path, I needed to defray suspicion for now, until I was ready to break away from the empire.

Alabaster accepted. Though neither of us apologised for the argument that had ended our previous meeting, we passed a pleasant enough time discussing a collection of the latest court poetry, which Alabaster's betrothed had sent to him along with her most recent correspondence. The conversation skirted around love and longing, though, which only deepened the pain that had lodged in my chest – the seeping wound I had dealt myself *and dealt Atar*? I wondered by reaching for more than she could give.

At the next full moon – the fourth since Atar and I had met beside the Blessed Oasis – I left the citadel by the servants' gate and walked alone to the Valley of Rulers. When I emerged from the catacombs, the music of the dance already rebounded from the valley walls. I hung back from the circle and watched from afar while Atar spun and leapt in a dance I had not yet seen. Her movements shifted from one step to the next, full of grace, sadness, anger, and regret. I sank to the sand, hugged my knees to my chest, and watched her, captured by the depth of feeling she expressed with a single turn of her wrist.

How had I imagined that such a person could love me? A leader of her people, master of the wind and the dance. A woman who might have had the captain of the fastest, sleekest ship in the windcallers' fleet if she wanted. And I a foreigner, a Foolish Cur, servant to her enemies and uncertain of my place in the world.

A shadow passed between me and the moon. With a grunt, and favouring one knee, Katiz lowered himself to the sand beside me. 'Atar was not certain you would return,' he said.

Something tightened in my chest. 'Did she want me to?'

'I think she hoped,' Katiz said. He cupped my shoulder in one thick, calloused hand.

A candle flame flickered to life in my chest, and with it a new fear. 'She rejected me, and she was right to.'

'I think she is as afraid as you are,' Katiz said.

I looked up at him, puzzled, but saw no trick in his sun-seamed face.

'On your first night here, you danced for us. You showed us your magic, and the Sienese would have killed you for it.' He squeezed my shoulder, then released me and leaned back, crossing his arms over his barrel chest. 'This is why I have come to trust you, Firecaller. You have not yet found your way of fighting them, but you have shown yourself to us and you have helped us. That is enough for a start. Now.' He grinned down at me. 'Atar tells me you wish to learn the Windcallers' Dance.'

I straightened. 'Are you willing to teach me?'

'I am,' Katiz said. 'But not tonight. The circle gathers for expression, not for learning. What will you dance tonight, Firecaller?'

A shiver ran down my spine as Atar called the wind and let her scarves unfurl. They spun around her like flying serpents that twined together, then split apart, each to follow its own spiralling, circuitous path.

'I'm sorry,' I said. 'I don't know if I have it in me.'

'You do,' Katiz insisted and nodded towards Atar. 'Just as she did. You should have seen her this last week, always with slumped shoulders and a sour expression. Even Shazir stayed well clear of her path. Yet she has come, and she dances and shares her truth. You too have come to the circle, and you too must dance.'

He levered himself to his feet, then offered me a hand. I took it, not knowing what dance I would perform but unwilling to insult him and the others at the circle by coming to watch while offering nothing of my own. Atar finished her dance as we joined the circle. Her eyes found mine, then darted away.

A longing to speak with her welled within me. I wanted to reassure her, to tell her that, though she might not feel the way I did, I did not want to sacrifice our friendship to salve the bruises on my heart. Perhaps it was the echo of my grand-mother in Atar's ferocity, in the hard line of her shoulders, in her unimpeachable defence of her culture and people, but I admired her far more than I desired her.

Was that a truth I could bring to the dance?

My turn came. Uncertain of what I would do, but with the first steps percolating in my body and my mind, I walked to the centre of the circle.

I began with the footwork of the Iron Dance, the first line of a poem I would write with steps and gestures, recalling the day

276

we had met and the first night of our friendship. Then, in the order that she had taught them, I moved through the dances of An-Zabat, performing each for a scant dozen steps, retelling the story of our time together. The loose, broad strokes of the scribe. The twirls and reversals of a merchant on the balls of my feet. A soldier's leaping precision. Lastly, a recreation of her dance earlier that night – as best I could capture it, having seen it only once and at a distance – with what echo I could muster of its beauty and sadness. But instead of scarves, I danced with twining lines of fire that curled through the air in a blazing spiral before dividing and swirling high to flash and fade against the backdrop of night. In the wake of their light and my sorcery, a chill trickled down my spine and a breeze curled out to fill a pair of silver-patterned scarves.

'You are doing it wrong,' Atar said.

She caught my wrists, curled my fingers to the proper form, and began the dance again.

'Follow my steps,' she said, and I did, though with a bare fraction of her grace and certainty. Her wind whirled up and down, drawing her scarves into the dance. My fire rose to meet them, encircling them, forming a double helix of wind, silk, and flame that spun around us to fill the night with warmth and colour.

'Someday, Nayen will call you home,' she said with no hint of exertion in her voice. 'That is your place, your fight.'

'Someday,' I said, breathless. 'Not today.'

She considered this while our dance pulled us apart, then drew us back together, and some of the sadness had gone out of her steps.

'Then I can promise you no more than today,' she said.

'That is enough.' My heart leapt, and not only from fatigue. 'More than enough.'

Her hand flashed out, caught mine, pulled me close. My

world filled with the scent of lavender, sweat, and honey, then with the soft press of her lips. Her scarves descended and draped themselves around us, shielding us from the circle in our moment of intimacy, for this alone we would not share.

'To today, then,' she whispered. 'And a hope of tomorrow.'

That night, when the dancers had drunk from Katiz's bowl and returned to the city, he, Atar, and I remained. I followed the steps as he showed them to me, but my feet wanted to flatten against the earth and the sweeping movements of my arms felt loose and impotent. The Iron Dance had taught me to tighten my core, but windcalling required fluid motion and Katiz refused to so much as mention magic until I had mastered the steps.

The moon swung low, and when I once again faltered in the early steps of the Windcallers' Dance, Katiz announced, with a heavy note of frustration, that our lesson was at an end. Without another word he departed and vanished into the tunnel that led back to the city. I collapsed to the sands in exhaustion, letting the cool pre-dawn wind wick the sweat from my brow.

Atar smiled down at me, the setting moon framing her head and filling the loose curls of her hair with pale light. 'It takes time,' she said, then lay down beside me. 'And a great deal of practice. I will help you through it.'

'Thank you,' I panted.

She shrugged. 'It is my duty as winddancer to pass on such knowledge.'

'Not only for that,' I said, struggling for the right words as I so often did with her, as with no one else – a sign, perhaps, of how much I cared not only for what she might think of me but for how well she understood. I had spent so little of my life trying to articulate the truth. Even with Oriole, there had always been a scaffolding of lies. 'You didn't have to dance with me.'

'That is true,' Atar said, 'but I wanted to, as I want to be here with you tonight. Do you think I stayed to help Katiz only because it would be amusing to watch you flail about aimlessly?'

I frowned at her and she burst out laughing.

'Your dignity is so easily bruised for a man soaked in his own sweat,' she said.

'We're in the desert!' I blurted. 'Everyone is sweaty all the time!'

'Indeed,' she agreed, 'but we An-Zabati understand this and accept it while the Sienese seem to melt into puddles of wilting fabric.'

'Was I not sweating when you kissed me?' I said, and immediately regretted it. That moment had felt like a brush with a new kind of magic, something not to be spoken of lest the memory of it crumble to dust.

She smiled, a hint of mischief – and something richer, stranger – lighting her eyes. She leaned towards me. Her breath brushed the line of my jaw. 'There is time yet before the sun rises,' she said. 'Time for one more dance.'

My pulse throbbed at my throat. Then, in a burst of motion, she was on her feet again.

'Come, Firecaller,' she said. 'You'll never learn if you just lie there in a heap.'

Disoriented, and disappointed in a vague way I dared not directly face, I stood and followed her through the steps once more. And then again the night after, and the night after that, until four weeks later – beneath another full moon, after dancing the dance of a windcaller at the centre of the circle – I earned my tattoos.

While those gathered to the circle watched, Katiz ground ink in a wide stone bowl, then sharpened the radius of a hawk into a hollow-tipped needle. 'Only thrice before have we given mastery of the wind to an outsider,' he said. 'They, like you, came to us already powerful in magic. They, like you, had lost their own people. They, as we hope for you, stayed with us for many years.'

'The first marks go here,' Atar said. She made three swirls with the tips of her fingers on the underside of my forearm, below my elbow. 'One day, if you have your own ship, the whole of both arms will be covered.'

A pleasant shiver ran up my arm at her touch. I doubted I would ever wear so many marks, and I was grateful that the tattoos would be so small. The sleeve of a Sienese robe would cover them easily, and I had yet to form any kind of plan to extricate myself from the citadel. There had been nothing to put my guard up since Cinder's visit to my office. I still had plenty of time.

'Do not be afraid to show pain,' Katiz said, raising a laugh from the gathered dancers. 'Everyone winces on the first few strikes.'

'My grandmother carved my hand with a stone knife. I doubt this will be worse.'

Katiz prodded me with the needle and I did wince, especially at the burn of the ink rubbed into my wounds. Atar teased me, then kissed my cheek. The moon had begun to descend by the time Katiz had finished, but all in the circle had remained to witness the rise of a new windcaller.

'Try not to move the arm more than necessary for the next few days,' Katiz warned me. 'And for Naphena's sake, do not wash it or the ink will smudge.'

I barely heard him. While he had prodded and inked my arm, I had felt the first trickles of a new power, cool and calming – like healing sorcery – but with a tumultuous undercurrent, like conjuring fire. There was a pang of disappointment as I realised that windcalling, too, was limited, as witchcraft was. But I had expected nothing less. Wherever I found magic, I found it bound, whether by the canon or by pacts forged long ago with the gods.

The moment Katiz was done, I sprang to my feet and reached for that power. Its gentle, almost invisible wake followed the slow arc of my arm. A gust billowed in the palm of my hand. I pushed forwards and down, and it rushed away from me.

'Look, Atar!' I leaped, grinning and giddy, for though this was not the deep knowledge I sought, it was beautiful. 'I can call the wind!'

She ran to me, and together we danced with the zephyrs of the desert until the setting of the moon.

21

The Tools of Empire

Sleep returned me to the Valley of Rulers, but alone and dressed in the plain clothes that my grandmother and I had always worn to the Temple of the Flame. A curl of wind stirred the sand, and when it passed the wolf god Okara stood at the bottom of the valley, where the dancers had made their circle and Katiz drew water from the earth.

'What sort of home is this for a wolf?' Okara said. He peered up at me, his eye staring from above his scar-seamed muzzle, no longer a carving of stone but a living, breathing god. And on meeting his gaze, I suffered the shuddering realisation that this was no mere figment of my sleeping mind – and had never been, when he had visited me before – but the god himself, speaking into my dream.

'I am happy here,' I managed to say. A paltry defence.

Okara growled and the sands shook with his anger. 'Stay, then. Here you might live as an outcast and make a paltry contribution to the coming war, but the boy who veered without pact – who drew the eyes of the gods – desired knowledge, not happiness,' the god snarled. 'Do you forget what you accomplished, when your mind was supple, unconstrained, like a witch of the old sort before they bound us with their pact? This windcalling is not the truth you seek, only another frame.'

282

'And how do you suggest I learn these truths when every teacher I have had seems ignorant of them?' I shot back. 'You speak only in riddles and allusion.'

I felt a sudden weightlessness, and in the blink of an eye the Blessed Oasis appeared before us, surrounded not by the city but by empty sands. Naphena stood tall beneath the stars, and in the haze of the dream she seemed not carved of sandstone but almost alive.

'You came seeking her, did you not?' Okara said.

'She is dead,' I replied.

'Yes, but there is one like her who might teach you. Another witch of the old sort.'

A gout of flame swirled out from Okara, whipped across the sand as by a wind from nowhere. It curled towards me, caught in my clothes, blistered my flesh, and I shut my eyes against its burning intensity. A scream boiled in my throat.

The flame receded and I found myself surrounded by stone columns, a forest of them stretching in every direction, into depthless dark. Strange symbols written in the colour of blood or old rust decorated them.

'There is a woman of the bones in the north of Nayen,' Okara said, 'in a temple that is no longer a temple. Seek her out. The pact allows me to say that much.'

'Do you mean *this*?' I brandished my right hand and the scars my grandmother had carved. 'Is this the pact? How does it bind you? It constrains magic – I know that much – but how can scars in human flesh bind a god?'

'Why should I answer when, by your actions, you reveal that your thirst for the truth was but a passing curiosity?' Okara glared at me, turned, and loped up the temple steps. 'Seek the woman of the bones, if you would seek magic as it belongs to you, in all its fullness and power.'

With that, the wolf god vanished beyond the gateway of the

temple. In his passing, a trickle of water began to flow, building to a stream, then a flood that swept my feet from under me.

I woke slowly, as though rising from the depths of the sea, my head thick with the residue of the dream. What did he mean, the *woman of the bones*? I had heard of no such thing, not in any legend of Nayen. And yet that made the wolf god's words ring more powerfully. Surely my dreaming mind could conjure nothing it did not already know. For a fraught moment I wondered if I, like Iron Claw, the first Sun King, had been chosen by the gods for power.

The notion made no sense. Why would the gods of Nayen choose a servant of the empire, flung far from his island home, neglectful of their ways? At any rate, to seek out this woman of the bones and the answer Okara had promised would mean a return to Nayen, and I had many reasons to stay in An-Zabat.

The sun was already high – I had returned from the valley at dawn – but I smelled no brewing tea, porridge, boiled eggs, or fried dough, nor did I hear the feet of servants scurrying about to prepare my outer rooms for the day. I called out for Jhin but received no answer. I dressed and went to the door but found it locked. I shook the handle and felt the weight of a wooden beam barring it shut.

'Jhin! What is the meaning of this?' I shouted.

My tattoos itched beneath their bandage, but it had been less than a night. How could anyone possibly know? I imagined Jhin leaning over me while I slept, drawing down the sheets to reveal my freshly tattooed arm.

'Steward Jhin!'

'Good morning, Hand Alder,' Alabaster said through the gap in the doorframe. I pressed my eye to the gap, but he stood beyond the narrow band of my vision. 'Or should I call you something else?' he purred. 'Alder is a Sienese name, after all.'

'What is this, Alabaster?' A deep breath did little to calm me.

'Voice Golden-Finch has known since Iron Town, but there were always suspicions,' Alabaster said. 'Hand Usher kept you from the executioner's grasp. He saw a way to use you. To be honest, I worried you might not earn the windcallers' trust, but you surpassed my expectations. Do you know what the penalty for treason is, Alder?'

'Let me out, Alabaster!' I yelled, sifting through his words, trying desperately to make sense of them. 'This is a mistake.'

'You thought we believed that shattered porcelain made all those intricate little marks, so carefully arranged around the seams of your palm?' Alabaster went on. 'Do you think we are blind?'

'Take me to Voice Rill,' I said, reaching for any chance I might have. 'I can explain. We will sort through this misunderstanding.'

'Do you think the emperor would give such power as sorcery to his Hands without knowing how they use it?' he went on with venom in his voice. 'He has been with you all along, in the palm of your left hand. He might not know your every thought, as he does his Voices, but he feels every ripple and wake of magic you wield, whether drawn from the canon or no.'

'You don't know what you're talking—'

'When you used Easterling magic at Iron Town – and again here in An-Zabat – it stood out to the emperor and his Voices like a clot flowing through the veins and arteries of transmission. We had little use for the magic of Nayen, but Hand Usher saw that your curiosity and foolishness might be a tool to benefit the empire. And he was right. We did not know how you would manage it, but you did. Rill came to us last night, the moment you wielded An-Zabati magic, the moment the emperor added it to the canon, and we all drank to your success. Soon, windships will sail under the imperial tetragram and An-Zabat will be ours in truth as well as in name. Cinder is sharpening his sword even as we speak. He has a reputation for keeping his victims alive until the last scrap of their skin comes free.' His eye appeared at the gap and I stumbled backwards. 'Goodbye, Easterling,' he laughed. 'I will see you at dawn, when your suffering reaches its peak and, at last, an ending.'

Only then, sitting stunned on the floor, Alabaster's laughter ringing in my ears, did I feel the weight of my mistake. The rumour Clear-River had used to threaten me with had been only that, a rumour, but one that struck at the truth. I had thought myself careful in my gamble and hoped to win the truths of magic, or at the very least acceptance, understanding, and love. But the dice had been loaded from the moment Usher had sealed my hand.

There was no time for the paralysis of self-hatred, no time to mull over the connections I should have made, the conclusions I should have drawn. I had to warn Atar, Katiz, and the other windshapers. The city was forfeit but they might still escape.

I scrambled to my feet and sought the black chest with three iron locks that I had brought from Nayen. I pressed the obsidian blade of my grandmother's knife to my left palm. I would need magic, but as long as I wore the tetragram Voice Rill and the emperor himself would know every spell I cast even as I cast it and add it to the canon, as they had added windcalling. I had conjured fire while wearing the tetragram, and in so doing betrayed one of Nayen's deepest secrets. Thankfully, the memory of twisted limbs and brittle bones had frightened me away from veering. There were some secrets yet kept safe.

I started to carve the canon away along with my branded flesh, biting back the pain. Blood spilled from my palm where the tetragram had been, and the well of power I had felt since Hand Usher branded me vanished at once. I stared at the ruin of my hand, the ruin of so many dreams – Koro Ha's, my father's, my own. No time for self-pity, either. I wrapped my hand in a scrap of linen, cradled it to my chest, and began searching for a way out of my rooms.

The door was locked, chained, and barred. The windows were shuttered and bolted from the outside. Through the slats I caught sight of Jhin, just on the other side of the bamboo grove, a bundle of laundry in his arms.

'Jhin!' I called out and pounded on the window with my good hand. He nearly dropped his burden in surprise. The steward glanced around, checking for prying eyes and ears, then crept around the bamboo grove to my window.

'I shouldn't speak to you,' he whispered. 'Please, Hand Alder, let me be.'

'What do they say I've done, Jhin?' I said.

'They say you've betrayed the empire.'

'How? By hiding the fact I was marked as a witch before I understood what that would mean? By trying to learn about this city and help its people? Where is the treason, Jhin?'

He shied away and I worried that he would abandon me.

'You betrayed the empire's trust, Alder. You hid things—'

'They betrayed mine as well,' I said. 'For two years they planned to use me to steal the windcallers' magic. They might have given me a chance to cooperate, but they hid it all from me – even the emperor himself, when I stood at the foot of his throne.'

He grimaced but leaned closer to the window. I pressed on.

'What happened in Toa Alon, Jhin?' I asked. 'I've read volumes of imperial history, but there is a gap there. You spoke of lessons hard learned. What did the empire do?'

Jhin shuddered and pressed his face close to the slats. A fire lit in his eyes. 'If not for the empire's mercy, we would all be dead, buried with the Stone Speakers in the ruins of Sor Cala. Things were hidden, truths the Stone Speakers kept from their people and from the empire, though they *performed* surrender and claimed they had shared all their arts. When the empire

found out ...' he shook his head. 'The Hands, even the Voices
... Your power is nothing like the emperor's. He is a god-man
out of the deep-cave legends, their names forgotten but their
faces carved in stone. The empire did not conquer Sor Cala. It
surrendered, its rulers lied, and the emperor himself *buried it.*'

'And you do not hate the emperor for this?' I said. 'For caus-
ing such death and destruction?'

Jhin took a deep breath. 'We were warned. The city was
emptied. Only the Stone Speakers and those who refused to
leave were killed.'

'So, they killed a few instead of all. I would not call it mercy
if I were forced to watch my home destroyed.'

'Is deception not a crime?' Jhin argued.

'One deserving of death?'

He shrugged. 'Am I a stone-carved god, that I should condemn?'

'Is the emperor? Is Voice Rill?'

That gave him pause. I lunged for the gap in his defences.

'What crime have the windcallers committed? They never
deceived the empire. They only protect the secret of their magic
to protect their own lives. The empire destroyed Sor Cala but
saved the Toa Aloni. Here, they will destroy the An-Zabati but
save An-Zabat. Not to punish a crime, not to avenge a slight,
but only to control trade across the Waste. Is that a thing worth
killing for?'

'Why should I believe you?' he asked. 'I have only your word,
and you are a traitor.'

'At the very least, you know they will kill me,' I said. 'If you
do nothing, then by your actions you agree I should die. Are
you a stone-carved god, that you should condemn?'

'And what would you have me do, Hand Alder?' he said,
glaring through the window slat. 'Fight to free you and condemn us both?'

'No,' I said. 'Just open the window.'

Jhin measured the opening with his eyes and frowned. 'It is too small.'

'I have my ways,' I said. 'Please, Jhin. I deceived the empire, but I was deceived in turn. If I did wrong, so did they. Why should I be punished while the empire does what it wills? Only because the empire is strong and I am weak?'

His gaze drifted from mine and settled on the bar that held the shutters closed. Away from the discursive field of Sienese philosophy – a familiar battleground – I could only hope that my arguments appealed to Jhin's sense of justice, complicated as it was by a mixture of Toa Aloni and Sienese sensibilities.

'These drapes need to be hung out to dry or they will mould,' he said and left the window.

'Jhin!' I shouted after him. 'Do what you know is right!'

He paused in mid-stride and looked over his shoulder, his brow deeply furrowed in thought, his eyes searching, his body taut.

'I ... need to think,' he said at last and left me.

I paced my floor and fought down nausea. Even if Jhin chose to open the window, I would have to become much, much smaller to fit through it.

Sometime later – perhaps an hour, perhaps longer – I heard a commotion outside my window, of feet and clattering steel. A squadron of guards, armed and in their battle harnesses, marched towards the main gate of the citadel. I felt as though I had swallowed a stone. Atar, Katiz, and the other windshapers would be hunted down and slaughtered because of me, and they would think that I had betrayed them.

There was no time to wait for Jhin. Again, I cast about the room. They had left my piles of books, my wall hangings, my brush, inkstone, and paperweights. I hefted one of the paper-weights and bashed it against the shutter. A few of the slats splintered, but the bar across the shutter held. At the fourth blow the paperweight cracked – a cheap piece – and at the fifth it broke in two.

A survey of my progress left me with little hope. The window would give way eventually, but by then I would have attracted attention and it would be too late to save Atar. I could conjure a flame to burn my way out, but fire could be more dangerous than helpful. If I'd had battle sorcery, I might have blasted the window apart. I felt foolish and impulsive. Cutting away the canon had left me without a valuable tool.

But of course the canon itself wasn't magic. I had cut away the bit and bridle but the horse was still there, if I could master it.

As I'd once reached blindly for the power to veer, now I reached for battle sorcery. It was like stepping onto an empty plain where once a vast palace had been. The pattern of the world was there, as it had been when I'd knelt in the Temple of the Flame, but it appeared only as shadows of sensation, as timid wakes in the world, dulled by my witch marks and long acclimation to the canon. I felt my way forwards, towards the faint feeling of warmth on my skin, of a cool breeze filling my lungs.

And then I was upon it, grasping the magic I knew as battle sorcery, and at once the warmth on my skin became the heat of a bonfire, the breeze in my lungs a bitter winter chill. My teeth chattered, clipping my tongue, as magic rushed through me. Lightning crackled from the tips of my fingers. Bolts tore through my table, my chair, a bookcase – everything but the window.

I panicked as flames licked at stacks of paper and smoke filled the room. The wake of my sorcery was overwhelming, like I was pressed between two iron plates, one frozen and the other white-hot. A vision rose in my mind's eye of Hand Cinder cackling as he felt this absurd wake and saw the smoke rising from my rooms.

I choked on a lungful of smoke, gritting my teeth to keep them from chattering. I shut my eyes and focused on the pattern of the world around me. Felt the wakes of the battle sorcery I wielded. Grasped them like the mane of a bucking steed. This was *my* power – not the empire's, not my grandmother's – and I would do with it what I willed.

Flames licked at the walls around me. I squinted through the heat, smoke, and glare, fixed my gaze on the window, and bore down with all my will, all my intent – all my desire to avenge myself, to warn Atar, to beg her forgiveness – as I had when I'd tried to bring Oriole back from the dead.

Now, no walls of the canon constrained me.

A bolt of lightning speared the window. The iron bar shattered into molten droplets; the shutters burst to cinders.

For the first time since the most terrifying moment of my life, I reached for the power to veer. Every muscle in my body clenched at once, then relaxed as I settled into my new form. I had no time to bask in this success, long in coming though it was.

In a flurry of feathers, I leapt to the windowsill and dragged myself out of the smoke, into the sky.

22

The Obelisks of An-Zabat

I rode desert thermals out into the Batir Waste and soared well beyond the Valley of Rulers before landing. If Cinder or Alabaster followed the wake of my magic, they would be led out onto the open sands. Twilight had fallen when I landed and released the spell. Standing on wobbly, cramping legs, I recalled the memory of carrying my grandmother back from the Temple of the Flame with a sympathy I'd never imagined feeling. With no one to carry me, I set off at a flagging jog towards the Valley of Rulers.

Though the sun had set, heat clung to the sand. I sucked my cheeks for saliva – anything to wet my throat – and wished I had Katiz's bronze-and-silver bowl. I had seen him draw water from the sands half a dozen times and thought I could recreate the spell, though neither he nor Atar had taught me how.

My cramps only worsened by the time I reached the valley, where I followed the path to the sandstone cliff, watched all the while by the dark gaze of the countless tombs. My left hand was a useless club of bandages and blood, but I managed to pull the heavy brass door open and shut it behind me. Without a lantern, I conjured flame for light, just a finger-wide tongue of fire, leaving little more wake than a water-walker on the surface of a puddle.

I moved as quickly as I could, often bracing myself against the wall when a spasm shook me. The carved walls of the tunnel scraped my shoulder and the heavy shadows cast by the thin light of my flame made the carvings a menagerie of shrouded demons, snarling at me from the dark. Were these the old, cruel gods of An-Zabat? I wondered. Would they, too, invade my dreams, speaking in tortured riddles and goading me down fraught, unknown paths? I was delirious from thirst, I decided, and my mind was addled by Jhin's talk of stone-carved gods.

I rounded a corner and, to my relief, saw the dull gleam of brass. I pushed through the second door and out into the alleyway behind Katiz's temple. The first stars pierced a thin veil that I took for clouds, until I smelled the fire and saw the orange glow to the south, above the elevated harbour.

I was too late. The second conquest of An-Zabat had already begun.

'Atar!' My tongue felt thick. Dizzy though I was, I ran towards the obelisk that rose from Katiz's temple, stumbling and bumping into walls and kicking through piles of refuse. 'Katiz!'

The doors of the temple stood open. Atar and Blade-of-the-Wind Shazir were on either side, shepherding people into the shelter. A wake of sorcery – hot, then cold – washed over me from the south, followed by the bright burst of a lightning strike and a rumble of thunder.

'Atar!' I gasped as another cramp seized my leg and I stumbled. She caught me and lowered me to sit against the temple wall. 'Thank the sages – the gods – Naphena! Thank Naphena you're all right!'

She glanced at my wounded hand, then searched my face and felt my cheeks. 'You are hurt. And feverish.'

'I came from the desert,' I said, clutching her arm. 'I had to warn you.'

'Shazir! Bring water!'

The blade-of-the-wind scowled. 'Winddancer, he—'

'Water. Now.' Atar glared up at Shazir, who did as he was bid.

'I had . . .' I swallowed, trying to work moisture into my throat.

'Quiet now, Firecaller,' she said. She reached up to stroke my brow and comfort me but hesitated, and I felt a piercing dread.

'I'm sorry,' I croaked.

Atar studied me, as though my eyes could testify to my guilt or innocence. I wanted to explain everything, but my voice refused.

Shazir returned with a copper cup and Katiz in tow. Atar pressed the rim of the cup to my lips. The water stung my chapped mouth but was blessedly wet and cool.

'What is this?' Katiz said, his face a thundercloud.

'We should lock him up and question him,' Shazir said. 'The storage room—'

'Why would he come back if he betrayed us?' Atar challenged. 'When he can speak, he will explain.'

Desperate to prove her right, I drank the last of the water in a rush.

'They knew every magic I worked,' I said, my voice regaining strength. 'They knew I was marked as a witch. And they knew my curiosity about magic was boundless. They brought me here as a gamble to steal windcalling for their canon.'

'And you did not know this?' Shazir snapped. 'How? You are schooled in their magic, are you not, Hand of the emperor?'

'I was never one of them,' I shot back, meeting her stare. 'They gave me power only to use me.'

'They made you a fool,' Shazir said. 'That is, if what you say is true. Why should we believe you?'

'Because he came to warn us,' Atar pointed out.

'Too late,' Shazir said. She turned to Katiz. 'Whether he betrayed us wittingly or not, we cannot trust him.'

'His hand,' Atar said. She cradled my left hand and began to unwrap it. When the bandage fell away, her eyes widened at the ruin of my palm.

'I cut the canon away,' I told her. 'They no longer know what magic I work, unless they are near enough to feel its wake. I am no longer their tool.'

'Another layer of deception, for all we know!' Shazir threw up her hands. 'Katiz, be reasonable! Trusting this man may have cost us the city.'

'The city may be lost, but we are not,' Katiz said. 'The empire knows how to call the wind, but Firecaller never learned to draw water. We can deny them their victory.'

Atar's eyes widened. 'Naphena's urn has poured for hundreds of years!'

'It can be made dry,' Katiz said. 'And there are enough among the people who have kept their cistern bowls and know the art. We can slip into the desert and leave the dried-out husk of this city to the empire. But once we begin, they will realise what we are doing and they will stop us. The Sienese have weapons that could destroy an obelisk in an instant, as they destroyed this temple years ago and even now destroy homes throughout the city.'

'Weapons we do not have,' Shazir said. 'This is not a plan but a dream, one as transient as a dewdrop!'

'I can get them for you,' I said, piecing Katiz's plan together. I remembered the bowl in the Valley of Rulers and its silver filigree, so like the decoration on the obelisk that loomed above us. And I remembered the citadel armoury, a squat building next to Cinder's archery range. 'I know where the grenades are kept. With my grandmother's magic I can disguise myself and steal them, if we hurry.'

'A foolish plan,' Shazir snapped. 'And we would be doubly foolish to trust this one. I should slit his throat, and we should be in the harbour to defend our ships.'

Katiz crossed his arms, his tattoos shifting like desert winds.

'Shazir, you go with him,' he said. 'Atar as well, if you are willing. And take two of our fastest runners. This is what will do.'

The streets around the Blessed Oasis were empty and quiet save for the distant rumble of battle sorcery. We were far enough from the fighting that I felt the magic like fingers brushing my skin, slight but unsettling. I led Atar, Shazir, and the runners Shazir had chosen towards the servants' gate. They carried crates stuffed with rags and wore the simple kaftans of porters. I was clad in Sienese armour that Katiz had captured the last time the empire had tried to steal the windcallers' secrets.

In my months of coming and going from the citadel, the servants' gate had always been left unlocked and was rarely guarded. It was hidden at the end of a long, winding alleyway that few people had reason to venture down, and thus was protected more by secrecy than by lock and key. The battle slowly consuming An-Zabat had likely prompted the posting of additional guards, and we had planned accordingly.

I took a deep breath to brace myself and focus my tired mind, gathered power, and hoped that my Sienese colleagues had fixed their attentions elsewhere. I had only ever seen my grandmother use this power to veer into the body of an eagle hawk, but there was no reason to think it could not be used for subtler changes. The magic was slow to take effect, exhausted as I was after my flight to the desert, but at last the bones of my face stretched and bent. My flesh rippled and shifted until it mirrored the appearance of the lieutenant who had led the squadron I had seen through the slats of my window. The two runners watched me, their eyes wide with fear.

Shazir spat in disgust and rubbed at her jaw, feeling the cramps caused by the wake of my spell. 'A hideous magic,' she said.

A part of me had to agree, and not only for the visceral disgust that accompanied shifting flesh and bending bones. I shuddered at the thought of such a power falling into the empire's hands. Windcallers and witches could see through the deception, sensing the wake that veered left through the world, but there were those who resisted the empire without the aid of magic. Young rebels who might share some intimate secret or private outrage only to find their friend or lover shifting into a Hand of the emperor ready to arrest them for treason, if not execute them on the spot.

Atar glowered at Shazir, then pushed past us both. 'Let us be about our work.'

The gate was locked, as I had feared. At my knock, a small inset window swung open. Jhin's face appeared in the window, scrutinising me.

'Lieutenant?' he said, then looked beyond me. 'Did Hand Alabaster forget something? Who are these An-Zabati?'

The plan had been to lie my way past the guard, then incapacitate him and make for the armoury. I had not expected to find Jhin at the gate.

With a bracing breath, I released the spell.

'Wh-what are you—' Atar stammered, feeling the wake of my magic fade.

'I know him,' I said in An-Zabati and moved my face close to the window, then went on in Sienese. 'Jhin, it's me. It's Alder.'

'Of course you know him!' Shazir cried. She grabbed my shoulder and reached for her sword. 'That was the point of the disguise! He has betrayed us, Winddancer.'

'Wait!' Atar commanded, placing a hand on Shazir's arm. 'This one, too, is not Sienese. Let them speak.'

'Who are these people?' Jhin asked nervously. He had not fled, though, which gave me hope.

'Jhin, I'm sorry,' I said. 'I need your help. I know you wish to take no part in war.'

'You escaped,' Jhin said. 'Why did you come back? I will not be party to murder, Alder.'

'We are not here to kill anyone,' I said, 'but I cannot tell you what we plan. Nor do you want to know, I think. I just need you to open the gate.'

'They will know I helped you,' he said. 'They will know, and they will kill me.'

'Then come with us. The windcallers can take you back to Toa Alon, if you want, or give you a berth on their ships. They are all leaving this city. You can, too, and leave the empire far behind.'

'I should turn you in,' Jhin said mournfully.

'Jhin, listen to me,' I said softly. 'If you could have stopped the destruction of Sor Cala, would you?'

'I ...' he shook his head. 'I take no side.'

A burst of lightning lit the southern sky.

'Enough jabbering,' Shazir snarled. 'Atar, let me kill them both and shape the wind to tear this door from its hinges!'

'By doing nothing, Jhin, you take the side of the powerful,' I argued, abandoning my appeals to his better nature. 'If you do nothing – or worse, if you help them – they will win. There is no middle ground in this. You must choose. Either the empire or those who fight them.'

'Is this how you became Hand of the emperor?' Jhin asked. 'By making the uncomplicated complicated and twisting things up with words?'

'Yes,' I replied. And I had, by twisting things up with words, by confusing myself into following a path that led to the empire's service, believing that a third, neutral path was somehow possible. 'But am I wrong?'

He took a deep breath. 'You are not wrong, Alder.'

There was a click and the door swung open.

'You see, Shazir?' Atar said. She shoved Shazir's crate back into her arms, then hefted her own. 'You do Firecaller an injustice.'

Jhin eyed my companions warily but ushered us inside. He handed me a ring of keys. 'I will wait here. Do whatever you must and I will let you out again.'

'Thank you, Jhin,' I said.

I restored the magic disguising my face and motioned for the An-Zabati to follow. We left Jhin behind and began to cross the garden. As I had instructed, Atar, Shazir, and the two runners followed at a brisk yet unhurried walk. If we were stopped, we would claim that Hand Cinder had sent me to fetch more grenades for the battle and that the An-Zabati were traitors to their city, promised rewards when the windcallers had been dealt with.

'Who was that?' Atar whispered as we passed the Pavilion of Soaring Verse. Its stream still burbled, fed by pipes from the Blessed Oasis, though it seemed forlorn in the darkness, unlit by lamps, empty of paper boats and cups of wine.

'My steward,' I replied. 'From Toa Alon. I promised him a place on your ships when this is done.'

'You had no right to make such an offer,' Shazir snapped.

'Quiet,' Atar hissed. Then, turning back to me, as though her words were more for my ears than Shazir's, she said quietly, 'There will be a place on Katiz's ship for all who help us this night.'

Warmth pulsed through me, and I began to wonder at the implications of her words.

'Atar,' I began, but my question was interrupted.

'Ho there! An-Zabati in the garden?' shouted a guard in Sienese, sauntering towards us, his hand on his sword. The archery range, and the armoury beside it, were at his back. 'Explain yourselves!'

I saw a captain's tetragram on his helmet and saluted. 'More grenades are needed at the front, sir.'

The guard squinted at me. 'Why aren't you carrying a lant—'

His voice faded mid-word and his eyes filled with shock. 'Lieutenant Jasper? But they carried you back on a stretcher!'

Shazir stepped around me, as fast as the wind. She shifted her crate to one hand and punched with the other. A frigid wake pulsed from her fist as from a boulder dropped into a pond, and behind the wake burst a cylinder of air. The guard captain's helmet cracked. Blood sprayed from the ruin of his face.

'Voice Rill could have seen that from the other side of the city!' I cried, grabbing her by the elbow. 'We are likely dead because of you!'

Shazir's hand was an iron vice on my wrist. 'We are here because of *you*, Firecaller.'

Atar pulled us apart and glared at me. 'Give me the keys, if you two would rather fight one another than the empire.'

I released Shazir, and a moment later she let go of my wrist. I led them both down to the armoury and opened the door. As they rushed in, I looked up at the artificial hill that separated the archery range from the Gazing Upon Lilies Pavilion. At any moment Rill might appear on the hilltop, raise a finger, and strike us all down with bolts of lightning. I released the spell that reshaped my face. No sense leaving a beacon burning.

'Firecaller,' Atar said urgently. 'Where are the grenades?'

By the faint lantern light that fell through the armoury's lone window, I led them past racks of swords and spears to a door marked with logograms that read *danger* and *flammable*. The squat room beyond smelled of sulphur and stale air. Crates stood in stacks. Six bandoleers already strung with grenades hung from hooks along one wall.

Katiz's runners took two bandoleers each and strapped them on, then pressed hands with Atar and Shazir and set off across the garden towards the servants' gate. I offered the remaining bandoleers to Atar.

'Find me,' she said, meeting my eyes as she took the grenades.

'When the last obelisk falls, Katiz and I will make for the dunes above the Valley of Rulers. There will be a place for you and your steward on our ships.'

I would have accepted her offer, but for my growing conviction that the wolf god was right, that this was not my place. After the arguments I had made to Jhin, could I stand by and take no part while the empire ground Nayen beneath its feet?

'I will find you,' I promised, and she ran to do her duty.

'While you watch her, the Sienese are burning down my city,' Shazir said angrily. She knelt beside a crate and tried to lift it.

'Drop one of those crates and you'll never have to worry about the empire again,' I told her. 'We need more bandoleers.'

While I searched for them, Shazir began to unload one of the crates. There was a quiet clink of clay on stone as she placed each grenade on the floor. Then she hefted the crate, tilted it from side to side, and nodded in satisfaction when none of the remaining grenades shifted within their nest of straw. 'You waste time, Firecaller,' she said, and made for the doorway.

A bloom of heat washed over my skin and a chill gripped my lungs. A thunderclap pounded my ears, followed by an explosion that shook the world around me, blasting the door to splinters. I found myself sprawled on the ground, my nose filled with smoke and plaster, amid gently rolling grenades, each one finally clinking to a stop.

Crates had cracked but not toppled. Dust poured from my clothes as I scrambled to my feet. Acrid smoke rolled along the ceiling. I covered my mouth and nose with a sleeve and felt my way along the wall and into the main room of the armoury.

Hand Cinder stood there over a blackened corpse.

'I shouldn't be surprised you came back,' he said, stepping over Shazir's body. A hissing whip of sorcery trailed from his hand. 'Foolish bravery and a lust for vengeance are common traits among you Easterlings. Yet you seemed so *refined*. So *rational*. So *Sienese* in your thinking.'

Swords hung on a rack beside me. I managed to draw one before Cinder's whip lashed out. The wood exploded, the blades clattering to the floor. He flourished his whip – a coiled, hissing serpent of blazing light, and I circled, stepping carefully around the fallen swords and a pile of shattered wood and plaster. Stars and the orange light of the burning city showed through a gap in the wall. Cinder lashed out and his whip cracked in the air between me and the broken wall.

'Shouldn't you be out in the city?' I said. 'This is a battle you've wanted for years.'

'I've fought enough battles. Alabaster needed an opportunity. Without at least one victory, he'll never be taken seriously in the capital.'

'You two never seemed friendly.' I stepped towards him.

'A charade,' he said. 'You're not alone in your capacity for deceit.'

He riffled his whip along the ground to menace my feet. If he had wanted to, he could have sent a bolt of lightning through my chest from where he stood, yet he played this game of distance, toying with me.

'Did you know that, all the while you thought you served as minister of trade, Alabaster intercepted your every decision? He let some of your policies slip through, just to keep up the illusion, but he did the bulk of the real work – most of it by night, so you wouldn't notice. You've only ever been our puppet, Easterling.'

I waited until Cinder cracked the whip again – there! – and retreated backwards, away from him, towards the broken wall. Flames licked at the ceiling behind him, crawling towards the ruined door and the crates beyond. I could not veer instantly. I needed to distract him.

'I tire of this pathetic chase,' Cinder said as I retreated again. 'For an Easterling, you lack ferocity. Perhaps that's your Sienese—'

I dropped my sword. The world sharpened in the wake of the flame I hurled at Cinder's face. It was met by ripples of feather-light cold. The fire swept around Cinder, curling into nothingness at the rim of his sorcerous shield.

He grinned as the last tongue of fire faded. 'Shielding magic, which you might have learned if you—'

While Cinder had crouched behind his shield, I had taken two steps to his right, clearing the way between myself and the room full of grenades. I called the wind and hurled it through the shattered door. Then I cast my third spell in as many heart-beats, gathering power and veering without waiting to hear the clink of grenades caught and shattered by the wind.

Cinder whirled towards the door even as I opened my wings to catch the blast wave, which carried me through the gap in the wall and into the smoke-filled skies of An-Zabat.

Shouts of alarm rose behind me as the armoury exploded, hurling strips of burning wood and broken weapons into the night air. A tidal bore of power surged out, giving me the mo-ment's warning I needed, and I dived quickly beneath a blade of lightning that burst from the wreckage and cut through the sky, so bright it dimmed the moon and stars.

Cinder stood in the ashes of the armoury, one arm hanging limp and blackened. His jaw was broken, his face charred. He poured his fury into another attack, but I was too far away and his sorcery spilled harmlessly into the night.

As it faded, a flash of light burst at the base of a nearby obelisk. The thunderclap of chemical grenades assaulted my still-ringing ears, followed by the grinding scrape of stone against stone and the shriek of tearing metal. The obelisk listed to one side and shed broken pieces that shattered where they fell. The red banner with its imperial tetragram fluttered as the obelisk, finally, collapsed.

There was another burst of light, a crack of thunder, and a rumble of falling stone. Then another, and the ancient, deep-rippling power beneath An-Zabat began to fade.

I left the city behind and rode thermals towards the Valley of Rulers. Another obelisk fell, and Cinder poured his rage into the roiling sky.

I followed the wake of Katiz's windcalling and landed on the prow of his windship. The moment I returned to my human form, Atar hurled herself into my arms and covered my cheeks with kisses. I held her close, buried my face in her hair, and tried to find the precise words for the scent of her so that I might always conjure it in poetry if not in fact.

'We thought you dead!' she exclaimed.

'Hand Cinder killed Shazir,' I told her.

'Her death was *naphnet*,' she replied, after a pause. 'Hers, and many others.' She gestured towards the city. No obelisks stood silhouetted by the fires that raged through An-Zabat and filled the billows of smoke with flickering orange light.

'They will wonder why we destroyed the obelisks before we fled,' Atar mused, walking towards the prow of the ship with her customary grace. Even in the aftermath of battle, she was beautiful and I wanted nothing more than to carry her to a cabin, to begin to build a life with her. But my gaze drifted to Jhin, who sat against the railing, watching the city skyline fade.

'I felt the Hand's sorcery and heard the explosion just as I was leaving the citadel,' Atar said. She met my eye and took my hand, twining her fingers through mine like dancing fire and silk. 'I brought the steward with me. As you promised, there is a place for him with us. As there is for you.'

'Atar ...' How could I explain? But she smiled sadly, leaned up to kiss my forehead, and I knew there was no need.

'They have windcalling now, and though Naphena's urn will run dry, they will try to cross the Waste,' Atar went on, running her thumb along the lines of my right hand, feeling the brush-wrought callouses on my thumb and the tips of my fingers, then the hair-thin scars of my witch marks. 'Their ships will be slower, for they will have to carry enough water for the journey, while we can draw on the blessing of our goddess, and we will not make their crossing easy. If you stay, you can help us fight them.'

I looked out across the desert. The dunes were orange tinged with purple shadows, an empty, undulating plain that reached from horizon to horizon. Plumes of sand rose behind the other windships as they scattered to the four corners of the Waste. Okara's words rose in my mind, as though spoken from the space where dreams are made.

There could be no third path through the world. I understood that now, as I should have understood it at Iron Town, where I was made to fight against my grandmother's people – my people. Service to the empire would always mean opposition to those who fought against it. To believe otherwise was to delude myself, to imagine that I might enjoy the fruits of the empire, such as education in magic – an empty promise, in the end – without participating in conquest. I could only ever be the emperor's tool, whether willingly or accidentally. Unless I followed in my grandmother's footsteps. Unless I fought back.

Resistance was the only path towards freedom.

And Okara had offered me a way to pursue the mastery I longed for, if I would use it against the empire. The woman of the bones. I would find her, learn all I could of magic, and wield that power to fight for Nayen, which I had for so long betrayed.

305

Yet following that path would mean leaving behind all I had found in An-Zabat.

I searched Atar's face, the arch of her cheeks, the emerald glint of her eyes, the slope of her neck, and carved them deep in my memory as once I had carved the doctrines and aphorisms of Sien. Let all my education, all my mastery, all that had earned me wealth and comfort be stripped away. Only let me remember her face.

'My battle isn't here,' I said. 'My grandmother—'

Atar pressed her forehead to mine and breathed deeply. 'I understand,' she said.

We stood together, her shoulder against mine, our hands entwined, her body tense, as we watched An-Zabat and the life she had known fade to a distant glow on the horizon. When even that had vanished from sight, she leaned close to my ear.

'Know this, Firecaller,' she said softly. 'You will have a place with us, always, should you need it.' Her hand tightened, then opened. She drew away from me and turned to Katiz.

'Windcaller!' she said. 'Strike an eastward course.'

At the edge of the Waste, where scrub and brush jutted from the sand, where mountains emerged from the haze of the eastern horizon, I called a wind that would carry me on falcon's wings across Sien and the sea. I bade each of the An-Zabati farewell in turn and, for a final time, thanked Jhin, who only nodded and returned to sulking at the rail, gazing south towards the Pillars of the Gods and Toa Alon.

At last, I stood before Atar. She touched my cheek and caught a tear that had gathered there. Regret gnawed at me, and again my mind and heart did battle, but tomorrow had come and our day had ended. She was my first love, a love born of shared struggle, of shared curiosity, of the resonance between two hearts entwining for the briefest moment before the pattern of the world carried them into separate futures. A love I would leave behind for the sake of a larger purpose at the prodding of a god.

'Farewell, Firecaller,' she said. 'Nayen calls you home.'

IV

A Witch of the Old Sort

23

Return

I made my way wide around even the smallest of settlements as I flew towards Nayen. Each night, I found a clearing or an abandoned cave in which to release my spell and curl into a ball of cramping muscles for a few hours of dreamless sleep. I ate an eagle hawk's diet – sparrows, rabbits, fish snatched on the wing – and wondered whether I could sustain myself indefinitely as a beast. When I became human again, would parasites and diseases that my eagle hawk body resisted return to afflict me? I mulled over these questions during the two-week journey east-wards over Sien's mountains and river valleys, if only to distract myself from deeper anxieties.

Was my grandmother still alive, even? Had she told my uncle about me? Would either one of them accept me, after all I had done? After Iron Town?

How would Oriole have felt, knowing I went to join his killers?

Fretting over such questions was fruitless. My first goal was to find this so-called woman of the bones. Okara had claimed that she would teach the deeper secrets of magic, beyond the canon, beyond even the witchcraft of my grandmother. If she did not exist or refused to teach me, I would find the rebellion and throw in my lot with them, if they would have me.

As I soared over the rolling sea – careful to avoid the imperial warships that patrolled the strait between Nayen and the mainland – I puzzled over the gods' interest in me. Perhaps it was as simple a thing as stealing a tool from the empire and turning it to their own purposes. Maybe it was enough for them to know that I *could* be turned. My grandmother had planted seeds of rebellion in my childhood. Then Atar had watered them and Okara had come to collect the harvest.

After two days on the wing, the familiar mountains of Nayen appeared on the horizon. My body ached and I longed to land on the shore, find a meal, release my spell, and sleep. But I had never spent so long in an unhuman body. Even the cramps and exhaustion I had felt after a single day left me incapacitated for hours.

I pressed on, flying past the beach, towards the interior of the island, now with a landing site in mind, a safe place – if it still stood.

I landed in the overgrown garden of the Temple of the Flame. The altar was dead and cold, as I had left it. My feathers – which became my clothes – were crusted from the salt air of the sea. Spasms worked up my arms and legs, across my chest, down my spine. The urge to sleep weighed heavily. I shrugged it off long enough to open the brass door and conjure a flame, which lit the coals there as though they were soaked in oil.

This done, I curled up, let warmth soothe my aching body, and prayed for a dream.

A shaft of light spilled through a torn window screen and woke me. I had little notion of how much time had passed, beyond a pressing need to relieve myself and a rumbling hunger. The wolf god had not visited me. I was left with no direction but *north* and a vague faith that Okara would not have called me back to Nayen if he did not have plans for me, and the intention to instruct me in those plans.

The first of my pressing needs was simple enough to satisfy; hunger was more difficult. I might have veered again and hunted some small creature – I had yet to experience any ill effects of living on an eagle hawk's diet – but I was still stiff and sore from returning to human form and shied from the possibility of worsening that condition.

My father's estate was a short walk away, and unless his business was suffering – which it might well have been, given my fall from imperial favour – his larder would be well stocked. My parents had escaped retribution for my grandmother and uncle's role in the Nayeni rebellion, but I was certain they would suffer for my treason. As the sage Traveller-on-the-Narrow-Way wrote, 'Fruit, sweet or sour, is a reflection upon the branch that bore it.' A preposterous idea, now that I considered it. I owed my character to Koro Ha, my grandmother, Hand Usher, Oriole, and Atar. My mother and father had borne me but not formed me.

I gathered a few of the books my grandmother had left behind. I could not carry them all, so I selected those that would teach me the most about Nayen: the myths and legends of the Sun King and his war to unify the island's warring states into a single nation. Age, experience, and my new frame of mind would reshape these stories, which I remembered only hazily, and leave me with a clearer view of the people I had chosen for my own.

As I left the Temple, I paused beside the statue of Okara. It seemed smaller than I remembered, more weathered. Vines crawled up one of its legs and its back was spattered with the stains of bird droppings. Yet the eyes held the same intensity, staring out from a familiar tangle of scars that I knew better from my dreams than from childhood memory.

Studying Okara's scars reminded me of my own, and I un-wrapped the blood-crusted linen that bound my left hand. The wound was healing, but slowly. At least there was no sign of infection. I rebound the wound with a strip from the hem of my sleeve and set off along the familiar overgrown path.

Facing my father would not be easy, especially if I had outrun news of what had happened in An-Zabat. It would fall to me to explain what I had done there, and why. Likely he would disown me, and any hope for reconciliation would die once I joined the rebellion.

What of my mother? She would curse me for following in her mother's and brother's footsteps, I feared. Yet I remembered her cool hand on my forehead, her care and kindness. She was not a callous woman. At least, I did not remember her as such.

A flock of tawny sparrows fluttered over the garden wall that I had climbed so many times in childhood. The late-spring afternoon was cool with a faint brushing of mist and the smell of green and growing things, and despite itself my heart filled with the warmth of nostalgia. I imagined my father in his reception hall, sipping the day's first cup of warm rice wine while he reviewed a letter from a distant business partner. Perhaps my mother sat nearby, humming to please his ear as she had often done when he was at home. Koro Ha was also present in this idyllic scene, reviewing my latest essay, tutting and shaking his head and smearing it with commentary. There was tea flavoured with citrus rinds waiting for me and a warm soup of freshly caught fish and fiery peppers. And a book I had yet to read, and a warm bed, and no need to fight in wars or wonder at the motivations of cagey, fierce-eyed gods.

A deep, shaky breath drew me back to reality, where I was a fugitive and there could be no going home.

I dropped from the wall, hissing in pain at the stiffness in my hips and knees, and ducked into a nearby stand of tall, fragrant grasses, watchful for any sign that I had been spotted. Two servant girls carried buckets to the spring at the north end of the garden, and a steward set off towards an isolated pavilion with a ledger under his arm, muttering and shaking his head. If my father were at home, smoke would have risen from the chimney of the audience hall and the servants would have bustled about bringing teas and fine wines.

My mother would be in her apartments, waiting for the evening meal she would eat alone. Propriety suggested I should request an audience from her stewardess and wait to be admitted to her apartments, but my mother wasn't Sienese and neither was I. I had known my grandmother and I had known Atar, yet the strongest impression I had of my mother was clothed in gossamer and silken drapery, distant and concerned but never active in my life, save in my sickness and in that fraught conversation just before my departure to An-Zabat.

Her door was open. She was alone in the house now, save for her servants, and she had no need to cloister herself from them. They too were means to my father's ends.

She sat beside the window, framed by the cool light that diffused through its paper screen. A serving girl poured tea while my mother paged through a book of poetry. Her hair, a black so deep I wondered how she dyed it, fell in two rivers that spilled over her shoulders and curled into ringlets at their tips. There was a reddish tint to her skin, most visible along her high cheekbones, but she was pale after so many years cloistered and out of the sun.

The teapot slipped from the serving girl's fingers. She did not scream, though her lips trembled as her wide eyes locked on mine. Her hand found my mother's wrist, and my mother followed the girl's gaze. At the sight of me she stood in shock, but her expression warmed with recognition.

'Alder—' Her voice caught in her throat.

'Mother,' I said. 'I've come home.'

'Orchid, fetch another teapot,' she instructed the serving girl.

'Tell the stewardess not to worry about the one that broke. I should have warned you that my son was coming.'

The girl forgot to bow as she left for the kitchen and eyed me warily but otherwise kept her composure. When she was gone, my mother rushed to me and wrapped her arms around me.

'Oh, my son!' she sobbed. Her arms were thin but warm. Her tears wet the kaftan I had been wearing when I left An-Zabat, now dirtied by the salt of sweat and sea and by many nights of sleeping on the earth. 'I thought they surely had you by now. When they came looking—' she gasped and shook her head, burying her face deeper into my shoulder. 'What have you *done*, Alder?'

There were words that would vindicate me, but I could not collect my thoughts well enough to speak. I wanted to weep. Her suffering, too, I laid at the feet of the empire.

The serving girl returned with green tea that smelled of moss. My mother released me and dabbed at her eyes with a kerchief.

'Put the pot on the table there,' she said, lowering herself into her chair. I took the seat opposite her. Orchid glanced from my mother to me and back again.

'It is all right, dear,' Mother said. 'It is only young Master Alder, come to visit me. I was not expecting him to arrive for a few more days.' She took a deep breath and smiled. 'It's overwhelming how much young men can change, isn't it? Run along, now. Why don't you have a ginger candy from the kitchen?'

The girl bowed and retreated from the room, though it was clear that her suspicion did not fade.

Mother poured tea. She stared at the earthenware cups and took slow breaths, regaining her composure, collecting her thoughts. I endured the silence until I could endure it no longer.

'I'm going to join grandmother in the North,' I said.

'Speak Nayeni,' she said sharply.

She placed one of the cups in front of me and went on, her sadness simmering into anger.

'Of course. You have no other choice now, do you? The magistrate himself came a week ago with a sealed letter from Voice Golden-Finch in hand. You've burned every bridge I built for you, shredded your every honour and distinction, and now there's nothing left for you but to die on a battlefield.'

'Mother—'

'I said to speak Nayeni!' she snapped. 'Have you lived with servants for so long that they are like mice and cockroaches to you? Every word we speak, they hear and will sell to the local magistrate if we talk of things like rebellion or say names like Broken Limb and Harrow Fox. Thank the sages your father hired these expensive servants from the mainland, else we would have no way to speak openly.'

'Fine, then. I will speak Nayeni.' I uncurled my fists and took a deep breath, which did nothing to calm me. 'Mother, can we talk of something else?'

'There is nothing else to talk of.' She sipped her tea.

'I followed the path that Father set in front of me,' I said. 'But now that I'm grown, I have made my own choice. The empire is cruel. You must see that.'

'You have chosen violence and stubbornness,' she said. 'Just as your grandmother and your uncle did. Children, the lot of you.'

'You chose to marry one of them!' I said, shocked at my own words but unable to stop them from pouring forth like water through a broken dam. 'You made yourself his possession, to be locked away in a single wing of his pleasure garden.'

'Do not speak of your father that way, or of things you cannot understand.'

'Yet you would speak of *my* choices, when you've never been shown a path and followed it into a pit of vipers?'

'I loved him, Alder.'

I looked at an empty corner of the room and tried not to grind my teeth. 'You loved him?'

'Yes.'

I thought of Atar, of her determination and ferocity, and felt the deep ache of longing in my chest. Then of my father, a simple man, over-fond of wine and interested in little but silver. For such a man, my mother had sacrificed her people.

'What about him is there to love?'

She set down her cup and slowed the pace of her speech. 'He was handsome and intelligent. He had a wit like I had never seen, and though he was never much of a poet, the simplicity of his expression struck me to the heart. He protected me when soldiers came to our town looking for women, and again when they came hunting the family of Harrow Fox.'

'You married him to protect yourself.' I raised my eyes, ready to challenge her, but she had turned her gaze to the window.

'No. I was already pregnant, then. He lived in Nayen as a merchant long before the empire sent its armies.' When she faced me again, her anger had faded to quiet frustration. 'I knew they would come, though. Your father taught me the logograms, and I studied his maps. The empire was always growing, and I knew it would swallow us eventually. Your grandmother and uncle dreamed of avenging themselves and restoring the Sun Throne. Idle dreams. Conquest was inevitable. But you would be one of them through your father's line, and you would have the best education your father could afford. I thought, perhaps, that our family could survive – thrive, even – in the new world.'

'You gave up before the battle began.'

'Did your grandmother teach you to think this way? To see everything as a battle? The world changes, Alder. We must change with it to survive.'

'Who fitted into their world better than me?' I almost shouted back at her. 'I had their education. I passed their examinations. I fought for them in the North and watched the best friend I will ever have broken and slaughtered!' The cup in my hand cracked. I set it down, pressed my thumb against a cut in my finger. 'I didn't choose to become their enemy, Mother. They had already drawn swords against me.'

My words hung for a moment. She sipped her tea, then leaned back and folded her hands. 'Your grandmother, too, saw persecution in their every act.'

'And you are blind to it!' I pounded a fist on the table, gritting my teeth against the pain when I realised it was the wounded left one. 'Do you forget what they did to your father?'

Her composure slipped. 'What has that to do with *you*? I should never have let her teach you. The sages know I tried to ...' her eyes drifted from my face to my hand, where blood oozed through my bandage and formed a thin trickle on the table.

'Nothing serious,' I said. 'When it became clear that the empire only valued me as a tool, I cut the tetragram from my palm.'

'Oh, Alder. Why?' She cupped my hand in her own. 'We are all the tools of others. Often unwittingly, but always. You have read the sages. We all serve things beyond ourselves.'

I pulled away from her, overcome with sudden loathing. She was blind to cruelty, even cruelty towards her own son. A cruel thought of my own found its way to my tongue.

'Why did you bear me, Mother?' I asked her.

Her back and shoulders went rigid. She regained her composure, restoring her expression of maternal concern. 'What sort of question is that? Because I loved your father and we wanted a child.'

'But only one? What if I had died? The early years are the most dangerous, aren't they? Most Sienese wives long to bear

319

their husbands two or even three sons, and some bear a host of daughters in the process.'

'We tried—'

'Did you?' Vindication gave my voice an edge, even as my sadness deepened. 'He could have cast you out when the soldiers came. It might have been easier, certainly safer. But you gave him a son, and that raised your station, elevated you in his eyes—'

'A foolish son pries into his parents' bedchamber,' she snapped, but I pressed on.

'We are all the tools of others, aren't we? He served your purpose, as you served his, and I served you both in different ways.'

'Get out.' Her voice was cold, her eyes like discs of iron.

'You would give up your only son?' I said. 'I suppose I'm more a liability than an asset, now.'

'What did she name you? Foolish Cur?' She stood, her hands and shoulders quivering with her rage, but she held it close, unwilling to raise her voice to match mine. 'You are her creature now. Leave, before I am forced to send a runner for the magistrate's guards.'

I faced her hard eyes, and all the fury and indignation fell out of me and left me hollow. This was not what I had wanted.

'Mother—' I said, switching to Sienese.

'*What?* Will you castigate me? Blame me for seeking safety, for setting you on a gilded path, the brightest possible in these hard days? Your accusations are darts that sink deep into my heart, but it is accustomed to wounds. Now go. Fight your stupid war. Become the tool of that dried-up old woman – kept alive by hate and rage, I'm sure. When I'm asked where my son is and how he serves the empire, I will say that he is dead.'

I swallowed bile and felt an echo of the primal terror a child feels when it believes its mother has abandoned it, never to return. I was astonished to find how much she mattered to me, this woman whose truths and hopes and fears I had come to understand even as I lost her.

'I'm sorry, Mother,' I said. 'Perhaps I shouldn't have come back to see you.'

'No,' she said firmly. She stared at me for a long moment, then slumped back into her chair, as though the heat of her fury had been holding her up. 'You have no place here, nor anywhere else in the empire. It would have been better for you to flee far into the West, never to return.' She leaned across the table and again cupped my left hand. 'But I *am* glad to have seen my son again, even if for the last time. My heart may break every day at the thought of this path you take, but it is only because I love you.'

'A mother's love should not be pain.'

She smiled, but there was deep sadness in her eyes. 'It has always been, for me.'

I could think of no response to that, but there was no need. We sat there while the tea cooled and the afternoon darkened to evening. Orchid returned to let us know that a meal had been prepared, and to ask whether we would like it served now or later.

'Now, thank you,' my mother said, and her voice broke the spell that bound us.

When the serving girl had gone, I stood, gathered my mother into a final embrace, and turned to leave.

'Alder,' she called after me as I reached the threshold. I turned and she opened a small chest in the centre of the table, retrieved three taels of silver, and handed them to me. 'Find a doctor to look at that hand. It's a dreadful wound and you have done a pitiful job of tending it.'

I promised her that I would, then crept away from my father's house, slipping over the wall as I had often done as a child.

321

I'd left before filling my grumbling stomach – though I filled my pockets with apricots from my father's favourite tree on my way through the garden – yet I felt full. We had spoken, and I understood her, though understanding brought with it a pain I had never imagined.

24

The Journey North

The moon and stars were out in full by the time I arrived in Ashen Clearing, the town nearest my father's estate. It had been a market day and a few townsfolk were still dismantling their stalls. I asked a woman of middle years where I might find a meal and a bed for the night. No bed, she told me, but I might find a bench or a patch of floor in the town common house.

Her directions led me to a wide, two-storey building in the centre of town that abutted a stable. Music drifted from its lamp-lit windows, played by Nayeni instruments – the two-stringed banjo, the reed flute, the ox-hide drum.

A table ran the length of the common room's ground floor, and farmers, merchants, and tradespeople alike crowded the benches. A young woman met me with a smile, wiped her hands on her apron, and showed me to a seat at the end of one table beside a weathered old farmer and his wife. I showed her one of my silver taels and her eyes opened wide in shock. It was likely more money than the common house made in a month. She said that the kitchens could slaughter a chicken for me, if I liked, but I told her there was no need and ordered a bowl of whatever the simplest fare of the evening happened to be.

The warmth of the room, the openness of its people – all were out of step with the life I had known. Certainly, some were dressed in simple clothes while others wore splashes of silk and velvet, and some ate roast fowl and steamed buns while others had only bowls of rice and vegetables stir-fried with scraps of fat, but the old farmer and his wife welcomed me without question the moment I took my seat, despite my rough appearance. Most stunning: men and women ate together. I had seen this in An-Zabat but taken it for a peculiarity of their culture. To find something so alien to my childhood – to my entire Sienese existence – only a few hours' walk from my father's estate was baffling.

I offered the farmer and his wife apricots, and they gave me a bun stuffed with cabbage and pork in exchange. They asked where I had come from, and I dissembled.

The old farmer put up a hand to stop me mid-sentence, not fooled for a moment by the explanation I had improvised for my strange, travel-worn garb. 'Don't worry,' he said. 'I'm not one to pry into the goings-on of the witch-carved.'

And I saw, to my further astonishment, a naming scar on his palm. But of course my grandmother had not begun with the intention of teaching me magic. That had come later, only when she felt she had no choice.

Before leaving Ashen Clearing, I bought a pair of hardy workmen's clothes, then fashioned my kaftan into a rough satchel. As spring gave way to summer, I moved north from common house to common house, enjoying the company of Nayen's folk and, on quieter nights, reading the texts of Nayeni myth and legend I had taken from the Temple of the Flame.

Inspired by those stories, I began to compose a narrative of my own, an account to make my grandmother and uncle understand the winding path my life had taken. I began with An-Zabat, refining the year I had spent there to capture the meaning of the experience in a series of vignettes. As I travelled, the narrative grew, stretching backwards to my childhood, then forwards again through Iron Town, then into the present moment. Soon I had a book of my own, carved in slats of bamboo that I'd harvested from the side of the road, bound with strips torn from my kaftan.

At each village, I kept an ear open for rumours of the rebellion. It still survived, divided into at least two bands. One, led by Frothing Wolf, had lain dormant for years. The other – which styled itself the Army of the Fox – was building strength, so the rumours went, in a place called Greyfrost Keep, nestled high in the mountains, not to be found on any map. The name rekindled a memory from early childhood, of when my mother chased her brother from our gate.

At the height of summer, I reached the village of River Oak. As I approached the common house in late afternoon, I saw Sienese soldiers lounging about near the stables, keeping watch over their officers' mounts. My first instinct was to press on to the next village, but would these men recognise me as the fugitive Hand Alder, wearing two months' growth of beard and commoner's clothes? It would be more suspicious, I considered, to move on without any guarantee of reaching the next village before dark. I bobbed my head in deference – one of the soldiers responded with a dismissive grunt – and ducked into the common room.

Two dozen soldiers lounged within, talking among themselves, or jeering the singers and servants, their affect more hostile than jovial. Other than a group of local girls who sang a Nayeni folk song accompanied by a pipe and drum, every woman in the room was a servant of some kind, carrying trays to and from the tables or refilling cups with tea and wine – an off-putting sight after my prior experiences with Nayeni women. It was impossible to imagine my grandmother, to say nothing of Frothing Wolf or Burning Dog, accepting such subjugation. Where Sienese soldiers went, it seemed, Sien's notions of gender followed, enforced in all likelihood by the sword. The few Nayeni men who sat near the door drank only tea, and quietly, without so much as a murmur.

I stopped at the threshold, stunned by the sight of a bow-legged, wispy-bearded doctor who went among the soldiers, checking blisters and taking pulses. Doctor Sho seemed plucked from my childhood, unmarked by the years that had passed.

I took a seat with the other Nayeni men and watched Doctor Sho go about his work. He diagnosed each patient with perfunctory speed, filled paper packets with herbs from his battered chest of drawers – which had aged far more than he – and pocketed the few coins offered in payment. When he finished with the last, I expected him to sit with them – he, too, was Sienese – but he hefted his chest and made for an unoccupied stretch at the end of the table. One of the hostesses brought him a bowl of pork and rice. He ate without looking up from his meal.

I moved to sit across from him. He only glanced at me with cold hostility, then again with uncertainty.

'What do you want?' he demanded.

I showed him my left hand. 'I've an injury. I promised my mother that I would have a doctor look at it.'

He ate another mouthful and, chewing, studied my palm. 'You'll have to pay.'

While he spoke, I unwrapped my bandage, and as the linen fell away his eyes widened. The vague recognition in them became a piercing certainty.

'You!' he gasped. 'What by the pissing sages are you doing *here*? And looking like *that*?'

'Travelling,' I said. 'How are *you* still alive?'

'I'm a doctor,' he replied, as though that were all the

explanation I needed. 'Weren't you Hand of the emperor? Don't be flattered. I've a good memory for idiot patients and I pride myself on keeping up with the empire's goings-on.' He again looked at my wounded palm. 'Though I must say, you stand out more than most idiots.'

'It's a long story,' I told him, 'one vital to the empire's goings-on, and one that not many in this part of the world have heard.'

'I gather it's not a safe one to be telling within hearing of that lot,' he said with a furtive glance at the soldiers. 'Which way are you headed?'

'North,' I said.

Doctor Sho nodded, dipping a few whiskers in his bowl. He leaned closer and whispered, 'To the rebels, then?'

'Maybe,' I said and nodded towards my injured hand.

He grumbled but shifted to my side of the table and began to examine the wound more closely. 'Just so happens I'm headed north too. There's a village called Burrow where I wait out the typhoons. I'll treat this and you can tell me your story on the way.'

He wrapped my wound in a poultice that stank like a chicken coop and made the scab itch and burn. I asked after the purpose of the medicine, which made him cackle and jab me in the ribs. When I asked again, he ordered another bowl of rice.

While we travelled, I shared my narrative with Doctor Sho, whose obvious distaste for the Sienese soldiers coupled with his other eccentricities made me trust him despite hardly knowing him. He asked no questions and in fact, though he had asked to hear it, showed little interest in my story. My description of Oriole's death – an old wound that still ached when I spoke of it – failed to elicit as much as a blink. Only when I told of the last time Okara visited my dreams and his instruction to seek out the woman of the bones did he react, a burst of laughter escaping from him, which he quickly suppressed.

'Do you know of her?' I asked him.

'Enough to know not to meddle with her, or with gods,' he said. 'But you've already pissed in the cistern, haven't you?'

'How do you know so much of magic?' I said. 'I've never seen you use it, and your hands are unmarked – though those wrinkles might hide anything.'

'Yes, mock the old man,' he said. 'I know of all the ailments that might afflict my patients, magic included. I've treated Hands of the emperor other than you, I'll have you know.'

'And yet you shy away from soldiers.'

Doctor Sho shrugged. 'We didn't offer to exchange stories, Foolish Cur. I fix your hand, you add to the library gathering dust between my ears. That was the deal. Now tell me this.' His tone became suddenly serious. 'Why in all the frigid hells do you want to join the rebellion?'

His question put me on my heels. 'The empire betrayed me. They tore apart my mother's family, buried Sor Cala, and destroyed An-Zabat.'

'They also gave you a life of luxury, something you'll not find among the rebels – who, as I recall, murdered your closest friend.'

'Frothing Wolf and her daughters did that,' I protested, troubled to hear my own doubts in his mouth. 'My grandmother and uncle had nothing to do with the siege at Iron Town, or his death.'

'I'm a doctor, and therefore accustomed to giving advice that isn't wanted and won't be heeded,' he said. 'You should chart your own road, boy. Do as I do. Stay out of all the mess.'

'I've the sense that it will find me, even if I try to run,' I said.

Doctor Sho harrumphed and said no more about it.

*

It was the first sunny day we had seen in a week, now that the storms of early summer had begun to wash across Nayen, warm but without the mugginess of rain. Songbirds flitted in the thick broad-leaf canopy overhead. We were in the foothills below the mountainous country of Nayen's far north, where Oriole had died and where I would find the woman of the bones.

We heard the rumble of carts and the echo of shouted Sienese, too distorted to make out clearly but with a commanding tone. Doctor Sho moved to the side of the road and unslung his medicine chest, as he often did while we waited for the Sienese patrols to pass – a more frequent occurrence the further north we journeyed. I moved to stand beside him and was careful to hide the palm of my left hand against my leg. Soon, twenty-odd soldiers emerged from around the bend. A few near the rear of the column seemed abashed, like scolded children. They patted their swords and scowled when they caught me watching them.

'What're you staring at?' one of them demanded.

'Leave off, Cutter,' said his companion. 'Captain'll tan us if you kill a couple locals too.'

'Bad luck for that last village we passed,' Doctor Sho said, when the patrol was out of earshot. 'Those bastards will need a place to stay through the typhoons. We'll have the first one any day now.'

I looked at the blue, cloudless sky. 'Really?'

Doctor Sho grunted. 'Calm before the storm. For a witch, you're terrible at reading the weather.'

'I spent most of my life indoors,' I said and followed him back onto the road.

As we rounded the bend, we saw blood on the cobbles, splashes of bright red standing out against the green moss and grey stone. A dog lay on the side of the road. One side of its face was matted with gore and a deep gash had split its eye.

'Bastards,' Doctor Sho hissed and spat on the ground. He

put his hand in front of the dog's nose. 'Still breathing, but not much. Quick, help me with this, or do you want the poor creature to die?'

The dog whined as I lifted its head. Doctor Sho wiped away the blood, revealing the pattern left by the wounds – long, thin cuts that crossed the dog's snout and sliced through its right eye. Scars I recognised, though I had seen them only in stone and dreams, never carved in living flesh.

'What are you, squeamish?' Doctor Sho said, rummaging through drawer after drawer. 'Hold its mouth open.'

I carefully prised the dog's jaws apart. Doctor Sho pressed a ball of herbs and suet on its tongue, then massaged its throat until it swallowed. He bade me cradle the poor animal while he bandaged its wounds.

'A one-eyed wild dog faces a hard life,' I said as he tied off the bandage.

Doctor Sho stroked the dog's back. 'We'll take him with us. There was a sedative in the medicine. You'll have to carry him.'

For all his gruff demeanour and miserly affect, it was this kindness of soul which must have led Doctor Sho into his trade. I wondered at what this said about the empire, that those whose role was to nurture and care – tutors and doctors – were such transient members of its society, travelling from student to student or patient to patient.

We waited on the road until the dog fell asleep. It was heavier than I had expected, and would slow us, but Doctor Sho said that we were close to Burrow now and would still arrive before all the stars were out and the common house was closed for the night.

By early afternoon, the clear sky had filled with clouds. A wind brought the sound of thunder from the east and it began to rain, gently stirring the canopy and undergrowth. As the road became muddy and the wind whipped at our clothes, I saw flashes of Oriole's death in every lightning strike.

The road crested a hill, then plunged into a valley where the lights of distant lamps shone like jewels. As we descended into the shadow of mountains to the east and north and hills to the south and west, the storm seemed to lessen even as I knew it was gaining strength.

'A good place for typhoon season!' I shouted to Doctor Sho. 'But why not spend the season in the South?'

'Shut up!' he yelled back.

The dog whimpered in my arms, startled by the thunder and lightning. I made comforting sounds and stroked its head.

As we approached Burrow, the palisade wall and the lone guard tower struck a familiar silhouette – too like Iron Town – and in the heavy rain I could see little of the surrounding landscape. My heart raced and my vision narrowed, and deep breaths did little to calm me. The dog must have sensed my anxiety. It whimpered again and stuck its tongue out between its bandages to lick my hand.

'It's all right,' I said, as though to comfort the dog. 'We're close to shelter.'

Shouts of recognition sounded from the gatehouse as we approached. The decorations on Doctor Sho's chest of drawers were recognisable even through the veil of mist and rain. The gate opened and one of the townsfolk on guard duty shepherded us to the common house – thankful, I think, for the chance to get out of the rain for a moment. Along the way he told Doctor Sho the local gossip. A few children and old folk were down with a summer fever, and a carpenter had broken his leg falling off a roof. Oh, and did we meet that band of soldiers on the road? Nasty lot. Half the hostesses in the common room wouldn't go near them, and with good reason. Lucky they moved on before the storm hit or Burrow'd be stuck with them all through typhoon season.

He assured us that the dog could have a place by the hearth, and if it recovered and was able to work, one of the farmers would take it when we moved on. Doctor Sho seemed relieved by this. I was not so sure the dog would be willing to stay.

The common house at Burrow was the largest we had visited, three storeys high and with four long tables on the bottom floor. The smell of a long-simmering stew had seeped into the wood-panelled walls, and though a band of musicians played, the air was so full of conversation that only the flautist's highest, most keening notes were audible.

Doctor Sho and I were not the only folk of the road planning to weather the storms in Burrow. There was a travelling tinsmith working through a stack of kitchenware and a bowl of stew in turns. Nearby sat a merchant and his guards, loudly gambling with a group of farmers, a young woman dressed in blacksmith's garb, and – I was surprised to see – a pair of Sienese men dressed in the uniforms of garrison troops. Like many of the larger towns, Burrow had a magistrate and a garrison, but usually the Sienese locals kept away from the common houses. Here they mingled with Nayeni women and showed no sign of offence.

I mentioned this to Sho while we shrugged out of our coats and hung them on the crowded pegs beside the door.

'The magistrate here makes a point permitting the Nayeni their ways,' he replied. 'He was born in this country and likely sat for the same examinations as you.'

This surprised me. Usually the empire sent magistrates far from their home province in the belief that the fewer ties the magistrate had to the people he ruled, the less opportunity there was for corruption or favouritism. And, more nefariously, dislocation meant that the magistrates were more comfortable with the prescriptions of imperial doctrine than the ways of the local populace. I wondered which of the young men in my cohort had been given such an unusual, indulgent posting.

Before I could ask Doctor Sho more about this strange magistrate, one of the hostesses led me to a table at the far end of the hall, near the musicians, where it was far too noisy to carry on a conversation without shouting. Doctor Sho set down his chest of drawers and went to join the card game. The hostess brought an old quilt for the dog and arranged it near the hearth, for which I thanked her, though her polite nod told me she did not hear a word.

A loud bang and the sound of the howling wind fell on the common room, stifling conversation like a blanket thrown over a flame. At once, every woman stood and hurried towards the stair to the first floor. The captain of the patrol we had passed earlier stood in the open doorway. Soldiers shuffled past him and the room rearranged itself to accommodate them as they took seats near the hearth. The rumble of thunder and drum-beat of the rain dissuaded any of the Nayeni men from leaving. They bunched together, travellers and townsfolk alike. I was unwilling to leave the dog's side and equally unwilling to move him. Doctor Sho left the dissolving card game and joined me.

'Warm up, men,' the captain said brusquely. 'I will inform the magistrate of our presence.' He faced one of the older Nayeni men, ignoring entirely the hostess who had been in charge of the common room before his arrival. 'I apologise for intruding upon you a second time. My soldiers require food and watered wine. As soon as the storm ends, we will be out of your way.'

The man – who was only a farmer, and in no way responsible for the common house – nodded, though it was clear that the better part of the captain's burst of Sienese had been lost on him. The patrol captain shut the door on his way back out into the storm, deepening the quiet, now broken only by the sounds of the soldiers dragging a bench over to the hearth and arranging their sodden cloaks to dry. One of them, whose scowling face I recognised from that afternoon, noticed the dog, then Doctor Sho and me, and he put on a mocking grin.

'Oy, Doctor, it was only a joke,' he said. 'What sort of fool wastes medicine on a dog?' He broke into a laugh, elbowing one of his companions until he too laughed, though his heart did not seem to be in it. They took seats across from us. Doctor Sho glowered but said nothing. The first soldier snickered.

'What? No sense of humour?' he said. He kicked off his boots. 'Well then, how about some work? My toes are a mess of blisters.' He waggled them and laughed again.

'Ten cash,' Doctor Sho said.

The soldier cocked his head. 'What was that?'

'Want me to come anywhere near those putrid stumps? Ten cash.'

'Now he asks for payment!' The soldier looked to his comrades, who seemed just as annoyed with him as Doctor Sho. 'He treats a mongrel dog for free, but from a defender of the empire he asks for coin.' He leaned across the table and jabbed a finger in Doctor Sho's face. 'What sort of loyalty is that? Maybe he's a rebel spy, eh? You know what we do to spies?' His grin became a snarl. 'Worse than we did to that dog.'

'Your breath smells like piss,' Doctor Sho said, slapping the hand away. 'I've a prescription to amend that, for fifteen cash.'

The soldier's face reddened. He leaned back in his seat and looked to his companions. 'You hear that? My breath smells like piss! Ha! Funny one, this doctor. Wonder if he'll still be laughing after we're through with him.'

'Enough,' I said, mustering some of the commanding tone I had learned leading men at Iron Town.

The guard was taken aback for a moment, then shifted his attention to me. 'Who's this? Your bodyguard? What, is he going to fight the lot of us?' Again, the uncertain glance at his companions.

'Leave off, Cutter, for the last time,' one of them muttered.

'You'll let this bastard insult the imperial legions?' Cutter said, acting hurt.

'You're no legion,' I said, tired of this foolishness. 'You're a road patrol. Lower than a garrison guard. They at least get a warm meal and a cot every night. Now leave us alone.'

Cutter's face darkened from red to purple. His arm whipped out to slap me and I brought up my hands to shield my face. A stupid mistake. Cutter stopped his swing and stared bug-eyed at my palms.

'He's witch-marked!' Cutter barked in surprise. 'And that scar on the ... Lads! It's the severed Hand!'

At Cutter's words, the atmosphere in the room shifted yet again. The subdued tension between Nayeni and Sienese became a taut wire between the soldiers, Doctor Sho, and me. A wire that snapped as the soldiers reached for their swords and Cutter caught my wrist in a calloused hand.

'Run for the captain!' someone shouted.

The world narrowed, a thousand possible ways the night might have gone collapsing at once as I made a fateful decision that seemed correct, if only in the blind rush of panic.

I sent a spear of wind through Cutter's eye. He flopped onto the table and I sprang to my feet, Sienese shouts of outrage mixing with Nayeni cries of alarm. And above it all, Doctor Sho screaming, 'What the *fuck* are you doing?'

I moved through the hall, dancing with the wind as Shazir had done, killing on her behalf, on behalf of the people of An-Zabat and Nayen and Toa Alon whose lives had been broken by the grasping hands of the empire. For my grandfather, who had lost his life before I could know him, and my grandmother, and my mother, forced to sacrifice dignity for safety. The soldiers in that common house became emblematic of the empire as a whole, and I took my vengeance.

The stink of blood and offal and the pleasant smell of that long-simmering stew mingled in a sickening bouquet. When I reached the door, a dozen soldiers lay dead behind me. Eight more stood before me, their swords drawn and faces full of terror. I paused, blades of wind swirling in my hands. In the lull, while the horror of what I had done settled in the back of my mind, Doctor Sho moved among the corpses, a roll of linen in hand, feeling for pulses and muttering curses under his breath.

There had been twenty-four, along with the captain and the aide who had accompanied him to the magistrate. Two still unaccounted for.

The door behind me flew open and a figure dressed in the robes of a magistrate strode out of the rain. A familiar splash of freckles marked his cheeks.

Clear-River paled to see the carnage I had wrought, even as he placed himself between me and his men. The captain followed at his heels, but a gesture from the magistrate made him stand back.

We studied each other, two men whose lives had crossed briefly in youth. He was no longer the whip-thin boy who had threatened me with a rumour. His freckles stood out on rounded cheeks, and his thick, reddish beard had been carefully groomed to frame his mouth. He wore silks while I wore peasant's clothes stained by the road. He did not gloat, nor comment on my fall from power. Yet I felt the urge to justify myself, to explain how the man who had bested him in the examinations had become this ragged, unkempt wanderer.

'What are you doing, Alder?' Clear-River demanded, recognising me more by my reputation than by my appearance, I was sure. 'Why did you come here?'

A few of the Nayeni sidled towards the door, as horrified as the Sienese, and I realised that I would have to kill everyone in the village to stop word of this massacre from spreading. Even then, in time a passing traveller or a patrol would stop, expecting to find a welcoming common house, and would carry news that would soon reach Voice Golden-Finch.

I had been walking the edge of a cliff and grown complacent, and now I had fallen.

'You've done well for yourself,' I said, stalling while my mind sought a way to escape without spilling any more blood. 'Someday I'd like to ask how you managed to secure an assignment in Nayen.'

'We'll never have that conversation,' Clear-River said. 'You're a murderer and a traitor. You should have listened to me all those years ago. The tale of the pollical cat proved a prophecy. They found your secret, as I knew they would.'

'Let me go,' I said, 'and no one else needs to die here.'

The captain stiffened. Clear-River put out a restraining hand. 'I know you could kill every man, woman, and child, soldier and townsfolk alike, if you wanted to,' he said. 'But I do not think you want to.'

'I do not need to,' I said. 'I only need to cut my way through you. The townsfolk will not pursue me. I am not their enemy. Let me go, Clear-River, and I will let you all live.'

'You *dare* threaten an imperial magistrate?' the captain bellowed, though his quaking hand betrayed his fear. 'Your Excellency, a severed Hand stands before us. We will be disgraced if we allow him his freedom!'

Clear-River took a steadying breath. The rain and the wind lashed the open doorway behind him. For a crazed moment, while we stood on the precipice of violence, I felt a pang of envy for his quiet life, working to make Burrow a place where Nayeni and Sienese could live side by side, growing to understand one another, to see humanity in place of an enemy. If the empire were ruled by those like Clear-River, there might be no need for rebellion, no need to destroy the obelisks of An-Zabat, no need for promising youths to die tortured in the rain.

A notion Atar would call foolish and optimistic.

Behind me, Doctor Sho spat a curse and stood from the last of my victims.

'What have you done with the position you stole from me?' Clear-River said. 'Destroyed a foreign city. Turned the emperor's ire on our home. Brought violence to this place of peace. You do not deserve to go free, as you did not deserve to wear the tetragram.'

'I did deserve it,' I said. 'I earned it. But I should never have wanted it, and I should have heeded your warning – as you must heed mine now, if you want this to end without more violence.'

Clear-River studied me, incredulous and outraged yet calculating weighing his duty to do everything he could to stop me against the likelihood that he would die in the attempt. When we were young, he had been willing to lie and manipulate his way into power, sacrificing honour for the sake of pragmatism. I had to trust that he would make the same sacrifice again.

'No more need die today,' he said firmly, then stepped to the side and bade the captain and his men do the same. 'Go, Alder.'

'What of the doctor?' the captain said. 'They were together on the road.'

'The doctor had no part in the killing,' I said. 'There is no need to cast him out.'

'Yes, there is,' Doctor Sho said. He shouldered his pack and came to my side, though he kept his eyes away from me. 'I arrived in your company. You think the friends of these dead will forgive that?'

'If he stays, he will either be murdered by a mob or he and I both will, unless I put him to death,' Clear-River said. 'Something you will not abide, I imagine. He goes as well.'

'There is one more thing,' I said and returned to the hearth, where the dog lay awake and agitated, whimpering and pawing at the floor. I gathered him into my arms. We collected our coats, all the while watching the naked blades of the soldiers around us. Did they know how easy it would be for them to cut my throat? Their minds reeled and wondered, I was sure, whether steel could hurt a man whose sword was the wind.

'All this over a dog,' Doctor Sho muttered, and we stepped out into the storm.

25

The Woman of the Bones

Thunder rolled and lightning crackled in the sky behind us. I flinched, fearing battle sorcery, but it was only the storm. The dog twisted in my arms. Though its sodden bandage had slipped off some time ago during the two days it had been with us, its wounds no longer bled.

We had not rested since leaving Burrow, and neither had the storm. Trees creaked and bent and snapped in the wind that howled around us. Doctor Sho plunged through the rain ahead of me, at the edge of the column of whirling winds I had called to shelter us. Though holding the spell was simpler than creating it had been, it still drained me. The phantom chill of its wake sent shivers pulsing through me. As flesh pushes out a thorn, so the pattern of the world pushed against my windshaping.

At least I no longer had to fear leaving a wake in the world. If any Hand felt my magic and was willing to brave the storm to hunt me, so be it. They were bound to come eventually, after what I had done.

Images of blood-smeared tables, of limbs scattered like bamboo beneath the scythe, had been painted in red on the back of my eyelids. Every blink returned me to the common house.

I had seen so much violence in my short life. It was an easy thing to reach for, as though the human mind sought it below the level of conscious thought. Yet it solved so little and caused so much suffering.

My foot slid out from under me. Burdened by the dog, I lost my balance and crashed to the muddy cobbles. The spell I had been holding slipped my grasp and the wind raked at us with renewed ferocity. The exhaustion that I had been fighting through the night and the long day reached deep into my bones to hold me down and drown me in the mud.

A warm tongue lapped at my chin. I had dropped the dog, and it now crouched beside me, licking insistently. I levered myself to my feet and prodded at my side for broken ribs. The dog took shelter behind my leg.

'It can walk now, can it?' Doctor Sho shouted. 'Guess it wasn't as bad off as it seemed. What about you?'

I nodded, taking deep breaths against the pain.

'Then whatever you were doing, start doing it again!' he yelled. 'My pack's catching the wind like a bloody sail!'

'We need to get out of the storm!' I shouted when I found my breath. 'I can't keep this up forever.'

'We *were* out of the storm!' he shouted back, an edge of outrage in his voice. 'Now we're at its mercy, thanks to you! If we camp, we'll like as not be buried by a mudslide. It'll take another day to reach the next village, at this pace. We'd be warm in Burrow if you hadn't ...' He trailed off, his expression strained. He shook his head and made a whirling motion with his hand. 'You're our shelter for now, boy!'

Reaching for magic was like dragging my hand through thick, clinging mud. The power to shape the wind was there. When I reached for it, I felt its wake – a cool breeze, incongruous against the muggy, soaking rain and howling storm. It was not exhaustion of the body that slowed me but of the mind, and the pattern of the world's resistance to my spell.

341

I squeezed my eyes shut and rebuilt the cyclone. It whirled out from me, pushing against the currents of the typhoon, slower and smaller than it had been. Quiet descended, as though we stood in the eye of the storm, though it was only a dozen steps across. The wake of the spell was not the cool breeze of wind-calling but a frigid chill that seeped into my spine and left me shivering.

'You look ill,' Doctor Sho said.

'I feel it,' I replied. 'I'm not sure I'll be able to do that again.'

'Then you'd best keep this one going.' He stood, adjusted the straps of his pack, and plunged ahead.

Darkness fell, and though the summer night was warm, shivers shook my body. Doctor Sho mashed a handful of herbs and rolled them into a soggy pill, which I swallowed but which did little to help me. The storm still roiled around us. Though I held it back, I could manage only a few steps before having to stop and rest.

The dog now raced ahead, into the brunt of the storm, always returning with spatters of mud along its tawny coat. It nuzzled my hand with its scarred nose, as though urging me on to some shelter that lay just around the next bend in the road.

'Come on,' Doctor Sho said. He put out an arm to brace me and looked at the cliff that bordered the left side of the road, a wall of rock topped with a cap of earth that threatened to fall on our heads as the wind and rain loosened it and prised it free. 'We can't rest here. You'd be hard-pressed to stop a landslide as well as a storm. We'll be away from these cliffs in a moment.'

With Doctor Sho's support, I managed to stagger a few more steps towards a bend in the road that led away from the cliff. Just a bit beyond that point, I told myself, I could sit for a moment to catch my breath and – hopefully – a scrap of warmth.

When we reached the bend, the dog barked and loped off the

road, disappearing into the undergrowth between a pair of pine trees that creaked and popped as they swayed, ready to snap and crash to the earth.

'Hey!' Doctor Sho called after it. He peered into the sodden undergrowth. 'What's got into it?'

The dog returned a moment later. It stood between the swaying pines and barked again, then vanished back into the forest.

'There's nothing that way but the face of a cliff,' Doctor Sho said. 'Bloody mutt's smelled some carrion along that deer trail, I'll wager.'

The dog returned, glared at Doctor Sho and then at me, and stamped its front legs. It barked again and turned its back on us yet stood where it was, looking over its shoulder.

'Stupid dog,' Doctor Sho muttered and waved it towards us. 'C'mere, you scoundrel. I didn't fix you up so you could lead us off to drown in a ditch.'

The dog huffed indignantly and fixed me with a long, reproachful stare. As I met its scarred, milky eye, I felt the same heady weight that had come upon me that first night at the Temple of the Flame when I'd stood before the stone gaze of the gods.

I pulled away from Doctor Sho.

'Where're you going?' he shouted after me.

I could offer him no explanation beyond my faith in the dog, which bore the same scars as the god who had called me back to Nayen.

'First you murder half a patrol, then you go wandering off into the woods in the middle of a typhoon!' Doctor Sho called after me, but I heard the squelch of his feet in the mud behind me. 'That'll teach me to take on a travelling companion. Pfa!'

The dog loped ahead of us, hale but for the angry red lines that criss-crossed its face, along a path that ran uphill, angling away from the road. The mud was slick and forced us to crouch and pull ourselves along, using trees and saplings for handholds. The dog stopped beside the basalt cliff, its tongue lolling and eyes expectant.

'See, I told you. Now let's head back to the road,' Doctor Sho said.

As he spoke, the dog vanished from view. Doctor Sho grumbled but we followed and found a narrow gap in the cliff face between two hexagonal columns of basalt. One rose straight from the ground, the other at an angle, so that they met several hand spans above my head. I saw no sign of the dog.

'It's a cave,' I said. 'Not a rotting carcass after all.'

'There's probably a dead animal somewhere in there,' Doctor Sho said. 'And if there's not, there soon will be. A cave in a typhoon! Nearly as stupid an idea as murdering a dozen men in the only town to be found for miles. We'll be trapped and drowned.'

As if in answer, a bark echoed from the opening.

'It's shelter,' I said. 'And we're uphill. The whole valley would have to flood for the water to reach us. Let's at least have a look inside.'

'You have no idea what could be in there,' Doctor Sho said. 'Bears ... something worse!'

'Would the dog lead us into a bear's den?'

'He might well lead us to something worse.'

'Why are you so afraid?' I asked.

'I'm just being sensible!'

'And I'm exhausted,' I said, and edged in after the dog.

'Boy!' Doctor Sho called after me, but I ignored him. The narrow cave made for slow going. It was just wide enough for me to fit sideways, with my back against one wall and my chest against the other. When I was out of the rain, I released the spell that had been holding the wind at bay.

Doctor Sho yelped and the wind whistled past the mouth of the cave.

'You could have given me some warning!' he shouted.

The fingers of cold that had gripped my spine finally un-clenched. Relief washed through me and I found the strength to conjure a flame. I held my right hand up to light the way.

'Come on,' I said. 'It's dry, and it looks like it widens out up ahead.'

'Fine, then, if you're going to be a bastard about it,' he mut-tered. 'But I'm not leaving my medicines behind.'

He pushed and I pulled, and though the chest of drawers lost a few more pieces of decoration, we managed to make steady progress. As we ventured deeper, I noticed stains on the walls, deep red and rich brown. I held my flame closer and saw that they were tiny, almost abstract images of people doing battle with a smear that might have been a bear, an oversized wolf, or a ferocious creature lost to time.

The cave doubled in width, then doubled again. The walls were no longer basalt but the older stone that lies at the heart of mountains. A narrow path wound through a forest of stalag-mites. Their deep shadows moved with us as we progressed.

'We should leave,' Doctor Sho said suddenly, his voice a whisper that nonetheless echoed through the cave.

I'd begun to ask him why when my light revealed the dog, sitting on its haunches at the feet of a woman. She was tall but stooped, with eyes that peered out from deep wrinkles. The skulls of birds hung braided in her long white hair. The cape of woven grass she wore glistened where it had been stitched with the feathers of crows and ravens.

'Do you fools know what it is that leads you?' she said, her voice deep and cracked as the cave.

'A dog,' I answered, 'marked like the wolf god Okara.'

'Huh! A lying, loathsome, cowardly bastard is what,' she

said. 'A dog! Ha! He's no more that dog than he is one of the countless statues your idiot ancestors built to him. And the favour they thanked him for? Hardly a favour at all.'

The dog blinked at the flame in my hand and huffed.

The woman peered past me and showed her yellow teeth. 'Been a while, Sho.'

Doctor Sho crossed his arms and glowered at her.

'Not even a greeting?' she said. 'Well, I'll learn how you got mixed up in this sooner or later.' She returned her attention to me. 'And you, what do you think you're doing wandering through my woods, tossing magic about like a tomcat tosses piss in breeding season?'

'I was holding back the storm,' I said, taken aback. 'Okara told me to seek a woman of the bones.'

She shook her head, clattering the skulls in her hair, and glared at the dog. 'Does the pact mean nothing?'

The dog whimpered. The woman rolled her eyes, then fixed them on me.

'I'm the one you seek,' she said. 'Call me ... Hissing Cat, I guess. There were other names, but that's a fine one for the mood I'm in.' She ventured further into the cave. I hesitated, unsure whether she meant for us to follow.

'It's not too late to turn back,' Doctor Sho murmured.

'You know her,' I whispered. 'If there's reason to be afraid, tell me.'

'Boy, you're in the company of a god and a witch of the old sort. What reason *isn't* there to be afraid? Let's be gone from here.'

'You'd prefer the storm to this ... Hissing Cat?'

'I would prefer to be flayed alive to her.'

'Why?' I demanded. 'Always you blame me for ignorance yet share nothing of your knowledge. Tell me why I should leave with you, and how she knows you, and I will *consider* leaving. You won't make it far on your own.'

Doctor Sho shifted from foot to foot and pulled at the wisps of his beard in agitation.

'Fine then,' I said and followed Hissing Cat. The dog – who I could no longer stop thinking of as Okara – fell into step at my side. A moment later, I heard Doctor Sho grumble and then his footsteps echoing behind me while he hurried to catch up. Hissing Cat had become a silhouette in the dark ahead of us. She carried no light – but what obstacle, the dark, to a woman on familiar terms with gods?

'So, you're coming after all,' she said.

'I would not give up this opportunity,' I said, trying to keep the fear she stirred in my gut from sounding in my voice. 'All my life I have longed for magic. Okara said you might teach me, and—'

'Did he now?' Hissing Cat crossed her arms and faced us. The wavering light made her face seem craggy as the stone. Okara shied behind my legs.

'I know a little already,' I said. 'I was Hand of the emperor, though ...' I showed her my left hand '... I cut myself free of them, and now I've struck out on my own. When I was young and had no witch marks, I tried to veer – unsuccessfully, but I worked the magic all the same. And now I can wield some Sienese sorcery, even without the tetragram, though not with any nuance.'

'Sien is an empire?' she asked. 'I've been away too long. And all you've told me is that you're sensitive, curious, and foolhardy. The first is your only asset.'

'I'm much less foolhardy than I was.'

She threw her head back and bellowed a laugh, and I feared the stalactites would crack and fall on our heads. 'Oh, my. That's one I'll need to write down.'

'Please,' I said. How could this path, too, lead to a dead end?

'Why should I teach you?' she replied.

'Because if you do not teach me, I will teach myself. I don't know the havoc I might wreak ... but I think you do.'

She considered this. 'I don't hear a threat. More a childish warning.'

'Does that mean you will teach me?'

'I won't teach you magic, child. The pact forbids it,' she said and returned to the path. 'But you have other questions, I'm sure. And I need something to do while I wait out this storm.'

'What is this pact?' I asked. What, if not magic, *would* her lessons be? 'Okara spoke of it as well. Something about the witches of the old sort holding the gods to an ancient agreement.'

'Oh, it binds us too – more than them, in many ways,' she said. 'That is something I can teach you, I suppose. Though not now. I like to sit down when I bloviate.'

As we delved deeper into the cave – Hissing Cat leading the way, Okara at my heel, and Doctor Sho muttering along behind – the paintings on the stalagmites and the walls became more frequent and more complex. Many showed scenes of hunting, like the one at the mouth of the cave, while others were more placid: a family gathered around a fire, a herd of antlered beasts grazing between stands of trees. One drew my eye and held it. It showed a seated figure surrounded by a fractal pattern in white chalk, like lightning but rounded and radiating out from the figure's head like a crown.

'Did you paint these?' I asked Hissing Cat.

The skulls in her hair clattered as she glared over her shoulder. 'How old do you think I am?'

I had no answer.

She saw the figure that held my attention. 'A witch of the *very* old sort,' she said wryly. 'No. These were here when I found

348

the place. The hands that painted them died long before I came spitting and yowling into the world.'

'What brought you here?' I said.

'A much longer journey than yours,' she said. 'And one I'll not tell standing in the middle of this cave, especially not when we'd be sitting 'round a warm fire by now if you'd stop asking so many questions.'

'I warned you that I was curious.'

The cave opened into a vast chamber. The roof was high enough that the light of my little flame never touched it. If not for the echo – and the stalactites jutting down out of the dark – we might have been walking beneath a night sky empty of stars.

At the centre of the chamber stood a column in the shape of an hourglass, formed by the meeting of a stalagmite and stalactite. Hundreds of handprints, all of different colours and sizes, covered the entire column, beginning at the floor and rising beyond the reach of my light.

'Yes, yes, it's very moving,' Hissing Cat muttered. 'Come. My home is just ahead.'

'How did they make it?' I asked.

'Sho, is there a way to shut him up?' she said.

'If you ignore him long enough, he gets all quiet and introspective,' Doctor Sho replied. 'That's been my strategy.'

'I'm not *that* talkative,' I protested. Okara whined – in solidarity with me, I told myself, and not in agreement with Hissing Cat.

The forest of stalagmites thinned and a warm light appeared ahead of us, which soon resolved into a smouldering campfire. Behind it, bathed in shadow, stood a house built in the old Nayeni fashion. Its roof was tiled like the Temple of the Flame and it had a timber-frame construction, the wood fitting together with pegs and glue rather than nails.

Beside the campfire stood a pile of what I at first took for flat stones, but as we drew nearer I saw that they were bones – bovine shoulder blades, dozens of them, piled like detritus. They were carved with letters I did not recognise.

'Before you ask,' Doctor Sho whispered. 'Those, and not the skulls, would be the *bones*. The skulls are new ... among other things.'

'What are they for?'

'So many questions!' Hissing Cat said. 'No more talking until after I eat. I had a soup ready when you fools wandered into my home. It's thin, but you're welcome to a cup. Mushrooms and ...' The skulls in her hair clattered as she turned and smiled. '... bone broth.'

We followed her into the single broad room of her house. A brazier full of old coals stood at its centre. A collection of shoulder blades hung on the walls, carved with the same strange letters and defaced with long, jagged cracks. She had hung them haphazardly on pegs, and I could deduce no reason why these, and not the others, deserved to be displayed rather than cast aside.

The soup was simple yet hearty and satisfying, and though I nursed a thousand questions my exhausted mind soon succumbed to my full stomach. Hissing Cat unrolled a straw mat for me and chuckled as I sprawled out and began to doze.

'This one? Really?' she said as Okara padded up to me. The dog barked and curled up in the small of my back. Hissing Cat shrugged and I realised as sleep took me that, in the flurry of all my questions, we had not thought to warn her of the danger that followed in our wake.

My mind swam through a scattered dream. A vision of surging oceans hurling high black waves that boiled into steam. The earth splitting wide and bathing primordial forests in flowing stone and flame. Towering figures strode through it all, like

350

great ships cutting their wakes deep into the pattern of the world, with ribbons of harsh light unfurling from their heads.

I woke to a sudden snapping noise and a smell like burning dust. Doctor Sho snored nearby, one arm tangled in the straps of his medicine chest. I rose, accidentally nudging Okara awake, and followed the sound and smell out into the cave.

Hissing Cat crouched over her fire, pressing the tip of a long needle into the coals. With her free hand she took a shoulder blade from the pile beside the fire. The runes that marked it seemed logographic, like Sienese writing, but written with symbols I had never seen before. She pressed the white-hot tip of the needle to the centre of the shoulder blade. With a curl of acrid smoke and a loud snap, the bone cracked. Hissing Cat studied the fractures, muttered to herself, and tossed the scapula into the darkness, where it shattered against the stone.

'As I recall – and I haven't been in society for some time, so I might be wrong – it's rude to stare at other people,' she said, and reached for another shoulder blade.

'I didn't want to disturb you,' I said.

'Then you should have stayed asleep,' she said. 'Or kept out of my cave. And before you ask, I'm trying to decide what to do about you and your … dog.'

'The bones give you your answers?'

She nodded. 'These runes are my question. When the bone cracks, it gives me an answer, sometimes as simple as yes or no – though not in this case. Sometimes I see the answer and feel relief. Sometimes I feel regret. Either way, I know the choice I should make.'

'That seems unnecessarily complex,' I said.

'When I and the world were young, the witches of the *very* old sort who could sense the pattern of the world, but who did not understand it, used this method to divine the pattern's will. They believed that, by fitting their actions to their divinations,

they could avoid calamity and prolong their lives. Which was
... partly true. Knowing that a volcano will erupt or a locust
swarm descend or a wildfire break out is useful, but knowing a
calamity will come is not always enough to avoid it. Sometimes
such knowledge is more a curse than a blessing.'

'Yet you keep their ways alive.'

'You are being very careful not to phrase your questions as
questions.'

'I don't want to overburden you.'

'Yet you felt no compunction about inserting yourself into
my life and demanding knowledge that I cannot give.'

'Because the pact forbids you to give it,' I said.

'Yes,' she said and pressed the needle to the bone. She studied
its cracks for a breath longer than the last, then set it down
beside the fire and motioned for me to sit. 'That knowledge, at
least, I can share. Though there is little to teach.'

I sat across from her and could not resist glancing at the
shoulder blade she had kept.

'I won't waste your time with tales of the war between the
gods at the world's dawn,' she said. 'Know only that there *was*
a war. One that filled the sky with lightning, sundered the
land, divided the waters, and bore mountains with fire for their
afterbirth. Into this chaos, humankind was born, cleverer than
its animal kin, able to discern the deeds of the gods from the
pattern of nature, and terrified of their power. In their fear,
many begged the gods for mercy and favour, but others nursed
their outrage and sought the power to shape the world as the
gods did.

'It was a power they already held, for humanity had something of the divine. Awareness, but more than awareness: the
power to consider, and to choose. Not all used that power, and
most lived straightforward lives, seeking pleasure and avoiding
pain with only a modicum of thought.

'But among those who *did* use that power, the first witch was born. Not when she crawled from her mother's womb, but when she reached out to the world, felt the shape of the pattern, and – as she might bend her own arm – bent *it* to her will. She taught others, who taught others, and soon there were enough to challenge the gods, to demand that they cease their endless war, to bring an end to all the calamities their conflict wrought upon the world. Of course, the gods refused. We were rude creatures in their minds. Would you accede to the demands of a dog?'

Okara yipped and Hissing Cat glared at him.

'The gods did not listen. And so the witches of the old sort waged against them a battle that threatened the end of all things. When the world seemed so brittle the slightest spell might break it, the gods and the witches of the old sort met, parlayed, and made a pact. No longer would the gods wage their war for dominion over the pattern of the world, nor would they interfere directly in human lives. But in exchange, the witches of the old sort would allow their power to be sealed.'

I held out my right hand to show the witch marks there. 'What of this?'

'That is the seal itself,' Hissing Cat said. 'The witches of the old sort were unwilling to give up all of their power. The gods agreed that any who showed the capacity should be taught, but that none could be trusted with the whole of magic. We each chose a few powers of our preference and taught them to our people.' She pointed her needle at the scars. 'That is the symbol of the pact I made with Okara, Tollu, and Ateri.'

'But my grandmother wielded magic beyond those limits,' I said, remembering when I had awoken in her arms returned to my human shape, aching but alive.

'Not so,' a voice echoed in my skull, like my own thoughts but placed there by another. A voice I knew from my dreams.

Okara lay in the doorway of Hissing Cat's house, watching

353

us, his scarred eye glinting in the firelight. 'She unmade your magic, Foolish Cur,' the voice said. 'She restored the pattern as it would have been had you never reshaped it to your will. The pact does not forbid such a thing, though the effort of it nearly killed her.'

'You can speak,' I said.

The dog barked.

'He's a god,' Hissing Cat pointed out. 'But speaking strays close to violating the pact, so he'll say as little as possible. Put a paw wrong, dog ...' She pointed her needle at him, then drew it across her throat.

'I am not the only one who strains the pact,' Okara said. 'You have hidden yourself long, Hissing Cat. Have you kept an eye on your peers?'

'How could she have done?' Doctor Sho said, emerging from the house and rubbing the small of his back. 'She's been in a bloody cave for the better half of a millennium.'

'I had passed on my pact and watched my students succumb to ambition and brutality, like the gods before them,' Hissing Cat said. 'Gods, beasts, humanity – none can endure peace for long. Always there must be war, and I tired of it. But enough of me. What's the dog talking about?'

'The emperor,' I muttered. The weight of his power had eclipsed even my dreams of the wolf gods.

Hissing Cat shrugged. 'What about him?'

'He's one of you,' I said, though I felt none of that awe when I looked at Hissing Cat. 'Only he made himself King of Sien and made Sien into an empire – one which conquered this island, along with everything east of the Batir Waste.'

'I knew of his little kingdom, and why should I care if it's grown and devoured its rivals?' Hissing Cat glared at Okara. 'Nation building is no violation of the pact.'

'But he gives power to his Hands and Voices,' I said.

'Transmission is the pact magic of Sien,' Hissing Cat said. 'Meant as a way of communication, or so Tenet – your emperor – led the gods of Sien to believe.'

'A magic suited to that already sprawling kingdom,' Okara cut in. 'Yet he has put it to uses we did not anticipate.'

'If he has broken pact, rain fury on his head,' Hissing Cat said with a dismissive wave. 'What has it to do with me?'

'Where the emperor conquers, he outlaws local customs,' Doctor Sho said, seated on the steps of Hissing Cat's house. 'Think, Cat. You know well enough what you stood to gain from the pact. Safety. A world that wasn't cracking apart at the seams. Did you ever stop to ponder what the gods got out of it all?'

'They got to survive, is what,' Hissing Cat said.

Doctor Sho stared at her, his expression drawn with stale frustration. An undercurrent ran beneath their exchange, speaking of a long, fraught familiarity. I recalled his hesitancy to enter the cave. Had he known we would find Hissing Cat here? What reason did he have to want to stay away?

'While you held onto a scrap of power, they held onto their rivalry,' Doctor Sho said. Who was this strange little man, with such knowledge of ancient things that appeared in no history I had ever read? I might have asked how he knew so much, but he still carried anger towards me after the massacre at Burrow, and I had no interest in diverting our conversation into such troubled waters while it seemed to flow so easily towards topics I had longed to discuss my entire life. 'The pact forbade them from waging open war,' he went on. 'So, rather than dominion over the pattern, they vied for worshippers and waged their contest on the battlefield of human culture.'

'Then the gods of Sien are losing,' I pointed out. 'Growing up, the only gods I knew were Nayeni. My father taught me to worship the emperor and the sages – a witch of the old sort and his servants.'

Doctor Sho nodded. 'The Sienese gods have lost, yes. Yet the borders of Sien are always expanding.'

'And the ranks of the emperor's Hand are always growing, and with it the canon,' I mused. I was seeing glimpses of the emperor's grand strategy, but I needed to better understand the rules of his game. 'Wherever Tenet conquers, he steals magic – or, at least, that's what he claims.'

In fact, I realised, with the sorcery of transmission he could add any magic at all to the canon, just as easily as he could wield any magic in the world. He was a witch of the old sort, after all. So why didn't he? Why go to all the trouble of using me to infiltrate the windcallers when he could have given his Hands the power to call the wind whenever he pleased? And why wasn't it a violation of the pact when he gave his Hands magic meant for the Girzan or the Toa Aloni?

'He isn't stealing magic,' Okara said. 'He is stealing the pacts themselves.'

I rubbed my forearms and thought back to the sting of Katiz's needle.

'A pact gives the right to power over certain aspects of the pattern,' Hissing Cat elaborated. 'The pacts were made with spells of the old magic, woven to restrict the changes a witch might make to the pattern. For example' – she gestured towards Okara – 'when we made our pact, I agreed that my followers would only veer and conjure flame, and so I crafted a spell and a seal, and carved it in flesh.'

'Thereby weakening your followers by constraining them,' I said, remembering Oriole in my arms, my desperate grasping at a deeper power beyond the sorcery of healing, and the impregnable wall that kept that power away. 'Once one Hand is marked by a pact and wields its magic, the Voices can learn it – they feel every magic a Hand touches. Then it can be added to the canon without the emperor teaching them himself and violating his own pact with the Sienese gods.'

Okara stood and his hackles rose. 'One witch might wear many marks without breaking pact. As you well know, Foolish Cur.'

'Each magic in the canon is permitted by a pact, but they were separated,' I continued. 'One by one, the emperor is joining them together, like the pieces of a puzzle. Yet at any moment he *could* transmit the old magic and make every Hand as powerful as a witch of the old sort.'

Okara wagged his tail and barked.

Hissing Cat scratched the dirt between her feet with the tip of her needle. 'That would violate the pact.'

'Which is why he progresses as he does,' I said, imagining a Stones board – the slow, subtle push into enemy territory, the constant need to disguise the purpose of every move even as it paved the way to victory.

The dog wriggled, hopping from one paw to the other. A slow whine built in its throat.

'I'm sorry,' I said. 'I don't see ... It can't be that he means to reignite the war with the gods, can it?'

'It can be nothing else,' Okara said.

'But that would mean the end of the world!'

'Not if he struck fast enough.' Hissing Cat stabbed her needle into the fire. 'If – *if* – you are right, the truly clever thing he's done is to find a way to make his own witches of the old sort. With transmission, he could turn 10,000 ordinary men into an army of sorcerers with the old magic at hand.'

'You speak as though you *want* him to do this,' Doctor Sho said.

'Age does little to kill old grudges,' she replied. 'As you and I both know.'

'But if he fails—' I began.

'This is all based in speculation, and by a child,' Hissing Cat groused. 'Oh, don't take offence. I've been alive for quite a while. Thirty is very, *very* young.'

'I'm twenty-three,' I mumbled.

She scoffed. 'Not a child, then – an infant! I know Tenet, your emperor. I need not speculate. He would not risk the world for petty revenge. Okara, you must chafe at the loss of your temples and witches. That is all that concerns your god, boy. The first and pettiest rivalry: the contest between divinities.'

I considered her words and found myself floundering in a sea of new information. Gods and witches of the old sort were beyond my comprehension, but there were a few certainties that I clung to, anchoring myself.

'I am not a god and have no stake in their rivalry,' I said. 'All I know is that I watched children hunt for rats in the streets of An-Zabat and that it was the An-Zabati, not the empire, who tried to feed them.'

'I've been all over this empire of his, and I can say that the boy is correct in this – the empire is cruel,' Doctor Sho said. 'It has a beauty of its own, and its culture is far from empty or meaningless, but it is self-centred and callous, as Tenet has always been. Whether or not he means war against the gods, he certainly plans to craft a world of his own design and rule over it forever. And it is not, I think, a world you would want to live in.'

Hissing Cat opened her mouth to speak but Doctor Sho put up a hand to silence her. 'You could go on living in this cave and pretend that what happens outside is not your concern, but you once fought to save humanity from the whims of the powerful. Why not do so again?'

'I always took you for a coward,' Hissing Cat muttered.

'Oh, I am,' Doctor Sho said with a heavy nod. 'But I'm also a doctor. What I prescribe for you may not be the medicine I need.'

'Will you teach me, then, if she will not?' I asked him.

His expression towards me hardened.

'I know I erred at Burrow,' I said, 'but—'

'He can't teach you,' Hissing Cat interrupted.

'Because of the pact?'

'Because I'm not a witch,' Doctor Sho said flatly. 'I'm just a doctor. A very, very good one.'

'That's impossible!' I blurted. 'No ordinary doctor could know as much as you do, about anything.'

'As I said, I am very good,' Doctor Sho repeated, turning the conversation back to Hissing Cat. 'And my history is not at issue here. Her decision is.'

The fire crackled. The dog, at last, lay quietly. I watched Hissing Cat stare into the flames.

'Every heart in the world should break when children starve,' Hissing Cat said, 'though at times that is where the pattern leads.' She reached for the bone she had kept at her side. The firelight played along its surface, filling the cracks and carved runes with shadow. 'You didn't give an honest answer when I asked before,' she said at last. 'Why do you want to learn?'

'Because I have seen the cruelty of the empire and I want to resist it,' I said and leaned towards the fire, letting hope rekindle in my chest.

The skulls in her hair clattered. 'No. You sought magic before – you said so yourself. Tell me truthfully.'

My mouth went dry. Like the imperial examinations, my answer to her question could open a door or forever seal it.

'My grandmother marked me,' I said. 'I feel a duty to—'

'No one ever sought magic from a sense of *duty*,' she snapped. 'Last chance, boy.'

She had asked for the truth. Would that be enough?

'When I was a child, I felt the wake of my grandmother's magic,' I said. 'It was true to me, and meaningful, in ways that her stories and my tutor's lessons never were. All my life I have been constrained by the paths others intended for me. I want to make my own way through the world, for my own reasons, based on my own understanding. And the first, true step is learning magic as I first touched it. Magic without the canon, without a pact.'

She studied me for a long moment and I felt nausea blossom in the pit of my stomach at the prospect of rejection.

'The pact forbids me to teach you magic beyond the pacts you wear,' she said, 'but I can teach you the pattern – the world as it is that you so long to comprehend. And when you have comprehended it, I can teach you how to do as your grandmother did when she made you whole, to restore the pattern as it ought to be and unmake the spells of your enemies. Who knows? If you're as bright as you claim, perhaps with what little guidance I can offer you'll arrive at the old magic on your own.'

I sat with her words, unable to believe her.

She was going to teach me. Here, I would find the answers to questions that had dogged me since childhood. Relief washed through me, and then excitement, fast and hot and energising as lightning.

'I'm hungry,' she muttered. 'There's smoked fish in the house. We can start after I've eaten.'

The shoulder blade whistled as she flung it through the air. It, too, shattered in the dark.

26

The Pattern of the World

'No, you idiot,' Hissing Cat snarled. 'Don't try to *do* anything yet. Just feel how the pattern changes and rewrites itself around the flame.'

I knelt beside her fire pit, my eyes bound by a cloth that stank of mould, my hands in my lap and my legs folded beneath me. The first autumn chill swept through the cave and pricked goosepimples on the back of my arms and neck. I focused on the sensation and dwelt within it until, like the pain in my knees and the stiffness of my shoulders, it no longer felt apart from me but core to my being.

The cold – and the heat that washed over my chest and thighs – was outside of me. The sensation was the shadow of the real, cast on the wall of my consciousness. The fevers and chills, cramps and weight that I had felt in the wake of magic were shadows just the same. The first step in comprehending the pattern, Hissing Cat had said, was to perceive the distinction between the self and the other, and to regard the other as its own reality.

'Do you feel how it burns but should not burn?' she asked. 'How no fuel is consumed, yet there is heat?'

Her voice was muted, as though far away. In my mind I was a sphere, as hard and smooth as jade, and all around that sphere the myriad things of the world revolved in an infinite, dizzying dance. I touched them with the same sense that had once touched the walls of the canon, and I felt the pattern as I had when I was a child, before I wore the witch marks.

There was another will with me in the pattern, like a spar of iron jutting down from some higher, unseen place, moving against the flow of the dance.

'I feel it,' I said.

'Good,' Hissing Cat said, her voice its own intrusion. 'Now extinguish the flame.'

I pressed against the spar but it was solid as the walls of the canon.

'Force it out like the thorn it is,' she instructed. 'Feel the world as it wants to be. Align your will with the pattern.'

I took a deep breath and opened myself further. *Align my will with the pattern ... align my will with the world as it was, is, and will be.*

But there were things I wanted that were not and could never be. I wanted to be on the Batir Waste, on the prow of Katiz's windship, fighting the empire side by side with Atar. I wanted to be in Voice Golden-Finch's garden, drinking and playing Stones with the only friend of my youth. Yet I saw only crumbling obelisks and Oriole's blood on the ground.

'Enough!' Hissing Cat barked. The spar vanished from the pattern and she tore the blindfold from my eyes. 'Useless fool.'

I opened my mouth to explain, but she waved a hand to silence me. 'I'm through for today, but you are not. Every teacher you've ever had has given you only their limited, narrow vision of what is possible. Until you see beyond that, you'll never grasp the pattern in its completeness. Resume the first exercises until you can feel the pattern with your eyes wide open and a monkey screaming in your ear. I'm going to do what I would be doing if that bloody dog had never led you here.'

I saw the bait but bit anyway. 'What's that?'

'Taking a nap.'

The door of her house banged shut.

I swallowed my frustration, shut my eyes, and tried to open myself, repeating the breathing exercises that had been Hissing Cat's first lesson. At twelve years old, I had veered by little more than instinct. It had been easy to imagine that I could change myself and the world with a thought and my force of will. Age and experience had taught me otherwise, however, had bound my mind with the rigidities of pact and canon.

After so many years, I had found someone willing – and *able* – to teach the deeper truths that had always lingered just beyond my comprehension, taunting me. Perhaps the canon had not only constrained my capacity for magic, but reshaped my mind, leaving me blind to the deeper truths of the pattern. No matter how Hissing Cat tried to teach me those truths, I might never be able to learn. A terrifying thought that filled my mind with heat and thunder, ruining any possibility of concentration.

I stood, massaging sore knees and a stiff back, and set off towards the mouth of the cave. When not learning from Hissing Cat or continuing to expand and refine the account of my life that I meant to give my uncle, I had taken to sketching and cataloguing the cave paintings. As I examined them by torchlight – Hissing Cat had forbidden me to so much as conjure a flame until I could extinguish hers – I marvelled at what they evidenced: that ancient people had lived lives different yet parallel to mine and walked these same caves thousands of years before.

How, I wondered, had they shaped the pattern? Which of their choices had rippled down through history to create the world I knew?

Footsteps echoed from the mouth of the cave. The light of another torch bobbed along the stone wall and revealed Doctor

Sho as he rounded the bend. His satchel bulged with the herbs and other medicines he had set out to collect. 'Seems one of us isn't having a very productive day,' he said, noting the paper and charcoal in my hand, taken from Hissing Cat's surprisingly robust supply. 'Still can't put the candle out, eh?'

'I could conjure a flame with the old magic, or veer, or even wield battle sorcery,' I said, 'but she won't let me do those things. She has me trying to stop *her* from wielding magic but won't tell me plainly how I'm meant to do that. But then, she's a witch of the old sort; is it any surprise her will is stronger than mine?'

'There were witches of the old sort who lost their sense of the pattern,' Doctor Sho said. 'They nearly broke the world in their effort to save it. She wants to be sure you won't make the same mistake.'

I glared at him. 'That does not sound like something a mere doctor could know, no matter how skilled. Do you intend ever to tell me the truth?'

'Do I *owe* you the truth?' he shot back. 'You've lived a life full of secrets, Alder. You know the value in keeping them.'

'You think you cannot trust me?' I asked.

'I watched you kill a dozen men at Burrow,' he said.

'I was fearing for my life!' I replied. 'You are right. I know the value of a secret, and those men had uncovered mine.'

'And in response you took their lives, in the process revealing your secret to dozens more who did not yet know it.' He took a deep breath and when he spoke again the edge had gone out of his voice. 'Someday, perhaps you will earn my trust. For now, you are still an impulsive youth, albeit a dangerously powerful one.'

I bristled at the insult but was too demoralised to mount any further self-defence. He was correct, wasn't he? My dozens of failures with Hissing Cat proved my lack of control.

'To the end of tempering that power, I am willing to help you learn the restraint that might make you trustworthy,' Doctor Sho went on. He set down his bags of herbs and sat beside me. 'Tell me what goes awry.'

I scoffed and thought to make a snide remark about the capacity of an ordinary doctor to help me in mastering magic. But the truth was that I needed help, and Hissing Cat was unlikely to offer anything more than another round of castigation.

'Whenever I think I'm getting close, I'm flooded by old memories,' I told him. 'I see Oriole's death again and again, as though the world never tires of reminding me. Or the collapse of an obelisk, or the blood on the table at Burrow.' I made a few lines on my sketch, as though I were still working, as though this confession of my weakness and frustration were of little consequence and that Doctor Sho should continue with his day as though it had not happened.

'Have you told her?' he asked quietly.

I took a deep breath. 'No.'

'Not even about Burrow?' He seemed surprised when I shook my head. 'Boy, we're likely to bring the whole empire down on our heads.'

'Hissing Cat seems more than capable of fending off a Hand or two,' I said.

'That isn't the point!' He tugged at his beard. 'Gods, *why* haven't you told her?'

'If I tell her of all the damage I have caused *without* the old magic, she will sooner kill me than help me.'

'You think so much of yourself, Foolish Cur,' he said. 'She was alive before the foundations of the empire were laid. She fought a war against the *gods*. You think she hasn't caused damage that she regrets? We all leave a wake in the world, often a destructive one. At best, we can make amends.'

'How can I make amends for An-Zabat?' I demanded, as

though he could speak for every person I had ever hurt. 'How can I make amends for Iron Town? For Oriole? Even now, the empire likely tortures my father and has buried my mother in some lightless dungeon. How can I make amends for *that*?'

'I don't know,' he said flatly. 'But if you think you can fight an empire without hurting a few people, you're not just foolish, you're delusional.'

'Why are you even still here?' I snapped. Rather than calming my frustration, he had stirred it, and now I spat lightning without thought. 'The typhoon season is over. Go back to grubbing copper coins from the margins of the empire.'

'I was with you at Burrow.' The torches flickered and I failed to meet his stare. He stood and walked away from me. 'I can't go back.'

I watched him, my sketch forgotten, and as his torchlight moved deeper into the cave, I suffered the weight of yet another regret.

Autumn gave way to winter and the hillside beyond the mouth of Hissing Cat's cave became dusted with snow. We spent most of our time huddled around the brazier in her house. She had stores for the winter but grumbled that Doctor Sho and I would devour her supply well before the thaw, and so we laid traps throughout the nearby woods. Okara went out on his own and always returned licking his lips, often with a rabbit or wild turkey to fill our bellies when the traps came up empty.

Cooped up in Hissing Cat's cave, I reread the autobiography I had written, considering revisions that might make it more palatable to my uncle. It chronicled how dogma and doctrine had bound me and dragged me down a path I would never have otherwise chosen. Yet such an account would do little to ingratiate me with the rebellion.

'What's that?' Hissing Cat asked one night as I sat by the

366

brazier, working on the book while I waited for Doctor Sho to serve a stew that had filled the cave with gamey scent. 'I've seen you writing in it before. Journaling your many, many failings?'

I set the book in its usual place beside my bedroll. 'Something like that.'

She harrumphed, drained her bowl, and asked for another helping.

'Eat something, Cur,' she said. 'There's time for a few more failures before we sleep.'

'I thought you could veer when you were a few years off your mother's tit?'

Hissing Cat paced the length of her house. I sat in the corner, muddling through that evening's attempt to extinguish her flame.

'The pattern of the world is on your side, boy! Everything, and I mean' – she waved her arms erratically, making the skulls in her hair shake and clatter – everything wants the flame to go out, except for me. How are you so shit at this?'

'He's trying, Cat,' Doctor Sho grumbled from his corner of the house, where he was reorganising his chest of drawers for the hundredth time.

'If he wasn't trying, I'd feel much better,' Hissing Cat said. 'Once more, and then again, until you get it right or pass out from exhaustion.'

A spar of iron jutted into the pattern of the world as tongues of flame licked at her fingers. I shut my eyes. It was a quick thing, now, to reach out and touch her will. The problem was what came next. Her spell was as intractable as a mountain – though, as I now knew from feeling the pattern, even mountains move.

Feel the world as it wants to be, she had said. As it would have been without the rupture of her will and its conjured flame. Don't focus on the rupture but on what had been disrupted

– the progression from one moment to the next. All that *will be* predicated on all that *was*, the present moment only a bridge between them.

I thought of my life, each transient moment born from its predecessor, such that the whole became nonsensical without each part. There could be no Foolish Cur in the cave with Hissing Cat if not for Alder in An-Zabat. No Alder in An-Zabat if not for the Alder who watched Oriole die. I was all of them and none of them. I was the bridge between that long, painful past and the unknown future.

As once I had observed Atar to learn the dances of An-Zabat, now I felt the rhythm of the pattern of the world and followed its steps, recognising them as chapters in the story of the world, like the chapters of my life, each one nonsensical without the one before. When I returned to the iron spar, I knew what belonged in its place. Yet there was something missing.

I understood the pattern. I knew what ought to replace the iron spar of Hissing Cat's flame, the wake her magic left in the world. I *willed* the pattern to push out the spar and make itself whole, yet I felt resistance – not from the spar but from the pattern itself.

Hissing Cat's flame went out, and not because of anything I had done.

She stood over me, her jaw set, her head tilted, and I felt not only the scrutiny of her eyes but the empty gaze of the skulls in her hair. 'That's enough for tonight,' she said.

I curled up on my pallet, disappointed, as I had done each night for the last two months.

I slept as deeply as I have ever slept, untroubled by dreams, and woke to a wet nose beneath my chin and Okara's insistent whining. I ruffled the dog's ears, but he backed away from me and yipped.

'What's wrong?' I said and dragged myself out from under the threadbare blanket. As I did, I felt a weight dragging through the pattern of the world – a weight I would always recognise. The maze of the canon, somewhere to the north and east.

A Voice of the emperor.

The house was empty, save for Okara and me. The brazier burned low. Doctor Sho's medicine chest was beside his pallet, where it had been these last two months. One thing was missing: the book of my life, which should have been beside my bed, was nowhere to be seen.

I heard the crackle of flames beyond the door.

Hissing Cat sat beside the fire pit. The skulls in her hair seemed to watch me as I approached. She kept her face down, buried in shadow, reading my confession.

'You've scrawled quite the mess of runes here, boy,' she said, her voice quiet and controlled. 'What do you say? Should I jab them with my needle and see how they crack?'

What could I say? It was not enough that I had accepted my own failings. To be in the world is to be with other people.

'You've read the account,' I said. 'What do you make of me?'

'Where you go, the world changes for the worse. People die. Cities crumble.' Her face twisted, like that of a mother who has lost a child, then went on. 'You speak of *preserving* things, and the starving children of An-Zabat, as though you *care*. Do you think those children survived the city's fall?'

'No,' I said. 'I mourn their deaths, as did Atar and Katiz. But their deaths were *naphnet*—'

'Keep that word from your tongue or I'll cut it out,' she snarled. 'I know what you are, now, and what you want. I thought you desired truth. I see now you want only power. A weapon. The means to avenge yourself.'

'I want to learn, Hissing Cat. I do.'

'How can you, when you carry all of this?' She waved the

369

book in the air, shook her head, and tossed it across the fire. The bamboo slats clattered at my feet. 'I've been wondering why you came so close but could never fit your will to the pattern of the world. Well ... there it is.'

I felt another shift in the distant weight of the canon. Hissing Cat felt it too and her expression darkened. 'Even now their battle distracts you. I gave you too much credit. Your first answer was the honest one. I never should have tried to teach you.'

'Can't it be both?' I asked. 'Can't I long for the truth *and* oppose the empire?'

'What does it matter to the pattern of the world what king sits where and what lines are drawn on human maps?'

'But you fought battles too! What of your war against the gods?'

'The pattern of the world was itself our battleground,' Hissing Cat said. 'We fought to make the world comprehensible, liveable, no longer shattered by their whims. What's at stake in this contest you would join? Surely you don't think a world under Nayeni rule would be free of death and cruelty.'

Again, I felt the wake of battle sorcery stirring the pattern of the world, yet I felt no answering wake of witchcraft.

'Even now, the rebellion you would fight for crumbles,' Hissing Cat said. 'By your own account it has been corroded by factionalism. Frothing Wolf and Harrow Fox. The competing ambitions which have always been the corruption at the heart of Nayen. What you feel is the empire's magic eating away the walls of Greyfrost Keep, where your uncle kept his holdfast for a time, though whether he is there at this moment I cannot say.'

'But it is winter,' I said as another wake of sorcery washed through the world. 'They would not go to war in winter.' But even as I spoke the words, I knew them for a lie. They had marched through the Batir Waste and left two out of every three soldiers a corpse on the sand. The Nayeni rebellion had controlled no commerce, no wealth, no power, unlike the wind-callers. They were a nuisance. One that could be safely tolerated.

Until, that was, I had defected, destroyed An-Zabat, and slaughtered a dozen men at Burrow. They had given me power and I had used it against them. Such a humiliation could not go unanswered.

'Why should you care, Foolish Cur?' Hissing Cat demanded. 'You fought the rebellion, and by your book they killed your only friend.'

'I was wrong then,' I replied sourly, shame and anger churning within me. 'I learned what the empire truly was in An-Zabat.'

'Didn't your grandmother tell you the truth of them that night she bound you to her pact? You knew all along but you became one of them anyway, because it was easy.' The crows' skulls clattered as she shook her head and matched their mirth-less smiles. 'A witch of the old sort ... pfa! The gods were fools to try and use you. You've hardly the capacity to make a single bloody choice.'

'And what would you have me do?' I shouted, my voice cracking. 'Stand aside and let the empire do what it will?'

'Yes!' Hissing Cat snapped.

A log cracked in the fire between us. A wake of distant sorcery ripped through the pattern and my stomach clenched, as though the truth she had spoken – bitter medicine though it was – had buried itself within me.

'You will not be able to accept the pattern of the world until you realise what you are,' Hissing Cat said, her voice calmer yet still as hard and sharp as a scalpel. 'And that means choosing not to live in the world as your elders would have you, or as your impulses would drive you, or as the culture of your birth would lead you. A choice to align to the pattern, apprehending it as it is, not distorted through those frames.'

I found my voice, halting though it was. 'You offer such a choice?'

'I do not hate you, Foolish Cur – Alder – whatever your name should be,' she said. 'You only frustrate me, and I tire of your indecisiveness. Your mind cannot apprehend the truths you seek while bound by the concerns of competing clans and warring tribes, of pact and canon.'

She held out her fingers. The iron spike of her will drove into the pattern and a candleflame lit in her hand.

'Extinguish the flame, boy,' she ordered, 'and let us move on to deeper things.'

Recognising this for the final chance it was, I shut my eyes and let my awareness descend to the pattern of the world, to become a sphere of jade resting above the ebb and flow of possibility, the ever-shifting dance of all things.

Abandon the petty war, to stand outside the frame of canon and pact, of Sien and Nayen, of conqueror and conquered, of competing constructions layered atop the deeper truths. Step back, expand my perspective, and understand the world as it truly was.

I felt the spike of Hissing Cat's will, carving her candle flame into the swell and churn of the pattern around me. Then, pulsing heavily, I felt another wake of distant battle sorcery, a reminder that beyond this cave a battle raged – insipid and petty though it may be – and people suffered. An-Zabat had been destroyed in the contest between conqueror and conquered, a contest that had cost Oriole his life, that had twice divided my mother from her family, and which led my grandmother to abandon me.

That suffering had to matter. At the very least, it mattered to me.

I opened my eyes and retreated from the pattern. Hissing Cat's face was a blur of shadows in the mingled light of the fire and conjured flame.

'Yet you have hardly set foot beyond this cave these last thousand years,' I said. 'Whom do you love? Whose suffering can touch you here, alone with your bones and your endless questions?'

'Do you seek understanding or not?' Hissing Cat said. 'It is as simple as that.'

'It isn't,' I argued. 'It can't be. As you say, to know the pattern of the world, I must know what I am, and what I am is the grandson of Broken Limb. The nephew of Harrow Fox. The student of Koro Ha and Hand Usher. The lover, however briefly, of Winddancing Atar. The friend of Oriole. And the killer of Frigid Cub. I dealt the massacre at Burrow and drew the empire into these mountains.'

'I was once many things to many people,' Hissing Cat said.

'Perhaps you still would be, if you had not hidden yourself away.'

She glowered over the flame. 'The pact bound me.'

'As it binds the emperor?'

She curled her lip and made as if to speak, but I pressed on.

'If the choice is between understanding some deeper truth or fighting for a chance to make good on all the harm I have done, then I choose to fight.'

Hissing Cat closed her fist and snuffed her conjured flame. The fire crackled between us and water dripped from stalactites overhead. Okara nuzzled the back of my calf and whined. Hissing Cat fixed him with her shadowed glare. 'Then go,' she snarled. 'Let yourself be a pawn of the gods. But do not seek me again.'

She lowered herself to her seat beside the fire, as though I were already forgotten. I moved automatically, first collecting the book of bamboo slats before stowing it and my few belongings into the rucksack I had fashioned from my kaftan. As I neared the bend towards the painted caves, I glanced back and saw her as I had on our first morning together, beside her fire and her pile of shoulder blades, cracking each bone for answers before tossing it into the dark.

Okara padded behind me as I moved on, bracing myself against the chill that swept in from the world outside.

Doctor Sho sat hunched on a flattened stalagmite by the cave mouth, watching a few flakes of snow swirl and drift between the white-dusted pines. 'So, she read it after all,' he said.

Okara whined into the pause between us.

'I'm sorry,' I said. 'If you want, I'm sure the rebellion—'

'I'll wait out the winter here, if it's all the same to you.'

'Where will you go?' I asked. 'You were with me at Burrow, remember.'

He shrugged, and his shoulders collapsed back to their hunched posture. 'The world is bigger than Nayen. There are doctors in Toa Alon, too. If I can smuggle myself aboard a ship, I doubt anyone would think to look for me there. Besides, we doctors tend to blend together, unless one of us is seen in the company of a wanted fugitive.'

'I'm sorry, Doctor Sho,' I said, my voice straining against the tightness in my throat. 'You tried to warn me away from all of this, years ago. I didn't listen, and in our meeting again I caused you nothing but trouble. I would say I hope we meet for a third time, but I doubt you would appreciate the sentiment.'

He chuckled wryly. 'Boy, if we meet again, it'll most likely be in a dungeon.' He pointed northwards. 'Greyfrost is nestled between two peaks, less than a day away as the crow flies.' He glanced down at Okara. 'What of this one?'

I ruffled the dog's ears for perhaps the final time. In that moment, I did not see the scheming divine who had lurked in my dreams and drawn me away from the Batir Waste. Only a wounded, loyal mountain dog.

'I go on the wing,' I said.

'It'll do me well to keep a guard dog, I think,' Doctor Sho said. 'If you want him back when all this is through, find me in Toa Alon. Try the executioners' field if you find the dungeon empty.'

'Thank you, Sho,' I said. 'And good luck.'

We clasped hands and I set out into the cold. The sky was clear save for wispy clouds, long and feathered like the lines of a calligrapher's brush. I set my heading by the next wake of battle sorcery. Okara's long, lonely howl gave me pause before I veered, launched myself into the frigid air, and flew to war.

27

Greyfrost Keep

Wakes of witchcraft and sorcery crashed through the pattern of the world, stirring all to chaos. As I drew nearer, I felt them more keenly and more frequently, and I hoped that the wake of my veering would be lost in the tumult.

The thin mountain winds led me around one peak and towards another, which rose from distant mist like the back of an ancient beast, furred in forest and armoured in stone. A basalt plateau rose from the valley between them, where Greyfrost Keep had been built, its walls flush with the cliffs, its causeway thin and winding. A sea of soldiers – at least 10,000, by my hasty count – filled a deforested battle plain around the plateau. Banners fluttered among them. All bore the emperor's tetragram, and beneath it another name, one I did not recognise at first. When I had last seen it, the logogram beginning Usher's name had been for *hand* rather than *voice*.

Corpses littered an empty stretch that spanned an arrow's flight from the walls, but Greyfrost had suffered in turn. One of its four towers had collapsed and the others bore the fractal scars of battle sorcery and the cracks and bruises of chemical grenades. The walls, too, were scored and scorched, and fires raged on the causeway, preventing an assault on the gates but sealing in the fortress's defenders.

Even as I approached, the swinging arms of siege engines hurled chemical grenades that spilled fire across the walls. Wake after wake of battle sorcery preceded bolts of raking lightning. At least three sorcerers had come to hunt me among the rebels.

I felt a swell of gratitude that I had never veered while wearing the tetragram, preserving that power for those who wore the Nayeni pact. A well-defended wall could still impede the empire, as long as it did not crumble.

I folded my wings and dived for the courtyard as lightning cut through the air behind me and filled my nose with the smell of thunder. Then I felt a wake that surprised me, for it did not belong to the canon I knew, though I should have expected it after An-Zabat. I called wind of my own and spun it around me. Spear met shield with a burst of pressure that rolled me in the air. I flared my wings to right myself and their next attacks splashed against the stone of the keep as my dive took me behind the curtain wall.

I veered back to my human form in the same moment I landed on the frozen, snow-dusted earth of the courtyard. As a wave of cramps washed through me, I stood and faced a bristling ring of drawn swords and lowered pikes.

I put up my hands to show my naming scar and witch marks, and some of the tension went out of the soldiers surrounding me. They were gaunt, their eyes bruised for want of sleep, and dressed in ill-fitting armour, many pieces stained with blood and rust.

'A witch!' one of them exclaimed, lowering his sword. 'Did one of the messengers make it? Is the Army of the Wolf on its way?'

'I am alone,' I said. 'My name is Foolish Cur, grandson of Broken Limb, nephew of Harrow Fox—'

The sword came up again, hovering a finger's width from my throat. 'We know of you,' the soldier said.

'Take me to my uncle,' I said. 'I am here to help, in whatever way I can.'

He scowled. 'We all know how you *helped* at Iron Town. Bind his hands. The Sun King will see justice done.'

The darkness in the hallways of Greyfrost Keep swam with the sputtering light of dying torches. The fortress shook beneath muted explosions and peals of thunder. Dust cascaded from the bare stone walls.

The soldiers surrounding me kept their distance and their weapons in hand. Their leader – I could not discern a rank, for their armour was mismatched and lacked insignia – led us through a broad hall where once a court must have gathered. No throne stood atop the dais, though, and the floor was scratched where tables and chairs had been hastily dragged to build barricades. A woman dressed in finer armour than the soldiers who had captured me stood guard at a door in the back of the hall. She regarded me with bright eyes rimmed with red paint.

'Who is this, Captain?' she said.

'I am—'

One of the soldiers cuffed me. I spat blood and resigned myself to silence. I could wait to speak for myself until I met my uncle.

'The traitor Foolish Cur,' the captain said. 'He seeks an audience with the Sun King.'

She recoiled from me and I felt the spike of her will in the pattern of the world as she reached for witchcraft. After a deep breath she regained her composure, yet she remained a moment's thought from conjuring flame.

'Wait here,' she said. 'I'll announce him.'

She opened the door, revealing a wide room dominated by a high map table, where an arrangement of wooden tokens abstracted the battle into something like a game of Stones. Of the many men and women who stood around that table, making reports and arguing over plans of action, one drew my eye: an old woman, stooped with age and more deeply wrinkled than I remembered, but unmistakably my grandmother.

The sight of her kindled hope in me, mingled with melancholy.

Beside my grandmother stood a man who could only have been Harrow Fox, though he had changed a great deal in the years since he had come to my father's estate. The iron scales of his armour fitted him well but bore the scars of many a deflected blow. No crown or insignia marked him as claimant to the Sun Throne. The pattern of that room – the way the others gave him space, deferring to his gaze and his furrowed brow – marked him as surely as the tetragram marked a Voice of the emperor.

The young witch who had guarded the door approached Harrow Fox and whispered in his ear. The crease in his brow deepened and his hand reached up to tug a streak of white that shot through his fiery beard from lip to chin.

'We have a visitor,' he said and the chatter in the room faded to silence.

The captain nudged me forwards. I half-stumbled into the room, my hands bound behind my back, and met my uncle's narrow, measuring gaze.

'I would say well met, Nephew,' Harrow Fox said, 'but I doubt any meeting between us could be so described.'

I fell to my knees and pressed my forehead to the floor. 'I must beg your forgiveness,' I said. 'I fought with a patrol in the town of Burrow. These legions come hunting me.'

'On your feet,' Harrow Fox said. 'We are Nayeni. We do not bow and scrape like the conquerors.'

I rose to my knees, then stood, helped by the rough arm of the soldier who had escorted me. 'Again, I beg forgiveness. I was raised among the Sienese and know their ways better than our own.'

'You also think too much of yourself.' Harrow Fox gestured to the maps. 'This is not to hunt a single man but to crush a rebellion. When they've cornered us before, our witches at least could escape to rebuild. Now, those we sent bearing word of this battle were cut down even as they crossed the walls – not by lightning but by the wind itself. A new magic the empire has dredged from their conquests. They've found a way to close our escape, and so have come to finish this long war of skirmishes and retreats with a final, decisive battle.'

'Then for that, too, I must beg forgiveness,' I said. 'The empire stole that magic from the people of An-Zabat, and I played a part in that theft. But in playing my part, I learned the cruelty of the empire.'

'And you have come here why?' Harrow Fox said. 'To die with us, and so earn absolution?'

'If that is what you ask of me, yes,' I said and looked past him, seeking my grandmother. She watched with hard eyes. 'I was named well, Uncle. I have long been a fool. What wisdom I have was hard won, and it tells me that I belong here, that I must make amends for my failures and misdeeds.'

'Better that you'd stayed away, I think,' he rumbled. 'We are trapped, Foolish Cur. We will die.' He struck the table with his palm, making the wooden markers jump and clatter. 'These plans are not to defeat the Sienese but to make their victory as costly as we can. That is all we can hope for now, to wound them deeply with our death throes.'

The walls shook with the explosion of another grenade and a distant rumbling sounded.

'Even now another tower falls,' Harrow Fox said. 'If you have truly chosen your people over the empire, then you have chosen too late.'

I felt his words like a blow. Again, my foolishness had shaped the pattern of the world for the worse.

'I, too, can command the wind,' I told him. 'Let me fight them. I might shield you and your witches while you escape, or at least draw their attention and buy you time.'

'You think you can stand alone against three Hands of the emperor?' Harrow Fox stroked his beard. 'They'll tear you apart in the space of a breath.'

'And you will have lost nothing,' I countered. 'Please, Uncle. Let me try.'

'The boy is strong,' my grandmother said. She stepped forwards, leaning heavily on a staff of gnarled wood. It had been a decade since I had last seen her, and time and war had not been kind. 'When he was only named and wore no witch marks, he was sensitive to magic – enough to wield it, however clumsily. If any among us can hold the Sienese at bay, it's him.'

'You speak as though he's one of us,' Harrow Fox said, crossing his arms. 'He is not.'

'Look at his hands,' my grandmother said. 'When he bowed, I saw them. He wears his witch marks still, but not the tetragram. He has chosen and carved himself with his choice.'

Harrow Fox rounded the table and spun me by the shoulder. His calloused fingers turned my wrist.

'He is your sister's son,' my grandmother said, 'and he has been a fool, but a fool can learn what is right. Let him stand between us and the empire. If he succeeds, we might endure, as we have long endured. If he fails ...' She took a deep breath and leaned heavily on her staff. 'Then, as he says, we lose nothing. All we sacrifice will be the chance to dig our fangs into the empire as we die, and all hope of a liberated Nayen will die with us.'

Harrow Fox released me and returned to his place beside the table. He picked up the wooden tokens, one at a time, and set them in their proper places on the map, each with a solid click of wood on stone, muffled by the paper between them.

'Very well,' he said. 'Unbind him.'

There was a moment of quiet hesitation before the captain cut my bonds. I rubbed my wrists and shrugged sore shoulders. The soldiers who had escorted me shrank away as though these small, human movements were the threatening postures of a demon.

'Thank you for your trust, Uncle,' I said.

'Don't speak to me of trust. You haven't earned it. But my mother is right,' he said and scattered the wooden tokens with a sweep of his hand. 'We will die anyway. This, at least, is a chance to live.'

Harrow Fox and his cadre of nine witches gathered in the centre of the courtyard. Flurries of snow dusted their mismatched armour. They had adorned themselves with fetishes that reminded me of Hissing Cat – feathers, the bones of small mammals, sigils of the creatures they had become in their veering. For luck, perhaps? Or as a means to identify corpses blackened by lightning?

Harrow Fox's paltry army, too, had gathered, save those who stood the walls and towers to keep the Sienese legions at bay with javelin and bow. My uncle moved among them, pressing hands, clapping shoulders, giving each a few words of courage in the face of death.

At last he came to stand beside me, at the centre of that sombre congregation. He swept his gaze over them and, in a voice that rose above the cracking of thunder and the roar of chemical grenades, he began to speak.

'Many of you have fought long beside me,' he said, his voice echoing from the hoary walls. 'You have wet your blades in Sienese blood. You have seen the tide of battle turn against us and have survived. And you know that, though many of us fall and mix our blood with the earth and water of our home, the rebellion must endure.

'I will not promise you that the blood you spill here today might deal the empire a fatal wound. Nor will I claim that your deaths are necessary. They are not. If we could all take wing and escape this place, we would. It is but an accident of birth, an accident of timing, an accident of divine whim that brings you to your deaths today.'

He held up a finger and met many a frightened eye.

'But that does not make your deaths meaningless – no. You have made yourselves a thorn in the side of the oppressors, when you might have stood aside and accepted the rule of the strong over the weak, when you might have forgotten the names of those who came before you. When you might have forgotten who you are and lived as the Sienese would have us live.

'You will die. But make your deaths *costly*. Now it is time to twist that thorn, to deal back to them in blood and pain a bare fraction of the suffering they have dealt to us.'

No cheer went up to answer him, but the fear in their faces hardened to determination. Their hands tightened on the hilts of swords and shafts of spears – poor weapons against a Hand of the emperor, yet capable of wounding, even killing with a stroke of luck.

'It is time, then,' Harrow Fox said and touched the shoulder of the young witch who had guarded his door. A quiet understanding passed between them, and with a breath of cinnamon scent the woman became a tawny owl.

'Nephew, let us test this plan of yours,' Harrow Fox said to me, and then, to the rest of his cadre: 'If she breaks free, we will follow her. If she does not, we will slit the throat of a Sienese dog for every drop of her blood they spill.'

My time with Hissing Cat may have ended in failure, but as familiarity with brush and ink improves the quality of handwriting, so familiarity with the pattern of the world gave me a finer hand at magic. I felt through the pattern, tracing the walls of Greyfrost Keep and the basalt plateau beneath them, then called the wind and set it to follow that curving line. Only a gentle breeze, but building, gathering snow and dust into a whirling barrier that grew around the fortress, until it caught grenades before they struck the walls and hurled them haphazardly into the forest. Until the wind roared around us, louder than the crack of any battle sorcery, drowning out the imperial trumpets as they sounded short bursts of alarm.

The stone maze of the canon hammered at the pattern, and new winds rose against mine. They clawed at the edges of my storm, trying to slow it, or break it, even as it grew. But I knew the wind better than they, and my spell was my own, conjured for this moment, this purpose, not an echo of a distant emperor's will.

I pushed the storm higher and higher, till it cut the clouds above. At my signal, the young witch took to the air. She flew a circuit of the fortress walls and I followed her with my will, shaping a second wind like a desert thermal that filled her wings and carried her up within the eye of the cyclone. The Sienese felt her wake and hurled wind and lightning, but the storm swallowed both, devouring their spears of wind and scattering their battle sorcery against the snow.

With a final push, I launched the witch over the top of the storm into frigid, thin air where not even Katiz could have called a wind. Her wake faded as she dived and glided high over Nayen and vanished into the east.

'She is away,' Harrow Fox said, his face slack with disbelief.

While the Sienese could do little to slow my storm, the pattern of the world pushed hard against it. Fatigue dragged at my limbs and brought me to my knees, just as the storm teetered on the brink of collapsing.

'Go, the rest of you!' my grandmother shouted. 'The boy cannot hold forever!'

I forgot all else but the storm and the thermals and the need to keep them spinning. The cadre leapt to the sky, one after the other, and rode the magic of An-Zabat to freedom.

'You next, Mother!' Harrow Fox yelled against the storm.

'Do you think these poor souls with their swords and spears will manage to deal a single wound alone?' she shouted back. 'The moment these winds fall, the Hands of the emperor will rush this courtyard and spill lightning down every hallway in this fortress. I'll stay and slow them to give your soldiers a chance to die well.'

'And what of survival?' shouted Harrow Fox. 'By your own words, it is better to endure.'

'For you!' she yelled. 'I am old, son. Let me die with my teeth deep in an imperial throat rather than wasting away in the bowels of some mouldering holdfast.'

He kissed her brow. I groaned beneath the strain of holding the whirlwind and roused them from a long, shared silence.

'Farewell, Mother,' Harrow Fox said. 'And farewell, Nephew. You've proven your quality, today. If you survive this, find me again and we may yet learn to trust one another.'

I could answer only with a nod. He became an eagle hawk and took flight, wheeling once above our heads before riding the thermal up and away. When his wake faded into the pattern of the world, I began to release the spell.

'Not yet, boy.' My grandmother lowered herself to the ground beside me. She cupped my chin, then wrapped me in her arms, and I felt wetness on my cheek. 'Oh, Foolish Cur. Oh, my child. I doubted, and I am sorry that I doubted. You have saved our hope.' She clasped my hand and traced the scars she cut long ago. 'From the moment I named you, I have asked too much. Let this be my last request. Show them the fullness of your power. Let our deaths be legend.'

The fullness of my power. The winds of An-Zabat, the fires

385

of Nayen, even the lightning of the Girzan steppe, though I had known it stripped and constrained by the canon of sorcery. I reached for them all, wove them together, as the disparate strands of those places and people had been woven into me. The upper reaches of the cyclone collapsed till it formed not a cylinder but a dome of wind. And within those winds I conjured flame, which caught and danced like spirits of living fire. Last, into the pattern itself, unmediated by canon or pact, I made what I could of battle sorcery, wild bolts of lightning ripping through the air.

I shut my eyes against the searing wall of light that spun around Greyfrost Keep. Heat washed over the courtyard, melted the frigid earth to mud. I collapsed and poured out everything of me. All my rage. All my grief. All my need for redemption. It blazed like a star, and for a heartbeat the world aligned to its gravity.

With a final push, I spun the hurricane of wind and flame and surging lightning outward, into the valley between the peaks. In the pattern I felt ancient pines burst from the heat and snow boil into steam. Soldiers screamed and fled and died, entombed in the molten ruins of their armour.

And then it was past. The fires went out. The conjured winds faded. The last bolt of lightning buried itself in the earth. Piece by piece, the pattern of the world rebuilt itself. Winds – natural winds – swirled in, stirred by the sudden heat. I rolled onto my back, stared upwards at the round scar my cyclone had dealt the sky, which was slowly being closed by the drift of brush-stroke clouds. Snow began to fall in a gentle downward dance.

'Yes,' my grandmother said, and I felt her hand on my shoulder, firm and strong. '*That* they will not forget.'

She cradled my head and I let myself believe that this would all end well. That my display had frightened off the Sienese.

That my uncle would soon return, embrace me, and give me the life among his people I had always been meant to live.

Footsteps sounded on the causeway beyond the gate and raised voices shouted in Sienese. I lifted my head as the gate squealed open and a dozen figures spilled into the courtyard, led by a man I knew at once by his wispy beard and his smile, small and ghostly and twitching with rage.

'Well now,' Voice Usher said. 'If it isn't our pollical cat.'

28

The Hand of the Sun King

I tried to stand, but exhaustion held me. Usher took slow steps towards us, his hands folded behind his back. The tetragram on his brow was bright with mercurial fire.

'Oh, Alder,' Usher said. 'You should have stayed away. We sought you, and hoped to find you here, but didn't know we would until you came diving out of the sky like the fool you always have been.'

'That is not his name,' my grandmother said in Sienese.

Usher regarded her with disdain. 'Another witch?' he muttered, then turned to the men who had followed him. 'Only an old woman. A good first test, wouldn't you say?'

I followed the line of his eyes and saw two faces, one that gave me a moment's pause while the other drove an icy blade into my heart. The first was Cinder, the left side of his face a mass of wet, fleshy scar tissue. The second was achingly familiar, with the same keen eyes I had watched over many a Stones board, but paler, thinner, and now dressed in the gilt armour of a Hand of the emperor. His gaze met mine and there was a moment's hesitation before he lifted his hand to my grandmother.

Cinder grabbed Pinion's wrist. 'You promised me revenge, Usher.'

'You will have it,' Usher said. 'But Hand Pinion deserves the opportunity to prove himself, does he not?'

'You rest, Foolish Cur,' Grandmother said and gently laid my head on the ground. 'It's my turn to make them bleed.'

She conjured flame, poured it into her gnarled staff, and hurled it like a javelin at Usher. The wake of the canon hammered at the world as Usher raised a shield of shimmering light. Her staff struck it, shattering to burning cinders, putting Usher on his back foot. While he recovered, she leapt into the air on an eagle hawk's wings and dived for Cinder.

A whip of battle sorcery lashed out from Cinder's hand, but she veered from hawk to mouse and the whip cut only the air around her. Cinder moved through the canon and curled his fist like a blade-of-the-wind. She veered again and fell on him with the bulk of a mountain wolf. Her jaws closed around his throat and she bowled him over into the mud.

Cinder rolled, spraying crimson, and she rounded on Pinion. Her teeth flashed with white foam flecked with red. The boy staggered away, and I saw a vision of Oriole, broken and battered, caked in his own blood.

I cried out, delirious, unwilling to watch my friend die a second time.

Grandmother hesitated. Only for a heartbeat, but enough time for Usher's will to race through the canon, casting a wake like a held breath and a heavy weight on my shoulders. Ribbons of light flicked out from his fingers and wrapped her, like chains, at elbow and knee.

A spasm worked through the muscles beneath her iron-grey fur. She howled in pain – increasingly human – as the ribbons of light contracted, forcing her back to her natural form. Her will drove into the world, reached for flame in a last desperate attack, mirroring her husband's fate so many years ago. In three strides Voice Usher reached her. The toe of his boot thudded into her jaw. She rolled, lay limp, and the spike of her witchcraft faded from the pattern.

I rolled onto my stomach and pushed at the mud, trying to rise to her defence. I reached for witchcraft, for windcalling, but I had poured myself into the hurricane of fire and lightning. All I had left was a candle flame, sputtering at the tips of my fingers, reaching out to Usher, who turned towards the wake of my witchcraft with a look of pity.

'Oh, Alder, my poor, brilliant, foolish boy,' he said, drawing a knife from his sash. 'I wish I could be kind.'

He stepped around me, kicking away my attempt to set fire to the hem of his robe. His knee pressed between my shoulder blades. A soft hand gripped my left arm and I felt a cold bite below my elbow, then fire, then dribbling wetness. He released that wrist and grasped the other, repeated the strokes of his knife, and I felt the sudden absence of the windcallers' pact, an emptiness that seemed to swallow every memory of Atar, of the Valley of Rulers, as though the part of me built in An-Zabat had been carved away.

'Grit your teeth,' he said. 'This last will hurt the most.'

Pain lanced down from the joint of my right wrist. A scream welled up, broke against my teeth, and stripped my throat raw well before Usher's task was done. I felt the last blow as on a raw nerve, and then the soothing, mocking warmth of healing sorcery.

'I'm sorry, Alder,' he said, his words a distant echo, 'but the empire still has a use for you.'

The last of my strength seeped into my wounds, drawn by Usher's healing sorcery, and I fell into blackness.

The echoes of clanging steel and agonised voices drew me up from the depths. There was no pain, though that had been my last memory – pain, and Oriole standing over my grandmother's corpse.

I blinked against torchlight. I was back in the map room, seated in a chair, my arms bound to my sides by ribbons of flickering light. Other ribbons wrapped my grandmother, who lay sprawled on the table. I tried to stand but the light held me as surely as iron chains.

'The fourth sorcery – actually the first added to the canon, though much more difficult to learn than lightning or healing, and the most useful,' Voice Usher said. He stepped between me and the table, holding a small silken bag and his knife.

At the sight of the knife, I looked down at my arms. My sleeves were torn. My windcaller's tattoos had been replaced by jagged scars and my right arm ended at the wrist in a pink, puckered stump.

'I warned you, didn't I?' Usher said. 'This is the fate of all failed Hands.'

'Why haven't you killed us?' I croaked, my throat dry and raw.

'Would that I could, Alder,' he said, placing the bag on the table beside my grandmother. 'As I was saying, binding sorcery does more than hold the body. In fact, it derives from the sorcery of transmission. It muddles the will and makes magic more difficult to use for the bound but allows the binder an unprecedented insight into the motions of that will. Enough to trace the working of any primitive magic. This, you will have realised – for you were always such a bright, *bright* student – is how the empire learns the magics of the conquered. The An-Zabati proved resistant to this method, able to withstand any torture even unto death rather than work their magic while bound. But you well know the ... unique solution we devised.'

'You would prise me for magic,' I said, sagging against my bonds. 'What magic? I have none now. You cut them all away.'

'There was lightning in that storm you conjured,' Voice Usher said. 'I am not a fool. I cut away the marks of your pacts to deny you the ease of familiar weapons, but I think you are more than capable of giving me what I need.'

'And what is that?'

The ghostly smile, tinged with anger, rose to his lips. He reached into his sleeve and produced a small bowl, glinting silver in the torchlight as he set it on the table between us.

'Water, Alder. The better half of An-Zabati magic.' He clapped his hands and motioned towards someone behind me. 'Which reminds me, I've forgotten hospitality! Would you like tea? Or something stronger? I didn't bring the plum wine you loved so much, sadly.'

A soldier placed a tray on the table beside my grandmother. Steam rose from the spout of a teapot, but there were no cups, only a bottle of the same harsh sorghum liquor Oriole and I had shared on the first night of our friendship.

I shook my head and let myself laugh at the absurdity of his gesture, and of his demand. 'I saw them draw water from the desert many times, but they never taught me how.'

'Oh, I doubt that,' Usher said. 'But perhaps they taught you some of their reticence as well. Once the ... prising, as you say, has begun, we shall see how that seal on your lips endures.'

Two fingers dipped into the silk bag and withdrew a dried seed. 'This is a simple plant. A crawling vine common in Toa Alon.' He held it up, inviting me to examine it. 'The Toa Aloni call it *nor kuhol*, which translates to something like carrion creeper. One need not master their language to grasp the subtleties of such a name. It much prefers to grow in rotting carcasses than in the soil, you see.'

The seed fell softly back into its bag. Usher set down the knife and draped his fingers on the handle of the teapot.

'Carrion creeper is common enough. Much rarer to find a

drug that addles the mind without dulling pain. But when one scours the whole of the world, one can find anything.'

He lifted the teapot and I flinched, but he reached for my grandmother. The blood drained from my face.

'Already?' Usher said. 'Cinder would be so disappointed. Ah, well. I much prefer things to end here, before the screams and the blood.'

My mouth opened, seeking a way to save her without betraying the last secret and hope of the An-Zabati.

'She's an old woman,' I blurted. 'How can you torture her? She is shielded by propriety!'

'But she is not Sienese and has rejected the empire, along with its doctrine,' Usher said and lifted the teapot. 'Shall we dispense with the moral debate and get to the point? Show me how to call water from the earth and she need not suffer.'

'I told you,' I said, seeking a way of escape. My will went to windcalling but found no well of power, then to witchcraft but there was only void. 'It is a secret I never learned.'

'Such a shame,' Usher said and grabbed my grandmother's jaw, where a bruise had blossomed at the join of her skull. He set the spout to her lips. She spluttered, spraying tea across the table. Usher pushed her head back, forcing her airway closed and her gullet open. He poured till the pot was empty, then set it aside and reached for the knife while she gagged and spasmed against her bonds.

'Not only healing, but the sixth and seventh channels, like the third, are from Toa Alon,' he said, 'a country rich in useful magics. The sixth channel is the sorcery of dowsing. Originally, the Toa Aloni used it to find veins of precious minerals in stone, which became the hearts of their idols, but it can be used to find any number of things.'

He traced the line of my grandmother's arm with the tip of

his knife, slicing through the sleeve of her shirt but not breaking skin.

'For example, the body has certain nodes. It is these that doctors feel to find the pulses. The pain dealt to such nodes is *quite* excruciating.'

All the while, the canon of sorcery had hung in the room, binding Usher to the emperor and his power. The iron spike of his will moved through it, carving the pattern of the world under the emperor's guidance. The knife in his hand began to vibrate gently, a quiver that intensified as it moved past my grandmother's elbow.

'There we are,' Usher said and released his dowsing sorcery. He made a small incision, drawing only a bead of blood, and set the knife aside. 'After our conquest of Toa Alon, after we learned dowsing and healing and thought the Toa Aloni had learned subservience, the bountiful terrace gardens of Sor Cala began to die,' he went on. 'There was a great deal of starvation, though not as much as An-Zabat now suffers. We thought it a pestilence, but it seemed not to touch the rural highlands, which we found odd. Until we caught one of their priests waving his hands over their fields by moonlight. Thus we discovered the sorcery of cultivation, which they had denied us and ceased to work in the lands we occupied. Cultivation has done more to spur the empire's growth than any other magic. Though, sadly, it still requires water, else An-Zabat would thrive and there would be no cause for this ... unpleasantness.'

He pinched the seed between thumb and forefinger and held it above the cut he had made in my grandmother's arm.

'Last chance,' he said.

'No matter the pain you inflict on her, or on me, it will not give me knowledge I do not have,' I said. 'You must believe me, Usher.'

'How can I?' he replied and pressed the seed beneath her

394

skin. 'You have worn so many lies, layered like the masks of a Face Changer.'

Usher splayed his fingers over my grandmother's arm. His will moved into the seventh channel of the canon and the silver lines of his tetragram flickered, then glowed golden as the summer sun. The room filled with the smell of fresh air and blood and the new growth of spring. A tendril sprouted from the wound and grew to maturity before my eyes, draping over the edge of the table. The skin of my grandmother's arm wriggled like wet, wormy earth. A groan bubbled from her throat, then became a scream, then a howl of pain that filled the room and echoed from the stone walls long after Usher released his spell.

My voice rose to join hers, begging Usher to stop, insisting that I had told the truth, that this cruelty was needless and would gain him nothing.

'Her suffering is yours to end,' Usher said and gestured at the silver bowl. 'We took that from the wreck of a pirate windship. I realise it might not function properly without being buried in the sand, but you can work the magic nevertheless.'

I could not tear my eyes from the distended ruin of my grandmother's arm, the bright green tips of new-growth vines sprouting from a dozen seeping wounds. Her howls had been replaced by muted, hiccuping sobs.

'No?' Usher scowled at me, opened the bottle of liquor, and took a long swallow. 'This is your doing,' he said, wiping his mouth and the wisps of his beard. 'Her pain arises from your stubbornness and nothing else. If you would only tell the *truth*!' He thumped the bottle onto its tray and reached again for the knife.

There was a knock at the door.

'Enter,' he said, the knife dangling loosely in his hand.

Pinion walked into my field of view, his sharp eyes glancing off the horror on the map table, drifting over me, and settling on Usher. 'The last holdouts have surrendered,' he said. 'The captives are in the courtyard. What should we do with them?'

'Let them stew a while,' Usher said. 'Come, Pinion. You should learn this, distasteful though it is. Hold her shoulders and be ready with healing sorcery.'

Pinion positioned himself beside my grandmother's head. His hands shook as he grasped her and held her writhing frame to the table. Usher began to dowse her other arm, the knife gently vibrating in his hand, and as I watched them a mirthless, spasming laugh began to work through me.

'You laugh at her misery?' Usher said.

I shook my head, fought the laughter, swallowed it. 'You told me the emperor wanted an end to war. A lasting peace. Does he truly believe he can win such a thing like this? With cruelty layered upon cruelty?'

'You are the one who mocks an old woman's pain,' Usher said. 'I do only what is necessary.'

'Necessary!' I bit back another burst of laughter. It was all so *preposterous* when you looked it in the face.

Yes, I was culpable for the suffering at Iron Town, in An-Zabat, and now as my grandmother writhed on the table. But I had done my best, lived as well as I could within the confines of the world the empire had built. It was those confines – doctrine, canon, propriety – that were cruel. Despite the beauty of its art and poetry, that cruelty defined the empire. For what could be more brutal than to tolerate – even endorse – the suffering of those who failed to meet some arbitrary standard, and to kill others for their honesty?

As life gives way to death, as winter to summer, so brutality would produce rebellion long after the cultures of Nayen, An-Zabat, and the other conquered lands had been forgotten. Such was the ebb and flow of the pattern of the world.

And with that realisation, I understood Hissing Cat's instruction: *Align your will to the pattern*. Not to stagnancy, but to the necessary outcome of every action in the interplay of all things, from moment to moment. Even those outcomes I longed to avert or wished to rewrite.

And, laughing, I let my will collapse. In Hissing Cat's cave, it had been a sphere of polished jade skimming along the surface of the pattern. Now it fell into the pattern's depths, seeing it not from above but from within, and I witnessed a deeper truth: that suffering is inescapable, for it is the dusk that must follow every dawn, but cruelty ... cruelty is a human invention, justified by doctrine and canon but far from *necessary*.

'Will you laugh even as she screams in agony?' Usher said and sliced open another wound, planting another seed. The spike of his will moved through the channels of the canon, which stood like a seaside cliff against the pulsing waves of the pattern. An intrusion. An artefact of empire.

The flow of magic was clear to me now, as it had not been since my first fumbling grasp for power, before my grandmother had marked me. I traced the pattern of the world in that room and felt the missing steps in the eternal dance. The truths of the world as it ought to be, and would have been, if not for the canon of transmission.

I threw my will against the walls of the canon, as I had done when I'd knelt over Oriole's corpse in Iron Town.

Extinguish the flame, Hissing Cat had said. Not a flame, this time, but the canon itself.

All the world was on my side, for the pattern always resisted magic. The wakes of magic were the shadow of that resistance, and the greatest wake of all was the stone-heavy maze of the canon.

I aligned my will to the wake of the emperor's transmission, the world's desperate attempt to free itself of this weapon of cruelty and conquest, this thing that should never have been.

Together, the pattern of the world and I pushed against its walls, and felt it crumble to dust.

As my grandmother had once undone the magic that had made me something between human and eagle hawk, now I undid the magic that bound Usher to the emperor and conveyed the canon to this remote place in the mountains of Nayen.

The light that bound me vanished, as it vanished from my grandmother, who lashed out in pain and fury. Pinion recoiled. I felt Usher's will move through the pattern, but without the guiding walls of the canon he floundered, ignorant and power-less. A single spark crackled between his fingertips.

'What is this?' Usher rounded on me, still digging at the pattern. 'What did you *do*?'

I stood, cradling the stump of my wrist. Pact and canon had been cut from me, leaving me naked before the pattern of the world. Unprotected, yet unconstrained. Able to extinguish the flame. Able to do so much more.

'Take Pinion and your men and leave,' I said, even as I began to carve my will into the pattern as Hissing Cat had done – as I had done years ago, and nearly destroyed myself in the process. But I knew much of magic now – far from all, yet enough to work the spells Usher had tried to take from me with the edge of his knife, even without the sheltering guidance of a pact. 'Flee Nayen,' I went on. 'The emperor has no more power here.'

A light like blazing quicksilver erupted from the tetragram on Usher's forehead and streamed to the west, seeking the emperor and the canon. Its wake in the world was like a river, and easily dammed by a motion of my will. Usher staggered backwards into the table and raised the knife between us.

'This is ... This is impossible!' he growled.

'Give up, Usher,' I said.

The ghostly smile touched his lips, then twisted into a sneer and he lunged and slashed with the knife. My feet found the first steps of the Iron Dance. My remaining hand lashed out, gripping a blade of wind instead of a dowel. Usher's fingers spun away, trailing blood, and the knife clattered on the floor.

'I don't want to kill you,' I told him.

'How are you *doing* this?' he snarled, clutching his wounded hand, then reached for battle sorcery, as I in my ignorance had once reached for the power to veer. 'No matter. I'll dig this and every other secret from your quivering, screaming flesh.'

A bolt of lightning lashed out from him and struck the wall, scoring black scars deep into the stone. Another ripped through the chair where I had been bound. Bolt after bolt speared the floor, the walls, the ceiling. It might have been possible to stop them as I had stopped the emperor's transmission, but they flashed into being with a speed I could not hope to match. One would surely kill me, or my grandmother, or Pinion before I learned their wakes well enough to unmake them as they struck.

I drove my will into the pattern and began to weave a sorcery I had seen at An-Zabat and in the courtyard mere hours ago but had never learned. The sensation of its wake was cool and crisp, and it manifested in the world as a shield built from curtains of light. The curtains appeared around Usher, enfolding him. Lightning struck them and rebounded, until the space between them was filled with screams, acrid smoke, and blue-white flame.

Usher's gaze found mine, wide and terrified, his mouth twisted in a hideous scream. No hint of that ghostly smile. With a final spark, his will faded from the world.

The curtains of light vanished and all that remained of Usher was a pile of bone and ash. I felt an odd pain – a wish that I could mourn his death – and turned to my grandmother.

'You killed him,' Pinion said flatly.

I met the horror in his eyes. 'He could have released his magic,' I told him. 'He did not. That is why he died. All I wanted was to shield the rest of us.' And it was easy to see how the world should be changed, and simple to find the magic of that change, when I knew what I truly wanted. 'I'll not hurt you, Pinion. The offer I made to Usher stands. Take your men and go.'

He raised his hand, but I felt no movement of his will. With Usher dead, there was no nearby Voice to transmit power to him. He would be helpless, until Voice Golden-Finch realised what had happened here and turned his attention – and the emperor's transmission – towards us.

'Do you think your brother would accept this?' I asked, gingerly touching my grandmother's tortured arm. She groaned but otherwise lay still, her breath shallow and full of grit. 'Would he have gone on fighting for an empire that caused such pain?'

'I cannot know,' Pinion muttered. 'The rebellion killed him. I will never have a chance to ask.'

'I cradled his head while he died,' I said. 'And I think he would have sooner driven that knife through Usher's throat than be party to such torment. Like you, I cannot know, but I believe that he too could have learned, just as I have learned. I would like to believe the same of you. Ask yourself – as you asked yourself at Oriole's grave when last we saw each other – does this seem right?'

The carrion crawler had made my grandmother's arm a twisted wreck of puckered flesh and glistening bone, all wrapped in the green of new-growth vines. No medicine could repair this damage, and healing sorcery would drain her to the brink of death.

As I had in the mud at Iron Town, I reached for magic beyond healing sorcery. Unhindered by the canon, I found it, took it, and felt it bind us.

I heard footsteps, the door opening, and orders shouted in Sienese, but I paid them little mind.

My thoughts returned to the overgrown path to the Temple

of the Flame, where my grandmother had found my broken body and rebuilt it. Now I did the same for her. With magic that I had once known as the witchcraft of Nayen, I reshaped her limb, pulling out the vine that had wound itself through her muscle and bone, knitted her wounds, and then felt a wave of weakness as the greater healing magic that bound us began to restore her life by draining mine.

The pattern of the world surged against me, for I was cheating death, one of its deepest certainties. But while I knew that the pattern should reject Usher's cruelty, I knew as well that it should accept this kindness. The world must change in the end. Let it change for the better.

As a leaden weariness filled me, I heaved myself onto the table. Clutching her hand, lying beside her, cradling her head with the stump of my right arm, I listened to her heartbeat deepen and grow in strength.

Bone-deep exhaustion, the slow drain of her healing, and the lullaby of her breath carried me to the space between sleeping and waking, where I found myself in the company of gods.

They surrounded the table. Some I knew – Ateri and Tollu, with their stone muzzles and blazing eyes. Others were strange but known from myth, like the man with hair and beard of wispy cloud and eyes like starlight who could be none other than the Skyfather, subject of many an old An-Zabati poem. There were creatures like living mountains shaped like human beings with forests for hair and molten pools of fire for eyes. Men and women with the heads of beasts. Creatures composed entirely of wings that unfolded like the petals of an infinite, fractal flower. There were others, too – strange, wonderful, terrifying – but I was too exhausted to feel anything but peace.

'This one has broken pact,' the Skyfather said in a voice as dry as the desert wind.

'He was ours before he was any of yours,' Ateri said. 'We

claim his fate.' She leapt onto the table, heat pulsing from her open mouth.

A woman with the head of a horse pushed her aside. 'You cannot claim him,' she said to Ateri. 'He broke pact with all of us.'

'What pact?'

Okara, in the body of the mountain dog, bounded through the doorway and mounted the table beside his mother. He glared a challenge at the other gods, each in turn, staring out from his web of scars.

'You know well what pact,' Ateri snapped. 'Many pacts, in truth.'

'Where are the marks carved in his flesh?' Okara asked.

The eyes of the gods searched the diamond scar on my palm, the wealed flesh below my elbows, the pink stump at the end of my right arm.

'He is of the old sort,' the Skyfather said.

'Of the old sort, but not present when the pacts were made,' Okara countered. 'And uncarved. Thus unbound and free to wield any magic.'

Ateri showed her teeth.

'Was this your doing, wolf of guile?' said one of the living mountains. 'Perhaps we should punish you instead.'

'You might point to the emperor of Sien and accuse him of worse than I have done,' Okara said. 'The pact does not bind this one, but he is on our side.'

'Our side of what?' snapped the Skyfather. 'We wage no war.'

'You have watched the peoples of your pacts crushed by Sien,' Okara said. 'That is Tenet's doing, and he will not be satisfied with mortal conquest. He seeks an end to every old order and a new pattern of his own design.'

'So say you,' a voice echoed from the depths of unfolding wings. 'Yet in this time, in this pattern of this world, we wage no war.'

'But what of the future?' Okara pressed. '*He* can fight Tenet on our behalf and break no pact. He can contain this conflict before the seas boil and the earth tears itself apart.'

Silence held between the gods. Ateri menaced her son, the elder wolf snarling, the mountain dog hunching low.

'If he has broken no pact, there is no punishment we can deliver without violating it in turn,' said Tollu, wolf-sister and daughter, breaking the tension. 'Let him live. But we consider him bound, as all witches of the old sort are from this moment. If he teaches the old magic, his life will be forfeit.'

'That is acceptable,' said the Skyfather, and vanished.

One by one, the gods assented and were gone, until only Okara and Ateri remained. He showed her his back and nuzzled my chin.

'Do not act as though you love him,' Ateri said. 'You would make of him a weapon, and an unwieldy one at that. Do not be surprised when it cuts you deepest of all.' Then, in a flash of flame and heat, she too departed.

Okara licked my chin and I stirred, rising from half-sleep, still weak and feeling the last of my strength drain into my grandmother. He dashed from the room. I heard his nails on the stone floor, then his bark and a muffled curse.

The door flew open and Okara rushed back in with Hissing Cat at his heels, the skulls in her hair clattering. She took one look at me and called out, 'Sho! He's nearly killed himself! Get in here!'

She crossed to the table and slapped me hard across the face. 'Enough of that, you fool. Do you want her to wake and find herself draped in your dried-out husk?'

I released my spell. Though I was weary, I no longer felt as though all my blood were half its thickness and every breath far too shallow. My grandmother was still sickly, but there was colour in her cheeks, her bruise had faded, and her arm was whole. The frayed remnants of the carrion crawler lay scattered across the floor.

Hissing Cat's gaze lingered on Usher's corpse and the lightning scars that lined the walls. 'So you saved the bloody rebellion, did you?' she asked. 'Are you satisfied?'

I pushed myself to my feet and found that I did, indeed, feel satisfied – a deep satisfaction I had last felt after passing the imperial examinations. The feeling that the path of my life had been leading me through trial after trial towards some purpose, finally achieved.

'How many survived?' I asked weakly.

'Enough to keep Sho well distracted,' Hissing Cat replied. Then she leaned out of the doorway and shouted, 'Hurry up, you old bastard! I'd like to know if he's going to drop dead!'

'What are you doing here?' I croaked. 'I thought you were finished with me.'

'I was,' she said, 'but you don't get to live as long as I have without regretting a few decisions. This was one. So, I put the issue to the bones.'

'And they told you to forgive me?'

'No. But I only listen to them half the time.'

Doctor Sho trundled into the room and thumped his chest of drawers down in the corner. 'There are twenty-eight people in that courtyard, several of them badly wounded,' he said. 'A doctor's duty is to the patient in front of him, not to the whims of whatever bee flew up your robe and made you care for the boy all of a sudden.'

He crossed to the table, felt my grandmother's pulse, then held out his hand for mine. Unthinking, I offered my right wrist.

'At least it healed well,' Sho said, 'but best I examine your other pulse.'

'You could repair it by veering,' Hissing Cat said.

I stared at the empty space above the pink stump while Doctor Sho prodded my left arm and returned to his chest of drawers.

'I might,' I said, and left it at that.

Hissing Cat crossed her arms. 'Well, it's your body. And from what I felt of the magic you wielded here, you've little need for hands.'

'You should hear what the soldiers are calling you,' Doctor Sho said, plucking herbs from their drawers and dropping them into a clay bowl, which he filled from a waterskin and offered to me. 'That should be warm, by the way.'

I took the bowl in my remaining hand and conjured a candle flame to dance along its base. 'What are they saying?'

'That you conjured the sun itself to defend the keep,' Doctor Sho said, preparing another dose for my grandmother. He looked up at me, his brow creased with concern. 'They say it's a sign. They call you Sun King.'

'They are confused,' I replied, remembering with amusement the Valley of Rulers and the last time I had earned a new name. 'My uncle fled, but not all of them were there to witness. Perhaps they thought he stayed behind.'

Who would want me, failure of failures, for their king? I laughed, shook my head, and sipped the tea. It was bitter but soothing, and I felt strength flow into my limbs as I drained the cup. Strange, I thought, how even after a battle fought with magic the only way to truly heal the body was with time and herbs, grown naturally, born out of the pattern of the world.

Doctor Sho and Hissing Cat exchanged a glance. Okara huffed.

'She will explain to them,' I said, helping Doctor Sho support my grandmother's head. 'When she wakes, she will tell them that I am only a Foolish Cur.'

Acknowledgements

Like any book, *The Hand of the Sun King* would not exist but for the support, influence, and help of dozens of people.

First I want to thank my parents, Jenny and Ward, who not only raised me but have always encouraged my creativity (even when my imaginary war-games in the front yard unnerved the neighbors). Further, they educated me for the majority of my childhood. Whoever I am, and whatever I am capable of, it is largely thanks to them.

I want also to thank my brothers, Seth and Nathan, who are full of creativity and intellect and a constant source of inspiration (and music recommendations!). Similarly, I want to thank Tom Schultz, who was the first person to tell me, in no uncertain terms, that I was an artist, not just someone who liked to draw and write for fun. In addition, I need to thank Dr. Anthony Clark, my academic mentor, whose guiding hand on my education in history is at the deepest root of Wen Alder's story.

The beta readers for this book – Jon Ficke, Erin Cairns, and Don Allmon – deserve enormous thanks for their feedback, which helped mold it from its earliest pupal stage. I also want to offer special thanks to Scott H. Andrews of Beneath Ceaseless Skies, the first editor to pluck me out of a slush pile and pay me at least $0.06 a word for my trouble when the story was finally ready.

I would be remiss, of course, not to thank Joshua Bilmes, my agent, for taking a second look at the first fifty pages of this book, sitting down with me at the 2018 San Jose Worldcon, and walking me through everything wrong with what I was doing (and even a few of the things I was doing right!). If not for his willingness to work with me on draft after draft, this novel would not have reached your hands. Deserving of mention also are Stevie Finegan, who found the perfect home for this book, and Brendan Durkin, my editor, whose incisive letter helped polish *The Hand of the Sun King* into the best version of itself.

Finally, I want to thank my wife Hannah, a brilliant artist in her own right who patiently (and sometimes enthusiastically!) listens while I ramble about wild worldbuilding notions; while I pare every movie we watch down to the narrative bones in search of useful lessons; while I pace the apartment muttering to myself about a sticky plot twist or a character arc that just won't bend right, and who loves me not in spite of these things but, at least in part, because of them. I love you, too.

Credits

J.T. Greathouse and Gollancz would like to thank everyone at Orion who worked on the publication of *The Hand of the Sun King* in the UK.

Editor
Brendan Durkin

Copy editor
Alan Heal

Proof reader
Jane Howard

Audio
Paul Stark
Amber Bates

Contracts
Anne Goddard
Paul Bulos
Jake Alderson

Design
Lucie Stericker
Rabab Adams

Joanna Ridley
Nick May

Editorial Management
Charlie Panayiotou
Jane Hughes

Finance
Jennifer Muchan
Jasdip Nandra
Afeera Ahmed
Elizabeth Beaumont
Sue Baker

Marketing
Folayemi Adebayo

Production
Paul Hussey

Publicity
Will O'Mullane

Sales
Jen Wilson
Esther Waters
Victoria Laws
Ellie Kyrke-Smith

Frances Doyle
Georgina Cutler

Operations
Jo Jacobs
Lisa Pryde
Lucy Brem